1976

VARIETIES OF
PERSONALITY
THEORY

HENDRIK M. RUITENBEEK was born in Leyden, Holland, in 1928. He took his doctorate at the University of Leyden and came to the United States in 1955. He is now a naturalized citizen. Dr. Ruitenbeek is a practicing psychoanalyst in New York City, and he also teaches psychology at New York University.

Dr. Ruitenbeek is the author of *The Rise and Origin of the Dutch Labour Party* (published in Holland in 1955) and of *The Individual and the Crowd: A Study of Identity in America* (1964). He has edited the following anthologies for the Dutton Paperbacks series: *Psychoanalysis and Social Science* (1962), *Psychoanalysis and Existential Philosophy* (1962), *Varieties of Classic Social Theory* (1963), *Varieties of Modern Social Theory* (1963), *The Dilemma of Organizational Society* (1963), *The Problem of Homosexuality in Modern Society* (1963), and *Psychoanalysis and Literature* (1964). He has also edited *Psychoanalysis and Contemporary American Culture* (1964) and *The Psychotherapy of Perversions*. Dr. Ruitenbeek is currently preparing a study of male homosexuality in America.

VARIETIES OF
PERSONALITY
THEORY

Edited, and with an introduction, by

HENDRIK M. RUITENBEEK

A Dutton  *Paperback*

NEW YORK
E. P. DUTTON & CO., INC.

SBN 0-525-47151-0

ACKNOWLEDGMENTS

Grateful acknowledgment is made to the following for permission
to quote from copyright material:

Sigmund Freud: *The Origin and Development of Psychoanalysis*.
Reprinted from *The American Journal of Psychology*, Vol. XXI,
No. 2, 1910, by permission of *The American Journal of Psychology*.

Carl Gustav Jung: *The Basic Postulates of Analytical Psychology*.
Reprinted from *Modern Man in Search of a Soul* by Carl Gustav
Jung, New York, Harcourt, Brace & World, Inc., 1933, by per-
mission of the publishers.

Alfred Adler: *Individual Psychology, Its Assumptions and Its
Results*. Reprinted from *The Practice and Theory of Individual
Psychology* by Alfred Adler, New York, Humanities Press, 1955,
by permission of the publishers.

Erich Fromm: *Selfishness and Self-Love*. Reprinted from *Psychiatry*, 1939, Vol. 2:507-523, by permission of the author and by
special permission of The William Alanson White Psychiatric
Foundation, Inc. Copyright, 1939, by The William Alanson White
Psychiatric Foundation, Inc.

Karen Horney: *Culture and Neurosis*. Reprinted from the
American Sociological Review, 1936, Vol. I:221-235, by permission of the editor and of The American Sociological Association.

Harry Stack Sullivan: *The Illusion of Personal Individuality*.
Reprinted from *The Fusion of Psychiatry and Social Science* by
Harry Stack Sullivan, New York, W. W. Norton & Company, Inc.,
1964. Copyright © 1964 by The William Alanson White Psychiatric Foundation, Inc.

Gordon W. Allport: *The Open System in Personality Theory*.
Reprinted from the *Journal of Abnormal and Social Psychology*,
1960, Vol. 61, No. 3: 301-310, by permission of the American
Psychological Association.

Carl R. Rogers: *Significant Aspects of Client-Centered Therapy*. Reprinted from *The American Psychologist*, 1946, Vol. I, No. 10: 415-22, by permission of the American Psychological Association.

Henry A. Murray: *Some Proposals for a Theory of Personality*. Reprinted from *Explorations in Personality* by Henry A. Murray, New York, Oxford University Press, Inc., 1938, by permission of the publishers. Copyright, 1938, by Oxford University Press, Inc.

Kurt Lewin: *The Conflict Between Aristotelian and Galileian Modes of Thought in Contemporary Psychology*. Reprinted from the *Journal of General Psychology*, 1931, Vol. V, pages 141-177, by permission of The Journal Press.

Kurt Goldstein: *On the Structure of Personality*. Reprinted from *Human Nature in the Light of Psychopathology* by Kurt Goldstein, Cambridge, Massachusetts, Harvard University Press, 1940, by permission of the publishers. Copyright, 1940, by the President and Fellows of Harvard College.

Gardner Murphy: *Affect and Perceptual Learning*. Reprinted from the *Psychological Review*, January 1956, Vol. 63, No. 1: 1-15, by permission of the American Psychological Association.

William H. Sheldon: *Constitutional Factors in Personality*. Reprinted from *Personality and the Behavior Disorders,* edited by J. McV. Hunt, New York, The Ronald Press Company, 1944, by permission of the publishers. Copyright, 1944, by The Ronald Press Company.

Abraham H. Maslow: *Notes on Being-Psychology*. Reprinted from the *Journal of Humanistic Psychology*, 1962, Vol. II, by permission of the author and the editor.

John Dollard and Neil Miller: *The Learning Process*. Reprinted from *Social Learning and Imitation* by John Dollard and Neil Miller, New Haven, Yale University Press, 1944, by permission of the publishers. Copyright, 1944, by Yale University Press.

CONTENTS

INTRODUCTION*

Intellectual disciplines, it has been said, multiply by fission and budding, rather like some forms of unicellular life. Thus, in the nineteenth century, we see psychology splitting away from philosophy and asserting itself as an independent field of study; later, personality theory budded off from psychology and although it has not yet separated from the parent growth —perhaps it may never do so—personality theory has certainly swelled large during the last five decades.

When scholars began to develop psychology as an independent discipline, the physical and biological sciences were beginning to achieve their current status as the most significant form of intellectual activity. Theology and philosophy continued to assert their ancient claims, but rather soon, as the span of human history is measured, both fell back; philosophy to devote increasing attention to critiques of scientific methodology, and theology to become a respected specialty of limited relevance (its claims currently are principally asserted by professionals—that is, the clergy of the principal Western faiths and by the highly influential literary persons who have created the "new criticism" in the United States and in England). Intellectual pursuits came to be considered "reputable," to use Thorstein Veblen's term, in so far as they could claim to be scientific—that is, to stress formally designed, controlled experimentation, careful measurement, and statistical validation. These tools were most readily applied to the study of perception and of learning. The psychologist came to be concerned with the more readily segmentable aspects of behavior, especially of animal behavior, which could be conveniently studied in the laboratory. He worked in the protected university environment, generally, and was untroubled by a need to communicate with anyone but his fellow scholars. Psychologists like Ebbinghous, Wundt, Helmholtz, and their disciples learned a great deal in this fashion; but much of what they dis-

* For much of the material which is included in the prefaces and introduction I have borrowed freely from that excellent text *Theories of Personality* by Calvin S. Hall and Gardner Lindzey— EDITOR.

covered seemed to have small relevance to what most people wanted to know about human behavior. It might be interesting to have information about how delicately people (or laboratory rats) could discriminate among sounds, colors, weights, smells. It could be useful to find out how human beings committed lists of nonsense syllables to memory. It might be necessary to know how widely people varied in their capacities. Yet very few of these data seemed to tell much of anything about the kinds of human behavior which was of real concern to other persons. For the scientific academic psychologist seemed to have as one of his objectives that of straining out of his laboratory situation and of the behavior of subjects in that situation nearly everything that bore resemblance to the complexity of actual human experience. The experimentalists and the psychometricians did indeed accumulate data and refine methods for handling those data, but the material so carefully collected and evaluated seemed to bear little meaningful relation to the behavior of human beings who, after all, usually acted as functioning wholes rather than assemblages of disparate parts. (So, for that matter, did animals, but consideration of that problem would carry us too far afield.)

While the psychologist was thus toiling to purge his discipline of involvement with the untidy and unruly actualities of behavior (always, of course, with the purpose of elucidating that behavior), the physicians, and particularly the psychiatrists, were obliged to deal with that actuality at its most recalcitrant, in the behavior of emotionally disturbed persons. The clinician had to treat those persons as wholes whether he found them confined in institutions or encountered them in his office practice. And, from the less immediately practical side of the situation, we have as a third group of influences on personality theory, the group headed by William Stern—the Gestaltists—who became convinced that human behavior had to be dealt with as a unity; efforts to understand behavior in more segmented fashion could only distort the data.

Personality theory has thus been played upon by three sets of pressures: those of academic psychology from which it derives and to which it is still rather loosely attached; those of intellectual dissidents from that discipline; and those of the clinicians. From the first two, personality theory draws its concern with experimental design and statistical evaluation, what may be labeled its "scientific conscience."

From the third, personality theory draws its interest in the functioning of the individual as a whole and in the role of motivation in determining that functioning.

Academic psychology, as has been mentioned, has its roots in the work of nineteenth-century scholars who operated in a university setting and concentrated on study in what they regarded as a wholly scientific manner. Academic psychology seeks to be a pure science as theoretical astrophysics, for example, once was considered to be pure. (In our complicated contemporary world few fields of inquiry can remain "pure," in the sense of being divorced from practical consequences.) Personality theory, as a bud of psychology, shares its roots but recognizes its own divergence from the path of purity; yet practitioners in the area do seek to remain on that path, so far as they can. Sometimes the personality theorist considers himself a specialist in uniting what the experimentalists have learned by dividing; that is—an effort to integrate into knowledge of the *whole* person what the latter have learned about perception, motor responses, learning, and the like. Personality theory is not a single-domain study, therefore, but a discipline which attempts to deal with a general picture. It is free to inquire into any variety of human behavior in its natural setting rather than to abstract some particular form of behavior and transfer it to the laboratory. Hence, in one sense, we might compare personality theory to old-fashioned natural history—which observed, let us say, the reproductive behavior of animals in the field—and compare academic psychology to physiological studies of similar behavior in animals confined to the laboratory where they can be manipulated as well as watched.

We have talked of the relationship between personality theory and academic psychology, but we have not yet said what personality theory actually is. This is especially difficult to do because *personality* is a very elusive term to define; *theory* is a rather disputable concept; and one may even argue that it is not correct to combine the two terms since few, if any, among the numerous intellectual constructs now labeled "personality theories" would be considered theories at all by persons who adhere to the rigorous modern concepts of the philosophy of science. Sometimes a theory is regarded as a set of concepts by which a mass of validated data is organized into a coherent (and preferably elegant) whole. More formally, a theory is a set of conventions which can generate propositions about relevant events. These propositions must be so stated as to be subject to validation. A useful theory—and note that this definition of a theory treats it as an appraisable instrument rather than as an entity to be evaluated as *true* or *false*—leads to new relevant observations of empirical relationships among data and provides a consistent framework into which such new findings may fit. By its very presence, however, a theory tends to direct attention and research into particular areas. This is true in the realm of personality study: personality, as a result, is apt to be defined in terms of the theory favored by a particular theoretician.

Consequently it is almost impossible to arrive at a definition of personality which will both satisfy all workers in the field and bear some relation to what the dictionary and the layman would recognize when the word is employed. The popular definition of personality concentrates on outstanding characteristics and the evaluation of social images. It can be applied to anything from the adroitness of a politician's conduct in press conferences to the lessons in cleanliness and deportment given by the "personality leader" of a high school class who encourages her fellow students to dress becomingly, extirpate blackheads, and cultivate the "nice" boys. Commonly, we say people have pleasing or repellent personalities or—devastatingly—we may say they have "no personality" at all.

If popular usage is vague, professional definitions are scarcely more precise: Hall and Lindzey* find at least fifty definitions of personality. These can be grouped into several categories: those which stress relationship to the environment; those which stress human uniqueness; and those which give up the attempt to achieve abstract coherence and merely list the concepts considered to be of primary significance in describing the individual. Thus *personality* may be defined as that which integrates the person's behavior, that which adjusts him to his environment, or which is his feedback response to the reaction of the "responding others" in that environment. The complex of behavior which sets one

---

* Calvin S. Hall and Gardner Lindzey, *Theories of Personality* (New York: John Wiley & Sons, Inc., 1957). This useful compendium presents a well-analyzed summary of the views of a number of personality theorists together with some appraisal of those views as meeting the requirements of what might be termed the "ideal model" of a theory.

person apart from all others may be called his personality. Or the label may be given to the sum of a person's responses to the problems of existence.

Should we proceed to combine the tentative definition of personality with the definition of theory, we might say that personality theory is a set of assumptions about human behavior accompanied by a group of empirical definitions of data concerning that behavior. Such a theory, to be useful, should enable workers in the area to make predictions adequate to deal with a wide range of human behavior, and it should generate a body of relevant research. Measured by this criterion, none of the personality theories presented in this anthology would deserve the label. Nearly all have given rise to some research, but few make their assumptions clear or explicit; as few derive consistent definitions from those assumptions. As regards research, the theories associated with Freud, with Lewin's field theory, and with the study of stimulus-response patterns have generated most formal inquiry; those associated with Karen Horney and Erich Fromm, least; and those associated with other theorists fall between these two poles, since rather inbred groups of investigators tend to cluster about a "master" and to explore a small number of problems with special techniques. Like the stimulus-response school of theorists, the researchers last mentioned tend to work in the manner of conventionally reputable scientific inquiry.

The anomalous character of the situation becomes clear when we look at personality theories in order to note the issues on which they tend to differ. In the earliest period of work on personality theory dispute turned on the question of purposiveness in behavior. Hence motivation assumed the key position which it has continued to have in the discipline. Personality theorists have argued about the role of unconscious factors in human behavior. Since Freud's work became known and accepted, there is little question about the significance of unconscious factors in motivation—and again motivation is a point of crucial interest—instead, personality theorists are concerned with the strength of these factors and the conditions under which they operate. Some theorists seem to imply that the "normality" of an individual's personality can be measured, or at least evaluated, in terms of the degree to which unconscious motivation appears to affect his behavior.

Other points of division come when we consider the distinction between those theorists who stress the genetic aspect of the personality and those who stress the role of the environment in creating it, or the dispute between those who stress knowledge of the role of past experience in understanding behavior as against those who emphasize the possibility of understanding current behavior primarily in terms of current situations. A third line of cleavage comes between theorists who want to study the personality as a unit and those who believe that although the personality is analogous to the field in physics and exists as a whole, it nevertheless can profitably be analyzed into a set of variables. Among the geneticists, Freud and Jung keep incongruous company with mathematical analysts like Cattell and Eysenck and with the physiological determinism of William Sheldon. On the issue of the role of understanding the past in order to comprehend the present, Freud stands at one pole and Carl Rogers, perhaps, at the other. Again, perhaps a little oddly, Lewin, a leading figure in developing a field theory of personality, a thoroughly holistic approach, is also an important figure in the effort to discover specific significant variables for dividing that field into portions which can be analyzed.

At present, as might be expected in a world uneasily aware of social pressures and imperatives bearing hard upon the individual, some personality theorists are stressing the importance of group membership and of role behavior in shaping the personality whereas others emphasize the importance of psychological experience, as against response to actuality, in creating the personality. Concepts like the self are also attracting an attention which might have seemed strange and unscientific in the 1930's. Again, the *self* is variously defined, with definitions falling into two broad categories: those centering on the processes determining behavior, and those centering on the attitudes of the individual concerning his particular self. As contemporary theorists view it, the concept of the self has tended to gain a metric and to lose many of its older, mystic overtones.

Earlier, we remarked that a really useful personality theory should be clear, explicit, and so closely related to the data that it could be employed to predict future behavior. We remarked, too, that none of the theories presented here met these standards too well. Might it be argued, then, that personality theory is a rather footling enterprise? Or at least that "theorizing" in this field should be set aside in favor of fuller and more careful empirical inquiry? Certainly, such inquiry is needed. Certainly, too, the discipline needs fuller exploration and more rigid formal appraisal of prevailing theories rather than new theories or attempts to create a theoretical consensus by abstracting and assembling what current formulations have in common. Nevertheless, it must be remembered that theory is not vain speculation, a kind of epiphenomenon of fact-finding. Theory is a necessary guide. The investigator who attempts to work without it, to be guided by data alone, actually works with premises of which he is not fully aware and which, therefore, he often fails to appraise properly. Better faulty theory, then, than no theory at all. Better still, ample research and rigorous testing of a theory consciously accepted.

This anthology presents a number of theories of personality in their relation to psychoanalytic thought in order to inform the general reader of what is being done in this field. Hopefully, it will also give readers more familiar with this type of material the stimulation of exposure to views different from those they have accepted.

HENDRIK M. RUITENBEEK

VARIETIES OF
PERSONALITY
THEORY

Sigmund Freud

THE ORIGIN AND DEVELOPMENT OF PSYCHOANALYSIS

"THE CLARK LECTURES"

Sigmund Freud was born in Moravia in 1856 and died in London in 1939. For nearly eighty years, however, he resided in Vienna and left that city when the Germans took over Austria. Freud's primary interests were in medicine, biology, and neurology. He obtained a medical degree in 1881 from the University of Vienna. His interest in neurology caused him to study the treatment of nervous disorders which in turn brought him to Paris to study with the famous French psychiatrist, Jean Charcot, who used hypnosis in the treatment of hysteria. The next link to psychoanalysis was his relationship with Joseph Breuer, a Viennese physician, who used to cure patients by letting them talk about their symptoms. For some time Freud and Breuer collaborated in writing up some of their cases of hysteria, but soon the men parted company over the importance of sexual factors in hysteria. In 1900 Freud published his first major work, The Interpretation of Dreams, *and soon was surrounded by a great many followers.*

Freud's contribution to personality theory is his attack upon the traditional psychology of consciousness and his discovery and introduction of the unconscious. In the vast domain of the unconscious, according to Freud, are found the urges, the passions and desires, and repressed feelings which control the conscious thoughts and deeds of man. In Freud's view a psychology which limits itself solely to the analysis of consciousness is inadequate for the understanding of the underlying motives of man's behavior. One can safely state that Freud presented us with the first comprehensive theory of personality.

The lectures printed here are those given on the occasion of his visit to Clark University in September, 1909, his first and only visit to the United States. These lectures contain the basic elements of Freud's theory of personality. Although presented in 1909, they are as valid and penetrating today as they were when first delivered in the lecture hall at Clark University in the presence of Freud's closest disciples Ernest Jones, Carl Jung, and Sandor Ferenczi.

THE ORIGIN AND DEVELOPMENT OF PSYCHOANALYSIS[1]

FIRST LECTURE

Ladies and Gentlemen: It is a new and somewhat embarrassing experience for me to appear as lecturer before students of the New World. I assume that I owe this honor to the association of my name with the theme of psychoanalysis, and consequently it is of psychoanalysis that I shall aim to speak. I shall attempt to give you in very brief form an historical survey of the origin and further development of this new method of research and cure.

Granted that it is a merit to have created psychoanalysis, it is not my merit. I was a student, busy with the passing of my last examinations, when another physician of Vienna, Dr. Joseph Breuer,[2] made the first application of this method to the case of an hysterical girl (1880–82). We must now examine the history of this case and its treatment, which can be found in detail in *Studien über Hysterie*, later published by Dr. Breuer and myself.[3]

But first one word. I have noticed, with considerable satisfaction, that the majority of my hearers do not belong to the medical profession. Now, do not fear that a medical education is necessary to follow what I shall have to say. We shall now accompany the doctors a little way, but soon we shall take leave of them and follow Dr. Breuer on a way which is quite his own.

Dr. Breuer's patient was a girl of twenty-one, of a high degree of intelligence. She had developed in the course of her two years' illness a series of physical and mental disturbances which well deserved to be taken seriously. She had a severe paralysis of both right extremities, with anesthesia, and at times the same affection of the members of the left side of the body; disturbance of eye movements, and much impairment of vision; difficulty in maintaining the position of the head, an intense *Tussis nervosa*, nausea when she attempted to take nourishment, and at one time for several weeks a loss of the power to drink, in spite of tormenting thirst. Her power of speech was also diminished, and this progressed so far that she could neither speak nor understand her mother tongue; and, finally, she was subject to states of "absence," of confusion, delirium, alteration of her whole personality. These states will later claim our attention.

When one hears of such a case, one does not need to be a physician to incline to the opinion that we are concerned here with a serious injury, probably of the brain, for which there is little hope of cure and which will probably lead to the early death of the patient. The doctors will tell us, however, that in one type of case with just as unfavorable symptoms, another, far more favorable, opinion is justified. When one finds such a series of symptoms in the case of a young girl whose vital organs (heart, kidneys) are shown by objective tests to be normal, but who has suffered from strong emotional disturbances, and when the symptoms differ in certain finer characteristics from what one might logically expect, in a case like this the doctors are not too much disturbed. They consider that there is present no organic lesion of the brain, but that enigmatical state, known since the time of the Greek physicians as hysteria, which can simulate a whole series of symptoms of various diseases. They consider in such a case that the life of the patient is not in danger and that a restoration to health will probably come about of itself. The differentiation of such an hysteria from a severe organic lesion is not always very easy. But we do not need to know how a differential diagnosis of this kind is made; you may be sure that the case of Breuer's patient was such that no skillful physician could fail to diagnose an hysteria. We may also add a word here from the history of the case. The illness first appeared while the patient was caring for her father, whom she tenderly loved, during the severe illness which led to his death, a task which she was compelled to abandon because she herself fell ill.

So far it has seemed best to go with the doctors, but we shall soon part company with them. You must not think that the outlook of a patient with regard to medical aid is essentially bettered when the diagnosis points to hysteria rather than to organic disease of the brain. Against the serious brain diseases medical skill is in most cases powerless, but also in the case of hysterical affections the doctor can do nothing. He must leave it to benign nature, when and how his hopeful prognosis will be realized.[4] Accordingly, with the recogni-

tion of the disease as hysteria, little is changed in the situation of the patient, but there is a great change in the attitude
of the doctor. We can observe that he acts quite differently
toward hystericals than toward patients suffering from organic diseases. He will not bring the same interest to the
former as to the latter, since their suffering is much less
serious and yet seems to set up the claim to be valued just
as seriously.

But there is another motive in this action. The physician,
who through his studies has learned so much that is hidden
from the laity, can realize in his thought the causes and
alterations of the brain disorders in patients suffering from
apoplexy or dementia, a representation which must be right
up to a certain point, for by it he is enabled to understand
the nature of each symptom. But before the details of hysterical symptoms, all his knowledge, his anatomical-physio-
logical and pathological education, desert him. He cannot
understand hysteria. He is in the same position before it
as the layman. And that is not agreeable to anyone who is
in the habit of setting such a high valuation upon his
knowledge. Hystericals, accordingly, tend to lose his sympathy; he considers them persons who overstep the laws of
his science, as the orthodox regard heretics; he ascribes to
them all possible evils, blames them for exaggeration and in-
tentional deceit, "simulation," and he punishes them by
withdrawing his interest.

Now, Dr. Breuer did not deserve this reproach in this
case; he gave his patient sympathy and interest, although at
first he did not understand how to help her. Probably this
was easier for him on account of those superior qualities
of the patient's mind and character, to which he bears witness in his account of the case.

His sympathetic observation soon found the means which
made the first help possible. It had been noticed that the
patient, in her states of "absence," of psychic alteration,
usually mumbled over several words to herself. These seemed
to spring from associations with which her thoughts were
busy. The doctor, who was able to get these words, put her
in a sort of hypnosis and repeated them to her over and over,
in order to bring up any associations that they might have.
The patient yielded to his suggestion and reproduced for him
those psychic creations which controlled her thoughts during
her "absences," and which betrayed themselves in these
single spoken words. These were fancies, deeply sad, often

poetically beautiful, daydreams, we might call them, which commonly took as their starting point the situation of a girl beside the sickbed of her father. Whenever she had related a number of such fancies, she was, as it were, freed and restored to her normal mental life. This state of health would last for several hours, and then give place on the next day to a new "absence," which was removed in the same way by relating the newly created fancies. It was impossible not to get the impression that the psychic alteration which was expressed in the "absence" was a consequence of the excitations originating from these intensely emotional fancy-images. The patient herself, who at this time of her illness strangely enough understood and spoke only English, gave this new kind of treatment the name "talking cure," or jokingly designated it as "chimney sweeping."

The doctor soon hit upon the fact that through such cleansing of the soul more could be accomplished than a temporary removal of the constantly recurring mental "clouds." Symptoms of the disease would disappear when in hypnosis the patient could be made to remember the situation and the associative connections under which they first appeared, provided free vent was given to the emotions which they aroused. "There was in the summer a time of intense heat, and the patient had suffered very much from thirst; for, without any apparent reason, she had suddenly become unable to drink. She would take a glass of water in her hand, but as soon as it touched her lips she would push it away as though suffering from hydrophobia. Obviously for these few seconds she was in her absent state. She ate only fruit, melons and the like, in order to relieve this tormenting thirst. When this had been going on about six weeks, she was talking one day in hypnosis about her English governess, whom she disliked, and finally told, with every sign of disgust, how she had come into the room of the governess, and how that lady's little dog, that she abhorred, had drunk out of a glass. Out of respect for the conventions the patient had remained silent. Now, after she had given energetic expression to her restrained anger, she asked for a drink, drank a large quantity of water without trouble, and woke from hypnosis with the glass at her lips. The symptom thereupon vanished permanently."[5]

Permit me to dwell for a moment on this experience. No one had ever cured an hysterical symptom by such means before, or had come so near understanding its cause. This would be a pregnant discovery if the expectation could be confirmed that still other, perhaps the majority of symptoms, originated in this way and could be removed by the same method. Breuer spared no pains to convince himself of this and investigated the pathogenesis of the other more serious symptoms in a more orderly way. Such was indeed the case; almost all the symptoms originated in exactly this way, as remnants, as precipitates, if you like, of affectively toned experiences, which for that reason we later called "psychic traumata." The nature of the symptoms became clear through their relation to the scene which caused them. They were, to use the technical term, "determined" (*determiniert*) by the scene whose memory traces they embodied, and so could no longer be described as arbitrary or enigmatical functions of the neurosis.

Only one variation from what might be expected must be mentioned. It was not always a single experience which occasioned the symptom, but usually several, perhaps many similar, repeated traumata co-operated in this effect. It was necessary to repeat the whole series of pathogenic memories in chronological sequence, and of course in reverse order, the last first and the first last. It was quite impossible to reach the first and often most essential trauma directly, without first clearing away those coming later.

You will of course want to hear me speak of other examples of the causation of hysterical symptoms beside this of inability to drink on account of the disgust caused by the dog drinking from the glass. I must, however, if I hold to my program, limit myself to very few examples. Breuer relates, for instance, that his patient's visual disturbances could be traced back to external causes, in the following way: "The patient, with tears in her eyes, was sitting by the sickbed when her father suddenly asked her what time it was. She could not see distinctly, strained her eyes to see, brought the watch near her eyes so that the dial seemed very large (macropia and strabismus conv.), or else she tried hard to suppress her tears, so that the sick man might not see them."[6]

All the pathogenic impressions sprang from the time when she shared in the care of her sick father. "Once she was watching at night in the greatest anxiety for the patient, who was in a high fever, and in suspense, for a surgeon was expected from Vienna, to operate on the patient. Her mother had gone out for a little while, and Anna sat by the sickbed, her right arm hanging over the back of her chair. She fell into a revery and saw a black snake emerge, as it were, from the wall and approach the sick man as though to bite him. (It is very probable that several snakes had actually been seen in the meadow behind the house, that she had already been frightened by them, and that these former experiences furnished the material for the hallucination.) She tried to drive off the creature, but was as though paralyzed. Her right arm, which was hanging over the back of the chair, had "gone to sleep," become anesthetic and paretic, and as she was looking at it, the fingers changed into little snakes with death's-heads (the nails). Probably she attempted to drive away the snake with her paralyzed right hand, and so the anesthesia and paralysis of this member formed associations with the snake hallucination. When this had vanished, she tried in her anguish to speak, but could not. She could not express herself in any language, until finally she thought of the words of an English nursery song, and thereafter she could think and speak only in this language." [7] When the memory of this scene was revived in hypnosis, the paralysis of the right arm, which had existed since the beginning of the illness, was cured and the treatment ended.

When, a number of years later, I began to use Breuer's researches and treatment on my own patients, my experiences completely coincided with his. In the case of a woman of about forty, there was a tic, a peculiar smacking noise which manifested itself whenever she was laboring under any excitement, without any obvious cause. It had its origin in two experiences which had this common element, that she attempted to make no noise, but that by a sort of counter-will this noise broke the stillness. On the first occasion, she had finally after much trouble put her sick child to sleep, and she tried to be very quiet so as not to awaken it. On the second occasion, during a ride with both her children in a thunderstorm the horses took fright, and she carefully avoided any noise for fear of frightening them still more.[8] I give this example instead of many others which are cited in the *Studien über Hysterie*.

Ladies and gentlemen, if you will permit me to generalize, as is indispensable in so brief a presentation, we may express our results up to this point in the formula: *Our hysterical patients suffer from reminiscences*. Their symptoms are the remnants and the memory symbols of certain (traumatic) experiences.

A comparison with other memory symbols from other sources will perhaps enable us better to understand this symbolism. The memorials and monuments with which we adorn our great cities are also such memory symbols. If you walk through London you will find before one of the greatest railway stations of the city a richly decorated Gothic pillar—Charing Cross. One of the old Plantagenet kings, in the thirteenth century, caused the body of his beloved queen Eleanor to be borne to Westminster, and had Gothic crosses erected at each of the stations where the coffin was set down. Charing Cross is the last of these monuments which preserve the memory of this sad journey.[9] In another part of the city, you will see a high pillar of more modern construction, which is merely called the "monument." This is in memory of the great fire which broke out in the neighborhood in the year 1666, and destroyed a great part of the city. These monuments are memory symbols like the hysterical symptoms; so far the comparison seems justified. But what would you say to a Londoner who today stood sadly before the monument to the funeral of Queen Eleanor, instead of going about his business with the haste engendered by modern industrial conditions, or rejoicing with the young queen of his own heart? Or to another, who before the "monument" bemoaned the burning of his loved native city, which long since has arisen again so much more splendid than before?

Now, hystericals and all neurotics behave like these two unpractical Londoners, not only in that they remember the painful experiences of the distant past, but because they are still strongly affected by them. They cannot escape from the past, and neglect present reality in its favor. This fixation of the mental life on the pathogenic traumata is an essential, and practically a most significant characteristic of the neurosis. I will willingly concede the objection which you are probably formulating, as you think over the history of Breuer's patient. All her traumata originated at the time when she was caring for her sick father, and her symptoms could only be regarded as memory symbols of his sickness and death. They corresponded to mourning, and a fixation on thoughts of the dead so short a time after death is certainly not pathological, but rather corresponds to normal emotional behavior. I concede this: there is nothing abnormal in the fixation of feeling on the trauma shown by Breuer's patient. But in other cases, like that of the tic that I have mentioned, the occasions for which lay ten and fifteen years back, the characteristic of this abnormal clinging to the past is very clear, and Breuer's patient would probably have developed it, if she had not come under the "cathartic treatment" such a short time after the traumatic experiences and the beginning of the disease.

We have so far only explained the relation of the hysterical symptoms to the life history of the patient; now by considering two further moments which Breuer observed, we may get a hint as to the processes of the beginning of the illness and those of the cure. With regard to the first, it is especially to be noted that Breuer's patient in almost all pathogenic situations had to suppress a strong excitement, instead of giving vent to it by appropriate words and deeds. In the little experience with her governess' dog, she suppressed, through regard for the conventions, all manifestations of her very intense disgust. While she was seated by her father's sickbed, she was careful to betray nothing of her anxiety and her painful depression to the patient. When, later, she reproduced the same scene before the physician, the emotion which she had suppressed on the occurrence of the scene burst out with especial strength, as though it had been pent up all along. The symptom which had been caused by that scene reached its greatest intensity while the doctor was striving to revive the memory of the scene, and vanished after it had been fully laid bare. On the other hand, experience shows that if the patient is reproducing the traumatic scene to the physician, the process has no curative effect if, by some peculiar chance, there is no development of emotion. It is apparently these emotional processes upon which the illness of the patient and the restoration to health are dependent. We feel justified in regarding "emotion" as a quantity which may become increased, derived, and displaced. So we are forced to the conclusion that the patient fell ill because the emotion developed in the pathogenic situation was prevented from escaping normally, and that the essence of the sickness lies in the fact that these "imprisoned" (*dingeklemmt*) emotions undergo a series of abnormal changes. In part they are preserved as a lasting charge and as a source of constant disturbance in psychical life; in part they undergo a change into unusual bodily innervations and inhibitions, which present themselves as the physical symptoms of the case. We have coined the name "hysterical conversion" for the latter process. Part of our mental energy is, under normal conditions, conducted off by way of physical innervation and gives what we call "the expression of emotions." Hysterical conversion exaggerates this part of the course of a mental process which is emotionally colored; it corresponds to a far more intense emotional expression, which finds outlet by new paths. If a stream flows in two channels, an overflow of one will take place as soon as the current in the other meets with an obstacle.

You see that we are in a fair way to arrive at a purely psychological theory of hysteria, in which we assign the first rank to the affective processes. A second observation of Breuer compels us to ascribe to the altered condition of consciousness a great part in determining the characteristics of the disease. His patient showed many sorts of mental states, conditions of "absence," confusion and alteration of character, besides her normal state. In her normal state she was entirely ignorant of the pathogenic scenes and of their connection with her symptoms. She had forgotten those scenes, or at any rate had dissociated them from their pathogenic connection. When the patient was hypnotized, it was possible, after considerable difficulty, to recall those scenes to her memory, and by this means of recall the symptoms were removed. It would have been extremely perplexing to know how to interpret this fact, if hypnotic practice and experiments had not pointed out the way. Through the study of hypnotic phenomena, the conception, strange though it was at first, has become familiar, that in one and the same individual several mental groupings are possible, which may remain relatively independent of each other, "know nothing" of each other, and which may cause a splitting of consciousness along lines which they lay down. Cases of such a sort, known as "double personality" (*"double conscience"*), occasionally appear spontaneously. If in such a division of personality consciousness remains constantly bound up with one of the two states, this is called the *conscious* mental state, and the other the *unconscious*. In the well-known phenomena of so-called posthypnotic suggestion, in which a command given in hypnosis is later executed in the normal state as though by an imperative suggestion, we have an excellent basis for understanding how the unconscious state can influence the conscious, although the latter is ignorant of the existence of the former. In the same way it is quite possible to explain the facts in hysterical cases. Breuer came to the conclusion that the hysterical symptoms originated in such peculiar mental states, which he called "hypnoidal states" (*hypnoide Zustände*). Experiences of an emotional nature, which occur during such hypnoidal states, easily become pathogenic, since such states do not present the conditions for a normal draining off of the emotion of the exciting processes. And as a result there arises a peculiar product of this exciting process, that is, the symptom, and this is projected like a foreign body into the normal state. The latter has, then, no conception of the significance of the hypnoidal pathogenic situation. Where a symptom arises, we also find an amnesia, a memory gap, and the filling of this gap includes the removal of the conditions under which the symptom originated.

I am afraid that this portion of my treatment will not seem very clear, but you must remember that we are dealing here with new and difficult views, which perhaps could not be made much clearer. This all goes to show that our knowledge in this field is not yet very far advanced. Breuer's idea of the hypnoidal states has, moreover, been shown to be superfluous and a hindrance to further investigation, and has been dropped from present conceptions of psychoanalysis. Later I shall at least suggest what other influences and processes have been disclosed besides that of the hypnoidal states, to which Breuer limited the causal moment.

You have probably also felt, and rightly, that Breuer's investigations gave you only a very incomplete theory and insufficient explanation of the phenomena which we have observed. But complete theories do not fall from Heaven, and you would have had still greater reason to be distrustful had any one offered you at the beginning of his observations a well-rounded theory, without any gaps; such a theory could only be the child of his speculations and not the fruit of an unprejudiced investigation of the facts.

SECOND LECTURE

Ladies and Gentlemen: At about the same time that Breuer was using the "talking-cure" with his patient, M. Charcot began in Paris, with the hystericals of the Salpetrière, those researches which were to lead to a new understanding of the disease. These results were, however, not yet known in Vienna. But when about ten years later Breuer and I published our preliminary communication on the psychic mechanism of hysterical phenomena, which grew out of the cathartic treatment of Breuer's first patient, we were both of us under the spell of Charcot's investigations. We made the pathogenic experiences of our patients, which acted as psychic traumata, equivalent to those physical traumata whose influence on hysterical paralyses Charcot had determined; and Breuer's hypothesis of hypnoidal states is itself only an echo of the fact that Charcot had artificially reproduced those traumatic paralyses in hypnosis.

The great French observer, whose student I was during the years 1885–86, had no natural bent for creating psychological theories. His student, P. Janet, was the first to attempt to penetrate more deeply into the psychic processes of hysteria, and we followed his example when we made the mental splitting and the dissociation of personality the central points of our theory. Janet propounds a theory of hysteria which draws upon the principal theories of heredity and degeneration which are current in France. According to his view hysteria is a form of degenerative alteration of the nervous system, manifesting itself in a congenital "weakness" of the function of psychic synthesis. The hysterical patient is from the start incapable of correlating and unifying the manifold of his mental processes, and so there arises the tendency to mental dissociation. If you will permit me to use a banal but clear illustration, Janet's hysterical reminds one of a weak woman who has been shopping and is now on her way home, laden with packages and bundles of every description. She cannot manage the whole lot with her two arms and her ten fingers, and soon she drops one. When she stoops to pick this up, another breaks loose, and so it goes on.

Now it does not agree very well with this assumed mental weakness of hystericals that there can be observed in hysterical cases, besides the phenomena of lessened functioning, examples of a partial increase of functional capacity, as a sort of compensation. At the time when Breuer's patient had forgotten her mother tongue and all other languages save English, her control of English attained such a level that if a German book was put before her she could give a fluent, perfect translation of its contents at sight. When later I undertook to continue on my own account the investigations begun by Breuer, I soon came to another view of the origin of hysterical dissociation (or splitting of consciousness). It was inevitable that my views should diverge widely and radically, for my point of departure was not, like that of Janet, laboratory researches, but attempts at therapy. Above everything else, it was practical needs that urged me on. The cathartic treatment, as Breuer had made use of it, presupposed that the patient should be put in deep hypnosis, for only in hypnosis was available the knowledge of his pathogenic associations, which were unknown to him in his normal state. Now hypnosis, as a fanciful and, so to speak, mystical aid, I soon came to dislike; and when I discovered that, in spite of all my efforts, I could not hypnotize by any means all of my patients, I resolved to give up hypnotism and to make the cathartic method independent of it.

Since I could not alter the psychic state of most of my patients at my wish, I directed my efforts to working with them in their normal state. This seems at first sight to be a particularly senseless and aimless undertaking. The problem was this: to find out something from the patient that the doctor did not know and the patient himself did not know. How could one hope to make such a method succeed? The memory of a very noteworthy and instructive proceeding came to my aid, which I had seen in Bernheim's clinic at Nancy. Bernheim showed us that persons put in a condition of hypnotic somnambulism, and subjected to all sorts of experiences, had only apparently lost the memory of those somnambulic experiences, and that their memory of them could be awakened even in the normal state. If he asked them about their experiences during somnambulism, they said at first that they did not remember, but if he persisted, urged, assured them that they did know, then every time the forgotten memory came back.

Accordingly I did this with my patients. When I had reached in my procedure with them a point at which they declared that they knew nothing more, I would assure them that they did know, that they must just tell it out, and I would venture the assertion that the memory which would emerge at the moment that I laid my hand on the patient's forehead would be the right one. In this way I succeeded, without hypnosis, in learning from the patient all that was necessary for a construction of the connection between the forgotten pathogenic scenes and the symptoms which they had left behind. This was a troublesome and in its length an exhausting proceeding, and did not lend itself to a finished technique. But I did not give it up without drawing definite conclusions from the data which I had gained. I had substantiated the fact that the forgotten memories were not lost. They were in the possession of the patient, ready to emerge and form associations with his other mental content, but hindered from becoming conscious, and forced to remain in the unconscious by some sort of force. The existence of this force could be assumed with certainty, for in attempting to drag up the unconscious memories into the consciousness of the patient, in opposition to this force, one got the sensation of his own personal effort striving to overcome it. One could get an idea of this force, which maintained the pathological situation, from the resistance of the patient.

It is on this idea of *resistance* that I based my theory of the psychic processes of hystericals. It had been found that in order to cure the patient it was necessary that this force should be overcome. Now, with the mechanism of the cure as a starting point, quite a definite theory could be constructed. These same forces, which in the present situation as resistances opposed the emergence of the forgotten ideas into consciousness, must themselves have caused the forgetting, and repressed from consciousness the pathogenic experiences. I called this hypothetical process "repression" (*Verdrängung*), and considered that it was proved by the undeniable existence of resistance.

But now the question arose: What were those forces, and what were the conditions of this repression, in which we were now able to recognize the pathogenic mechanism of hysteria? A comparative study of the pathogenic situations, which the cathartic treatment has made possible, allows us to answer this question. In all those experiences, it had happened that a wish had been aroused which was in sharp opposition to the other desires of the individual, and was not capable of being reconciled with the ethical, aesthetic, and personal pretensions of the patient's personality. There had been a short conflict, and the end of this inner struggle was the repression of the idea which presented itself to consciousness as the bearer of this irreconcilable wish. This was, then, repressed from consciousness and forgotten. The incompatibility of the idea in question with the "ego" of the patient was the motive of the repression; the ethical and other pretensions of the individual were the repressing forces. The presence of the incompatible wish, or the duration of the conflict, had given rise to a high degree of mental pain; this pain was avoided by the repression. This latter process is evidently in such a case a device for the protection of the personality.

I will not multiply examples, but will give you the history of a single one of my cases, in which the conditions and the utility of the repression process stand out clearly enough. Of course, for my purpose I must abridge the history of the case and omit many valuable theoretical considerations. It is that of a young girl, who was deeply attached to her father, who had died a short time before, and in whose care she had shared—a situation analogous to that of Breuer's patient.

When her older sister married, the girl grew to feel a peculiar sympathy for her new brother-in-law, which easily passed with her for family tenderness. This sister soon fell ill and died, while the patient and her mother were away. The absent ones were hastily recalled, without being told fully of the painful situation. As the girl stood by the bedside of her dead sister, for one short moment there surged up in her mind an idea, which might be framed in these words: "Now he is free and can marry me." We may be sure that this idea, which betrayed to her consciousness her intense love for her brother-in-law, of which she had not been conscious, was the next moment consigned to repression by her revolted feelings. The girl fell ill with severe hysterical symptoms, and, when I came to treat the case, it appeared that she had entirely forgotten that scene at her sister's bedside and the unnatural, egoistic desire which had arisen in her. She remembered it during the treatment, reproduced the pathogenic moment with every sign of intense emotional excitement, and was cured by this treatment.[10]

Perhaps I can make the process of repression and its necessary relation to the resistance of the patient more concrete by a rough illustration, which I will derive from our present situation.

Suppose that here in this hall and in this audience, whose exemplary stillness and attention I cannot sufficiently commend, there is an individual who is creating a disturbance, and, by his ill-bred laughing, talking, by scraping his feet, distracts my attention from my task. I explain that I cannot go on with my lecture under these conditions, and thereupon several strong men among you get up and, after a short struggle, eject the disturber of the peace from the hall. He is now "repressed," and I can continue my lecture. But in order that the disturbance may not be repeated, in case the man who has just been thrown out attempts to force his way back into the room, the gentlemen who have executed my suggestion take their chairs to the door and establish themselves there as a "resistance," to keep up the repression. Now, if you transfer both locations to the psyche, calling this "consciousness," and the outside the "unconscious," you have a tolerably good illustration of the process of repression.

We can see now the difference between our theory and that of Janet. We do not derive the psychic fission from a congenital lack of capacity on the part of the mental apparatus to synthesize its experiences, but we explain it dynam-

ically by the conflict of opposing mental forces; we recognize
in it the result of an active striving of each mental complex
against the other.

New questions at once arise in great number from our
theory. The situation of psychic conflict is a very frequent
one; an attempt of the ego to defend itself from painful memories can be observed everywhere, and yet the result is not a
mental fission. We cannot avoid the assumption that still
other conditions are necessary, if the conflict is to result in
dissociation. I willingly concede that with the assumption of
"repression" we stand, not at the end, but at the very beginning of a psychological theory. But we can advance only one
step at a time, and the completion of our knowledge must
await further and more thorough work.

Now, do not attempt to bring the case of Breuer's patient
under the point of view of repression. This history cannot be
subjected to such an attempt, for it was gained with the help
of hypnotic influence. Only when hypnosis is excluded can
you see the resistances and repressions and get a correct idea
of the pathogenic process. Hypnosis conceals the resistances
and so makes a certain part of the mental field freely accessi-
ble. By this same process the resistances on the borders of
this field are heaped up into a rampart, which makes all beyond inaccessible.

The most valuable things that we have learned from
Breuer's observations were his conclusions as to the connection of the symptoms with the pathogenic experiences or
psychic traumata, and we must not neglect to evaluate this
result properly from the standpoint of the repression theory.
It is not at first evident how we can get from the repression
to the creation of the symptoms. Instead of giving a complicated theoretical derivation I will return at this point to the
illustration which I used to typify repression.

Remember that with the ejection of the rowdy and the establishment of the watchers before the door the affair is not
necessarily ended. It may very well happen that the ejected
man, now embittered and quite careless of consequences,
gives us more to do. He is no longer among us; we are free
from his presence, his scornful laugh, his half-audible remarks; but in a certain sense the repression has miscarried,
for he makes a terrible uproar outside, and by his outcries
and by hammering on the door with his fists interferes with
my lecture more than before. Under these circumstances it
would be hailed with delight if possibly our honored presi-

dent, Dr. Stanley Hall, should take upon himself the role of peacemaker and mediator. He would speak with the rowdy on the outside, and then turn to us with the recommendation that we let him in again, provided he would guarantee to behave himself better. On Dr. Hall's authority we decide to stop the repression, and now quiet and peace reign again. This is in fact a fairly good presentation of the task devolving upon the physician in the psychoanalytic therapy of neuroses. To say the same thing more directly: we come to the conclusion, from working with hysterical patients and other neurotics, that they have not fully succeeded in repressing the idea to which the incompatible wish is attached. They have, indeed, driven it out of consciousness and out of memory, and apparently saved themselves a great amount of psychic pain, *but in the unconscious the suppressed wish still exists,* only waiting for its chance to become active, and finally succeeds in sending into consciousness, instead of the repressed idea, a disguised and unrecognizable surrogate creation (*Ersatzbildung*), to which the same painful sensations associate themselves that the patient thought he was rid of through his repression. This surrogate of the suppressed idea —the symptom—is secure against further attacks from the defenses of the ego, and instead of a short conflict there originates now a permanent suffering. We can observe in the symptom, besides the tokens of its disguise, a remnant of traceable similarity with the originally repressed idea; the way in which the surrogate is built up can be discovered during the psychoanalytic treatment of the patient, and for his cure the symptom must be traced back over the same route to the repressed idea. If this repressed material is once more made part of the conscious mental functions—a process which supposes the overcoming of considerable resistance— the psychic conflict which then arises, the same which the patient wished to avoid, is made capable of a happier termination, under the guidance of the physician, than is offered by repression. There are several possible suitable decisions which can bring conflict and neurosis to a happy end; in particular cases the attempt may be made to combine several of these. Either the personality of the patient may be convinced that he has been wrong in rejecting the pathogenic wish, and he may be made to accept it either wholly or in part; or this wish may itself be directed to a higher goal which is free from objection, by what is called sublimation (*Sublimierung*); or the rejection may be recognized as rightly motivated, and the automatic and therefore insuf-ficient mechanism of repression be reinforced by the higher, more characteristically human mental faculties: one succeeds in mastering his wishes by conscious thought.

Forgive me if I have not been able to present more clearly these main points of the treatment which is today known as "psychoanalysis." The difficulties do not lie merely in the newness of the subject.

Regarding the nature of the unacceptable wishes, which succeed in making their influence felt out of the unconscious, in spite of repression; and regarding the question of what subjective and constitutional factors must be present for such a failure of repression and such a surrogate or symptom crea-tion to take place, we will speak in later remarks.

THIRD LECTURE

Ladies and Gentlemen: It is not always easy to tell the truth, especially when one must be brief, and so today I must correct an incorrect statement that I made in my last lecture.

I told you how when I gave up using hypnosis I pressed my patients to tell me what came into their minds that had to do with the problem we were working on; I told them that they would remember what they had apparently for-gotten, and that the thought which irrupted into consciousness (*Einfall*) would surely embody the memory for which we were seeking. I claimed that I substantiated the fact that the first idea of my patients brought the right clue and could be shown to be the forgotten continuation of the memory. Now, this is not always so; I represented it as being so simple only for purposes of abbreviation. In fact, it would only happen the first times that the right forgotten material would emerge through simple pressure on my part. If the experience was continued, ideas emerged in every case which could not be the right ones, for they were not to the purpose, and the patients themselves rejected them as incor-rect. Pressure was of no further service here, and one could only regret again having given up hypnosis. In this state of perplexity I clung to a prejudice which years later was proved by my friend C. G. Jung, of the University of Zurich, and his pupils to have a scientific justification. I must confess that it is often of great advantage to have prejudices. I put a high value on the strength of the determination of mental processes, and I could not believe that any idea which

occurred to the patient, which originated in a state of concentrated attention, could be quite arbitrary and out of all
relation to the forgotten idea that we were seeking. That
it was not identical with the latter could be satisfactorily explained by the hypothetical psychological situation. In the
patients whom I treated there were two opposing forces: on
the one hand the conscious striving to drag up into consciousness the forgotten experience which was present in the unconscious; and on the other hand the resistance which we
have seen, which set itself against the emergence of the
suppressed idea or its associates into consciousness. In case
this resistance was nonexistent or very slight, the forgotten
material could become conscious without disguise (*Enstel-
lung*). It was then a natural supposition that the disguise
would be the more complete, the greater the resistance to
the emergence of the idea. Thoughts which broke into the
patient's consciousness, instead of the ideas sought for, were
accordingly made up just like symptoms; they were new,
artificial, ephemeral surrogates for the repressed ideas, and
differed from these just in proportion as they had been more
completely disguised under the influence of the resistances.
These surrogates must, however, show a certain similarity
with the ideas which are the object of our search, by virtue
of their nature as symptoms; and when the resistance is
not too intensive it is possible from the nature of these irrup-
tions to discover the hidden object of our search. This must
be related to the repressed thought as a sort of allusion, as a
statement of the same thing in *indirect* terms.

We know cases in normal psychology in which analogous
situations to the one which we have assumed give rise to similar experiences. Such a case is that of wit. By my study of
psychoanalytic technique I was necessarily led to a consideration of the problem of the nature of wit. I will give one
example of this sort, which, too, is a story that originally
appeared in English.

The anecdote runs: Two unscrupulous businessmen had
succeeded by fortunate speculations in accumulating a large
fortune, and then directed their efforts to breaking into good
society. Among other means they thought it would be of advantage to be painted by the most famous and expensive
artist of the city, a man whose paintings were considered as
events. The costly paintings were first shown at a great
soirée, and both hosts led the most influential connoisseur
and art critic to the wall of the salon on which the portraits

were hung, to elicit his admiring judgment. The artist looked for a long time, looked about as though in search of something, and then merely asked, pointing out the vacant space between the two pictures, "And where is the Saviour?"[11]

I see that you are all laughing over this good example of wit, which we will not attempt to analyze. We understand that the critic means to say, "You are a couple of malefactors, like those between whom the Saviour was crucified." But he does not say this; he expresses himself instead in a way that at first seems not to the purpose and not related to the matter in hand, but which at the next moment we recognize as an *allusion* to the insult at which he aims, and as a perfect surrogate for it. We cannot expect to find in the case of wit all those relations that our theory supposes for the origin of the irruptive ideas of our patients, but it is my desire to lay stress on the similar motivation of wit and irruptive idea. Why does not the critic say directly what he has to say to the two rogues? Because, in addition to his desire to say it straight out, he is actuated by strong opposite motives. It is a proceeding which is liable to be dangerous to offend people who are one's hosts, and who can call to their aid the strong arms of numerous servants. One might easily suffer the same fate that I used in the previous lecture to illustrate repression. On this ground, the critic does not express the particular insult directly, but in a disguised form, as an allusion with omission. The same constellation comes into play, according to our hypothesis, when our patient produces the irruptive idea as a surrogate for the forgotten idea which is the object of the quest.

Ladies and gentlemen, it is very useful to designate a group of ideas which belong together and have a common emotive tone, according to the custom of the Zurich school (Bleuler, Jung, and others), as a "complex." So we can say that if we set out from the last memories of the patient to look for a repressed complex, we have every prospect of discovering it, if only the patient will communicate to us a sufficient number of the ideas which come into his head. So we let the patient speak along any line that he desires, and cling to the hypothesis that nothing can occur to him except what has some indirect bearing on the complex that we are seeking. If this method of discovering the repressed complexes seems too circumstantial, I can at least assure you that it is the only available one.

In practicing this technique, one is further bothered by the fact that the patient often stops, is at a standstill, and considers that he has nothing to say; nothing occurs to him. If this were really the case and the patient were right, our procedure would again be proved inapplicable. Closer observation shows that such an absence of ideas never really occurs and that it only appears to, when the patient holds back or rejects the idea which he perceives, under the influence of the resistance, which disguises itself as critical judgment of the value of the idea. The patient can be protected from this if he is warned in advance of this circumstance, and told to take no account of the critical attitude. He must say anything that comes into his mind, fully laying aside such critical choice, even though he may think it unessential, irrelevant, nonsensical, especially when the idea is one which is unpleasant to dwell on. By following this prescription we secure the material which sets us on the track of the repressed complex.

These irruptive ideas, which the patient himself values little, if he is under the influence of the resistance and not that of the physician, are for the psychologist like the ore, which by simple methods of interpretation he reduces from its crude state to valuable metal. If one desires to gain in a short time a preliminary knowledge of the patient's repressed complexes, without going into the question of their arrangement and associations, this examination may be conducted with the help of the association experiments, as Jung[12] and his pupils have perfected them. This procedure is to the psychologist what qualitative analysis is to the chemist; it may be dispensed with in the therapy of neurotic patients, but is indispensable in the investigation of the psychoses, which have been begun by the Zurich school with such valuable results.

This method of work with whatever comes into the patient's head when he submits to psychoanalytic treatment is not the only technical means at our disposal for the widening of consciousness. Two other methods of procedure serve the same purpose: the interpretation of his dreams and the evaluation of acts which he bungles or does without intending to (*Fehl-und Zufallshandlungen*).

I might say, esteemed hearers, that for a long time I hesitated whether instead of this hurried survey of the whole field of psychoanalysis, I should not rather offer you a thorough consideration of the analysis of dreams; a purely subjective and apparently secondary motive decided me against this. It seemed rather an impropriety that in this country, so devoted to practical pursuits, I should pose as "interpreter of dreams," before you had a chance to discover what significance the old and despised art can claim.

Interpretation of dreams is in fact the *via regia* to the interpretation of the unconscious, the surest ground of psychoanalysis, and a field in which every worker must win his convictions and gain his education. If I were asked how one could become a psychoanalyst, I should answer, through the study of his own dreams. With great tact all opponents of the psychoanalytic theory have so far either evaded any criticism of the *"Traumdeutung"*[13] or have attempted to pass over it with the most superficial objections. If, on the contrary, you will undertake the solution of the problems of dream life, the novelties which psychoanalysis present to your thoughts will no longer be difficulties.

You must remember that our nightly dream productions show the greatest outer similarity and inner relationship to the creations of the insane, but on the other hand are compatible with full health during waking hours. It does not sound at all absurd to say that whoever regards these normal sense illusions, these delusions and alterations of character as matter for amazement instead of understanding, has not the least prospect of understanding the abnormal creations of diseased mental states in any other than the lay sense. You may with confidence place in this lay group all the psychiatrists of today. Follow me now on a brief excursion through the field of dream problems.

In our waking state we usually treat dreams with as little consideration as the patient treats the irruptive ideas which the psychoanalyst demands from him. It is evident that we reject them, for we forget them quickly and completely. The slight valuation which we place on them is based, with those dreams that are not confused and nonsensical, on the feeling that they are foreign to our personality, and, with other dreams, on their evident absurdity and senselessness. Our rejection derives support from the unrestrained shamelessness and the immoral longings which are obvious in many dreams. Antiquity, as we know, did not share this light valuation of dreams. The lower classes of our people today stick close to the value which they set on dreams; they, however, expect from them, as did the ancients, the revelation of the future. I confess that I see no need to adopt mystical hypotheses to fill out the gaps in our present knowledge, and so I have never been able to find anything that supported the hypothesis of the prophetic nature of dreams. Many other things, which are wonderful enough, can be said about them.

And first, not all dreams are so foreign to the character of the dreamer, are incomprehensible and confused. If you will undertake to consider the dreams of young children from the age of a year and a half on, you will find them quite simple and easy to interpret. The young child always dreams of the fulfillment of wishes which were aroused in him the day before and were not satisfied. You need no art of interpretation to discover this simple solution; you need only to inquire into the experiences of the child on the day before (the "dream day"). Now it would certainly be a most satisfactory solution of the dream riddle if the dreams of adults, too, were the same as those of children, fulfillments of wishes which had been aroused in them during the dream day. This is actually the fact; the difficulties which stand in the way of this solution can be removed step by step by a thorough analysis of the dream.

There is, first of all, the most weighty objection, that the dreams of adults generally have an incomprehensible content, which shows wish fulfillment least of anything. The answer is this: These dreams have undergone a process of disguise; the psychic content which underlies them was originally meant for quite different verbal expression. You must differentiate between the *manifest dream content*, which we remember in the morning only confusedly, and with difficulty clothe in words which seem arbitrary, and the *latent dream thoughts*, whose presence in the unconscious we must assume. This distortion of the dream (*Traumentstellung*) is the same process which has been revealed to you in the investigations of the creations (*symptoms*) of hysterical subjects; it points to the fact that the same opposition of psychic forces has its share in the creation of dreams as in the creation of symptoms.

The manifest dream content is the disguised surrogate for the unconscious dream thoughts, and this disguising is the work of the defensive forces of the ego, of the resistances. These prevent the repressed wishes from entering consciousness during the waking life; and even in the relaxation of sleep they are still strong enough to force them to hide themselves by a sort of masquerading. The dreamer, then, knows just as little the sense of his dream as the hysterical knows the relation and significance of his symptoms. That there are

latent dream thoughts and that between them and the manifest dream content there exists the relation just described—of
this you may convince yourselves by the analysis of dreams, a
procedure the technique of which is exactly that of a psychoanalysis. You must abstract entirely from the apparent connection of the elements in the manifest dream and seek for the
irruptive ideas which arise through free association, according
to the psychoanalytic laws, from each separate dream element. From this material the latent dream thoughts may be
discovered, exactly as one divines the concealed complexes of
the patient from the fancies connected with his symptoms and
memories. From the latent dream thoughts which you will
find in this way, you will see at once how thoroughly justified
one is in interpreting the dreams of adults by the same rubrics
as those of children. What is now substituted for the manifest dream content is the real sense of the dream, is always
clearly comprehensible, associated with the impressions of the
day before, and appears as the fulfilling of an unsatisfied
wish. The manifest dream, which we remember after waking,
may then be described as a *disguised* fulfillment of *repressed*
wishes.

It is also possible by a sort of synthesis to get some insight
into the process which has brought about the disguise of the
unconscious dream thoughts as the manifest dream content.
We call this process "dream work" (*Traumarbeit*). This deserves our fullest theoretical interest, since here as nowhere
else we can study the unsuspected psychic processes which
are existent in the unconscious, or, to express it more exactly,
between two such separate systems as the conscious and the
unconscious. Among these newly discovered psychic processes, two, condensation (*Verdichtung*) and displacement or
transvaluation, change of psychic accent (*Verschiebung*),
stand out most prominently. Dream work is a special case
of the reaction of different mental groupings on each other,
and as such is the consequence of psychic fission. In all essential points it seems identical with the work of disguise, which
changes the repressed complex in the case of failing repression into symptoms.

You will furthermore discover by the analysis of dreams,
most convincingly your own, the unsuspected importance of
the role which impressions and experiences from early childhood exert on the development of men. In the dream life the
child, as it were, continues his existence in the man, with a
retention of all his traits and wishes, including those which

he was obliged to allow to fall into disuse in his later years. With irresistible might it will be impressed on you by what processes of development, of repression, sublimation, and re-action there arises out of the child, with its peculiar gifts and tendencies, the so-called normal man, the bearer and partly the victim of our painfully acquired civilization. I will also direct your attention to the fact that we have discovered from the analysis of dreams that the unconscious makes use of a sort of symbolism, especially in the presentation of sexual complexes. This symbolism in part varies with the indi-vidual, but in part is of a typical nature, and seems to be identical with the symbolism which we suppose to lie behind our myths and legends. It is not impossible that these latter creations of the people may find their explanation from the study of dreams.

Finally, I must remind you that you must not be led astray by the objection that the occurrence of anxiety dreams (*Angsttraüme*) contradicts our idea of the dream as a wish fulfillment. Apart from the consideration that anxiety dreams also require interpretation before judgment can be passed on them, one can say quite generally that the anxiety does not depend in such a simple way on the dream content as one might suppose without more knowledge of the facts and more attention to the conditions of neurotic anxiety. Anxiety is one of the ways in which the ego relieves itself of repressed wishes which have become too strong, and so is easy to ex-plain in the dream, if the dream has gone too far toward the fulfilling of the objectionable wish.

You see that the investigation of dreams was justified by the conclusions which it has given us concerning things other-wise hard to understand. But we came to it in connection with the psychoanalytic treatment of neurotics. From what has been said you can easily understand how the interpreta-tion of dreams, if it is not made too difficult by the resistance of the patient, can lead to a knowledge of the patient's concealed and repressed wishes and the complexes which he is nourishing. I may now pass to that group of everyday mental phenomena whose study has become a technical help for psychoanalysis.

These are the bungling of acts (*Fehlhandlungen*) among normal men as well as among neurotics, to which no signifi-cance is ordinarily attached; the forgetting of things which one is supposed to know and at other times really does know (for example, the temporary forgetting of proper names);

mistakes in speaking (*Versprechen*), which occur so frequently; analogous mistakes in writing (*Verschreiben*) and in reading (*Verlesen*), the automatic execution of purposive acts in wrong situations (*Vergreifen*), and the loss or breaking of objects, and so on. These are trifles, for which no one has ever sought a psychological determination, which have passed unchallenged as chance experiences, as consequences of absent-mindedness, inattention, and similar conditions. Here, too, are included the acts and gestures executed without being noticed by the subject, to say nothing of the fact that he attaches no psychic importance to them; as playing and trifling with objects, humming melodies, handling one's person and clothing, and the like.[14]

These little things, the bungling of acts, like the symptomatic and chance acts (*Symptom- und Zufallshandlungen*), are not so entirely without meaning as is generally supposed by a sort of tacit agreement. They have a meaning, generally easy and sure to interpret from the situation in which they occur, and it can be demonstrated that they either express impulses and purposes which are repressed, hidden if possible from the consciousness of the individual, or that they spring from exactly the same sort of repressed wishes and complexes which we have learned to know already as the creators of symptoms and dreams.

It follows that they deserve the rank of symptoms, and their observation, like that of dreams, can lead to the discovery of the hidden complexes of the psychic life. With their help one will usually betray the most intimate of his secrets. If these occur so easily and commonly among people in health, with whom repression has on the whole succeeded fairly well, this is due to their insignificance and their inconspicuous nature. But they can lay claim to high theoretic value, for they prove the existence of repression and surrogate creations even under the conditions of health. You have already noticed that the psychoanalyst is distinguished by an especially strong belief in the determination of the psychic life. For him there is in the expressions of the psyche nothing trifling, nothing arbitrary and lawless; he expects everywhere a widespread motivation, where customarily such claims are not made; more than that, he is even prepared to find a manifold motivation of these psychic expressions, while our supposedly inborn causal need is satisfied with a single psychic cause.

Now keeping in mind the means which we possess for the discovery of the hidden, forgotten, repressed things in the soul

life: the study of the irruptive ideas called up by free association, the patient's dreams, and his bungled and symptomatic
acts; and adding to these the evaluation of other phenomena
which emerge during the psychoanalytic treatment, on which
I shall later make a few remarks under the heading of "transfer" (*Uebertragung*), you will come with me to the conclusion that our technique is already sufficiently efficacious for
the solution of the problem of how to introduce the pathogenic psychic material into consciousness, and so to do away
with the suffering brought on by the creation of surrogate
symptoms.

The fact that by such therapeutic endeavors our knowledge
of the mental life of the normal and the abnormal is widened
and deepened can of course only be regarded as an especial
attraction and superiority of this method.

I do not know whether you have gained the impression
that the technique through whose arsenal I have led you is a
peculiarly difficult one. I consider that on the contrary, for
one who has mastered it, it is quite adapted for use. But so
much is sure, that it is not obvious, that it must be learned no
less than the histological or the surgical technique.

You may be surprised to learn that in Europe we have
heard very frequently judgments passed on psychoanalysis by
persons who knew nothing of its technique and had never
practiced it, but who demanded scornfully that we show the
correctness of our results. There are among these people
some who are not in other things unacquainted with scientific
methods of thought, who for example would not reject the
result of a microscopical research because it cannot be confirmed with the naked eye in anatomical preparations, and
who would not pass judgment until they had used the micro-
scope. But in matters of psychoanalysis circumstances are
really more unfavorable for gaining recognition. Psychoanalysis will bring the repressed in mental life to conscious acknowledgment, and every one who judges it is himself a
man who has such repressions, perhaps only maintained with
difficulty. It will consequently call forth the same resistances
from him as from the patient, and this resistance can easily
succeed in disguising itself as intellectual rejection, and bring
forward arguments similar to those from which we protect
our patients by the basic principles of psychoanalysis. It is
not difficult to substantiate in our opponents the same impairment of intelligence produced by emotivity which we
may observe every day with our patients. The arrogance of

consciousness which for example rejects dreams so lightly, belongs—quite generally—to the strongest protective apparatus which guards us against the breaking through of the unconscious complexes, and as a result it is hard to convince people of the reality of the unconscious, and to teach them anew what their conscious knowledge contradicts.

FOURTH LECTURE

Ladies and Gentlemen: At this point you will be asking what the technique which I have described has taught us of the nature of the pathogenic complexes and repressed wishes of neurotics.

One thing in particular: Psychoanalytic investigations trace back the symptoms of disease with really surprising regularity to impressions from the sexual life, show us that the pathogenic wishes are of the nature of erotic impulse components (*Triebkomponente*), and necessitate the assumption that to disturbances of the erotic sphere must be ascribed the greatest significance among the etiological factors of the disease. This holds of both sexes.

I know that this assertion will not willingly be credited. Even those investigators who gladly follow my psychological labors are inclined to think that I overestimate the etiological share of the sexual moments. They ask me why other mental excitations should not lead to the phenomena of repression and surrogate creation which I have described. I can give them this answer: that I do not know why they should not do this, I have no objection to their doing it, but experience shows that they do not possess such a significance, and that they merely support the effect of the sexual moments, without being able to supplant them. This conclusion was not a theoretical postulate; in the *Studien über Hysterie*, published in 1895 with Dr. Breuer, I did not stand on this ground. I was converted to it when my experience was richer and had led me deeper into the nature of the case. Gentlemen, there are among you some of my closest friends and adherents, who have traveled to Worcester with me. Ask them, and they will tell you that they all were at first completely skeptical of the assertion of the determinative significance of the sexual etiology, until they were compelled by their own analytic labors to come to the same conclusion.

The conduct of the patients does not make it any easier to convince one's self of the correctness of the view which I have

expressed. Instead of willingly giving us information concerning their sexual life, they try to conceal it by every means
in their power. Men generally are not candid in sexual matters. They do not show their sexuality freely, but they wear
a thick overcoat—a fabric of lies—to conceal it, as though it
were bad weather in the world of sex. And they are not
wrong; sun and wind are not favorable in our civilized society
to any demonstration of sex life. In truth no one can freely
disclose his erotic life to his neighbor. But when your patients
see that in your treatment they may disregard the conventional restraints, they lay aside this veil of lies, and then only
are you in a position to formulate a judgment on the question
in dispute. Unfortunately, physicians are not favored above
the rest of the children of men in their personal relationship
to the questions of the sex life. Many of them are under the
ban of that mixture of prudery and lasciviousness which determines the behavior of most *Kulturmenschen* in affairs of
sex.

Now to proceed with the communication of our results. It
is true that in another series of cases psychoanalysis at first
traces the symptoms back not to the sexual, but to banal traumatic experiences. But the distinction loses its significance
through other circumstances. The work of analysis which is
necessary for the thorough explanation and complete cure of
a case of sickness does not stop in any case with the experience of the time of onset of the disease, but in every case it
goes back to the adolescence and the early childhood of the
patient. Here only do we hit upon the impressions and circumstances which determine the later sickness. Only the
childhood experiences can give the explanation for the sensitivity to later traumata, and only when these memory traces,
which almost always are forgotten, are discovered and made
conscious is the power developed to banish the symptoms.
We arrive here at the same conclusion as in the investigation
of dreams—that it is the incompatible, repressed wishes of
childhood which lend their power to the creation of symptoms. Without these the reactions upon later traumata
discharge normally. But we must consider these mighty
wishes of childhood very generally as sexual in nature.

Now I can at any rate be sure of your astonishment. Is
there an infantile sexuality? you will ask. Is childhood not
rather that period of life which is distinguished by the lack of
the sexual impulse? No, gentlemen, it is not at all true that
the sexual impulse enters into the child at puberty, as the

devils in the gospel entered into the swine. The child has his sexual impulses and activities from the beginning; he brings them with him into the world, and from these the so-called normal sexuality of adults emerges by a significant development through manifold stages. It is not very difficult to observe the expressions of this childish sexual activity; it needs rather a certain art to overlook them or to fail to interpret them.[15]

As fate would have it, I am in a position to call a witness for my assertions from your own midst. I show you here the work of one Dr. Sanford Bell, published in 1902 in the *American Journal of Psychology*. The author was a fellow of Clark University, the same institution within whose walls we now stand. In this thesis, entitled "A Preliminary Study of the Emotion of Love between the Sexes," which appeared three years before my *Drei Abhandlungen zur Sexualtheorie*, the author says just what I have been saying to you: "The emotion of sex love . . . does not make its appearance for the first time at the period of adolescence as has been thought." He has, as we should say in Europe, worked by the American method, and has gathered not less than 2,500 positive observations in the course of fifteen years, among them 800 of his own. He says of the signs by which this amorous condition manifests itself: "The unprejudiced mind, in observing these manifestations in hundreds of couples of children, cannot escape referring them to sex origin. The most exacting mind is satisfied when to these observations are added the confessions of those who have as children experienced the emotion to a marked degree of intensity, and whose memories of childhood are relatively distinct." Those of you who are unwilling to believe in infantile sexuality will be most astonished to hear that among those children who fell in love so early not a few are of the tender ages of three, four, and five years.

It would not be surprising if you should believe the observations of a fellow countryman rather than my own. Fortunately, a short time ago from the analysis of a five-year-old boy who was suffering from anxiety, an analysis undertaken with correct technique by his own father,[16] I succeeded in getting a fairly complete picture of the bodily expressions of the impulse and the mental productions of an early stage of childish sexual life. And I must remind you that my friend Dr. C. G. Jung read you a few hours ago in this room an observation on a still younger girl who from the same cause as my patient—the birth of a little child in the family—betrayed certainly almost the same secret excitement, wish, and complex creation. Accordingly, I am not without hope that you may feel friendly toward this idea of infantile sexuality that was so strange at first. I might also quote the remarkable example of the Zurich psychiatrist, E. Bleuler, who said a few years ago openly that he faced my sexual theories incredulous and bewildered, and since that time by his own observations had substantiated them in their whole scope.[17] If it is true that most men, medical observers and others, do not want to know anything about the sexual life of the child, the fact is capable of explanation only too easily. They have forgotten their own infantile sexual activity under the pressure of education for civilization, and do not care to be reminded now of the repressed material. You will be convinced otherwise if you begin the investigation, by a self-analysis, by an interpretation of your own childhood memories.

Lay aside your doubts and let us evaluate the infantile sexuality of the earliest years.[18] The sexual impulse of the child manifests itself as a very complex one; it permits of an analysis into many components, which spring from different sources. It is entirely disconnected from the function of reproduction which it is later to serve. It permits the child to gain different sorts of pleasure sensations, which we include, by the analogues and connections which they show, under the term "sexual pleasures." The great source of infantile sexual pleasure is the autoexcitation of certain particularly sensitive parts of the body; besides the genitals are included the rectum and the opening of the urinary canal, and also the skin and other sensory surfaces. Since in this first phase of child sexual life the satisfaction is found on the child's own body and has nothing to do with any other object, we call this phase after a word coined by Havelock Ellis, that of "autoerotism." The parts of the body significant in giving sexual pleasure we call "erogenous zones." The thumb-sucking (*Ludeln*) or passionate sucking (*Wonnesaugen*) of very young children is a good example of such an autoerotic satisfaction of an erogenous zone. The first scientific observer of this phenomenon, a specialist in children's diseases in Budapest by the name of Lindner, interpreted these rightly as sexual satisfaction, and described exhaustively their transformation into other and higher forms of sexual gratification.[19] Another sexual satisfaction of this time of life is the excitation of the genitals by masturbation, which has such a great significance for later life and, in the case of many individuals, is never fully overcome. Besides this and other autoerotic manifestations we see very early in the child the impulse components of *sexual pleasure*, or, as we may say, of the *libido*, which presupposes a second person as its object. These impulses appear in opposed pairs, as active and passive. The most important representatives of this group are the pleasure in inflicting pain (sadism), with its passive opposite (masochism), and active and passive exhibition pleasure (*Schaulust*). From the first of these later pairs splits off the curiosity for knowledge, as from the latter the impulse toward artistic and theatrical representation. Other sexual manifestations of the child can already be regarded from the viewpoint of object-choice, in which the second person plays the prominent part. The significance of this was primarily based upon motives of the impulse of self-preservation. The difference between the sexes plays, however, in the child no very great role. One may attribute to every child, without wronging him, a bit of the homosexual disposition.

The sexual life of the child, rich, but dissociated, in which each single impulse goes about the business of arousing pleasure independently of every other, is later correlated and organized in two general directions, so that by the close of puberty the definite sexual character of the individual is practically finally determined. The single impulses subordinate themselves to the overlordship of the genital zone, so that the whole sexual life is taken over into the service of procreation, and their gratification is now significant only so far as they help to prepare and promote the true sexual act. On the other hand, object-choice prevails over autoerotism, so that now in the sexual life all components of the sexual impulse are satisfied in the loved person. But not all the original impulse components are given a share in the final shaping of the sexual life. Even before the advent of puberty certain impulses have undergone the most energetic repression under the impulse of education, and mental forces like shame, disgust, and morality are developed, which, like sentinels, keep the repressed wishes in subjection. When there comes, in puberty, the high tide of sexual desire it finds dams in this creation of reactions and resistances. These guide the outflow into the so-called normal channels, and make it impossible to revivify the impulses which have undergone repression.

The most important of these repressed impulses are coprophilism, that is, the pleasure in children connected with the excrements; and, further, the tendencies attaching themselves to the persons of the primitive object-choice.

Gentlemen, a sentence of general pathology says that every process of development brings with it the germ of pathological dispositions in so far as it may be inhibited, delayed, or incompletely carried out. This holds for the development of the sexual function, with its many complications. It is not smoothly completed in all individuals, and may leave behind either abnormalities or disposition to later diseases by the way of later falling back or *regression*. It may happen that not all the partial impulses subordinate themselves to the rule of the genital zone. Such an impulse which has remained disconnected brings about what we call a perversion, which may replace the normal sexual goal by one of its own. It may happen, as has been said before, that the autoerotism is not fully overcome, as many sorts of disturbances testify. The originally equal value of both sexes as sexual objects may be maintained and an inclination to homosexual activities in adult life result from this, which, under suitable conditions, rises to the level of exclusive homosexuality. This series of disturbances corresponds to the direct inhibition of development of the sexual function; it includes the perversions and the general *infantilism* of the sex life that are not seldom met with.

The disposition to neuroses is to be derived in another way from an injury to the development of the sex life. The neuroses are related to the perversions as the negative to the positive; in them we find the same impulse components as in perversions, as bearers of the complexes and as creators of the symptoms; but here they work from out the unconscious. They have undergone a repression, but in spite of this they maintain themselves in the unconscious. Psychoanalysis teaches us that overstrong expression of the impulse in very early life leads to a sort of fixation (*Fixirung*), which then offers a weak point in the articulation of the sexual function. If the exercise of the normal sexual function meets with hindrances in later life, this repression, dating from the time of development, is broken through at just that point at which the infantile fixation took place.

You will now perhaps make the objection, "But all that is not sexuality." I have used the word in a very much wider sense than you are accustomed to understanding it. This I willingly concede. But it is a question whether you do not rather use the word in much too narrow a sense when you restrict it to the realm of procreation. You sacrifice by that the understanding of perversions; of the connection between perversion, neurosis, and normal sexual life; and have no means of recognizing, in its true significance, the easily observable beginning of the somatic and mental sexual life of the child. But however you decide about the use of the word, remember that the psychoanalyst understands sexuality in that full sense to which he is led by the evaluation of infantile sexuality.

Now we turn again to the sexual development of the child. We still have much to say here, since we have given more attention to the somatic than to the mental expressions of the sexual life. The primitive object-choice of the child, which is derived from his need of help, demands our further interest. It first attaches to all persons to whom he is accustomed, but soon these give way in favor of his parents. The relation of the child to his parents is, as both direct observation of the child and later analytic investigation of adults agree, not at all free from elements of sexual accessory excitation (*Miterregung*). The child takes both parents, and especially one, as an object of his erotic wishes. Usually he follows in this the stimulus given by his parents, whose tenderness has very clearly the character of a sex manifestation, though inhibited so far as its goal is concerned. As a rule, the father prefers the daughter, the mother the son; the child reacts to this situation, since, as son, he wishes himself in the place of his father, as daughter, in the place of the mother. The feelings awakened in these relations between parents and children, and, as a resultant of them, those among the children in relation to each other, are not only positively of a tender, but negatively of an inimical sort. The complex built up in this way is destined to quick repression, but it still exerts a great and lasting effect from the unconscious. We must express the opinion that this with its ramifications presents the *nuclear complex* of every neurosis, and so we are prepared to meet with it in a not less effectual way in the other fields of mental life. The myth of King Oedipus, who kills his father and wins his mother as a wife, is only the slightly altered presentation of the infantile wish, rejected later by the opposing barriers of incest. Shakespeare's tale of Hamlet rests on the same basis of an incest complex, though better concealed. At the time when the child is still ruled by the still unrepressed nuclear complex, there begins a very significant part of his mental activity which serves sexual interest. He begins to investigate the question of where children come from and guesses more than adults imagine of the true relations by deduction from the signs which he sees. Usually his interest in this investigation is awakened by the threat to his welfare through the birth of another child in the family, in whom at first he sees only a rival. Under the influence of the partial impulses which are active in him he arrives at a number of "infantile sexual theories," as that the same male genitals belong to both sexes, that children are conceived by eating and born through the opening of the intestine, and that sexual intercourse is to be regarded as an inimical act, a sort of overpowering.

But just the unfinished nature of his sexual constitution and the gaps in his knowledge brought about by the hidden condition of the feminine sexual canal cause the infant investigator to discontinue his work as a failure. The facts of this childish investigation itself, as well as the infant sex theories created by it, are of determinative significance in the building of the child's character, and in the content of his later neuroses.

It is unavoidable and quite normal that the child should make his parents the objects of his first object-choice. But his libido must not remain fixed on these first chosen objects, but must take them merely as a prototype and transfer from these to other persons in the time of definite object-choice. The breaking loose (*Ablösung*) of the child from his parents is thus a problem impossible to escape if the social virtue of the young individual is not to be impaired. During the time that the repressive activity is making its choice among the partial sexual impulses, and later, when the influence of the parents, which in the most essential way has furnished the material for these repressions, is lessened, great problems fall to the work of education, which at present certainly does not always solve them in the most intelligent and economic way.

Gentlemen, do not think that with these explanations of the sexual life and the sexual development of the child we have too far departed from psychoanalysis and the cure of neurotic disturbances. If you like, you may regard the psychoanalytic treatment only as a continued education for the overcoming of childhood remnants (*Kindheitsresten*).

FIFTH LECTURE

Ladies and Gentlemen: With the discovery of infantile sexuality and the tracing back of the neurotic symptoms to erotic impulse components we have arrived at several unexpected formulas for expressing the nature and tendencies of neurotic diseases. We see that the individual falls ill when in consequence of outer hindrances or inner lack of adaptability the satisfaction of the erotic needs in the sphere of reality is denied. We see that he then flees to sickness, in order to find with its help a surrogate satisfaction for that denied him. We recognize that the symptoms of illness contain fractions of the sexual activity of the individual, or his whole sexual life, and we find in the turning away from reality the chief tendency and also the chief injury of the sickness. We may guess that the resistance of our patients against the cure is not a simple one, but is composed of many motives. Not only does the ego of the patient strive against the giving up of the repressions by which it has changed itself from its original constitution into its present form but also the sexual impulses may not renounce their surrogate satisfaction so long as it is not certain that they can be offered anything better in the sphere of reality.

The flight from the unsatisfaying reality into what we call, on account of its biologically injurious nature, disease, but which is never without an individual gain in pleasure for the patient, takes place over the path of regression, the return to earlier phases of the sexual life, when satisfaction was not lacking. This regression is seemingly a twofold one, a *temporal,* in so far as the libido or erotic need falls back to a temporally earlier stage of development, and a *formal,* since the original and primitive psychic means of expression are applied to the expression of this need. Both sorts of regression focus in childhood and have their common point in the production of an infantile condition of sexual life.

The deeper you penetrate into the pathogenesis of neurotic diseases, the more the connection of neuroses with other products of human mentality, even the most valuable, will be revealed to you. You will be reminded that we men, with the high claims of our civilization and under the pressure of our repressions, find reality generally quite unsatisfactory and so keep up a life of fancy in which we love to compensate for what is lacking in the sphere of reality by the production of wish fulfillments. In these fantasies is often contained very much of the particular constitutional essence of personality and of its tendencies, repressed in real life. The energetic and successful man is he who succeeds by dint of labor in transforming his wish fancies into reality. Where this is not successful in consequence of the resistance of the outer world and the weakness of the individual, there begins the turning away from reality. The individual takes refuge in his satisfying world of fancy. Under certain favorable conditions it still remains possible for him to find another connecting link between these fancies and reality, instead of permanently becoming a stranger to it through the regression into the infantile. If the individual who is displeased with reality is in possession of that *artistic talent* which is still a psychological riddle, he can transform his fancies into artistic creations. So he escapes the fate of a neurosis and wins back his connection with reality by this roundabout way.[20] Where this opposition to the real world exists, but this valuable talent fails or proves insufficient, it is unavoidable that the libido, following the origin of the fancies, succeeds by means of regression in revivifying the infantile wishes and so producing a neurosis. The neurosis takes, in our time, the place of the cloister, in which were accustomed to taking refuge all those whom life had undeceived or who felt themselves too weak for life. Let me give at this point the main result at which we have arrived by the psychoanalytic investigation of neurotics, namely, that neuroses have no peculiar psychic content of their own, which is not also to be found in healthy states; or, as C. G. Jung has expressed it, neurotics fall ill of the same complexes with which we sound people struggle. It depends on quantitative relationships, on the relations of the forces wrestling with each other, whether the struggle leads to health, to a neurosis, or to compensatory overfunctioning (*Ueberleistung*).

Ladies and gentlemen, I have still withheld from you the most remarkable experience which corroborates our assumptions of the sexual impulse forces of neurotics. Every time that we treat a neurotic psychoanalytically, there occurs in him the so-called phenomenon of *transfer* (Nebertragung), that is, he applies to the person of the physician a great amount of tender emotion, often mixed with enmity, which has no foundation in any real relation, and must be derived in every respect from the old wish fancies of the patient which have become unconscious. Every fragment of his emotive life, which can no longer be called back into memory, is accordingly lived over by the patient in his relations to the physician, and only by such a living of them over in the "transfer" is he convinced of the existence and the power of these unconscious sexual excitations. The symptoms, which, to use a simile from chemistry, are the precipitates of earlier love experiences (in the widest sense), can only be dissolved in the higher temperature of the experience of transfer and transformed into other psychic products. The physician plays in this reaction, to use an excellent expression of S. Ferenczi,[21] the role of a *catalytic ferment,* which temporarily attracts to itself the affect which has become free in the course of the process.

The study of transfer can also give you the key to the understanding of hypnotic suggestion, which we at first used with our patients as a technical means of investigation of the unconscious. Hypnosis showed itself at that time to be a therapeutic help, but a hindrance to the scientific knowledge of the real nature of the case, since it cleared away the psychic resistances from a certain field, only to pile them up in an unscalable wall at the boundaries of this field. You must not think that the phenomenon of transfer, about which I can unfortunately say only too little here, is created by the influence of the psychoanalytic treatment. The transfer arises spontaneously in all human relations and in the relations of the patient to the physician; it is everywhere the especial bearer of therapeutic influences, and it works the stronger the less one knows of its presence. Accordingly psychoanalysis does not create it; it merely discloses it to consciousness, and avails itself of it, in order to direct the psychic processes to the wished-for goal. But I cannot leave the theme of transfer without stressing the fact that this phenomenon is of decisive importance to convince not only the patient but also the physician. I know that all my adherents were first convinced of the correctness of my views through their experience with transfer, and I can very well conceive that one may not win such a surety of judgment so long as he makes no psychoanalysis, and so has not himself observed the effects of transfer.

Ladies and gentlemen, I am of the opinion that there are, on the intellectual side, two hindrances to acknowledging the value of the psychoanalytic viewpoint: first, the fact that we are not accustomed to reckoning with a strict determination of mental life, which holds without exception, and second, the lack of knowledge of the peculiarities through which unconscious mental processes differ from those conscious ones with which we are familiar. One of the most widespread resistances against the work of psychoanalysis with patients as with persons in health reduces to the latter of the two moments. One is afraid of doing harm by psychoanalysis; one is anxious about calling up into consciousness the repressed sexual impulses of the patient, as though there were danger that they could overpower the higher ethical strivings and rob him of his cultural acquisitions. One can see that the patient has sore places in his soul life, but one is afraid to touch them, lest his suffering be increased. We may use this analogy. It is, of course, better not to touch diseased places when one can only cause pain. But we know that the surgeon does not refrain from the investigation and reinvestigation of the seat of illness, if his invasion has as its aim the restoration of lasting health. Nobody thinks of blaming him for the unavoidable difficulties of the investigation or the phenomena of reaction from the operation, if these only accomplish their purpose, and gain for the patient a final cure by temporarily making his condition worse. The case is similar in psychoanalysis; it can lay claim to the same things as surgery; the increase of pain which takes place in the patient during the treatment is very much less than that which the surgeon imposes upon him, and especially negligible in comparison with the pains of serious illness. But the consequence which is feared, that of a disturbance of the cultural character by the impulse which has been freed from repression, is wholly impossible. In relation to this anxiety we must consider what our experiences have taught us with certainty, that the somatic and mental power of a wish, if once its repression has not succeeded, is incomparably stronger when it is unconscious than when it is conscious, so that by being made conscious it can only be weakened. The unconscious wish cannot be influenced, is free from all strivings in the contrary direction, while the conscious is inhibited by those wishes which are also conscious and which strive against it. The work of psychoanalysis accordingly presents a better substitute, in the service of the highest and most valuable cultural strivings, for the repression which has failed.

Now, what is the fate of the wishes which have become free by psychoanalysis? By what means shall they be made harmless for the life of the individual? There are several ways. The general consequence is that the wish is consumed during the work by the correct mental activity of those better tendencies which are opposed to it. The repression is supplanted by a condemnation carried through with the best means at one's disposal. This is possible, since for the most part we have to abolish only the effects of earlier developmental stages of the ego. The individual for his part only repressed the useless impulse, because at that time he was himself still incompletely organized and weak; in his present maturity and strength he can, perhaps, conquer without injury to himself that which is inimical to him. A second issue of the work of psychoanalysis may be that the revealed unconscious impulses can now arrive at those useful applications which, in the case of undisturbed development, they would have found earlier. The extirpation of the infantile wishes is not at all the ideal aim of development. The neurotic has lost, by his repressions, many sources of mental energy whose contingents would have been very valuable for his character building and his life activities. We know a far more purposive process of development, the so-called *sublimation* (*Sublimierung*), by which the energy of infantile wish excitations is not secluded, but remains capable of application, while for the particular excitations, instead of becoming useless, a higher, eventually no longer sexual, goal is set up. The components of the sexual instinct are especially distinguished by such a capacity for the sublimation and exchange of their sexual goal for one more remote and socially more valuable. To the contributions of the energy won in such a way for the functions of our mental life we probably owe the highest cultural consequences. A repression taking place at an early period excludes the sublimation of the repressed impulse; after the removal of the repression the way to sublimation is again free.

We must not neglect, also, to glance at the third of the possible issues. A certain part of the suppressed libidinous excitation has a right to direct satisfaction and ought to find it in life. The claims of our civilization make life too hard for the greater part of humanity, and so further the aversion to reality and the origin of neuroses, without producing an excess of cultural gain by this excess of sexual repression. We ought not to go so far as fully to neglect the original animal part of our nature; we ought not to forget that the happiness of individuals cannot be dispensed with as one of the aims of our culture. The plasticity of the sexual components, manifest in their capacity for sublimation, may cause a great temptation to accomplish greater culture effects by a more and more far-reaching sublimation. But just as little as with our machines we expect to change more than a certain fraction of the applied heat into useful mechanical work, just as little ought we to strive to separate the sexual impulse in its whole extent of energy from its peculiar goal. This cannot succeed, and if the narrowing of sexuality is pushed too far it will have all the evil effects of a robbery.

I do not know whether you will regard the exhortation with which I close as a presumptuous one. I only venture the indirect presentation of my conviction, if I relate an old tale, whose application you may make yourselves. German literature knows a town called Schilda, to whose inhabitants were attributed all sorts of clever pranks. The wiseacres, so the story goes, had a horse, with whose powers of work they were well satisfied, and against whom they had only one grudge, that he consumed so much expensive oats. They concluded that by good management they would break him of this bad habit, by cutting down his rations by several stalks each day, until he had learned to do without them altogether. Things went finely for a while, the horse was weaned to one stalk a day, and on the next day he would at last work without fodder. On the morning of this day the malicious horse was found dead; the citizens of Schilda could not understand why he had died. We should be inclined to believe that the horse had starved, and that without a certain ration of oats no work could be expected from an animal.

I thank you for calling me here to speak, and for the attention which you have given me.

NOTES

[1] Lectures delivered at the Celebration of the Twentieth Anniversary of the Opening of Clark University, September, 1909; translated from the German by Harry W. Chase, Fellow in Psychology, Clark University, and revised by Professor Freud.

[2] Dr. Joseph Breuer, born in 1842, corresponding member of the Kaiserliche Akademie der Wissenschaften, is known by works on respiration and the physiology of the sense of equilibrium.

[3] *Studien über Hysterie*, Vienna, Deuticke, 1895; 2nd ed. 1909. Parts of my contributions to this book have been translated into English by Dr. A. A. Brill, of New York (*Selected Papers on Hysteria and Other Psychoneuroses*, by S. Freud).

[4] I know that this view no longer holds today, but in the lecture I take myself and my hearers back to the time before 1880. If things have become different since that time, it has been largely due to the work the history of which I am sketching.

[5] *Studien über Hysterie*, 2d ed., p. 26.

[6] *Ibid.*, p. 31.

[7] *Ibid.*, p. 30.

[8] *Ibid.*, pp. 43-46. A selection from this book, augmented by

several later treatises on hysteria, lies before me, in an English translation by Dr. A. A. Brill, of New York. It bears the title *Selected Papers on Hysteria and Other Psychoneuroses*, 1909 (No. 4 of the Nervous and Mental Disease Monograph Series, New York).

⁹ Or rather the later copy of such a monument. The name "Charing" is itself, as Dr. E. Jones tells me, derived from the words *chère reine.*

¹⁰ This case has been translated by Dr. Brill in *Selected Papers on Hysteria,* p. 31–F4.

¹¹ *Der Witz und seine Beziehung zum Unbewussten,* Vienna, Deuticke, 1905, p. 59.

¹² C. C. Jung, *Diagnostische Assoziationsstudien,* B. 1, 1906.

¹³ *Die Traumdeutung,* 2nd ed., Vienna, Deuticke, 1909.

¹⁴ *Zur Psychopathologie des Alltagslebens,* 3rd ed., Berlin, S. Kargar, 1910.

¹⁵ *Drei Abhandlungen zur Sexualtheorie,* 2nd ed., Vienna, Deuticke, 1908.

¹⁶ "Analyse der Phobie eines 5-jährigen Knaben," *Jahrbuch f. Psychoanalytische u. psychopathologische Forschungen,* B. 1, H. 1., 1909.

¹⁷ Bleuler, "Sexuelle Abnormitäten der Kinder," *Jahrbuch der schweizer,* Gesellschaft für Schulgesundheitspflege, IX, 1908.

¹⁸ *Drei Abhandlungen zur Sexualtheorie.*

¹⁹ *Jahrbuch f. Kinderheilkunde,* 1879.

²⁰ Cf. Otto Rank, *Der Künstler, Ansätze zu einer Sexual-Psychologie,* Vienna, Heller & Co., 1907, 56 pp.

²¹ "Introduction und Uebertragung," *Jahrbuch f. psychoanal. u. psychopath., Forschungen,* Bd. 1, H. 2., 1909.

Carl Gustav Jung

THE BASIC POSTULATES
OF ANALYTICAL PSYCHOLOGY

Carl Gustav Jung was born in Kesswyl in Switzerland on July 26, 1875. He spent his childhood in Basel, where his father was a pastor in the Swiss Reformed Church. He studied at the University of Basel with the intention of becoming a classical philologist and possibly an archaeologist. It has been mentioned that a dream aroused his interest in medicine and the natural sciences. He became an assistant in the famous Burghölzli Mental Clinic in Zurich and started a career in psychiatry, working closely with the famous psychiatrist Eugen Bleuler, who developed the concept of schizophrenia.

In 1909 Jung terminated his work at the clinic and devoted his full time to private practice, training, research, and writing. He traveled in 1909 with Freud to America, where, like Freud, he delivered a series of lectures at Clark University. He died in 1961 and his autobiographical notes have recently been published in the books called Memories, Dreams, Reflections *(1963). In this magnificent work Jung writes about his own life in the following words ". . . my life has been singularly poor in outward happenings. I cannot tell much about them, for it would strike me as hollow and insubstantial. I can understand myself only in the light of inner happenings. It is these that make up the singularity of my life. . . ."*

In his theory of personality Jung also emphasizes the unconscious processes, but he differs notably with Freud's theory of personality. He combines teleology with causality in his view of man. Both man's past (causality) as well as his future (teleology) determine his behavior. In Jung's words "the person lives by aims as well as by causes." The insistence upon the role of the destiny or purpose of man sets Jung clearly apart from Freud, for whom there is only the endless repetition of instinctual themes until death intervenes. Jung also emphasizes the racial origins of personality, while Freud stresses the infantile origins of personality. In Jung's theory of personality, as is demonstrated in the following essay, the psyche consists of a number of separate but interacting systems. The main ones are the ego, the personal unconscious and its complexes, the collective unconscious and its archetypes, the persona, the anima or animus, and the shadow. Added to all this there are the attitudes of introversion and extraversion, and the functions of thinking, sensing, feeling, and intuiting.

THE BASIC POSTULATES OF ANALYTICAL PSYCHOLOGY

It was universally believed in the Middle Ages as well as in the Greco-Roman world that the soul is a substance.† Indeed, mankind as a whole has held this belief from its earliest beginnings, and it was left for the second half of the nineteenth century to develop a "psychology without the soul"‡ Under the influence of scientific materialism, everything that could not be seen with the eyes or touched with the hands was held in doubt; such things were even laughed at because of their supposed affinity with metaphysics. Nothing was considered "scientific" or admitted to be true unless it could be perceived by the senses or traced back to physical causes. This radical change of view did not begin with philosophical materialism, for the way was being prepared long before. When the spiritual catastrophe of the Reformation put an end to the Gothic Age with its impetuous yearning for the heights, its geographical confinement, and its restricted view of the world, the vertical outlook of the European mind was forthwith intersected by the horizontal outlook of modern times. Consciousness ceased to grow upward, and grew instead in breadth of view, as well as in knowledge of the terrestrial globe. This was the period of the great voyages, and of the widening of man's ideas of the world by empirical discoveries. Belief in the substantiality of the spirit yielded more and more to the obtrusive conviction that material things alone have substance, till at last, after nearly four hundred years, the leading European thinkers and investigators came to regard the mind as wholly dependent on matter and material causation.

† Substance: *i.e.*, that which has independent existence. (*Trans.*)

‡ *"Psychologie ohne Seele"*—compare the works of F. A. Lange (1828-1875). It is to be noted that the German word *Seele* means psyche as well as soul. (*Trans.*)

We are certainly not justified in saying that philosophy or nature science has brought about this complete *volte-face*. There were always a fair number of intelligent philosophers and scientists who had enough insight and depth of thought to accept this irrational reversal of standpoint only under protest; a few even resisted it, but they had no following and were powerless against the popular attitude of unreasoned, not to say emotional, surrender to the all-importance of the physical world. Let no one suppose that so radical a change in man's outlook could be brought about by reasoning and reflection, for no chain of reasoning can prove or disprove the existence of either mind or matter. Both these concepts, as every intelligent man today may ascertain for himself, are mere symbols that stand for something unknown and unexplored, and this something is postulated or denied according to man's mood and disposition or as the spirit of the age dictates. There is nothing to prevent the speculative intellect from treating the psyche, on the one hand, as a complicated biochemical phenomenon, and at bottom a mere play of electrons, or, on the other, from regarding the unpredictable behavior of electrons as the sign of mental life even in them.

The fact that a metaphysics of the mind was supplanted in the nineteenth century by a metaphysics of matter is a mere trick if we consider it as a question for the intellect; yet regarded from the standpoint of psychology, it is an unexampled revolution in man's outlook upon the world. Otherworldliness is converted into matter-of-factness; empirical boundaries are set to man's discussion of every problem, to his choice of purposes, and even to what he calls "meaning." Intangible, inner happenings seem to have to yield place to things in the external, tangible world, and no value exists if it is not founded on a so-called fact. At least, this is how it appears to the simple mind.

It is futile, indeed, to attempt to treat this unreasoned change of opinion as a question of philosophy. We had better not try to do so, for if we maintain that mental phenomena arise from the activity of glands, we are sure of the thanks and respect of our contemporaries, whereas if we explain the breakup of the atom in the sun as an emanation of the creative *Weltgeist*, we shall be looked down upon as intellectual freaks. And yet both views are equally logical, equally metaphysical, equally arbitrary, and equally symbolic. From the standpoint of epistemology it is just as admissible to derive animals from the human species, as man from animal species. But we know how ill Professor Daqué fared in his academic career because of his sin against the spirit of the age, which will not let itself be trifled with. It is a religion, or—even more—a creed which has absolutely no connection with reason, but whose significance lies in the unpleasant fact that it is taken as the abolute measure of all truth and is supposed always to have common sense upon its side.

The spirit of the age cannot be compassed by the processes of human reason. It is an inclination, an emotional tendency that works upon weaker minds, through the unconscious, with an overwhelming force of suggestion that carries them along with it. To think otherwise than our contemporaries think is somehow illegitimate and disturbing; it is even indecent, morbid, or blasphemous, and therefore socially dangerous for the individual. He is stupidly swimming against the social current. Just as formerly the assumption was unquestionable that everything that exists takes its rise from the creative will of a God who is spirit, so the nineteenth century discovered the equally unquestionable truth that everything arises from material causes. Today the psyche does not build itself a body, but on the contrary, matter, by chemical action, produces the psyche. This reversal of outlook would be ludicrous if it were not one of the outstanding features of the spirit of the age. It is the popular way of thinking, and therefore it is decent, reasonable, scientific, and normal. Mind must be thought to be an epiphenomenon of matter. The same conclusion is reached even if we say not "mind" but "psyche," and in place of matter speak of brain, hormones, instincts, or drives. To grant the substantiality of the soul or psyche is repugnant to the spirit of the age, for to do so would be heresy.

We have now discovered that it was intellectually unjustified presumption on our forefathers' part to assume that man has a soul; that that soul has substance, is of divine nature, and therefore immortal; that there is a power inherent in it which builds up the body, supports its life, heals its ills, and enables the soul to live independently of the body; that there are incorporeal spirits with which the soul associates; and that beyond our empirical present there is a spiritual world from which the soul receives knowledge of spiritual things whose origins cannot be discovered in this visible world. But people who are not above the general level of consciousness have not yet discovered that it is just as presumptuous and fantastic for us to assume that matter produces spirit; that

apes give rise to human beings; that from the harmonious in-
terplay of the drives of hunger, love, and power Kant's
Critique of Pure Reason should have arisen; that the brain
cells manufacture thoughts, and that all this could not possibly be other than it is.

What or who, indeed, is this all-powerful matter? It is once
more man's picture of a creative god, stripped this time of
his anthropomorphic traits and taking the form of a universal
concept whose meaning everyone presumes to understand.
Consciousness today has grown enormously in breadth and
extent, but unfortunately only in spatial dimensions; its temporal reach has not increased, for were that the case we
should have a much more living sense of history. If our consciousness were not of today only, but had historical continuity, we should be reminded of similar transformations of the
divine principle in Greek philosophy, and this might dispose
us to be more critical of our present philosophical assumptions. We are, however, effectively prevented from indulging
in such reflections by the spirit of the age. It looks upon history as a mere arsenal of convenient arguments that enables
us, on occasion, to say: "Why, even old Aristotle knew that."
This being the state of affairs, we must ask ourselves how the
spirit of the age attains such an uncanny power. It is without
doubt a psychic phenomenon of the greatest importance—at
all events a prejudice so deeply rooted that until we give it
proper consideration we cannot even approach the problem
of the psyche.

As I have said, the irresistible tendency to account for everything on physical grounds corresponds to the horizontal
development of consciousness in the last four centuries, and
this horizontal perspective is a reaction against the exclusively vertical perspective of the Gothic Age. It is a manifestation of the crowd mind, and as such is not to be treated
in terms of the consciousness of individuals. Resembling in
this the primitives, we are at first wholly unconscious of our
actions, and only discover long afterward why it was that we
acted in a certain way. In the meantime, we content ourselves with all sorts of rationalized accounts of our behavior,
all of them equally inadequate.

If we were conscious of the spirit of the age, we should
know why we are so inclined to account for everything on
physical grounds; we should know that it is because, up till
now, too much was accounted for in terms of the spirit. This
realization would at once make us critical of our bias. We

should say: most likely we are now making as serious an error on the other side. We delude ourselves with the thought that we know much more about matter than about a "metaphysical" mind, and so we overestimate physical causation and believe that it alone affords us a true explanation of life. But matter is just as inscrutable as mind. As to the ultimate we can know nothing, and only when we admit this do we return to a state of equilibrium. This is in no way to deny the close connection of psychic happenings with the physiological structure of the brain, with the glands, and the body in general. We are once for all deeply convinced of the fact that the contents of consciousness are to a large part determined by our sense perceptions. We cannot fail to recognize that unalterable characteristics of a physical as well as of a psychic nature are unconsciously ingrained in us by heredity, and we are deeply struck by the power of the instincts which inhibit or reinforce or otherwise modify our mental capacities. Indeed, we must admit that as to cause, purpose, and meaning, the human psyche—however we approach it—is first and foremost a close reflection of everything we call corporeal, empirical, and mundane. And finally, in the face of all these admissions, we must ask ourselves if the psyche is not after all a secondary manifestation—an epiphenomenon—and completely dependent upon the body. In the light of reason and of our commitments as practical men to an actual world, we say yes. It is only our doubts as to the omnipotence of matter which could lead us to examine in a critical way this verdict of science upon the human psyche.

The objection has already been raised that this approach reduces psychic happenings to a kind of activity of the glands; thoughts are regarded as secretions of the brain, and so we achieve a psychology without the psyche. From this standpoint, it must be confessed, the psyche does not exist in its own right; it is nothing in itself, but is the mere expression of physical processes. That these processes have the qualities of consciousness is just an irreducible fact—were it otherwise, so the argument runs, we could not speak of the psyche at all; there would be no consciousness, and so we should have nothing to say about anything. Consciousness, therefore, is taken as the *sine qua non* of psychic life—that is to say, as the psyche itself. And so it comes about that all modern "psychologies without the psyche" are studies of consciousness which ignore the existence of unconscious psychic life.

Yet there is not *one* modern psychology—there are several.

This is curious enough when we remember that there is only one science of mathematics, of geology, zoology, botany, and so forth. But there are so many psychologies that an American university was able to publish a thick volume under the title *Psychologies of 1930*. I believe there are as many psychologies as philosophies, for there is also no one single philosophy, but many. I mention this for the reason that philosophy and psychology are linked by indissoluble bonds which are kept in being by the interrelation of their subject matters. Psychology takes the psyche for its subject matter, and philosophy—to put it briefly—takes the world. Until recently psychology was a special branch of philosophy, but now we are coming to something which Nietzsche foresaw— the ascendance of psychology in its own right. It is even threatening to swallow philosophy. The inner resemblance of the two disciplines consists in this, that both are systems of opinion about subject matter which cannot be fully experienced and therefore cannot be comprehended by a purely empirical approach. Both fields of study thus encourage speculation, with the result that opinions are formed in such variety and profusion that heavy volumes are needed to contain them all, whether they belong to the one field or to the other. Neither discipline can do without the other, and the one always furnishes the implicit—and frequently even unconscious—primary assumptions of the other.

The modern preference for physical grounds of explanation leads, as already remarked, to a "psychology without the psyche"—I mean, to the view that the psyche is nothing but a product of biochemical processes. As for a modern, scientific psychology which starts from the mind as such, there simply is none. No one today would venture to found a scientific psychology upon the postulate of an independent psyche that is not determined by the body. The idea of spirit in and for itself, of a self-contained world system of the spirit that is the only adequate postulate for the belief in autonomous, individual souls, is extremely unpopular with us, to say the least. But I must remark that, in 1914, I attended at Bedford College, London, a joint session of the Aristotelian Society, the Mind Association, and the British Psychological Society, at which a symposium was held on the question Are individual minds contained in God or are they not? Should anyone in England dispute the scientific standing of these societies, he would not receive a very cordial hearing, for their membership includes the outstanding minds of the country. And perhaps I was the only person in the audience who listened with surprise to arguments that had the ring of the thirteenth century. This instance may serve to show that the idea of an autonomous spirit whose existence is taken for granted has not died out everywhere in Europe or become a mere fossil left over from the Middle Ages.

If we keep this in mind, we can perhaps summon up the courage to consider the possibility of a "psychology with the psyche—that is, of a field of study based on the assumption of an autonomous psyche. We need not be alarmed at the unpopularity of such an undertaking, for to postulate mind is no more fantastic than to postulate matter. Since we have literally no idea of the way in which what is psychic can arise from physical elements, and yet cannot deny the reality of psychic events, we are free to frame our assumptions the other way about for once, and to hold that the psyche arises from a spiritual principle which is as inaccessible to our understanding as matter. To be sure, this will not be a modern psychology, for to be modern is to deny such a possibility. For better or worse, therefore, we must turn back to the teachings of our forefathers, for they it was who made such assumptions. The ancient view held that spirit was essentially the life of the body, the life breath, or a kind of life force which assumed spatial and corporeal form at birth or after conception, and left the dying body again after the final breath. The spirit in itself was considered as a being without extension, and because it existed before taking corporeal form and afterward as well, it was considered as timeless and hence immortal. From the standpoint of modern, scientific psychology, this conception is of course pure illusion. But as it is our intention to indulge in "metaphysics," even of a modern variety, we will examine this time-honored notion for once in an unprejudiced way, and test its empirical justification.

The names people give to their experiences are often quite enlightening. What is the origin of the word *Seele*? Like the English word "soul," it comes from the Gothic *saiwala* and the Old German *saiwalô*, and these can be connected with the Greek *aiolos*, mobile, colored, iridescent. The Greek word *psyche* also means butterfly. *Saiwalô* is related on the other side to the old Slavonic word *sila*, meaning strength. From these connections light is thrown on the original meaning of the word *Seele*: it is moving force, that is, life force.

The Latin words *animus*, spirit, and *anima*, soul, are the same as the Greek *anemos*, wind. The other Greek word for wind, *pneuma*, means also spirit. In Gothic we find the same word in *us-anan*, to breathe out, and in Latin *an-helare*, to pant. In Old High German, *spiritus sanctus* was rendered by *atun*, breath. In Arabic, wind is *rīh*, and *rūh* is soul, spirit. There is a quite similar connection with the Greek *psyche*, which is related to *psycho*, to breathe, *psychos*, cool, *psychros*, cold, and *phusa*, bellows. These affinities show clearly how in Latin, Greek, and Arabic the names given to the soul are related to the notion of moving air, the "cold breath of the spirit." And this also is why the primitive point of view endows the soul with an invisible breath-body.

It is quite evident that, since breath is the sign of life, breath is taken for life, as are also movement and moving force. According to another primitive view the soul is regarded as fire or flame, because warmth also is a sign of life. A very curious, but by no means rare, primitive conception identifies the soul with the name. The name of an individual is his soul, and hence arises the custom of using the ancestor's name to reincarnate the ancestral soul in the newborn child. We can infer from this that the ego consciousness was recognized as an expression of the soul. Not infrequently the soul is identified with the shadow, for which reason it is a deadly insult to tread upon a person's shadow. For the same reason, noonday, the ghost hour of southern latitudes, is considered threatening; the shadow then grows small, and this means that life is endangered. This conception of the shadow contains an idea which was indicated by the Greeks in the word *synopados*, "he who follows behind." They expressed in this way the feeling of an intangible, living presence—the same feeling which led to the belief that the souls of the departed were shadows.

These indications may serve to show how primitive man experienced the psyche. To him the psyche appears as the source of life, the prime mover, a ghost-like presence which has objective reality. Therefore the primitive knows how to converse with his soul; it becomes vocal within him because it is not he himself and his consciousness. To primitive man the psyche is not, as it is to us, the epitome of all that is subjective and subject to the will; on the contrary, it is something objective, contained in itself, and living its own life.

This way of looking at the matter is empirically justified, for not only on the primitive level, but with civilized man as well, psychic happenings have an objective side. In large measure they are withdrawn from our conscious control. We are unable, for example, to suppress many of our emotions; we cannot change a bad mood into a good one, and we cannot command our dreams to come or go. The most intelligent man may at times be obsessed with thoughts which he cannot drive away with the greatest effort of will. The mad tricks that memory plays sometimes leave us in helpless amazement, and at any time unexpected fantasies may run through our minds. We only believe that we are masters in our own house because we like to flatter ourselves. Actually, however, we are dependent to a startling degree upon the proper functioning of the unconscious psyche, and must trust that it does not fail us. If we study the psychic processes of neurotic persons, it seems perfectly ludicrous that any psychologist could take the psyche as the equivalent of consciousness. And it is well known that the psychic processes of neurotics differ hardly at all from those of so-called normal persons—for what man today is quite sure that he is not neurotic?

This being so, we shall do well to admit that there is justification for the old view of the soul as an objective reality—as something independent, and therefore capricious and dangerous. The further assumption that this being, so mysterious and terrifying, is at the same time the source of life, is also understandable in the light of psychology. Experience shows us that the sense of the "I"—the ego consciousness—grows out of unconscious life. The small child has psychic life without any demonstrable ego consciousness, for which reason the earliest years leave hardly any traces in memory. Where do all our good and helpful flashes of intelligence come from? What is the source of our enthusiasms, inspirations, and of our heightened feeling for life? The primitive senses in the depths of his soul the springs of life; he is deeply impressed with the life-dispensing activity of his soul, and he therefore believes in everything that affects it—in magical practices of every kind. That is why, for him, the soul is life itself. He does not imagine that he directs it, but feels himself dependent upon it in every respect.

However preposterous the idea of the immortality of the soul may seem to us, it is nothing extraordinary to the primitive. After all, the soul is something out of the common. While everything else that exists takes up a certain amount of room, the soul cannot be located in space. We suppose, of course, that our thoughts are in our heads, but when it comes to our feelings we begin to be uncertain; they appear to dwell in the region of the heart. Our sensations are distributed over the whole body. Our theory is that the seat of consciousness is in the head, but the Pueblo Indians told me that Americans were mad because they believed their thoughts were in their heads, whereas any sensible man knows that he thinks with his heart. Certain Negro tribes locate their psychic functioning neither in the head nor in the heart, but in the belly.

To this uncertainty about the localization of psychic functions another difficulty is added. Psychic contents in general are nonspatial except in the particular realm of sensation. What bulk can we ascribe to thoughts? Are they small, large, long, thin, heavy, fluid, straight, circular, or what? If we wished to form a vivid picture of a nonspatial being of the fourth dimension, we should do well to take thought, as a being, for our model.

It would all be so much simpler if we could only deny the existence of the psyche. But here we are with our immediate experiences of something that *is*—something that has taken root in the midst of our measurable, ponderable, three-dimensional reality, that differs bafflingly from this in every respect and in all its parts, and yet reflects it. The psyche may be regarded as a mathematical point and at the same time as a universe of fixed stars. It is small wonder, then, if, to the unsophisticated mind, such a paradoxical being borders on the divine. If it occupies no space, it has no body. Bodies die, but can something invisible and incorporeal disappear? What is more, life and psyche existed for me before I could say "I," and when this "I" disappears, as in sleep or unconsciousness, life and psyche still go on, as our observation of other people and our own dreams inform us. Why should the simple mind deny, in the face of such experiences, that the "soul" lives in a realm beyond the body? I must admit that I can see as little nonsense in this so-called superstition as in the findings of research regarding heredity or the basic instincts.

We can easily understand why higher and even divine knowledge was formerly ascribed to the psyche if we remember that in ancient cultures, beginning with primitive times, man always resorted to dreams and visions as a source of information. It is a fact that the unconscious contains subliminal perceptions whose scope is nothing less than astounding. In recognition of this fact, primitive societies used dreams and visions as important sources of information.

Great and enduring civilizations like those of the Hindus and Chinese built upon this foundation and developed from it a discipline of self-knowledge which they brought to a high pitch of refinement both in philosophy and in practice.

A high regard for the unconscious psyche as a source of knowledge is by no means such a delusion as our Western rationalism likes to suppose. We are inclined to assume that, in the last resort, all knowledge comes from without. Yet today we know for certain that the unconscious contains contents which would mean an immeasurable increase of knowledge if they could only be made conscious. Modern investigation of animal instinct, as for example in insects, has brought together a rich fund of empirical findings which show that if man acted as certain insects do he would possess a higher intelligence than at present. It cannot, of course, be proved that insects possess conscious knowledge, but common sense cannot doubt that their unconscious action patterns are psychic functions. Man's unconscious likewise contains all the patterns of life and behavior inherited from his ancestors, so that every human child, prior to consciousness, is possessed of a potential system of adapted psychic functioning. In the conscious life of the adult, as well, this unconscious, instinctive functioning is always present and active. In this activity all the functions of the conscious psyche are prepared for. The unconscious perceives, has purposes and intuitions, feels and thinks as does the conscious mind. We find sufficient evidence for this in the field of psychopathology and the investigation of dream processes. Only in one respect is there an essential difference between the conscious and the unconscious functioning of the psyche. While consciousness is intensive and concentrated, it is transient and is directed upon the immediate present and the immediate field of attention; moreover, it has access only to material that represents one individual's experience stretching over a few decades. A wider range of "memory" is artificially acquired and consists mostly of printed paper. But matters stand very differently with the unconscious. It is not concentrated and intensive, but shades off into obscurity; it is highly extensive and can juxtapose the most heterogeneous elements in the most paradoxical way. More than this, it contains, besides an indeterminable number of subliminal perceptions, an immense fund of accumulated inheritance factors left by one generation of men after another, whose mere existence marks a step in the differentiation of the species. If it were permissible to personify the unconscious, we might call it a collective human being combining the characteristics of both sexes, transcending youth and age, birth and death, and, from having at his command a human experience of one or two million years, almost immortal. If such a being existed, he would be exalted above all temporal change; the present would mean neither more nor less to him than any year in the one hundredth century before Christ; he would be a dreamer of age-old dreams and, owing to his immeasurable experience, he would be an incomparable prognosticator. He would have lived countless times over the life of the individual, of the family, tribe, and people, and he would possess the living sense of the rhythm of growth, flowering, and decay.

Unfortunately—or rather let us say, fortunately—this being dreams. At least it seems to us as if the collective unconscious, which appears to us in dreams, had no consciousness of its own contents—though of course we cannot be sure of this, any more than we are in the case of insects. The collective unconscious, moreover, seems not to be a person, but something like an unceasing stream or perhaps an ocean of images and figures which drift into consciousness in our dreams or in abnormal states of mind.

It would be positively grotesque for us to call this immense system of experience of the unconscious psyche an illusion, for our visible and tangible body itself is just such a system. It still carries within it the discernible traces of primeval evolution, and it is certainly a whole that functions purposively—for otherwise we could not live. It would never occur to anyone to look upon comparative anatomy or physiology as nonsense. And so we cannot dismiss the collective unconscious as illusion, or refuse to recognize and study it as a valuable source of knowledge.

Looked at from without, the psyche appears to us to be essentially a reflection of external happenings—to be not only occasioned by them, but to have its origin in them. And it also seems to us that the unconscious can be understood only from without and from the side of consciousness. It is well known that Freud has attempted an explanation from this side—an undertaking which could succeed only if the unconscious were actually something which came into being with the existence and consciousness of the individual. But the truth is that the unconscious is always there beforehand as a potential system of psychic functioning handed down by generations of man. Consciousness is a late-born descendant of the unconscious psyche. It would certainly show perversity if we tried to explain the lives of our ancestors in terms of their late descendants; and it is just as wrong, in my opinion, to regard the unconscious as a derivative of consciousness. We are nearer the truth if we put it the other way round.

But this was the standpoint of past ages, which always held the individual soul to be dependent upon a world system of the spirit. They could not fail to do so, because they were aware of the untold treasure of experience lying hidden beneath the threshold of the transient consciousness of the individual. These ages not only formed an hypothesis about the world system of the spirit, but they assumed without question that his system was a being with a will and consciousness—was even a person—and they called this being God, the quintessence of reality. He was for them the most real of beings, the first cause, through whom alone the soul could be understood. There is psychological justification for this supposition, for it is only appropriate to call divine an almost immortal being whose experience, compared to that of man, is nearly eternal.

In the foregoing I have shown where the problems lie for a psychology that does not explain everything upon physical grounds, but appeals to a world of the spirit whose active principle is neither matter and its qualities nor any state of energy, but God. We might be tempted at this juncture by modern philosophy to call energy or the *élan vital* God, and thus to blend into one spirit and nature. As long as this undertaking is restricted to the misty heights of speculative philosophy, no great harm is done. But if we should operate with this idea in the lower realm of practical psychology, where our way of explaining things bears fruit in daily conduct, we should find ourselves involved in the most hopeless difficulties. We do not profess a psychology shaped to the academic taste, or seek explanations that have no bearing on life. What we want is a practical psychology which yields approvable results—one which helps us to explain things in a way that is justified by the outcome for the patient. In practical psychotherapy we strive to fit people for life, and we are not free to set up theories which do not concern our patients or which may even injure them. Here we come to a question which is often attended by mortal danger—the question whether we base our explanations upon matter or upon spirit. We must never forget that everything spiritual is illusion from the naturalistic standpoint, and that the spirit, to ensure its own existence, must often deny and overcome an obtrusive, physical fact. If I recognize only naturalistic values, and explain everything in physical terms, I shall depreciate, hinder, or even destroy the spiritual development of my patients. And if I hold exclusively to a spiritual interpretation, then I shall misunderstand and do violence to the natural man in his right to existence as a physical being. More than a few suicides in the course of psychotherapeutic treatment are to be laid at the door of such mistakes. Whether energy is God or God is energy concerns me very little, for how, in any case, can I know such things? But to give appropriate psychological explanations—this I must be able to do.

The modern psychologist occupies neither the one position nor the other, but finds himself between the two, dangerously committed to "this as well as that"—a situation which invitingly opens the way to a shallow opportunism. This is undoubtedly the danger of the *coincidentia oppositorum*—of intellectual liberation from the opposites. How should anything but a formless and aimless uncertainty result from giving equal value to contradictory postulates? In contrast to this, we can readily appreciate the advantage of an explanatory principle that is unequivocal. It allows of a standpoint which can serve as a point of reference. Undoubtedly we are confronted here with a very difficult problem. We must be able to appeal to an explanatory principle founded on reality, and yet it is no longer possible for the modern psychologist to believe exclusively in the physical aspect of reality when once he has given the spiritual aspect its due. Nor will he be able to put weight on the latter alone, for he cannot ignore the relative validity of a physical interpretation.

The following train of thought shows my way of attempting the solution of this problem. The conflict of nature and mind is itself a reflection of the paradox contained in the psychic being of man. This reveals a material and a spiritual aspect which appear a contradiction as long as we fail to understand the nature of psychic life. Whenever, with our human understanding, we must pronounce upon something that we have not grasped or cannot grasp, then—if we are honest—we must be willing to contradict ourselves, and we must pull this something into its antithetical parts in order to deal with it at all. The conflict of the material and spiritual aspects of life only shows that the psychic is in the last resort an incomprehensible something. Without a doubt psychic happenings constitute our only immediate experience. All that I experience is psychic. Even physical pain is a psychic event that belongs to my experience. My sense impressions—for all that they force upon me a world of impenetrable objects occupying space—are psychic images, and these alone are my immediate experience, for they alone are the immediate objects of my consciousness. My own psyche even transforms and falsifies reality, and it does this to such a degree that I must resort to artificial means to determine what things are like apart from myself. Then I discover that a tone is a vibration of the air of such and such a frequency, or that a color is a wavelength of light of such and such a length. We are in all truth so enclosed by psychic images that we cannot penetrate to the essence of things external to ourselves. All our knowledge is conditioned by the psyche which, because it alone is immediate, is superlatively real. Here there is a reality to which the psychologist can appeal—namely, psychic reality.

If we go more deeply into the meaning of this concept, it seems to us that certain psychic contents or images are derived from the material environment to which our bodies also belong, while others, which are in no way less real, seem to come from the mental source which appears to be very different from the physical environment. Whether I picture to myself the car I wish to buy, or try to imagine the state in which the soul of my dead father now is—whether it is an external fact or a thought that occupies me—both happenings are psychic reality. The only difference is that one psychic happening refers to the physical world, and the other to the mental world. If I change my concept of reality in such a way as to admit that all psychic happenings are real—and no other use of the concept is valid—this puts an end to the conflict of matter and mind as contradictory explanatory principles. Each becomes a mere designation for the particular scource of the psychic contents that crowd into my field of consciousness. If a fire burns me I do not question the reality of the fire, whereas if I am beset by the fear that a ghost will appear I take refuge behind the thought that it is only an illusion. But just as the fire is the psychic image of a physical process whose nature is unknown, so my fear of the ghost is a psychic image from a mental source; it is just as real as the fire, for my fear is as real as the pain caused by the fire. As for the mental process that finally underlies my fear of the ghost—it is as unknown to me as the ultimate nature of matter. And just as it never occurs to me to account for the nature of fire except by the concepts of chemistry and physics, so I would never think of trying to explain my fear of ghosts except in terms of mental processes.

The fact that all immediate experience is psychic and that immediate reality can only be psychic explains why it is that primitive man puts the appearance of ghosts and the effects of magic on a plane with physical events. He has not yet torn his naïve experiences into their antithetical parts. In his world mind and matter still interpenetrate each other, and his gods still wander through forest and field. He is like a child, only half born, still enclosed in a dream state within his own psyche and the world as it actually is, a world not yet distorted by the difficulties in understanding that beset a dawning intelligence. When the primitive world disintegrated into spirit and nature, the West rescued nature for itself. It was prone to a belief in nature, and only became the more entangled in it with every painful effort to make itself spiritual. The East, on the contrary, took mind for its own, and by explaining away matter as mere illusion (*maya*), continued to dream in Asiatic filth and misery. But since there is only *one* earth and *one* mankind, East and West cannot rend humanity into two different halves. Psychic reality exists in its original oneness, and awaits man's advance to a level of consciousness where he no longer believes in the one part and denies the other, but recognizes both as constituent elements of one psyche.

We may well point to the idea of psychic reality as the most important achievement of modern psychology, though it is scarcely recognized as such. It seems to me only a question of time for this idea to be generally accepted. It must be accepted, for it alone enables us to do justice to psychic manifestations in all their variety and uniquesness. Without this idea it is unavoidable that we should explain our psychic experiences in a way that does violence to a good half of them, while with it we can give its due to that side of psychic experience which expresses itself in superstition and mythology, religion and philosophy. And this aspect of psychic life is not to be undervalued. Truth that appeals to the testimony of the senses may satisfy reason, but it offers nothing that stirs our feelings and expresses them by giving a meaning to human life. Yet it is most often feeling that is decisive in matters of good and evil, and if feeling does not come to the aid of reason, the latter is usually powerless. Did reason and good intentions save us from the World War, or have they ever saved us from any other catastrophic non-sense? Have any of the great spiritual and social revolutions sprung from reasoning—let us say the transformation of the Greco-Roman world into the age of feudalism, or the explosive spread of Islamic culture?

As a physician I am of course not directly concerned with these world questions; my duties lie with people who are ill. Medicine has until recently gone on the supposition that illness should be treated and cured by itself; yet voices are now heard which declare this view to be wrong, and demand the treatment of the sick person, and not of the illness. The same demand is forced upon us in the treatment of psychic suffering. More and more we turn our attention from the visible disease and direct it upon the man as a whole. We have come to understand that psychic suffering is not a definitely localized, sharply delimited phenomenon, but rather the symptom of a wrong attitude assumed by the total personality. We can therefore not hope for a thorough cure to result from a treatment restricted to the trouble itself, but only from a treatment of the personality as a whole.

I am reminded of a case which is very instructive in this connection. It concerns a highly intelligent young man who had worked out a detailed analysis of his own neurosis after a serious study of medical literature. He brought me his findings in the form of a precise and well-written monograph fit for publication, and asked me to read the manuscript and to tell him why he was not cured. He should have been according to the verdict of science as he understood it. After reading his monograph I was forced to grant him that, if it were only a question of insight into the causal connections of a neurosis, he should in all truth be cured. Since he was not, I supposed this must be due to the fact that his attitude to life was somehow fundamentally wrong—though I had to admit that his symptoms did not betray it. In reading his account of his life I had noticed that he often spent his winters at St. Moritz or Nice. I therefore asked him who paid for these holidays, and it thereupon came out that a poor schoolteacher who loved him had cruelly deprived herself to indulge the young man in these visits to pleasure resorts. His want of conscience was the cause of his neurosis, and it is not hard to see why scientific understanding failed to help him. His fundamental error lay in his moral attitude. He found my way of looking at the question shockingly unscientific, for morals have nothing to do with science. He supposed that, by invoking scientific thought, he could spirit away the immorality which he himself could not stomach. He would not even admit that a conflict existed, because his mistress gave him the money of her free will.

We can take what scientific position we choose; there remains the fact that the large majority of civilized persons simply cannot tolerate such behavior. The moral attitude is a real factor in life with which the psychologist must reckon if he is not to commit the gravest errors. The psychologist must also remember that certain religious convictions not founded on reason are a necessity of life for many persons. It is again a matter of psychic realities which can cause and cure diseases. How often have I heard a patient exclaim, "If only I knew that my life had some meaning and purpose, then there would be no silly story about my nerves!" Whether the person in question is rich or poor, has family and social position or not, alters nothing, for outer circumstances are far from giving his life a meaning. It is much more a question of his unreasoned need of what we call a spiritual life, and this he cannot obtain from universities, libraries, or even churches. He cannot accept what these have to offer because it touches only his head, and does not stir his heart. In such cases, the physician's recognition of the spiritual factors in their true light is vitally important, and the patient's unconscious helps him in his need by producing dreams whose contents are undeniably religious. Not to recognize the spiritual source of such contents means faulty treatment and failure.

General conceptions of a spiritual nature are indispensable constituents of psychic life. We can point them out among all peoples whose level of consciousness makes them in some degree articulate. Their relative absence or their denial by a civilized people is therefore to be regarded as a sign of degeneration. Whereas in its development up to the present psychology has dealt chiefly with psychic processes in the light of physical causation, the future task of psychology will be the investigation of their spiritual determinants. But the natural history of the mind is no further advanced today than was natural science in the thirteenth century. We have only begun to take scientific note of our spiritual experiences.

If modern psychology can boast of having removed any of the coverings which concealed the picture of the human psyche, it is only that one which hid from the investigator its biological aspect. We may compare the present situation with the state of medicine in the sixteenth century, when people began to study anatomy but had not as yet even the faintest idea of physiology. The spiritual aspect of the psyche is at present known to us only in a fragmentary way. We have learned that there are spiritually conditioned processes of transformation in the psyche which underlie, for example, the well-known initiation rites of primitive peoples and the states induced by the practice of Hindu yoga. But we have not yet succeeded in determining their particular uniformities or laws. We know only that a large part of the neuroses arises from a disturbance in these processes. Psychological research has not as yet drawn aside all the many veils from the picture of the human psyche; it remains as unapproachable and obscure as all the deep secrets of life. We can speak only of what we have tried to do, and what we hope to do in the future, in the way of attempting a solution of the great riddle.

Alfred Adler

INDIVIDUAL PSYCHOLOGY, ITS ASSUMPTIONS AND ITS RESULTS

Alfred Adler was born in Vienna in 1870 and died in Aberdeen, Scotland, in 1937, while on a lecture tour. Like Freud, he attended the University of Vienna and received a medical degree in 1895. After some practice in general medicine he became a psychiatrist. He was one of the founders of the Vienna Psychoanalytic Society and a regular member of the "Wednesday" meetings at Freud's house. In 1911 Adler resigned as president of the Society and a few months later broke completely with Freudian psychoanalysis. He was the founder of Individual Psychology and attracted followers throughout the world. In 1935 Adler came to the United States, continued to practice psychiatry, and also served as Professor of Medical Psychology at the Long Island College of Medicine.

Adler wrote hundreds of books and articles. His book The Practice and Theory of Individual Psychology, *published in 1927, is probably the best introduction to Adler's theory of personality. Adler differed sharply with both Freud and Jung on the interpretation of man's behavior. He believed that man is motivated primarily by social urges. Man is a social being engaged in social activities—in short, he has acquired a style of life which is predominantly social in orientation. Adler believed that social interest was inborn and that the specific relationships with people and social activities were determined by the society in which the individual was born. Adler also introduced the concept of the creative self in the field of personality theory. This concept of a creative self was totally new to psychoanalytic theory, and it somewhere compensated for the extreme objectivity of classical psychoanalysis. Adler also stressed the uniqueness of personality and minimized the sexual instinct which played such an important role in Freud's personality theory. In the end, Adler stressed the consciousness of man's personality and thus really differed with Freud who had made the theory of the unconsciousness a central theme of his teaching.*

Adler believed man to be capable of planning and guiding his actions with a real awareness of their meaning.

INDIVIDUAL PSYCHOLOGY, ITS ASSUMPTIONS AND ITS RESULTS

A survey of the views and theories of most psychologists indicates a peculiar limitation both in the nature of their field of investigation and in their methods of inquiry. They act as if experience and knowledge of mankind were, with conscious intent, to be excluded from our investigations, and all value and importance denied to artistic and creative vision as well as to intuition itself. While the experimental psychologists collect and devise phenomena in order to determine types of reaction—that is, are concerned with the physiology of the psychical life properly speaking—other psychologists arrange all forms of expression and manifestations in old customary, or at best slightly altered, systems. By this procedure they naturally rediscover the interdependence and connection in individual expressions, implied from the very beginning in their schematic attitude toward the psyche.

Either the foregoing method is employed or an attempt is made by means of small, if possible measurable, individual phenomena of a physiological nature, to construct psychical states and thought by means of an equation. The fact that all subjective thinking and subjective immersion on the part of the investigator are excluded—although in reality they dominate the very nature of these connections—is from this viewpoint regarded as an advantage.

The method employed, and the very importance it seems to possess as a preparation for the human mind, reminds us of the type of natural science completely antiquated today, with its rigid systems, replaced everywhere now by views that attempt to grasp living phenomena and their variations as connected wholes, biologically, philosophically, and psychologically. This is also the purpose of that movement in psychology that I have called *"comparative individual psychology."* By starting with the assumption of the *unity of the individual,* an attempt is made to obtain a picture of this unified personality regarded as a variant of individual life manifestations and forms of expression. The individual traits are then compared with one another, brought into a common plane, and finally fused together to form a composite portrait that is, in turn, individualized.[1]

It may have been noticed that this method of looking upon man's psychic life is by no means either unusual or even particularly daring. This type of approach is particularly noticeable in the study of child psychology, in spite of other lines of inquiry also used there. It is the essence and the nature above all of the work of the artist, be he painter, sculptor, musician, or particularly poet, so to present the minute traits of his creations that the observer is able to obtain from them the general principles of personality. He is thus in a position to reconstruct those very things that the artist when thinking of his *finale* had previously hidden therein. Since life in any given society, life without any of the preconceptions of science, has always been under the ban of the question "whither?" we are warranted in definitely stating that, scientific views to the contrary notwithstanding, no man has ever made a judgment about an event without endeavoring to strain toward the point which seems to bind together all the psychic manifestations of an individual, even to an *imagined goal* if necessary.

When I hurry home, I am certain to exhibit to any observer the carriage, expression, the gait, and the gestures that are to be expected of a person returning home. My reflexes indeed might be different from those anticipated; the causes might vary. The essential point to be grasped psychologically, and the one which interests us exclusively and practically and psychologically more than all others, *is the path followed.*

Let me observe that if I know the goal of a person I know in a general way what will happen. I am in a position to bring into their proper order each of the successive movements made, to view them in their connections, to correct them and to make, where necessary, the required adaptations for my approximate psychological knowledge of these associations. If I am acquainted only with the causes, know only the reflexes, the reaction times, the ability to repeat, and such facts, I am aware of nothing that actually takes place in the soul of the man.

We must remember that the person under observation would not know what to do with himself were he not oriented toward some goal. As long as we are not acquainted with the objective which determines his "life line," the whole system of his recognized reflexes, together with all their causal conditions, can give us no certainty as to his next series of movements. They might be brought into harmony with practically any psychic resultant. This deficiency is most clearly felt in association tests. I would never expect a man suffering from some great disappointment to associate "tree" with "rope." The moment I knew his objective, however, namely suicide, then I might very well expect that particular sequence of thoughts—expect it with such certainty that I would remove knives, poison, and weapons from his immediate vicinity.

If we look at the matter more closely, we shall find the following law holding in the development of all psychic happenings: *We cannot think, feel, will, or act without the perception of some goal.* For all the causalities in the world would not suffice to conquer the chaos of the future nor obviate the planlessness to which we would be bound to fall a victim. All activity would persist in the stage of uncontrolled gropings; the economy visible in our psychic life unattained; we should be unintegrated and in every aspect of our physiognomy, in every personal touch, similar to organisms of the rank of the amoeba.

No one will deny that by assuming an objective for our psychic life we accommodate ourselves better to reality. This can be easily demonstrated. For its truth in individual examples, where phenomena are torn from their proper connections, no doubt exists. Only watch, from this point of view, the attempts at walking made by a small child or a woman recovering from a confinement. Naturally, he who approaches this whole matter without any theory is likely to find its deeper significance escape him. Yet it is a fact that before the first step has been taken the objective of the person's movement has already been determined.

In the same way it can be demonstrated that all psychic activities are given a direction by means of a previously determined goal. All the temporary and partially visible objectives, after the short period of psychic development of childhood, are under the domination of an imagined terminal goal, of a final point felt and conceived of as definitely fixed. In other words the psychic life of man is made to fit into the fifth act like a character drawn by a good dramatist.

The conclusion thus to be drawn from the unbiased study of any personality viewed from the standpoint of individual psychology leads us to the following important proposition: *Every psychic phenomenon, if it is to give us any under-*

*standing of a person, can only be grasped and understood if
regarded as a preparation for some goal.*

To what an extent this conception promotes our psychological understanding is clearly apparent as soon as we become aware of the *multiplicity of meaning of those psychical processes that have been torn from their proper context.* Take, for example, the case of a man with a "bad memory." Assume that he is quite conscious of this fact and that an examination discloses an inferior capacity for the repetition of meaningless syllables. According to present usage in psychology, which we might more properly call an abuse, we would have to make the following inference: the man is suffering, from hereditary or pathological causes, from a deficient capacity for repetition. Incidentally, let me add, that in this type of investigation we generally find the inference already stated in different words in the premises. In this case, for example, we have the following proposition: if a man has a bad memory, or if he remembers only a few words—then he has an inferior capacity for repetition.

The procedure in individual psychology is completely different. After excluding the possibility of all organic causes, we would ask ourselves what is the objective of this weakness of memory? This we could determine only if we were in possession of an intimate knowledge of the whole individual, so that an understanding of one part becomes possible only after we have understood the whole. And we should probably find the following to hold true in a large number of cases: this man is attempting to prove to himself and to others that for certain reasons of a fundamental nature, that are either not to be named or have remained unconscious, *but which can most effectively be represented by poorness of memory,* he must not permit himself to perform some particular act or to come to a given decision (change of profession, studies, examination, marriage). We should then have unmasked this weakness of memory as tendentious and could understand its importance as a weapon against a contemplated undertaking. In every test of ability to repeat we should then expect to find the deficiency due to the secret life plan of an individual. The question then to be asked is how such deficiencies or evils arise. They may be simply "arranged" by purposely underlining general physiological weaknesses and interpreting them as personal sufferings. Others may succeed either by subjective absorption into an abnormal condition or by preoccupation with dangerous pessimistic anticipations, in so weakening their faith in their own capacities, that their strength, attention, or will power are only partially at their disposal.

A similar observation may be made in the case of affects. To give one more example, take the case of a woman subject to outbreaks of anxiety recurring at certain intervals. As long as nothing of greater significance than this was discernible, the assumption of some hereditary degeneration, some disease of the vasomotor system, of the vagus nerve, and so on, sufficed. It is also possible that we might have regarded ourselves as having arrived at a fuller understanding of the case, if we had discovered in the previous history of the patient some frightful experience or traumatic condition and attributed the disease to it. As soon, however, as we examined the personality of this individual and inquired into her directive lines we discovered an excess of will-to-power, with which anxiety as a weapon of aggression had associated itself, an anxiety which was to become operative as soon as the force of the will power had abated and the desired resonance was absent, a situation occurring, for example, when the patient's husband left the house without her consent.

Our science demands a markedly individualizing procedure and is consequently not much given to generalizations. For general guidance I would like to propound the following rule: *As soon as the goal of a psychic movement or its life plan has been recognized, then we are to assume that all the movements of its constituent parts will coincide with both the goal and the life plan.*

This formulation, with some minor provisos, is to be maintained in the widest sense. It retains its value even if inverted: *The properly understood part-movements must, when combined, give the picture of an integrated life plan and final goal.* Consequently, we insist that, without worrying about the *tendencies, milieu, and experiences,* all psychical powers are under the control of a directive idea and all expressions of emotion, feeling, thinking, willing, acting, dreaming, as well as psychopathological phenomena, are permeated by one unified life plan. Let me, by a slight suggestion, prove and yet soften down these heretical propositions: more important than tendencies, objective experience and milieu is *the subjective evaluation,* an evaluation which stands, furthermore, in a certain, often strange, relation to realities. Out of this evaluation however, which generally results in the development of a permanent mood *of the nature of a feeling of inferiority*, there arises, depending upon the unconscious technique of our thought apparatus, an imagined goal, an attempt at a planned final compensation, and a life plan.

I have so far spoken a good deal of men who have "grasped the situation." My discussion has been as irritating as that of the theorists of the "psychology of understanding" or of the psychology of personality, who always break off just when they are about to show us what exactly it is they have understood, as for instance, Jaspers. The danger of discussing briefly this aspect of our investigations, namely, *the results of individual psychology*, is sufficiently great. To do so we should be compelled to force the dynamics of life into static words and pictures, overlook differences in order to obtain unified formulas, and have, in short, in our description to make that very mistake that in practice is strictly prohibited: of approaching the psychic life of the individual with a dry formula, as the Freudian school attempt.

This, then, being my assumption, I shall in the following present to you the most important results of our study of psychic life. Let me emphasize the fact that the dynamics of psychic life that I am about to describe hold equally for healthy and diseased. What distinguishes the nervous from the healthy individual is the stronger safeguarding tendency with which the former's life plan is filled. With regard to the "positing of a goal" and the life plan adjusted to it, there are no fundamental differences.

I shall consequently speak of a general goal of man. A thoroughgoing study has taught us that we can best understand the manifold and diverse movements of the psyche as soon as our *most general presupposition*, that the psyche has as its objective the *goal of superiority*, is recognized. Great thinkers have given expression to much of this; in part everyone knows it, but in the main it is hidden in mysterious darkness and comes definitely to the front only in insanity or in ecstatic conditions. Whether a person desires to be an artist, the first in his profession, or a tyrant in his home, to hold converse with God or humiliate other people; whether he regards his suffering as the most important thing in the world to which everyone must show obeisance, whether he is chasing after unattainable ideals or old deities, overstepping all limits and norms, at every part of his way he is guided and spurred on by his longing for superiority, the thought of his godlikeness, the belief in his special magical power. In his love he desires to experience his power over his partner. In his purely optional choice of profession the goal floating before his mind manifests itself in all sorts of exaggerated anticipations and fears, and, thirsting for revenge, he experiences in suicide a triumph over all obstacles. In order to gain control over an object or over a person, he is capable of proceeding along a straight line, bravely, proudly, over-bearing, obstinate, cruel; or he may on the other hand prefer, forced by experience, to resort to bypaths and circuitous routes, to gain his victory by obedience, submission, mild-ness, and modesty. Nor have traits of character an independent existence, for they are also adjusted to the individual life plan, really representing the most important preparations for conflict possessed by the latter.

This goal of complete superiority, with its strange appearance at times, does not come from the world of reality. Inherently we must place it under "fictions" and "imaginations." Of these, Vaihinger (*The Philosophy of "As If"*) rightly says that their importance lies in the fact that whereas in themselves without meaning, they nevertheless possess in practice the greatest importance. For our case this coincides to such an extent that we may say *that this fiction of a goal of superiority, so ridiculous from the viewpoint of reality, has become the principal conditioning factor of our life as hitherto known*. It is this that teaches us to differentiate, gives us poise and security, molds and guides our deeds and activities, and forces our spirit to look ahead and to perfect itself. There is of course also an obverse side, for *this goal introduces into our life a hostile and fighting tendency*, robs us of the simplicity of our feelings, and is always the cause for an estrangement from reality, since it puts near to our hearts the idea of attempting to overpower reality. Whoever takes this goal of godlikeness seriously or literally will soon be compelled to flee from real life, and compromise by seeking a life within life; if fortunate in art, but more generally in pietism, neurosis, or crime.

I cannot give you particulars here. A clear indication of this supermundane goal is to be found in every individual. Sometimes this is to be gathered from a man's carriage; sometimes it is disclosed only in his demands and expectations. Occasionally one comes upon its track in obscure memories, fantasies and dreams. If purposely sought it is rarely obtained. However, every bodily or mental attitude indicates clearly its origin in a striving for power, and carries within itself the ideal of a kind of perfection and infallibility. In those cases that lie on the confines of neurosis there is always to be discovered a reinforced pitting of oneself against the environment, against the dead or heroes of the past.

A test of the correctness of our interpretation can be easily made. If everyone possesses within himself an ideal of superiority, such as we find to an exaggerated degree among the nervous, then we ought to encounter phenomena whose purpose is the oppression, the minimizing, and undervaluation of others. Traits of character such as intolerance, dogmatism, envy, pleasure at the misfortune of others, conceit, boastfulness, mistrust, avarice—in short, all those attitudes that are the substitutes for a struggle, force their way through to a far greater extent, in fact, than self-preservation demands.

Similarly, either simultaneously or interchangingly, depending upon the zeal and the self-confidence with which the final goal is sought, we see emerging indications of pride, emulation, courage, the attitudes of saving, bestowing, and directing. A psychological investigation demands so much objectivity that a moral evaluation will not disturb the survey. In fact *the different levels of character traits* actually neutralize our good will and our disapproval. Finally we must remember that these hostile traits, particularly in the case of the nervous, are often so concealed that their possessor is justifiably astonished and irritated when attention is drawn to them. For example, the elder of two children can create quite an uncomfortable situation in trying to arrogate to himself, through defiance and obstinacy, all authority in the family. The younger child pursues a wiser course, poses as a model of obedience, and succeeds in this manner in becoming the idol of the family and in having all wishes gratified. As ambition spurs him on, all willingness to obey becomes destroyed and pathological compulsion phenomena develop, by means of which every parental order is nullified even when the parents notice that the child is making efforts to remain obedient. Thus we have an act of obedience immediately nullified by means of a compulsion thought. We get an idea of the circuitous path taken here in order to arrive at the same objective as that of the other child.

The whole weight of the personal striving for power and superiority passes, at a very early age in the case of the child, into the form and the content of its striving, its thought being able to absorb for the time being only so much as the eternal, real, and physiologically rooted *community feeling* permits. Out of the latter are developed tenderness, love of neighbor, friendship and love, the desire for power unfolding itself in a veiled manner and seeking secretly to push its way along the path of group consciousness.

At this place let me go out of my way to endorse an old fundamental conception of all who know human nature. Every marked attitude of a man can be traced back to an origin in childhood. In the nursery are formed and prepared all of man's future attitudes. Fundamental changes are produced only by means of an exceedingly high degree of introspection or among neurotics by means of the physician's individual psychological analysis.

Let me, on the basis of another case, one which must have happened innumerable times, discuss in even greater detail the positing of goals by nervous people. A remarkably gifted man who by his amiability and refined behavior had gained the love of a girl of high character became engaged to her. He then forced upon her his ideal of education which made severe demands upon her. For a time she endured these unbearable orders but finally put an end to all further ordeals by breaking off relations. The man then broke down and became a prey to nervous attacks. The individual-psychological examination of the case showed that the superiority goal in the case of this patient—as his domineering demands upon his bride indicated—had long ago pushed from his mind all thought of marriage, and that his object really was to work secretly toward a break, secretly because he did not feel himself equal to the open struggle in which he imagined marriage to consist. *This disbelief in himself* itself dated from his earliest childhood, to a time during which he, an only son, lived with an early widowed mother somewhat cut off from the world. During this period, spent in continuous family quarrels, he had received the ineradicable impression, one he had never openly admitted to himself, that he was not sufficiently virile and would never be able to cope with a woman. These psychical attitudes are comparable to a permanent inferiority feeling, and it is easily understood how they had decisively interfered in his life and compelled him to obtain prestige along lines other than those obtainable through the fulfillment of the demands of reality.

It is clear that the patient attained just what his concealed preparations for bachelordom aimed at, and what his fear of a life partner, with the quarrels and restless relationship this implied, had awakened in him. Nor can it be denied that he took the same attitude toward both his bride and his mother, namely, the wish to conquer. This attitude induced by a longing for victory has been magnificently misinterpreted by the Freudian school as the permanently incestuous condition of being enamored of the mother. As a matter of fact this reinforced childhood feeling of inferiority occasioned by the patient's painful relation to his mother spurred this man on to prevent any struggle in later life with a wife by providing himself with all kinds of safeguards. Whatever it is we understand by love, in this particular case it is simply *a means to an end*, and that end is the final securing of a triumph over some suitable woman. Here we have the reason for the continual tests and orders and for the canceling of the engagement. This solution had not just "happened," but had on the contrary been artistically prepared and arranged with the old weapons of experience employed previously in the case of his mother. A defeat in marriage was out of the question because marriage was prevented.

Although we consequently realize nothing puzzling in the behavior of this man and should recognize in his domineering attitude simply aggression *posing as love*, some words of explanation are necessary to clear up the less intelligible nervous breakdown. We are here entering upon the real domain of the psychology of neuroses. As in the nursery so here our patient has been worsted by a woman. The neurotic individual is led in such cases to strengthen his protections and to retire to a fairly great distance from danger. Our patient is utilizing his breakdown in order to feed an evil reminiscence, to bring up the question of guilt again, to solve it in an unfavorable sense for the woman, so that in future he may either proceed with even greater caution or take final leave of love and matrimony! This man is thirty years old now. Let us assume that he is going to carry his pain along with him for another ten or twenty years and that he is going to mourn for his lost ideal for the same length of time. He has thereby protected himself against every love affair and permanently saved himself from new defeat.

He interprets his nervous breakdown by means of old, now strengthened, weapons of experience, just as he had as a child refused to eat, sleep, or to do anything, and played the role of a dying person. His fortunes ebb and *his beloved carries all the stigma;* he himself rises superior to her in both culture and character, and lo and behold: he has attained

that for which he longed, for he is the superior person, becomes the better man, and his partner, like all girls, is the
guilty one. Girls cannot cope with the man in him. In this
manner he has consummated what as a child he had already
felt, the duty of demonstrating his superiority over the fe-
male sex.

We can now understand that this nervous reaction can
never be sufficiently definite or adequate. *He is to wander
through the world as a living reproach against women.*

Were he aware of his secret plans he would realize how
ill-natured and evil-intentioned all his actions have been.
However he would, in that case, not succeed in attaining his
object of elevating himself above women. He would see himself just as we see him, falsifying the weights, and how everything he has done has only led to a goal previously set.
His success could not be described as due to "fate," nor as-
suredly would it represent any increased prestige. But his
goal, his life plan, and his life falsehood demand this prestige! In consequence it so "happens" that the *life plan remains in the unconscious,* so that the patient may believe
that an *implacable fate,* and not a long-prepared and long-
meditated plan for which he alone is responsible, is at work.

I cannot go into a detailed description of what I call the
"distance" that the neurotic individual places between himself and the final issue, which in this case is marriage. The
discussion of the manner in which he accomplishes it I must
also postpone. . . . I should like to point out here, however,
that the "distance" expresses itself clearly in the "hesitating
attitudes," the principles, the point of view, and the life
falsehood. In its evolution, neurosis and psychosis play leading roles. The appropriation for this purpose of perversions
and every type of impotence arising from the latter is quite
frequent. Such a man concludes his account and reconciles
himself with life by constructing one or a number of "if"
clauses. "If conditions had been different . . ."

The importance of the educational questions that arise and
upon which our school lays the greatest stress (*Heilen und
Bilden,* Munich, 1913) follows from what has been discussed.

From the method of presentation of the present work it is
to be inferred that as in the case of a psychotherapeutic cure,
our analysis proceeds backward examining first the *superiority* goal, explaining by means of it the type of *conflict attitude*[2] adopted particularly by nervous patients, and only

then attempting to investigate the sources of the vital psychic mechanism. One of the bases of the psychical dynamics we have already mentioned, the presumably unavoidable artistic trait of the psychical apparatus which, by means of the *artistic artifice of the creation of a fiction and the setting of a goal,* adjusts itself to and extends itself into the world of possible reality. I shall now proceed to explain briefly how the goal of godlikeness transforms the relation of the individual to his environment into hostility, and how the struggle drives an individual toward a goal either along a direct path, such as aggressiveness, or along byways suggested by precaution. If we trace the history of this aggressive attitude back to childhood, we always come upon the outstanding fact that *throughout the whole period of development, the child possesses a feeling of inferiority in its relations both to parents and the world at large.* Because of the immaturity of his organs, his uncertainty and lack of independence, because of his need for dependence upon stronger natures and his frequent and painful feeling of subordination to others, a sensation of inadequacy develops that betrays itself throughout life. This feeling of inferiority is the cause of his continual restlessness as a child, his craving for action, his playing of roles, the pitting of his strength against that of others, his anticipatory pictures of the future, and his physical as well as mental preparations. The whole potential educability of the child depends upon this feeling of insufficiency. In this way the future becomes transformed into the land that will bring him compensations. His conflict attitude is again reflected in his feeling of inferiority; and only conflict does he regard as a compensation which will do away permanently with his present inadequate condition and will enable him to picture himself as elevated above others. Thus the child arrives at the positing of a goal, an imagined goal of superiority, whereby his poverty is transformed into wealth, his subordination into domination, his suffering into happiness and pleasure, his ignorance into omniscience, and his incapacity into artistic creation. The longer and more definitely the child feels his insecurity, the more he suffers either from physical or marked mental weakness, the more he is aware of life's neglect, the higher will this goal be placed and the more faithfully will it be adhered to. He who wishes to recognize the nature of this goal should watch a child at play, at optionally selected occupations or when fantasying about his future profession. The apparent change in these phenomena is purely external, for in every new goal the child imagines a predetermined triumph. A variant of this weaving of plans, one frequently found among weakly aggressive children, among girls and sickly individuals, might be mentioned here. This consists of so misusing their frailties that they compel others to become subordinate to them. They will later on pursue the same method until their life plan and life falsehood have been clearly unmasked.

The attentive observer will find the nature of the *compensatory dynamics* presenting a quite extraordinary aspect as soon as he permits the sexual role to be relegated to one of minor importance, and realizes that it is the former that is impelling the individual toward superhuman goals. In our present civilization both the girl and the youth will feel themselves forced to extraordinary exertions and maneuvers. A large number of these are admittedly of a distinctively progressive nature. To preserve this progressive nature but to ferret out those bypaths that lead us astray and cause illness, to make these harmless, that is our object, and one that takes us far beyond the limits of medical art. It is to this aspect of our subject that society, child education and folk education may look for germs of a far-reaching kind. *For the aim of this point of view is to gain a reinforced sense of reality, the development of a feeling of responsibility, and a substitution for latent hatred of a feeling of mutual good will, all of which can be gained only by the conscious evolution of a feeling for the common weal and the conscious destruction of the will to power.*

He who is looking for the power fantasies of the child will find them drawn with a master hand by Dostoevski in his novel entitled *A Raw Youth.* I found them blatantly apparent in one of my patients. In the dreams and thoughts of this individual the following wish recurred repeatedly: others should die so that he might have enough room in which to live, others should suffer privations so that he might obtain more favorable opportunities. This attitude reminds one of the inconsiderateness and heartlessness of many men who trace all evil back to the fact that there are already too many people in the world; impulses that have unquestionably made the World War more palatable. The feeling of certainty, in fictions of this kind, has been taken over in the above-mentioned case from the basic facts of capitalistic trade, where, admittedly, the better the condition of one individual, the worse that of another. "I want to be a grave digger," said a four-year-old boy to me; "I want to be the person who digs graves for others."

NOTES

[1] William Stern has come to the same conclusions starting from a different method of approach.

[2] The "struggle for existence," the "struggle of all against all," etc., are merely other perspectives of the same kind.

Erich Fromm

HISTORICAL AND ETHICAL PSYCHOANALYSIS — SELFISHNESS AND SELF-LOVE

Erich Fromm, one of the most outstanding psychoanalysts of today, was born in Frankfurt in 1900 and studied psychology and sociology at the Universities of Heidelberg, Frankfurt, and Munich. He received his medical degree from Heidelberg in 1922 and was subsequently trained in psychoanalysis in Munich and at the Berlin Psychoanalytic Institute. He came to the United States in 1933 and is now Professor of Psychology at New York University and Professor of Psychoanalysis at the National University in Mexico City.

Fromm has written widely in the field of psychoanalysis, sociology, religion and philosophy. The essential theme in his work is his concept of the lonely and isolated man. Man has become separated from the world and from his fellow men. This condition of isolation, Fromm feels, is inherent in the human situation. The child, after severing the primary ties with his parents, finds himself isolated and helpless. The medieval peasant secured his freedom only to find himself adrift in an alien world. In his most important book, Escape from Freedom, *Fromm sets forth the thesis that as man gained more freedom throughout the ages he has also become increasingly alone. In the essay which follows here Fromm develops this notion in a clear and stimulating manner. Man, according to Fromm, presents us with basic contradictions, the contradiction of man being both a part of nature and separate from it. Fromm points to five specific needs of man: the need for identity, the need for roots, the need for transcendence, the need for relatedness, and the need for a frame of orientation. Fromm is greatly concerned about man's relations to society, and it is a recurrent theme in all his works. Fromm describes his ideal of society as "a society which gives him the possibility of transcending nature by creating rather than by destroying, in which everyone gains a sense of self by experiencing himself as the subject of his powers rather than by conformity, in which a system of orientation and devotion exists without man's needing to distort reality and to worship idols."*

HISTORICAL AND ETHICAL PSYCHOANALYSIS—
SELFISHNESS AND SELF-LOVE

Modern culture is pervaded by a taboo on selfishness. It teaches that to be selfish is sinful and that to love others is virtuous. To be sure, this doctrine is not only in flagrant contradiction to the practices of modern society but it also is in opposition to another set of doctrines which assumes that the most powerful and legitimate drive in man is selfishness and that each individual by following this imperative drive also does the most for the common good. The existence of this latter type of ideology does not affect the weight of the doctrines which declare that selfishness is the arch-evil and love for others the main virtue. Selfishness, as it is commonly used in these ideologies, is more or less synonymous with self-love. The alternatives are either to love others, which is a virtue, or to love oneself, which is a sin.

This principle has found its classic expression in Calvin's theology. Man is essentially bad and powerless. He can do nothing—absolutely nothing—good on the basis of his own strength or merits. "We are not our own," says Calvin,[1] "therefore neither our reason nor our will should predominate in our deliberations and actions. We are not our own; therefore, let us not propose it as our end, to seek what may be expedient for us according to the flesh. We are not our own; therefore, let us, as far as possible, forget ourselves and all things that are ours. On the contrary, we are God's; to him, therefore, let us live and die. For, as it is the most devastating pestilence which ruins people if they obey themselves, it is the only haven of salvation not to know or to want anything by oneself but to be guided by God who walks before us."[2] Man should not only have the conviction of his absolute nothingness. He should do everything to humiliate himself. "For I do not call it humility," says Calvin, "if you suppose that we have anything left. . . . we cannot think of ourselves as we ought to think without utterly despising everything that may be supposed an excellence in us. This humility is unfeigned submission of a mind overwhelmed with a weighty sense of its own misery and poverty; for such is the uniform description of it in the word of God."[3]

This emphasis on the nothingness and wickedness of the individual implies that there is nothing he should like about himself. This doctrine is rooted in contempt and hatred for oneself. Calvin makes this point very clear; he speaks of "Self-love" as of a "pest."[4]

If the individual finds something in himself "on the strength of which he finds pleasure in himself," he betrays this sinful self-love. This fondness for himself will make him sit in judgment over others and despise them. Therefore, to be fond of oneself, to like anything about oneself is one of the greatest imaginable sins. It excludes love for others[5] and is identical with selfishness.[6]

There are fundamental differences between Calvin's theology and Kant's philosophy, yet the basic attitude toward the problem of love for oneself has remained the same. According to Kant, it is a virtue to want the happiness of others, while to want one's own happiness is ethically "indifferent," since it is something which the nature of man is striving for and a natural striving cannot have positive ethical sense.[7] Kant admits that one must not give up one's claims for happiness; under certain circumstances it can even be a duty to be concerned with one's happiness; partly because health, wealth, and the like, can be means which are necessary to fulfill one's duty, partly because the lack of happiness—poverty—can seduce a person from fulfilling his duty.[8] But love for oneself, striving for one's own happiness, can never be a virtue. As an ethical principle, the striving for one's own happiness "is the most objectionable one, not merely because it is false, . . . but because the springs it provides for morality are such as rather undermine it and destroy its sublimity. . . ."[9] Kant differentiates in egotism, self-love, *philantia*—a benevolence for oneself; and arrogance—the pleasure in oneself. "Rational self-love" must be restricted by ethical principles; the pleasure in oneself must be battered down and the individual must come to feel humiliated in comparing himself with the sanctity of moral laws.[10] The individual should find supreme happiness in the fulfillment of his duty. The realization of the moral principle—and, therefore, of the individual's happiness—is only possible in the general whole, the nation, the state. Yet, "the welfare of the state—*salus rei publicae suprema lex est*—is not identical with the welfare of the citizens and their happiness."[11]

In spite of the fact that Kant shows a greater respect for the integrity of the individual than did Calvin or Luther, he states that even under the most tyrannical government the individual has no right to rebel and must be punished no less than with death if he threatens the sovereign.[12] Kant emphasizes the native propensity for evil in the nature of man,[13] for the suppression of which the moral law, the categorical imperative, is necessary unless man should become a beast and human society should end in wild anarchy.

In discussing Calvin's and Kant's systems, their emphasis on the nothingness of man has been stressed. Yet, as already suggested, they also emphasize the autonomy and dignity of the individual, and this contradiction runs through their writings. In the philosophy of the enlightenment period the individual's claims and happiness have been emphasized much more strongly by others than by Kant, for instance by Helvetius. This trend in modern philosophy has found an extreme expression by Stirner and Nietzsche. In the way that they often phrase the problem—though not necessarily in their real meaning—they share one basic premise of Calvin and Kant: that love for others and love for oneself are alternatives. But in contradiction to those authors, they denounce love for others as weakness and self-sacrifice and postulate egotism, selfishness, and self-love—they too confuse the issue by not clearly differentiating between these phenomena—as virtue. Thus Stirner says: "Here, egoism, selfishness must decide, not the principle of love, not love motives like mercy, gentleness, good-nature, or even justice and equity—for *iustitia* too is a phenomenon of love, a product of love: love knows only sacrifice and demands self-sacrifice."[14]

The kind of love denounced by Stirner is the masochistic dependence which makes the individual a means for achieving the purposes of somebody or something outside himself. With this conception of love could he scarcely avoid a formulation which postulated ruthless egotism as a goal. The formulation is, therefore, highly polemical and overstates the point. The positive principle with which Stirner was concerned[15] was directed against an attitude which had run through Christian theology for many centuries—and which was vivid in the German idealism which was passing in his time; namely, to bend the individual to submit to and find his center in a power and a principle outside of himself. To be sure, Stirner was not a philosopher of the stature of Kant or Hegel, yet he had the courage to make a radical rebellion against that side of idealistic philosophy which negated the concrete individual and thus helped the absolute state to retain its oppressive power over the individual. Although there is no comparison between the depth and scope of the two philosophers, Nietzsche's attitude in many respects is similar to that of Stirner. Nietzsche also denounces love and altruism as the expressions of weakness and self-negation. For Nietzsche, the quest for love is typical of slaves who cannot fight for what they want and, therefore, try to get it through "love." Altruism and love for mankind is thus a sign of degeneration.[16] For him, it is the essence of a good and healthy aristocracy that is ready to sacrifice countless people for its interests without having a guilty conscience. Society should be a "foundation and scaffolding by means of which a select class of beings may be able to elevate themselves to their higher duties, and in general to their higher existence."[17] Many quotations could be added to document this spirit of sadism, concept, and brutal egotism. This side of Nietzsche has often been understood as *the* philosophy of Nietzsche. Is this true; is this the "real" Nietzsche?

To answer this question would require a detailed analysis of his work which cannot be attempted here. There are various reasons which made Nietzsche express himself in the sense mentioned above. First of all, as in the case of Stirner, his philosophy is a reaction—a rebellion—against the philosophical tradition of subordinating the empirical individual to a power and a principle outside of himself. His tendency to overstatements shows this reactive quality. Second, there were traits in Nietzsche's personality, a tremendous insecurity and anxiety, which explain that, and why he had sadistic impulses which led him to those formulations. Yet, these trends in Nietzsche do not seem to me to be the "essence" of his personality nor the corresponding views the essence of his philosophy. Finally, Nietzsche shared some of the naturalistic ideas of his time as they were expressed in the materialistic-biologistic philosophy, for which the concepts of the physiological roots of psychic phenomena and the "survival of the fittest" were characteristic. This interpretation does not do away with the fact that Nietzsche shared the view that there is a contradiction between love for others and love for oneself. Yet, it is important to notice that Nietzsche's views contain the nucleus from development of which this wrong dichotomy can be overcome. The "love" which he attacks is one which is rooted not in one's own strength, but in one's own weakness. "Your neighbor love is your bad love for ,yourselves. You flee into your neighbor from yourselves and would fain make a virtue thereof. But I fathom your 'unself-ishness.'" He states explicitly, "You cannot stand yourselves and you do not love yourselves sufficiently."[18] The individual has for Nietzsche "an enormously great significance."[19] The "strong" individual is the one who has "true kindness, nobil-ity, greatness of soul, which does not give in order to take, which does not want to excell by being kind;—'waste' as type of true kindness, wealth of the person as a premise."[20]

He expresses the same thought also in *Thus Spake Zara-thustra:* "The one goeth to his neighbor because he seeketh himself, the other one because would he fain lose himself."[21]

The essence of these views is: love is a phenomenon of abundance, its premise is the strength of the individual who can give. Love is affirmation, "it seeketh to create what is loved!"[22] To love another person is only a virtue if it springs from this inner strength, but it is detestable if it is the ex-pression of the basic inability to be oneself.[23]

However, the fact remains that Nietzsche left the problem of the relationship between self-love and love for others as unsolved antinomy, even if by interpreting him one may sur-mise in what direction his solution would have been found.[24]

The doctrine that selfishness is the arch-evil that one has to avoid and that to love oneself excludes loving others is by no means restricted to theology and philosophy. It is one of the stock patterns used currently in home, school, church, movies, literature, and all the other instruments of social sug-gestion. "Don't be selfish" is a sentence which has been im-pressed upon millions of children, generation after generation. It is hard to define what exactly it means. Consciously, most parents connect with it the meaning not to be egotistical, in-considerate, without concern for others. Factually, they gen-erally mean more than that. "Not to be selfish" implies not to do what one wishes, to give up one's own wishes for the sake of those in authority; that is, the parents, and later the authorities of society. "Don't be selfish," in the last analysis, has the same ambiguity that we have seen in Calvinism. Aside from its obvious implication, it means, "Don't love yourself," "Don't be yourself," but submit your life to some-thing more important than yourself, be it an outside power or the internalization of that power as "duty." "Don't be self-ish" becomes one of the most powerful ideological weapons in suppressing spontaneity and the free development of per-sonality. Under the pressure of this slogan one is asked for every sacrifice and for complete submission: only those aims are "unselfish" which do not serve the individual for his own sake but for the sake of somebody or something outside of him.

This picture, we must repeat, is in a certain sense one-sided. Beside the doctrine that one should not be selfish, the opposite doctrine is propagandized in modern society: Have your own advantage in mind, act according to what is best for you—and by doing so, you will also bring about the greatest advantage for all others. As a matter of fact, the idea that the pursuit of individual egotism is the basis for the development of general welfare is the principle on which competitive capitalism has been built. It may seem strange that two such seemingly contradictory principles could be taught side by side in one culture. Of the fact, there can be no doubt. One result of this contradiction of ideological patterns certainly is confusion in the individual. To be torn between the one and the other doctrine is a serious blockage in the process of integration of personality and has often led to neurotic character formation.[25]

One must observe that this contradictory pair of doctrines has had an important social function. The doctrine that everybody should pursue his individual advantage obviously was a necessary stimulus for private initiative on which the modern economic structure is built. The social function of the doctrine "Don't be selfish" was an ambiguous one. For the broad masses of those who had to live on the level of mere subsistence, it was an important aid to resignation to having wishes which were unattainable under the given socio-economic system. It was important that this resignation should be one which was not thought of as being brought about by external pressure, since the inevitable result of such a feeling has to be a more or less conscious grudge and a defiance against society. By making this resignation a moral virtue, such a reaction could to a considerable extent be avoided. While this aspect of the social function of the taboo on selfishness is obvious, another, its effect upon the privileged minority, is somewhat more complicated. It becomes clear only if we consider further the meaning of "selfishness." If it means to be concerned with one's economic advantage, certainly the taboo on selfishness would have been a severe handicap to the economic initiative of businessmen. But what it really meant, especially in the earlier phases of English and American culture was, as has been pointed out before: Don't do what you want, don't enjoy yourself, don't spend money or energy for pleasure, but feel it as your duty to work, to be successful, to be prosperous.

It is the great merit of Max Weber[26] to have shown that this principle of what he calls *innerweltliche Askese* (inner-worldly asceticism) was an important condition for creating an attitude in which all energy could be directed toward work and the fulfillment of duty. The tremendous economic achievements of modern society would not have been possible if this kind of asceticism had not absorbed all energy to the purpose of thrift and relentless work. It would transcend the scope of this paper to enter into an analysis of the character structure of modern man as he emerged in the sixteenth century. Suffice it to say here, that the economic and social changes in the fifteenth and sixteenth centuries destroyed the feeling of security and "belonging" which was typical of the members of medieval society.[27] The socio-economic position of the urban middle class, the peasantry, and the nobility were shaken in their foundations;[28] impoverishment, threats to traditional economic positions, as well as new chances for economic success, arose. Religious and spiritual ties which had established a rounded and secure world for the individual had been broken. The individual found himself completely alone in the world, paradise was lost for good, his success and failure were decided by the laws of the market; the basic relationship to everyone else had become one of merciless competition. The result of all this was a new feeling of freedom attended, however, by an increased anxiety. This anxiety, in its turn, created a readiness for new submission to religious and secular authorities even more strict than the previous ones had been. The new individualism on the one hand, anxiety and submission to authority on the other, found their ideological expression in Protestantism and Calvinism. At the same time, these religious doctrines did much to stimulate and increase these new attitudes. But even more important than the submission to external authorities was the fact that the authorities were internalized, that man became the slave of a master inside himself instead of one outside. This internal master drove the individual to relentless work and striving for success and never allowed him to be himself and enjoy himself. There was a spirit of distrust and hostility directed not only against the outside world, but also toward one's own self.

This modern type of man was selfish in a twofold sense: he had little concern for others and he was anxiously concerned

with his own advantage. But was this selfishness really a concern for himself as an individual, with all his intellectual and
sensual potentialities? Had "he" not become the appendix of
his socio-economic role, a cog in the economic machine, even
if sometimes an important cog? Was he not the slave of this
machine even if he subjectively felt as if he were following
his own orders? Was his selfishness identical with self-love or
was it instead rooted in the very lack of it?

We must postpone answering these questions, since we
have still to finish a brief survey of the doctrine of selfishness
in modern society. The taboo on selfishness has been reinforced in the authoritarian systems. One of the ideological
cornerstones of National Socialism is the principle: "Public
good takes precedence over private good."[29] According to
the original propaganda technique of National Socialism, the
thought was phrased in a form purposed to permit the
workers to believe in the "Socialist" part of the Nazi program.
However, if we consider its meaning in the context of the
whole Nazi philosophy, the implication is this: The individual should not want anything for himself; he should find his
satisfaction in the elimination of his individuality and in par-
ticipating as a small particle in the greater whole of the race,
the state or its symbol, the leader. While Protestantism and
Calvinism emphasized individual liberty and responsibility
even as it emphasized the nothingness of the individual,
Nazism is focused essentially on the latter. Only the "born"
leaders are an exception, and even they should feel themselves as instruments of someone higher up in the hierarchy
—the supreme leader as an instrument of destiny.

The doctrine that love for oneself is identical with "selfishness" and that it is an alternative to love for others has pervaded theology, philosophy, and the pattern of daily life; it
would be surprising if one would not find the same doctrine
also in scientific psychology, but here as an allegedly objective statement of facts. A case in point is Freud's theory
on narcissism. He says, in short, that man has a certain quantity of libido. Originally, in the infant, all this libido has as
its objective the child's own person, *primary narcissism*. Later
on, the libido is directed from one's own person toward other
objects. If a person is blocked in his "object-relationships,"
the libido is withdrawn from the objects and returned to
one's own person, *secondary narcissism*. According to Freud,
there is an almost mechanical alternative between ego-love
and object-love. The more love I turn toward the outside

world, the less love I have for myself, and vice versa. Freud is thus moved to describe the phenomenon of falling in love as an impoverishment of one's self-love because all love is turned to an object outside of oneself. Freud's theory of narcissism expresses basically the same idea which runs through Protestant religion, idealistic philosophy, and the everyday patterns of modern culture. This by itself does not indicate that he is right or wrong. Yet, this translation of the general principle into the categories of empirical psychology gives us a good basis for examining the principle.

These questions arise: Does psychological observation support the thesis that there is a basic contradiction and the state of alternation between love for oneself and love for others? Is love for oneself the same phenomenon as selfishness? Is there a difference or are they in fact opposites?

Before we turn to the discussion of the empirical side of the problem, it may be noted that from a philosophical viewpoint, the notion that love for others and love for oneself are contradictory is untenable. If it is a virtue to love my neighbor as a human being, why must not I love myself too? A principle which proclaims love for man but which taboos love for myself exempts me from all other human beings. The deepest experience of human existence, however, is to have this experience with regard to oneself. There is no solidarity of man in which I myself am not included. A doctrine which proclaims such an exclusion proves its objective insincerity by this very fact.[30]

We have come here to the psychological premises on which the conclusions of this paper are built. Generally, these premises are: Not only others, but also we ourselves are the "object" of our feelings and attitudes; the attitude toward others and toward ourselves, far from being contradictory, runs basically parallel.[31] With regard to the problem under discussion this means: Love for others and love for ourselves are not alternatives. Neither are hate for others and hate for ourselves alternatives. On the contrary, an attitude of love for themselves will be found in those who are at least capable of loving others. Hatred against oneself is inseparable from hatred against others, even if on the surface the opposite seems to be the case. In other words, love and hatred, in principle, are indivisible as far as the difference between "objects" and one's own self is concerned.

To clarify this thesis, it is necessary to discuss the problem of hatred and love. With regard to hatred one can differentiate between "reactive hatred" and "character-conditioned hatred." By reactive hatred I mean a hatred which is essentially a reaction to an attack on one's life, security, or ideals or on some other person that one loves and identifies oneself with. Its premise is one's positive attitude toward one's life, toward other persons, and toward ideals. If there is a strong affirmation of life, a strong hatred necessarily is aroused if life is attacked. If there is love, hatred must be aroused if the loved one is attacked. There is no passionate striving for anything which does not necessitate hatred if the object of this striving is attacked. Such hatred is the counterpoint of life. It is aroused by a specific situation, its aim is the destruction of the attacker and, in principle, it ends when the attacker is defeated.[32]

Character-conditioned hatred is different. To be sure, the hatred rooted in the character structure once arose as a reaction to certain experiences undergone by the individual in his childhood. It then became a character trait of the person; he *is* hostile. His basic hostility is observable even when it is not giving rise to manifest hatred. There is something in the facial expression, gestures, tone of voice, kind of jokes, little unintentional reactions which impress the observer as indications of the fundamental hostility, which also could be described as a continuous *readiness* to hate. It is the basis from which active hatred springs if and when it is aroused by a specific stimulus. This hate reaction can be perfectly rational; as much so, as a matter of fact, as is the case in the situations which were described as arousing reactive hatred. There is, however, a fundamental difference. In the case of reactive hatred it is the situation which *creates* the hatred. In the case of character-conditioned hatred an "idling" hostility is *actualized* by the situation. In the case where the basic hatred is aroused, the person involved appears to have something like a feeling of relief, as though he were happy to have found the rational opportunity to express his lingering hostility. He shows a particular kind of satisfaction and pleasure in his hatred which is missing in the case of an essentially reactive hatred.

In the case of a proportionality between hate reaction and external situation, we speak of a "normal" reaction, even if it is the actualization of character-conditioned hatred. From this normal reaction to an "irrational" reaction found in the neurotic or psychotic person, there are innumerable transitions and no sharp demarcation line can be drawn. In the irrational hate-reaction, the emotion seems disproportionate to the actual situation. Let me illustrate by referring to a reaction which psychoanalysts have ample opportunity to observe; an analysand has to wait ten minutes because the analyst is delayed. The analysand enters the room, wild with rage at the offense done to him by the analyst. Extreme cases can be observed more clearly in psychotic persons; in those the disproportionality is still more striking. Psychotic hatred will be aroused by something which from the standpoint of reality is not at all offensive. Yet, from the standpoint of his own feeling it is offensive, and thus the irrational reaction is irrational only from the standpoint of external objective reality, not from the subjective premises of the person involved.

The lingering hostility can also be purposely aroused and turned into manifest hatred by social suggestion; that is, propaganda. If such propaganda which wants to instill people with hatred toward certain objects is to be effectual, it must build upon the character-conditioned hostility in the personality structure of the members of the groups to which it appeals. A case in point is the appeal of Nazism to the group which formed its nucleus, the lower middle class. Latent hostility was peculiarly the lot of the members of this group long before it was actualized by Nazi propaganda, and that is why they were such fertile soil for this propaganda.

Psychoanalysis offers ample opportunity to observe conditions responsible for the existence of hatred in the character structure.

The decisive factors for arousing character-conditioned hatred may be stated to be all the different ways by which spontaneity, freedom, emotional and physical expansiveness, the development of the "self" of the child are blocked or destroyed.[33] The means of doing this are manifold; they vary from open, intimidating hostility and terror, to a subtle and "sweet" kind of "anonymous authority," which does not overtly forbid anything but says: "I know you will or will not like this or that." Simple frustration of instinctual impulses does not create deep-seated hostility; it creates only a reactive hate reaction. Yet, this was Freud's assumption and his concept of the Oedipus complex is based on it; it implies that the frustration of sexual wishes directed toward the father or the mother creates hatred which in its turn leads to anxiety and submission. To be sure, frustration often appears as a symptom of something which does create hostility: not taking the child seriously, blocking his expansiveness, not allowing him to be free. But the real issue is not isolated frustration but the fight of the child against those forces which tend to suppress his freedom and spontaneity. There are many forms in which the fight for freedom is fought and many ways in which the defeat is disguised. The child may be ready to internalize the external authority and be "good"; it may overtly rebel and yet remain dependent. It may feel that it "belongs" by completely conforming to the given cultural patterns at the expense of the loss of its individual self—the result is always a lesser or greater degree of inner emptiness, the feeling of nothingness, anxiety, and resulting from all that a chronic hatred, and *ressentiment*, which Nietzsche characterized very well as *Lebensneid*, envy of life.

There is a slight difference, however, between hatred and this envy of life. The aim of hatred is in the last analysis the destruction of the object outside of my self. By destroying it I attain strength in relative, although not in absolute, terms. In envy of life, the begrudging attitude aims at the destruction of others too; not, however, in order to gain relative strength, but to have the satisfaction that others are being denied the enjoyment of things which—for external or inner reasons—I cannot enjoy myself. It aims at removing the pain, rooted in my own inability for happiness, by having nobody else who by his very existence demonstrates what I am lacking.[34]

In principle, the same factors condition the development of chronic hatred in a group. The difference here as in general between individual psychology and social psychology is only to be found in this: while in individual psychology, we are looking for the individual and accidental conditions which are responsible for those character traits by which one individual varies from other members of his group, in social psychology we are interested in the character traits by which one individual varies from other members of his group; in social psychology we are interested in the character structure as far as it is common to and, therefore, typical of the majority of the members of that group. As to the conditions, we are not looking for accidental individual conditions like an overstrict father or the sudden death of a beloved sister, but for those conditions of life which are a common experience for the group as such. This does not mean the one or the other isolated trait in the whole mode of life, but the structure of basic life experiences as they are essentially conditioned by the socio-economic situation of a particular group.[35]

The child is imbued with the "spirit" of a society long before it makes the direct acquaintance with it in school. The parents represent in their own character structure the spirit prevalent in their society and class, and transmit this atmosphere to the child from the day of his birth onward. The family thus is the "psychic agency" of society.

The bearing on our problem of the differentiation in hatred will have become clear by now. While in the case of reactive hatred the stimulus which is at the same time the object, constitutes the "cause" for the hatred; in the case of character-conditioned hatred, the basic attitude, the readiness for hatred, exists regardless of an object and before a stimulus makes the chronic hostility turn into manifest hatred. As has been indicated, originally, in childhood, this basic hatred was brought into existence by certain people, but later it has become part of the personality structure, and objects play but a secondary role. Therefore, in its case, there is, in principle, no difference between objects outside of myself and my own self. The idling hostility is always there; its outside objects change according to circumstances, and it but depends on certain factors whether I myself become one of the objects of my hostility. If one wants to understand why a certain person is hated in one case, why I myself am hated in another case, one has to know the specific factors in the situation which make others or myself the object of manifest hatred. What interests us in this context, however, is the general principle that character-conditioned hatred is something radiating from an individual and, like a searchlight, focusing sometimes on this and sometimes on that object, among them myself.

The strength of basic hatred is one of the major problems of our culture. In the beginning of this paper, it has been shown how Calvinism and Protestantism pictured man as essentially evil and contemptible. Luther's hatred against the revolting peasants is of extraordinary intensity.

Max Weber has emphasized the distrust for and hostility toward others which runs through the Puritan literature replete with warnings against having any confidence in the help and friendliness of our fellow man. Deep distrust even toward one's closest friend is recommended by Baxter. Th. Adams says: "He—the 'knowing' man—is blind in no man's cause but best sighted in his own. He confines himself to the circle of his own affairs and thrusts not his fingers in needless fires. . . . . He sees the falseness of it [the world] and, therefore, learns to trust himself ever, others so far as not to be damaged by their disappointments."[36]

Hobbes assumed that man's nature was that of a predatory animal, filled with hostility, set to kill and rob. Only by the consensus of all, submitting to the authority of the state, could peace and order be created. Kant's opinion of man's nature is not too distant from Hobbes', he too thought that man's nature had a fundamental propensity for evil. Among psychologists, chronic hatred as an inherent part of human nature has been a frequent assumption. William James considered it as being so strong that he took for granted that we all feel a natural repulsion against physical contact with other persons.[37] Freud, in his theory of the death instinct, assumed that, for biological reasons, we all are driven by an irresistible force to destroy either others or ourselves.

Although some of the philosophers of the enlightenment period believed that the nature of man was good and that his hostility was the product of the circumstances under which he lives, the assumption of hostility as an inherent part of man's nature runs through the ideas of representative thinkers of the modern era from Luther up to our days. We need not discuss whether this assumption is tenable. At any rate, the philosophers and psychologists who held this belief were good observers of man within their own culture, even though they made the mistake of believing that modern man in his essence is not a historical product but is as nature made him to be.

While important thinkers clearly saw the strength of hostility in modern man, popular ideologies and the convictions of the average man tend to ignore the phenomenon. Only a relatively small number of people have an awareness of their fundamental dislike for others. Many have only a feeling of just having little interest or feeling for others. The majority are completely unaware of the intensity of the chronic hatred in themselves as well as in others. They have adopted the feelings that they know they are supposed to have: to like people, to find them nice, unless or until they have actually committed an act of aggression. The very indiscriminateness of this "liking people" shows its thinness, or rather its compensatory quality a basic lack of fondness.

While the frequency of underlying distrust and dislike

for others is known to many observers of our social scene, the dislike for oneself is a less clearly recognized phenomenon. Yet, this self-hatred may be considered rare only so long as we think of cases in which people quite overtly hate or dislike themselves. Mostly, this self-dislike is concealed in various ways. One of the most frequent indirect expressions of self-dislike are the inferiority feelings so widespread in our culture. Consciously, these persons do not feel that they dislike themselves: what they do feel is only that they are inferior to others, that they are stupid, unattractive, or whatever the particular content of the inferiority feelings is.[38]

To be sure, the dynamics of inferiority feelings are complex, and there are factors other than the one with which we are dealing. Yet, this factor is never missing, and dislike for oneself or at least a lack of fondness for one's own person is always present and is dynamically an important factor.

A still more subtle form of self-dislike is the tendency toward constant self-criticism. These people do not feel inferior, but if they make one mistake, discover something in themselves which should not be so, their self-criticism is entirely out of proportion to the significance of the mistake or the shortcoming. They must either be perfect according to their own standards, or at least perfect enough according to the standards of the people around them so that they get affection and approval. If they feel that what they did was perfect or if they succeed in winning other people's approval, they feel at ease. But whenever this is missing they feel overwhelmed by an otherwise repressed inferiority feeling. Here again, the basic lack of fondness for themselves is one source from which the attitude springs. This becomes more evident if we compare this attitude toward oneself with the corresponding one toward others. If, for example, a man who believes that he loves a woman should feel if she makes any mistake that she is no good, or if his feeling about her is entirely dependent on whether others criticize or praise her, we cannot doubt that there is a fundamental lack of love for her. It is the person who hates who seizes every opportunity to criticize another person and who does not miss any blunder.

The most widespread expression of the lack of fondness for oneself, however, is the way in which people treat themselves. People are their own slavedrivers; instead of being the slaves of a master outside of themselves, they have put the master within. This master is harsh and cruel. He does not give them a moment's rest, he forbids them the enjoyment of any pleasure, does not allow them to do what they want. If they do so, they do it furtively and at the expense of a guilty conscience. Even the pursuit of pleasure is as compulsory as is work. It does not lead them away from the continual restlessness which pervades their lives. For the most part, they are not even aware of this. There are some exceptions. Thus, the banker, James Stillman, who, when in the prime of life, had attained wealth, prestige, and power reached only by but few people said: I never in my life have done what I wanted and never shall do so.[39]

The role of "conscience" as the internalization of external authorities and as the bearer of deep-seated hostility against oneself has been seen clearly by Freud in the formulation of his concept of the Super-Ego. He assumed that the Super-Ego contains a great deal of the basic destructiveness inherent in man and turns it against him in terms of duty and moral obligation. In spite of objections to Freud's Super-Ego theory, which cannot be presented here,[40] Freud undoubtedly has sensed keenly the hostility and cruelty contained in the "conscience" as it was conceived in the modern era.

What holds true of hostility and hatred holds also true of love. Yet, love for others and self-love is by far a more difficult problem to discuss; and this for two reasons. One is the fact that while hatred is a phenomenon to be found everywhere in our society and, therefore, an easy object for empirical observation and analysis, love is a comparatively rare phenomenon, which lends itself to empirical observation only under difficulties; and discussion of love, therefore, implies the danger of being unempirical and merely speculative. The other difficulty is perhaps even greater. There is no word in our language which has been so much misused and prostituted as the word "love." It has been preached by those who were ready to condone every cruelty if it served their purpose; it has been used as a disguise under which to force people into sacrificing their own happiness, into submitting their whole self to those who profited from this surrender. It has been used as the moral basis for unjustified demands. It has been made so empty that for many people *love* may mean no more than that two people have lived together for twenty years just without fighting more often than once a week. It is dangerous and somewhat embarrassing to use such a word. Yet a psychologist may not properly succumb to this embarrassment. To preach love is at best bad taste. But to make a cool and critical analysis of the phenomenon of love and to unmask pseudo-love—tasks which cannot be separated from each other—is an obligation that the psychologist has no right to avoid.

It goes without saying that this paper will not attempt to give an analysis of love. Even to describe the psychological phenomena which are conventionally covered by the term "love" would require a good part of a book. One must attempt, however, the presentation necessary to the main trend of thought of this paper.

Two phenomena closely connected with each other are frequently presented as love—the masochistic and sadistic *love*. In the case of masochistic *love*, one gives up one's self, one's initiative and integrity in order to become submerged entirely in another person who is felt to be stronger. Because of deep anxieties which give rise to the feeling that one cannot stand on one's own feet, one wants to be rid of one's own individual self and to become part of another being, thus becoming secure and finding a center which one misses in oneself. This surrender of one's own self has often been praised as the example of "the great love." It is actually a form of idolatry, and also an annihilation of the self. The fact that it has been conceived as love has made it the more seductive and dangerous.

The sadistic *love* on the other hand springs from the desire to swallow its object to make him a will-less instrument in one's own hands. This drive is also rooted in a deep anxiety and an inability to stand alone, but instead of finding increased strength by being swallowed, strength and security are found in having a limited power over the other person. The masochistic as well as the sadistic kind of love are expressions of one basic need which springs from a basic inability to be independent. Using a biological term, this basic need may be called a "need for symbiosis." The sadistic *love* is frequently the kind of love that parents have for their children. Whether the domination is overtly authoritarian or subtly "modern" makes no essential difference. In either case, it tends to undermine the strength of the self of the child and leads in later years to the development in him of the very same symbiotic tendencies. The sadistic love is not infrequent among adults. Often in relationships of long duration, the respective roles are permanent, one partner representing the sadistic, the other one the masochistic pole of the symbiotic relationship. Often the roles change constantly—a continuous struggle for dominance and submission being conceived as *love*.

It appears from what has been said that love cannot be separated from freedom and independence. In contradiction to the symbiotic pseudo-love, the basic premise of love is freedom and equality. Its premise is the strength, independence, integrity of the self, which can stand alone and bear solitude. This premise holds true for the loving as well as for the loved person. Love is a spontaneous act, and spontaneity means—also literally—the ability to act of one's own free volition. If anxiety and weakness of the self makes it impossible for the individual to be rooted in himself, he cannot love.

This fact can be fully understood only if we consider what love is directed toward. It is the opposite of hatred. Hatred is a passionate wish for destruction; love is a passionate affirmation of its "object."[41] That means that love is not an "affect" but an active striving, the aim of which is the happiness, development, and freedom of its "object." This passionate affirmation is not possible if one's own self is crippled, since genuine affirmation is always rooted in strength. The person whose self is thwarted can love only in an ambivalent way; that is, with the strong part of his self he can love, with the crippled part he must hate.[42]

The term *passionate affirmation* easily leads to misunderstanding; it does not mean intellectual affirmation in the sense of purely rational judgment. It implies a much deeper affirmation, in which one's personality takes part as a whole: one's intellect, emotion and senses. One's eyes, ears and nose are often as good or better organs of affirmation than one's brain. If it is a deep and passionate one, the affirmation is related to the essence of the "object," not merely toward partial qualities. There is no stronger expression of God's love for man in the Old Testament than the saying at the end of each day of creation: "And God saw that it was good."

There is another possible misunderstanding which should particularly be avoided. From what has been said, one might come to the conclusion that every affirmation is love, regardless of the worthiness of the object to be loved. This would mean that love is a purely subjective feeling of affirmation and that the problem of objective values does not enter into it. The question arises: Can one love the evil? We come here to one of the most difficult problems of psychology and philosophy, a discussion of which can scarcely be attempted here. I must repeat, however, that affirmation in the sense here used is not something entirely subjective. Love is affirmation of life, growth, joy, freedom; and by definition, therefore, the evil which is negation, death, compulsion cannot be loved. Certainly, the subjective feeling can be a pleasurable excitement, consciously conceived in the conventional term of love. The person is apt to believe that he loves, but analysis of his mental content reveals a state very different from what I have discussed as love. Much the same question arises with regard to certain other problems in psychology, for instance, the problem as to whether happiness is an entirely subjective phenomenon or whether it includes an objective factor. Is a person who feels "happy" in dependence and self-surrender happy because he feels to be so, or is happiness always dependent on certain values like freedom and integrity? One has always used the argument that the people concerned are "happy" to justify their suppression. This is a poor defense. Happiness cannot be separated from certain values, and is not simply a subjective feeling of satisfaction. A case in point is masochism. A person can be satisfied with submission, with torture, or even with death, but there is no happiness in submission, torture or death. Such considerations seem to leave the ground of psychology and to belong to the field of philosophy or religion. I do not believe that this is so. A sufficiently refined psychological analysis, which is aware of the difference in the qualities of feelings according to the underlying personality structure, can show the difference between *satisfaction* and *happiness*. Yet, psychology can be aware of these problems only if it does not try to separate itself from the problem of values. And in the end does not shrink from the question of the goal and purpose of human existence.

Love, like character-conditioned hatred, is rooted in a basic attitude which is constantly present; a readiness to love, a *basic sympathy* as one might call it. It is started, but not caused, by a particular *object*. The ability, the readiness to love is a character trait just as is the readiness to hate.[43] It is difficult to say what the conditions favoring the development of this *basic sympathy* are. It seems that there are two main conditions, a positive and a negative one. The positive one is simply to have experienced love from others as a child. While conventionally, parents are supposed to *love* their children as a matter of course, this is rather the exception than the rule. This positive condition is, therefore, frequently absent. The negative condition is the absence of all those factors, discussed above, which make for the existence of a chronic hatred. The observer of childhood experiences may well doubt that the absence of these conditions is frequent.

From the premise that actual love is rooted in a *basic sympathy* there follows an important conclusion with regard to the *objects* of love. The conclusion is, in principle, the same as was stated with regard to the objects of chronic hatred: the objects of love do not have the quality of exclusiveness. To be sure, it is not accidental that a certain person becomes the *object* of manifest love. The factors conditioning such a specific choice are too numerous and too complex to be discussed here. The important point, however, is that love for a particular *object* is only the actualization and concentration of lingering love with regard to one person; it is not, as the idea of *romantic love* would have it, that there is only *the* one person in the world whom one could love, that it is the great chance of one's life to find that person, and that love for him or her results in a withdrawal from all others. The kind of love which can only be experienced with regard to one person demonstrates by this very fact that it is not love, but a symbiotic attachment. The basic affirmation contained in love is directed toward the beloved person as an incarnation of essentially human qualities. Love for one person implies love for man as such. The kind of "division of labor," as William James calls it, namely, to love one's family, but to be without feeling for the "stranger," is a sign of a basic inability to love. Love for man as such is not, as it is frequently supposed to be, an abstraction coming "after" the love for a specific person, or an enlargement of the experience with a specific *object*; it is its premise, although, genetically, it is acquired in the contact with concrete individuals.

From this, it follows that my own self, in principle, is as much an object of my love as another person. The affirmation of my own life, happiness, growth, freedom is rooted in the presence of the basic readiness of and ability for such an affirmation. If an individual has this readiness, he has it also toward himself; if he can only *love* others, he cannot love at all. In one word, love is as indivisible as hatred with regard to its *objects*.

The principle which has been pointed out here, that hatred

and love are actualizations of a constant readiness, holds true for other psychic phenomena. Sensuality, for instance, is not simply a reaction to a stimulus. The sensual or, as one may say, the erotic person, has a basically erotic *attitude* toward the world. This does not mean that he is constantly excited sexually. It means that there is an erotic *atmosphere* which is actualized by a certain object, but which is there underneath before the *stimulus* appears. What is meant here is not the physiologically given ability to be sexually excited, but an atmosphere of erotic readiness, which under a magnifying glass could be observed also when the person is not in a state of actual sexual excitement. On the other hand, there are persons in whom this erotic readiness is lacking. In them, sexual excitement is essentially caused by a stimulus operating on the sexual instinct. Their threshold of stimulation can vary between wide limits, but there is a common quality in this type of sexual excitement; namely, its separateness from the whole personality in its intellectual and emotional qualities. Another illustration of the same principle is the sense of beauty. There is a type of personality who has a readiness to see beauty. Again, that does not mean that he is constantly looking at beautiful pictures or people or scenery; yet, when he sees them a continuously present readiness is actualized, and his sense of beauty is not simply *aroused* by the object. Here too, a very refined observation shows that this type of person has a different way of looking at the world, even when he looks at objects which do not stimulate an acute perception of beauty. We could give many more examples for the same principle, if space permitted. The principle should already be clear: While many psychological schools[44] have thought of human reactions in terms of stimulus-response, the principle presented here is that character is a structure of numerous *readinesses* of the kind mentioned, which are constantly present and are actualized but not caused by an outside stimulus. This view is essential for such a dynamic psychology as psychoanalysis is.

Freud assumed that all these readinesses are rooted in biologically given instincts. It is here assumed that although this holds true for some of them, many others have arisen as a reaction to the individual and social experiences of the individual.

One last question remains to be discussed. Granted that love for oneself and for others in principle runs parallel, how do we explain the kind of *selfishness* which obviously is in contradiction to any genuine concern for others. The *selfish* person is interested only in himself, wants everything for himself, is unable to give with any pleasure but is anxious only to take; the world outside himself is conceived only from the standpoint of what he can get out of it; he lacks interest in the needs of others, or respect for their dignity and integrity. He sees only himself, judges everyone and everything from the standpoint of its usefulness to him, is basically unable to love. This selfishness can be manifest or disguised by all sorts of unselfish gestures; dynamically it is exactly the same. It seems obvious that with this type of personality there is a contradiction between the enormous concern for oneself and the lack of concern for others. Do we not have the proof here that there exists an alternative between concern for others and concern for oneself? This would certainly be the case if selfishness and self-love were identical. But this assumption is the very fallacy which has led to so many mistaken conclusions with regard to our problem. Selfishness and self-love, far from being identical, actually are opposites.

Selfishness is one kind of greediness.[45] Like all greediness, it contains an insatiability, as a consequence of which there is never any real satisfaction. Greed is a bottomless pit which exhausts the person in an endless effort to satisfy the need without ever reaching satisfaction. This leads to the crucial point: close observation shows that while the selfish person is always anxiously concerned with himself, he is never satisfied, is always restless, always driven by the fear of not getting enough, of missing something, of being deprived of something. He is filled with burning envy of anyone who might have more. If we observe still closer, especially the unconscious dynamics, we find that this type of person is basically not fond of himself but deeply dislikes himself. The puzzle in this seeming contradiction is easy to solve. The selfishness is rooted in this very lack of fondness for oneself. The person who is not fond of himself, who does not approve of himself, is in a constant anxiety concerning his own self. He has not the inner security which can exist only on the basis of genuine fondness and affirmation. He must be concerned about himself, since basically his own self lacks security and satisfaction. The same holds true with the so-called narcissistic person, who is not so much overconcerned with getting things for himself as with admiring himself. While on the surface it seems that these persons are very much in love with themselves, they actually are not fond of themselves, and their narcissism—like selfishness—is an overcompensation for the basic lack of self-love. Freud has pointed out that the narcissistic person has withdrawn his love from others and turned it toward his own person. While the first part of this statement is true, the second one is a fallacy. He neither loves others nor himself.[46]

It is easier to understand this mechanism when we compare it with overconcern and overprotectiveness for others. Whether it is an oversolicitous mother or an overconcerned husband, sufficiently deep observation shows always one fact: While these persons consciously believe that they are particularly fond of the child or husband, there actually is a deep repressed hostility toward the very objects of their concern. They are overconcerned because they have to compensate not only for a lack of fondness but for an actual hostility.

The problem of selfishness has still another aspect. Is not the sacrifice of one's own person the extreme expression of unselfishness, and, on the other hand, could a person who loves himself make that supreme sacrifice? The answer depends entirely on the kind of sacrifice that is meant. There is one *sacrifice*, as it has been particularly emphasized in recent years by Fascist philosophy. The individual should give himself up for something outside of himself which is greater and more valuable; the Leader, the race. The individual by himself is nothing and by the very act of self-annihilation for the sake of the higher power finds his destiny. In this concept, sacrificing oneself for something or someone greater than oneself is in itself the greatest attainable virtue. If love for oneself as well as for another person means basic affirmation and respect, this concept is in sharp contrast to self-love. But there is another kind of sacrifice: If it should be necessary to give one's life for the preservation of an idea which has become part of oneself or for a person whom one loves, the sacrifice may be the extreme expression of self-affirmation. Not, of course, an affirmation of one's physical self, but of the self in the sense of the kernel of one's total personality. In this case the sacrifice in itself is not the goal; it is the price to be paid for the realization and affirmation of one's own self. While in this latter case, the sacrifice is rooted in self-affirmation, in the case of what one might call the masochistic sacrifice, it is rooted in the lack of self-love and self-respect; it is essentially nihilistic.

The problem of selfishness has a particular bearing on psychotherapy. The neurotic individual often is *selfish* in the sense that he is blocked in his relationship to others or overanxious about himself. This is to be expected, since to be *neurotic* means that the integration of a strong self has not been achieved successfully. To be *normal* certainly does not mean that it has. It means for the majority of *well-adapted* individuals that they have lost their own self at an early age and replaced it completely by a *social self* offered to them by society. They have no neurotic conflicts because they themselves and, therefore, the discrepancy between their selves and the outside world has disappeared. Often the neurotic person is particularly *unselfish*, lacking in self-assertion and blocked in following his own aims. The reason for this *unselfishness* is essentially the same as for the *selfishness*. What he is practically always lacking is self-love. This is what he needs to become *well*. If the *neurotic* becomes well, he does not become *normal* in the sense of the conforming *social self*. He succeeds in realizing his self, which never had been completely lost and for the preservation of which he was struggling by his neurotic symptoms. A theory, therefore, as Freud's on narcissism which rationalizes the cultural pattern of denouncing self-love by identifying it with *selfishness*, can have but devastating effects therapeutically. It increases the taboo on self-love. Its effects can only be called *positive* if the aim of psychotherapy is not to help the individual to be himself; that is, free, spontaneous, and creative—qualities conventionally reserved for *artists*—but to give up the fight for his self and conform to the cultural pattern peacefully and without the noise of a neurosis.

In the present era, the tendency to make of the individual a powerless atom is increasing. The authoritarian systems tend to reduce the individual to a will-less and feelingless instrument in the hands of those who hold the reins; they batter him down by terror, cynicism, the power of the state, large demonstrations, fierce orators, and all other means of suggestion. When finally he feels too weak to stand alone, they offer him satisfaction by letting him participate in the strength and glory of the greater whole, whose powerless part he is. The authoritarian propaganda uses the argument that the individual of the democratic state is *selfish* and that he should become unselfish and socially minded. This is a lie. Nazism substituted the most brutal selfishness of the leading bureaucracy and of the state for the selfishness of the average man. The appeal for unselfishness is the weapon to make the average individual still more ready to submit or to renounce. The criticism of democratic society should not be that people are too selfish; this is true, but it is only a consequence of something else. What democracy has not succeeded in is to make the individual love himself; that is, to have a deep sense of affirmation for his individual self, with all his intellectual, emotional, and sensual potentialities. A Puritan-Protestant inheritance of self-denial, the necessity of subordinating the individual to the demands of production and profit, have made for conditions from which Fascism could spring. The readiness for submission, the pervert *courage* which is attracted by the image of war and self-annihilation, is only possible on the basis of a—largely unconscious—desperation, stifled by martial songs and shouts for the Führer. The individual who has ceased to love himself is ready to die as well as to kill. The problem of our culture, if it is not to become a Fascist one, is not that there is too much selfishness but that there is no self-love. The aim must be to create those conditions which make it possible for the individual to realize his freedom, not only in a formal sense, but by asserting his total personality in his intellectual, emotional, sensual qualities. This freedom is not the rule of one part of the personality over another part—conscience over nature, Super-Ego over Id—but the integration of the whole personality and the factual expression of all the potentialities of this integrated personality.

Notes

[1] Johannes Calvin, *Institutes of the Christian Religion* (translated by John Allen), Philadelphia, Presbyterian Board of Christian Education, 1928 (1:688 pp.), in particular Book III, Chap. 7, par. 1, p. 619.

[2] From "For as it is . . ." the translation is mine from the Latin original (Johannes Calvini *Institutes Christianae Religionis*, Editionem curavit A. Tholuk; Berolini, 1845, par. 1, p. 445). The reason for this shift is that Allen's translation slightly changes the original in the direction of softening the rigidity of Calvin's thought. Allen translates this sentence: "For as compliance with their own traditions leads men most effectually to ruin, so to place no dependency on our own knowledge or will, but merely to follow the guidance of the Lord, is the only way of safety." However,

the Latin *sibi ipsis obtemperant* is not equivalent to "follow one's own inclinations" but "to obey oneself." To forbid following one's inclinations has the mild quality of Kantian ethics that man should suppress his natural inclinations and by doing so follow the orders of his conscience. On the other hand, forbidding to obey oneself is a denial of the autonomy of man. The same subtle change of meaning is reached by translating *ita unicus est salutis portis nihil nec sapere, nec velle per se ipsum* "to place no dependence on our knowledge nor will." While the formulation of the original straightforwardly contradicts the motto of enlightenment philosophy: *sapere aude*—dare to know, Allen's translations warns only of a dependence on one's own knowledge, a warning which is by far less contradictory to modern thought. I mention these deviations of the translation from the original which I came across accidentally, because they offer a good illustration of the fact that the spirit of an author is "modernized" and colored—certainly without any intention of doing so—just by translating him.

3 Reference Footnote 1, Chap. 12, par. 6, p. 681.

4 Cf. reference Footnote 1, Chap. 7, par. 4, p. 622.

5 It should be noted, however, that even love for one's neighbor, while it is one of the fundamental doctrines of the New Testament, has not been given a corresponding weight by Calvin. In blatant contradiction to the New Testament, Calvin says: "For what the schoolmen advance concerning the priority of charity to faith and hope, is a mere reverie of a distempered imagination. . . ." Cf. reference Footnote 1, Chap. 24, par. 1, p. 531.

6 Despite Luther's emphasis on the spiritual freedom of the individual, his theology, different as it is in many ways from Calvin's, is pervaded by the same conviction of man's basic powerlessness and nothingness.

7 Cf. Immanuel Kant, *Kant's Critique of Practical Reason and Other Works on the Theory of Ethics* (translated by Thomas Kingsmill Abbott), London, New York, Longmans Greene, 1909 (xiv and 369 pp.)—in particular Part I, Book I, Chap. 1, par. 8, Remark II, p. 126.

8 Cf. reference Footnote 7—in particular Part I, Book I, Chap. III, p. 186.

9 Reference Footnote 7—in particular *Fundamental Principles of the Metaphysics of Morals*, second section, p. 61.

10 Cf. reference Footnote 7—in particular Part I, Book I, Chap. III, p. 165.

11 Immanuel Kant, *Immanuel Kants Werke*, Berlin, Cassierer (8:xxix and 468 pp.)—in particular "Der Rechtslehre Zweiter" Teil I. Abschnitt, par. 49, p. 124. I translate from the German text, since this part is omitted in the English translation of *The Metaphysics of Ethics* by I. W. Semple (Edinburgh, 1871).

12 Cf. reference Footnote 11—in particular p. 126.

13 Cf. Immanuel Kant, *Religion Within the Limits of Reason*

Alone (translated by Th. M. Greene and H. H. Hudson), Chicago, Open Court, 1934 (xxxv and 200 pp.)—in particular Book I.

[14] Max Stirner, *The Ego and His Own* (translated by Steven T. Byington), London, A. C. Fifield, 1912 (xx and 506 pp.)—in particular p. 339.

[15] One of his positive formulations, for example, is: "But how does one use life? In using it up like the candle one burns. . . . Enjoyment of life is using life up."—Reference Footnote 14, p. 426. Engels has clearly seen the onesidedness of Stirner's formulations and has attempted to overcome the false alternative between love for oneself and love for others. In a letter to Marx in which he discovers Stirner's book, Engels writes: "If, however, the concrete and real individual is the true basis for our 'human' man, it is self-evident that egotism—of course not only Stirner's egotism of reason, but also the egotism of the heart—is the basis for our love of man" (*Marx-Engels Gesamtausgabe*, Berlin, Marx-Engels Verlag, 1929 [1:1 and 540 pp.]—in particular p. 6).

[16] Friedrich Nietzsche, *The Will to Power* (translated by Anthony M. Ludovici), Edinburgh and London, T. N. Foulis, 1910 (1:xiv and 384 pp.) and (2:xix and 432 pp.)—in particular stanzas 246, 362, 369, 373, and 728.

[17] Friedrich Nietzsche, *Beyond Good and Evil* (translated by Helen Zimmer), New York, Macmillan, 1907 (xv and 268 pp.)—in particular Stanza 258, p. 225.

[18] Friedrich Nietzsche, *Thus Spake Zarathustra* (translated by Thomas Common), New York, Modern Library (325 pp.)—in particular p. 75.

[19] Reference Footnote 16, Stanza 785.

[20] Reference Footnote 16, Stanza 935.

[21] Reference Footnote 18, p. 76.

[22] Reference Footnote 18, p. 102.

[23] See reference Footnote 16, Stanza 820, and Friedrich Nietzsche, *The Twilight of Idols* (translated by A. M. Ludovici), Edinburgh, T. N. Foulis, 1911 (xviii and 281 pp.), Stanza 35. Friedrich Nietzsche, *Ecce Homo* (translated by A. M. Ludovici), New York, Macmillan, 1911 (xiv and 207 pp.), Stanza 2. Friedrich Nietzsche, *Nachlass, Nietzsches Werke*, Leipzig, A. Kroener (14:x and 442 pp.), pp. 63-64.

[24] Cf. the important paper by Max Horkhelmer, "Egoismus und Freiheitzbewegung," *Zeitschr. f. Socialforshung* (1936), 5:167, which deals with the problem of egotism in modern history.

[25] This point has been emphasized by Karen Horney, *The Neurotic Personality of Our Time*, New York, Norton, 1937 (xii and 290 pp.), and by Robert S. Lynd, *Knowledge for What*, Princeton, Princeton University Press, 1939 (x and 268 pp.).

[26] Max Weber, *The Protestant Ethic and the Spirit of Capitalism* (translated by Talcott Parsons), London, Allan, 1930 (xi and 292 pp.).

[27] Harry Stack Sullivan has given particular emphasis to the need for security as one of the basic motivating forces in man, while orthodox psychoanalytical literature has not paid sufficient attention to this factor.

[28] Cf. R. Pascal, *The Social Basis of the German Reformation*, London, Watts, 1933 (viii and 243 pp.). Johann Babtist Kraus, *Scholastik, Puritanismus und Kapitalismus*, München, Dunker, 1930 (329 pp.). R. H. Tawney, *Religion and the Rise of Capitalism*, London, John Murray, 1926 (xiii and 339 pp.).

[29] "Gemeinnutz geht vor Eigennutz."

[30] This thought is expressed in the biblical "Love thy neighbor as thyself!" The implication is that respect of one's own integrity and uniqueness, love for and understanding of one's own self, cannot be separated from respect, love, and understanding with regard to another individual. The discovery of my own self is inseparably connected with the discovery of any other self.

[31] This viewpoint has been emphasized by Karen Horney, *New Ways in Psychoanalysis*, New York, Norton, 1939 (313 pp.); in particular chapters 5 and 7.

[32] Nietzsche has emphasized the creative function of destruction. Reference Footnote 23, *Ecce Homo*, Stanza 2.

[33] In recent years, a number of psychologists were interested in the problem of uncovering the hostility, consciously or unconsciously present in children. Some of them were very successful in demonstrating the presence of strong hostility in very young children. A method which proved to be particularly fruitful was to arrange play situations in which the children expressed their hostility very clearly. According to Lauretta Bender and Paul Schilder, "Aggressiveness in Children," *Genetic Psychology Monographs* (1936), 18:410-425, the younger the children were, the more directly they expressed hostility, while with the older ones the hate reaction was already repressed but could be clearly observed in a play situation. Cf. also David M. Levy, *Studies in Sibling Rivalry V*, New York, American Orthopsychiatric Association, 1937 (96 pp.). L. Murphy and G. Lerner have found normal children who seem quite conventionally adjusted to the nursery-school play group, revealing intense aggression in a free play situation, alone with one adult. J. Louise Despert has come to similar conclusions: See her "A Method for the Study of Personality Reactions in Preschool Age Children by Means of Analysis of Their Play," *J. Psychol.* (1940), 9:17-29. A. Hartoch and E Schachtel have found expression of strong aggressiveness in Rorschach tests in two- to four-year-old children who did not show proportionate amount of manifest aggressiveness in their behavior.

[34] It should be noted that sadism has to be differentiated from hatred. As I see it, the aim of sadism is not destruction of the subject, but a seeking to have absolute power over it, to make it

an instrument of oneself. Sadism can be blended with hatred; in this case it will have the cruelty usually implied in the notion of sadism. It can also be blended with sympathy, in which case the impulse is to have the object as an instrument and, at the same time, to further him in any way excepting in one: letting him be free.

35 See, on the method of analytic social psychology, Erich Fromm, "Zur Aufgabe und Methode einer analytischen Sozial-psychologie," *Zeitschr. f. Sozialforschung* (Leipzig) (1932), 1:28-54.

36 *Work of the Puritan Divines* (quoted by Weber). Reference Footnote 26—in particular begin p. 222.

37 William James, *Principles of Psychology*, New York, Holt, 1893 (1:xii and 689 pp.), and (2:vi and 704 pp.)—in particular, 2:348.

38 Industry, for instance, capitalizes the unconscious self-dislike by terrorizing people with the threat of "body odor." The unconscious dislike the average person has for himself makes him an easy prey for this suggestion.

39 Cf. Anna Robeson (Brown), *The Portrait of a Banker: James Stillman*, New York, Duffield, 1927 (x and 370 pp.).

40 See my discussion of the Super-Ego in the psychological part of *Studien über Autorität und Familie* (Max Horkheimer, ed.), Paris, Alcan, 1936 (xv and 947 pp.).

41 Object is put into quotation marks because in a love relationship the "object" ceases to be an object; that is, something opposite to and separated from the subject. Not accidentally do "object" and "objection" have the same root.

42 Sullivan has approached this formulation in his lectures. He states that the era of preadolescence is characterized by the appearance of impulses in interpersonal relations which make for a new type of satisfaction in the pleasure of the other person (the chum). Love, according to him, is a situation in which the satisfaction of the loved one is exactly as significant and desirable as that of the lover.

43 It would be most unfortunate to assume that these respective readinesses are characteristics of different personalities. Many people present concomitant readinesses of both varieties.

44 Although the reflexological viewpoint seems to be similar to the one taken here, this similarity is only a superficial one. The reflexological viewpoint means a pre-formed readiness of neurones to react in a certain way to a certain stimulus. Our viewpoint is not concerned with these physical conditions and, what is more important, by *readiness* we mean an actually present but only lingering, or idling attitude, which makes for a basic atmosphere or *Grundstimmung*.

⁴⁵ The German word *Selbstsucht* (addiction of self) very adequately expresses this quality common to all *Sucht*.

⁴⁶ Since Freud thinks only in the framework of his instinctual concepts, and since a phenomenon like love in the sense used here does not exist in his system, the conclusions to which he comes are all but inevitable.

Karen Horney

PSYCHOANALYSIS WITHOUT LIBIDO — CULTURE AND NEUROSIS

Karen Horney was born in Hamburg in 1885 and died in New York on December 4, 1952. She studied medicine at the University of Berlin and was affiliated with the Berlin Psychoanalytic Institute from 1918 until 1932. Franz Alexander invited her to come to the United States and she was Associate Director of the Chicago Psychoanalytic Institute for two years. She moved to New York in 1934 and taught for some time at the New York Psychoanalytic Institute. After her break with orthodox psychoanalysis she founded the Association for the Advancement of Psychoanalysis and the American Institute of Psychoanalysis.

In her approach to personality theory Horney prefers to work within the framework of Freudian psychology. But she aspires to eliminate the fallacies of Freudian thinking, which fallacies, according to Horney, have their root in the mechanistic and biological orientation of Freud's thinking. She formulates her position in the following words: "My conviction, expressed in a nutshell, is that psychoanalysis should outgrow the limitations set by its being an instinctivistic and a genetic psychology."

Horney presents us with ten basic neurotic needs which the individual has acquired in order to find solutions for the problem of disturbed human relationships: 1) the need for affection and approval, 2) the need for a "Partner" who will take over one's life, 3) the need to restrict one's life within narrow borders, 4) the need for power, 5) the need to exploit others, 6) the need for prestige, 7) the need for personal admiration, 8) the ambition for personal achievement, 9) the need for self- sufficiency and independence, 10) the need for perfection and unassailability.

All of these conflicts that arise in man's life are avoidable or resolvable if the young child is raised in a home where there is security, trust, and warmth. Unlike Freud and Jung, Horney feels that conflict is built in the realm of social conditions and not in the nature of man, as she formulates in her own words: "The person who is likely to become neurotic is

111

one who has experienced the culturally determined difficulties in an accentuated form, mostly through the medium of childhood experience."

PSYCHOANALYSIS WITHOUT LIBIDO— CULTURE AND NEUROSIS

In the psychoanalytic concept of neuroses a shift of emphasis has taken place: whereas originally interest was focused on the dramatic symptomatic picture, it is now being realized more and more that the real source of these psychic disorders lies in character disturbances, that the symptoms are a manifest result of conflicting character traits, and that without uncovering and straightening out the neurotic character structure we cannot cure a neurosis. When analyzing these character traits, in a great many cases one is struck by the observation that, in marked contrast to the divergency of the symptomatic pictures, character difficulties invariably center upon the same basic conflicts.

These similarities in the content of conflicts present a problem. They suggest, to minds open to the importance of cultural implications, the question of whether and to what extent neuroses are molded by cultural processes in essentially the same way as "normal" character formation is determined by these influences; and, if so, how far such a concept would necessitate certain modifications in Freud's views of the relation between culture and neurosis.

In the following remarks I shall try to outline roughly some characteristics typically recurring in all our neuroses. The limitations of time will allow us to present neither data—good case histories—nor method, but only results. I shall try to select from the extremely complex and diversified observational material the essential points.

There is another difficulty in the presentation. I wish to show how these neurotic persons are trapped in a vicious circle. Unable to present in detail the factors leading up to the vicious circle, I must start rather arbitrarily with one of the outstanding features, although this in itself is already a complex product of several interrelated, developed mental factors. I start, therefore, with the problem of competition.

The problem of competition, or rivalry, appears to be a never-failing center of neurotic conflicts. How to deal with competition presents a problem for everyone in our culture; for the neurotic, however, it assumes dimensions which generally surpass actual vicissitudes. It does so in three respects:

1. There is a constant measuring up with others, even in situations which do not call for it. While striving to surpass others is essential for all competitive situations, the neurotic measures up even with persons who are in no way potential competitors and have no goal in common with him. The question as to who is the more intelligent, more attractive, more popular is indiscriminately applied toward everyone.

2. The content of neurotic ambitions is not only to accomplish something worth while, or to be successful, but to be absolutely best of all. These ambitions, however, exist in fanstasy mainly—fantasies which may or may not be conscious. The degree of awareness differs widely in different persons. The ambitions may appear in occasional flashes of fantasy only. There is never a clear realization of the powerful dramatic role these ambitions play in the neurotic's life, or of the great part they have in accounting for his behavior and mental reactions. The challenge of these ambitions is not met by adequate efforts which might lead to realization of the aims. They are in queer contrast to existing inhibitions toward work, toward assuming leadership, toward all means which would effectually secure success. There are many ways in which these fantastic ambitions influence the emotional lives of the persons concerned: by hypersensitivity to criticism, by depressions or inhibitions following failures, et cetera. These failures need not necessarily be real. Everything which falls short of the realization of the grandiose ambitions is felt as failure. The success of another person is felt as one's own failure.

This competitive attitude not only exists in reference to the external world, but is also internalized, and appears as a constant measuring up to an ego ideal. The fantastic ambitions appear on this score as excessive and rigid demands toward the self, and failure in living up to these demands produces depressions and irritations similar to those produced in competition with others.

3. The third characteristic is the amount of hostility involved in neurotic ambition. While intense competition implicitly contains elements of hostility—the defeat of a competitor meaning victory for oneself—the reactions of neurotic persons are determined by an insatiable and irrational expectation that no one in the universe other than themselves

should be intelligent, influential, attractive, or popular. They become infuriated, or feel their own endeavors condemned to futility, if someone else writes a good play or a scientific paper or plays a prominent role in society. If this attitude is strongly accentuated, one may observe in the analytical situation, for example, that these patients regard any progress made as a victory on the part of the analyst, completely disregarding the fact that progress is of vital concern to their own interests. In such situations they will disparage the analyst, betraying, by the intense hostility displayed, that they feel endangered in a position of paramount importance to themselves. They are as a rule completely unaware of the existence and intensity of this "no one but me" attitude, but one may safely assume and eventually always uncover this attitude from reactions observable in the analytical situation, as indicated above.

This attitude easily leads to a fear of retaliation. It results in a fear of success and also in a fear of failure: "If I want to crush everyone who is successful, then I will automatically assume identical reactions in others, so that the way to success implies exposing me to the hostility of others. Furthermore: if I make any move toward this goal and fail, then I shall be crushed." Success thus becomes a peril and any possible failure becomes a danger which must at all costs be avoided. From the point of view of all these dangers, it appears much safer to stay in the corner, be modest and inconspicuous. In other and more positive terms, this fear leads to a definite recoiling from any aim which implies competition. This safety device is assured by a constant, accurately working process of automatic self-checking.

This self-checking process results in inhibitions, particularly inhibitions toward work, but also toward all steps necessary to the pursuit of one's aims, such as seizing opportunities, or revealing to others that one has certain goals or capacities. This eventually results in an incapacity to stand up for one's own wishes. The peculiar nature of these inhibitions is best demonstrated by the fact that these persons may be quite capable of fighting for the needs of others or for an impersonal cause. They will, for instance, act like this:

When playing an instrument with a poor partner, they will instinctively play worse than he, although otherwise they may be very competent. When discussing a subject with someone less intelligent than themselves, they will compulsively descend below his level. They will prefer to be in the rank and file, not to be identified with the superiors, not even to get an increase in salary, rationalizing this attitude in some way. Even their dreams will be dictated by this need for reassurance. Instead of utilizing the liberty of a dream to imagine themselves in glorious situations, they will actually see themselves, in their dreams, in humble or even humiliating situations.

This self-checking process does not restrict itself to activities in the pursuit of some aim, but, going beyond that, tends to undermine the self-confidence, which is a prerequisite for any accomplishment, by means of self-belittling. The function of self-belittling in this context is to eliminate oneself from any competition. In most cases these persons are not aware of actually disparaging themselves, but are aware of the results only as they feel themselves inferior to others and take for granted their own inadequacy.

The presence of these feelings of inferiority is one of the most common psychic disorders of our time and culture. Let me say a few more words about them. The genesis of inferiority feelings is not always in neurotic competition. They present complex phenomena and may be determined by various conditions. But that they do result from, and stand in the service of, a recoiling from competition is a basic and ever-present implication. They result from a recoiling inasmuch as they are the expression of a discrepancy between high-pitched ideals and real accomplishment. The fact, however, that these painful feelings at the same time fulfill the important function of making secure the recoiling attitude itself, becomes evident through the vigor with which this position is defended when attacked. Not only will no evidence of competence or attractiveness ever convince these persons, but they may actually become scared or angered by any attempt to convince them of their positive qualities.

The surface pictures resulting from this situation may be widely divergent. Some persons appear thoroughly convinced of their unique importance and may be anxious to demonstrate their superiority on every occasion, but betray their insecurity in an excessive sensitivity to every criticism, to every dissenting opinion, or every lack of responsive admiration. Others are just as thoroughly convinced of their incompetence or unworthiness, or of being unwanted or unappreciated; yet they betray their actually great demands in that they react with open or concealed hostility to every frustration of their unacknowledged demands. Still others will waver constantly in their self-estimation between feeling themselves all-important and feeling, for instance, honestly amazed that anyone pays any attention to them.

If you have followed me thus far, I can now proceed to outline the particular vicious circle in which these persons are moving. It is important here, as in every complex neurotic picture, to recognize the vicious circle, because if we overlook it and simplify the complexity of the processes going on by assuming a simple cause-effect relation, we either fail to get an understanding of the emotions involved or attribute an undue importance to some one cause. As an example of this error, I might mention regarding a highly emotion-charged rivalry attitude as derived directly from rivalry with the father. Roughly, the vicious circle looks like this:

The failures, in conjunction with a feeling of weakness and defeat, lead to a feeling of envy toward all persons who are more successful or merely more secure or better contented with life. This envy may be manifest or it may be repressed under the pressure of the same anxiety which led to a repression of, and a recoiling from, rivalry. It may be entirely wiped out of consciousness and represented by the substitution of a blind admiration; it may be kept from awareness by a disparaging attitude toward the person concerned. Its effect, however, is apparent in the incapacity to grant to others what one has been forced to deny oneself. At any rate, no matter to what degree the envy is repressed or expressed, it implies an increase in the existing hostility against people and consequently an increase in the anxiety, which now takes the particular form of an irrational fear of the envy of others.

The irrational nature of this fear is shown in two ways: (1) it exists regardless of the presence or absence of envy in the given situation; and (2) its intensity is out of proportion to the dangers menacing from the side of the envious competitors. This irrational side of the fear of envy always remains unconscious, at least in nonpsychotic persons; therefore it is never corrected by a reality-testing process, and is all the more effective in the direction of reinforcing the existing tendencies to recoil.

Consequently, the feeling of one's own insignificance grows, the hostility against people grows, and the anxiety grows. We thus return to the beginning, because now the fantasies come up, with about this content: "I wish I were more powerful, more attractive, more intelligent than all the others; then I should be safe, and besides, I could defeat them and step on them." Thus we see an ever-increasing deviation of the ambitions toward the stringent, fantastic, and hostile.

This pyramiding process may come to a standstill under various conditions, usually at an inordinate expense in loss of expansiveness and vitality. There is often some sort of resignation as to personal ambitions, in turn permitting the diminution of anxieties as to competition, with the inferiority feelings and inhibitions continuing.

It is now time, however, to make a reservation. It is in no way self-evident that ambition of the "no-one-but-me" type must necessarily evoke anxieties. There are persons quite capable of brushing aside or crushing everyone in the way of their ruthless pursuit of personal power. The question then is: Under what special condition is anxiety invoked in neurotically competitive people?

The answer is that they at the same time want to be loved. While most persons who pursue an asocial ambition in life care little for the affection or the opinion of others, the neurotics, although possessed by the same kind of competitiveness, simultaneously have a boundless craving for affection and appreciation. Therefore, as soon as they make any move toward self-assertion, competition, or success, they begin to dread losing the affection of others, and must automatically check their aggressive impulses. This conflict between ambition and affection is one of the gravest and most typical dilemmas of the neurotics of our time.

Why are these two incompatible strivings so frequently present in the same individual? They are related to each other in more than one way. The briefest formulation of this relationship would perhaps be that they both grow out of the same sources, namely, anxieties, and they both serve as a means of reassurance against the anxieties. Power and affection may both be safeguards. They generate each other, check each other, and reinforce each other. These interrelations can be observed most accurately within the analytic situation, but sometimes are obvious from only a casual knowledge of the life history.

In the life history may be found, for instance, an atmosphere in childhood lacking in warmth and reliability, but rife with frightening elements—battles between the parents, injustice, cruelty, oversolicitousness—generation of an increased need for affection—disappointments—development of an outspoken competitiveness—inhibition—attempts to get affection on the basis of weakness, helplessness, or suffering.

We sometimes hear that a youngster has suddenly turned to ambition after an acute disappointment in his need for affection, and then given up the ambition on falling in love.

Particularly when the expansive and aggressive desires have been severely curbed in early life by a forbidding atmosphere, the excessive need for reassuring affection will play a major role. As a guiding principle for behavior, this implies a yielding to the wishes or opinions of others rather than asserting one's own wishes or opinions; an overvaluation of the significance for one's own life of expressions of fondness from others, and a dependence on such expressions. And, similarly, it implies an overvaluation of signs of rejection and a reacting to such signs with apprehension and defensive hostility. Here again a vicious circle begins easily and reinforces the single elements: In diagram it looks somewhat like this:

> Anxiety plus repressed hostility
> Need for reassuring affection
> Anticipation of, sensitivity to, rejection
> Hostile reactions to feeling rejected

These reactions explain why emotional contact with others that is attained on the basis of anxiety can be at best only a very shaky and easily shattered bridge between individuals, and why it always fails to bring them out of their emotional isolation. It may, however, serve to cope with anxieties and even get one through life rather smoothly, but only at the expense of growth and personality development, and only if circumstances are quite favorable.

Let us ask now, which special features in our culture may be responsible for the frequent occurrence of the neurotic structures just described?

We live in a competitive, individualistic culture. Whether the enormous economic and technical achievements of our culture were and are possible only on the basis of the competitive principle is a question for the economist or sociologist to decide. The psychologist, however, can evaluate the personal price we have paid for it.

It must be kept in mind that not only is competition a driving force in economic activities but also that it pervades our personal life in every respect. The character of all our human relationships is molded by a more or less outspoken competition. It is effective in the family between siblings, at school, in social relations (keeping up with the Joneses), and in love life.

In love, it may show itself in two ways: the genuine erotic wish is often overshadowed or replaced by the merely competitive goal of being the most popular, having the most dates, love letters, lovers, being seen with the most desirable man or woman. Again, it may pervade the love relationship itself. Marriage partners, for example, may be living in an endless struggle for supremacy, with or without being aware of the nature or even of the existence of this combat.

The influence on human relations of this competitiveness lies in the fact that it creates easily aroused envy toward the stronger ones, contempt for the weaker, distrust toward everyone. In consequence of all these potentially hostile tensions, the satisfaction and reassurance which one can get out of human relations are limited, and the individual becomes more or less emotionally isolated. It seems that here, too, mutually reinforcing interactions take place, so far as insecurity and dissatisfaction in human relations in turn compel people to seek gratification and security in ambitious strivings, and vice versa.

Another cultural factor relevant to the structure of our neurosis lies in our attitude toward failure and success. We are inclined to attribute success to good personal qualities and capacities, such as competence, courage, enterprise. In religious terms this attitude was expressed by saying that success was due to God's grace. While these qualities may be effective—and in certain periods, such as the pioneer days, may have represented the only conditions necessary—this ideology omits two essential facts: (1) that the possibility for success is strictly limited; even external conditions and personal qualities being equal, only a comparative few can possibly attain success; and (2) that factors other than those mentioned may play the decisive role, such as, for example, unscrupulousness or fortuitous circumstances. Inasmuch as these factors are overlooked in the general evaluation of success, failures, besides putting the person concerned in a factually disadvantageous position, are bound to reflect on his self-esteem.

The confusion involved in this situation is enhanced by a sort of double moral. Although, in fact, success meets with adoration almost without regard to the means employed in securing it, we are at the same time taught to regard modesty and an undemanding, unselfish attitude as social or religious virtues, and are rewarded for them by praise and affection. The particular difficulties which confront the individual in our culture may be summarized as follows: for the competitive struggle he needs a certain amount of available aggressiveness; at the same time, he is required to be modest, unselfish, even self-sacrificing. While the competitive life situation with the hostile tensions involved in it creates an enhanced need of security, the chances of attaining a feeling of safety in human relations—love, friendship, social contacts—are at the same time diminished. The estimation of one's personal value is all too dependent on the degree of success attained, while at the same time the possibilities for success are limited and the success itself is dependent, to a great extent, on fortuitous circumstances or on personal qualities of an asocial character.

Perhaps these sketchy comments have suggested to you the direction in which to explore the actual relationship of our culture to our personality and its neurotic deviations. Let us now consider the relation of this conception to the views of Freud on culture and neurosis.

The essence of Freud's views on this subject can be summarized, briefly, as follows: Culture is the result of a sublimation of biologically given sexual and aggressive drives—"sexual" in the extended connotation Freud has given the term. Sublimation presupposes unwitting suppression of these instinctual drives. The more complete the suppression of these drives, the higher the cultural development. As the capacity for sublimating is limited, and as the intensive suppression of primitive drives without sublimation may lead to neurosis, the growth of civilization must inevitably imply a growth of neurosis. Neuroses are the price humanity has to pay for cultural development.

The implicit theoretical presupposition underlying this train of thought is the belief in the existence of biologically determined human nature, or, more precisely, the belief that oral, anal, genital, and aggressive drives exist in all human beings in approximately equal quantities.[1] Variations in character formation from individual to individual, as from culture to culture, are due, then, to the varying intensity of the suppression required, with the addition that this suppression can affect the different kinds of drives in varying degrees.

This viewpoint of Freud's seems actually to encounter difficulties with two groups of data. (1) Historical and anthropological findings[2] do not support the assumption that the growth of civilization is in a direct ratio to the growth of instinct suppression. (2) Clinical experience of the kind indicated in this paper suggests that neurosis is due not simply to the quantity of suppression of one or the other instinctual drives, but rather to difficulties caused by the conflicting character of the demands which a culture imposes on its individuals. The differences in neuroses typical of different cultures may be understood to be conditioned by the amount and quality of conflicting demands within the particular culture.

In a given culture, those persons are likely to become neurotic who have met these culturally determined difficulties in accentuated form, mostly through the medium of childhood experiences; and who have not been able to solve their difficulties, or have solved them only at great expense to personality.

NOTES

[1] I pass over Freud's recognition of individual constitutional difference.

[2] Ruth Benedict, *Patterns of Culture*; Margaret Mead, *Sex and Temperament in Three Primitive Societies*.

Harry Stack Sullivan

A THEORY OF INTERPERSONAL RELATIONS — THE ILLUSION OF PERSONAL INDIVIDUALITY

Harry Stack Sullivan was born near Norwich, New York, in 1892 and died in 1949, in Paris, on his way home from a professional meeting in Amsterdam. He received his medical degree in 1917 from the Chicago College of Medicine and Surgery. In 1922 Sullivan became affiliated with Saint Elizabeths Hospital in Washington, D.C., and was influenced strongly by William Alanson White, one of the leaders in American neuropsychiatry. He became president of the William Alanson White Foundation in 1933 and held that office until 1943. He founded and became director of the Washington School of Psychiatry, which is a training institution of the Foundation. Besides William Alanson White, others who have influenced Sullivan are Freud, Adolf Meyer, George Mead, Edward Sapir, and Ruth Benedict.

In his personality theory Sullivan became known for his interpersonal theory of psychiatry. Its major theme is that personality is the relatively enduring pattern of recurrent personal situations which are characterizing a human life. Personality cannot be separated from interpersonal situations. In Sullivan's view personality consists chiefly of interpersonal behavior. The individual cannot exist and does not exist apart from his relations with other people. Man is the product of social interactions, and personality is a purely hypothetical entity. However, Sullivan accepts personality as a dynamic center of various processes that occur in a series of interpersonal fields. These processes are identified by Sullivan in three categories: dynamisms, personifications, and cognitive processes.

Sullivan gained a great deal of his empirical knowledge of personality from work with patients suffering from various types of personality disorders, but chiefly with schizophrenics. He held that the psychiatrist was much more than an observer, that he was a vital participant in an interpersonal situation. The following essay illustrates in detail Sullivan's questioning of the concept of individuality.

A THEORY OF INTERPERSONAL RELATIONS— THE ILLUSION OF PERSONAL INDIVIDUALITY*

When one has the notion of studying personality before him, the ideas of maturation, growth, and development ought certainly never to be too far from consciousness. And if you will have those ideas in mind at the beginning, I will avoid talking about them for some time.

A word that is much more common in all discussions of personality is adjustment, and I would like to state the idea of this paper as a special use of the term "adjustment"; namely, the adjustment of potentialities to necessities—just as, for example, each person who is going to be a full-fledged person very early adjusts his potentialities for learning to do tricks with his speech apparatus, to the overweening necessity of learning the mother tongue of his family. Now the learning of language, which is terribly important in any approach to the study of personality on a general scale, is the classical and perhaps the most important single instance of adjustment in the sense of an immensely capable organism— the vast potentialities of which have perhaps never been adequately envisaged, much less explored—adjusting itself to the necessity for verbal communication with significant people.

Another great word in thinking about personality is experience, and I have never found any better definition of experience than that which is, I believe, embalmed as the first meaning of the term in all good English dictionaries: experience is anything lived, undergone, or the like. But to add slightly to this very general notion, let me say that experience can usefully be considered as of two kinds: *direct* experience, in which you are directly undergoing, living, or the like; and *mediate* experience, in which that which has been previously undergone or lived is passed in review. Another form of the mediate experience occurs when we take select excerpts from the past and string them together on the basis of probability, in which case we are engaged in prospective experience, commonly called foresight. Now, experience is quite clearly susceptible of consideration from another standpoint; namely, what happens in awareness, consciousness, or in what we like to term our mental life. And from this stand-

* This paper was given before the Society on the Theory of Personality, New York Academy of Medicine in New York City, May 3, 1944.

point, experience is either noted or unnoticed or, in the first case, formulated. In other words, we note many things which we do not formulate; that is, about which we do not develop clear ideas of what happened to us. And there is also experience which we do not notice but which can be demonstrated to have occurred in explaining subsequent events.

All of us have developed some view of the world, and in general the routes over which we have moved in developing these views of the world are capable of being put under three rubrics. These rubrics that I shall use are terms with pretty definite meaning in certain biological fields, and I am using these terms in a much more general sense; but I think you will see that they have some justification. They are viewpoints. We develop our views of the world from the viewpoint of *morphology*, of our understanding of the way that material is organized; and from *physiology*, in which we gradually come to understand how functional activity, the working of things, is organized; and *ecology*, in which we finally begin to see that materials interpenetrate and that materials and activity are related in some more or less enduring way. So, from these three standpoints—the organization of material things, the way that activity is or the pattern that activities tend to follow, and the interpretation and interrelation of the whole—we gradually develop our views of the world. I should say that these views are, in their currently best form, either notions of a pluralist universe or notions along the line of the doctrine of organism, which is, while it sounds monistic, very different indeed from any monistic philosophy. Now, a pluralist universe is probably not unassimilable to the doctrine of organism, but be that as it may. Wherever we have a great deal of data assembled, and free ourselves from prejudices that obscure our study of that data, we discover that there are the three aspects that I have already mentioned, including very importantly the interrelation, the interdependence of this and that.

A classical instance of this interdependence is the organism's relation with oxygen. Every seventh-grade grammar school boy, I am sure, knows that oxygen is a gas which is an ingredient of the atmosphere and that this gas is in some fashion vital to life. It is a very clever seventh-grade boy who knows that the oxygen gets out of the atmosphere into the body and is presently returned to the atmosphere in the shape of carbon dioxide; but what very few seventh-grade pupils know, and some fourth-grade medical students have not yet quite captured, is the notion that there is very little storage of oxygen and that life is dependent on the continual, almost uninterrupted, exchange between the oxygen of the atmosphere, the oxygen in the body, the carbon dioxide in the body and in the atmosphere. They interpenetrate through marvelously capable cells in the lungs, and the balance of the oxygen in the body is very delicately adjusted by a most elaborate apparatus. But life without an atmosphere including oxygen is not possible for man, and, similarly, an atmosphere which could not receive or would not take the oxygen which we have processed would rapidly prove fatal. There is a continuous interchange which can be called communal existence, if you please, of the organism and its necessary environment.

In this development of a world view, nearly all of us start —not because it is the first thing that intrudes itself upon us but it is the first thing that we can grasp—with some element of the physicochemical world, the world of the nonliving objects and their relations. And then we go from that to the idea of the biological world, the world of the living, living objects and their relations, realizing, as I say, certainly from the seventh grade onward, that the biological world requires some part of the physicochemical world to live. And only as we get well along do we contemplate the world of people, although they are the first things that impress themselves upon us; and it is at this point—the field of the psychiatrist's interest, the social scientist's interest, the educator's, the lawyer's, and so on—that views of the world are most poignantly deficient in breadth or depth, or both. All these worlds are encountered through their significant relation with us in our roles of experiencers and formulators. It is probably true that we can experience almost anything for an indefinite length of time; and if we do not fortunately run it through the process which we call formulating, we don't really know what we are doing—although we may get more and more clever at eluding unpleasantness, and so on—and we certainly can't tell our children about it. So the double role of undergoing or living through things and having more or less descriptive and defining thoughts or formulas is the common route by which these various aspects of the universe—the various worlds, if you please—come to be encountered. Because we know of the universe by way of our experience and according to the skill of our formulating faculties, it becomes clear to the thoughtful that whatever the perduring, the long-continuing entities of the universe may be, and however curious their relations may be, in some respects these will forever be unknown to us because we have no channels for experiencing these things and therefore nothing to formulate. And more in keeping with what I intend to talk about in this paper, the current views which are entertained about any of these worlds and their relations are almost inevitably going to undergo change, the rapidity of change in these views probably being greatest in the world of people and slowest in the physicochemical world with which serious people have been seriously concerned for the longest time.

Now, there is a word which is not particularly an ingredient of common speech but has long since delighted me—it pleased Whitehead also, so at least I am in good company for the moment. I believe that the word in its parental Greek tongue meant "knot"; the word I mean is *nexus,* the place where things get together and are snarled up or tangled. The nexus of all this experience by which we form views of the world, the universe, our place in it, and so on, is always in the experience of me-and-my-mind, or you-and-your-mind if you feel very separate from me. And in this you-and-your-mind there are some things which are fairly clearly capable of being named which go on in experiencing and formulating. We analyze and understand the past, and to understand means that we see certain relations in certain parts of it with the still earlier past, which has gradually taken on personal meaning. We symbolize and formulate the present—and by "symbolize" we mean we relate it to things, thought forms, words, and so on, which will stand for it. With this conversion of something—which for all I know may be unique—into more or less familiar things that stand for it, one becomes able to throw it into statements and conclusions, to deduce relationships which may not have been clear in the experience, and so on and so forth. And as I said before, we project the future by juggling with past symbolizations, understandings, and present formulations in terms of probable future events. To the extent that we project well—that is, we are careful in deciding the probabilities of certain courses of events—we sometimes exercise foresight and are prepared for what happens.

The mind—you know I am now talking about me-and-my-mind or you-and-your-mind—the mind is phenomenologically coterminous with consciousness; that is, so far as anything that you can observe or can get anyone else to observe about your mind or his mind, anything that can be sensed and perceived, will be of the same extent as the state of mind called consciousness; and the various ingredients, the contents of consciousness, which cover a wonderful bunch of alleged or real entities, are what one ordinarily means when he talks about his "mental life." In this we find a marvelous congeries of things, some things being just terms invented by psychologists, and others being such anciently associated labels that we may assume that they pertain to things: sensations; perceptions; feelings of pleasantness and unpleasantness; sundry wishes, desires, and personal needs; beliefs and ideas, of various orders of abstraction—some that refer to very concrete entities, some that refer to classes of entities, some that refer to some totality of all entities, such as the idea of the universe; thoughts and reveries; and even recollected dreams. Besides these, we find rather less clear, less easily communicable, less easily describable ingredients, such as "the exercise of choice," the manifestation of volition, the state of having intention—always good if you are anything like fully human—and the manifestation of decision; and occasionally, of course, indecision, perplexity, and that peculiarly unpleasant experience which is properly called anxiety—about which, if I am lucky, I will have quite a bit to say presently. And most exciting of all the things that one finds in one's mind is the feeling of power and effectiveness which is connected with objectifying "the mental life," which is ordinarily done by thoughts or remarks about I-and-myself.

Now, perhaps all of you or most of you are so familiar with thinking about I-and-myself that you don't realize how delightfully powerful you feel many times when the time comes to say, "I believe so and so." That reaches out and changes things, and only disagreeable people fail to be swayed by the power that you are experiencing and indicating, so that while you-and-your-mind are, so far as phenomena are concerned, coterminous with consciousness, I-and-myself are rather more powerful, more forceful entities, you see, which are in fact somewhat slower in appearing in life than is me-and-myself. The way the "myself" part—you know, that sort of Old Dog Tray that follows along—fits into life gets to be obscure when a patient tells you, "Well, I shall hold myself to doing it." Now, I have often tried to picture this process and usually experience a mild tailspin. But it is certainly very reassuring to the patient to announce that he is going to hold himself to something or other, or force himself to do something or other; it's really the most safe and therefore the most sane field in which to exercise power when you don't have it.

In this audience it is scarcely necessary to stress the fact that the content of consciousness, the mental life to which people are really referring when they talk about their minds, is entirely inadequate to account for events, or to exercise very powerful influence directly on the course of events, or even actually to control the contents of consciousness. And for a very long time the science of mind, psychology, was in rather a rum position because its events—in contradistinction to those of the respectable, natural scientific world and even in rather inferior contrast to the growing world of biological knowledge—were discrete and didn't follow each other with due proper copulas and connections but instead were erratic and unpredictable. It is hard to build a science where things have gaps between them. Who knows what's in the gap? And so, as I say, psychology wasn't doing very well with the conscious life as a subject matter for scientific formulation. But things changed a great deal when, through Freud's and Breuer's careful observations and Freud's brilliant thinking, it became possible to postulate the unconscious. The unconscious, from the way I have actually presented the thing, is quite clearly that which cannot be experienced directly, which fills all the gaps in the mental life. In that rather broad sense, the postulate of the unconscious has, so far as I know, nothing in the world the matter with it. As soon as you begin to arrange the furniture in something that cannot be directly experienced, you are engaged in a work that requires more than parlor magic and you are apt to be embarrassed by some skeptic. And so I say, the postulate of the unconscious as that which fills the gaps explains the discontinuity in the conscious life; that's bully, but don't be tempted to tell the world all about the unconscious because someone is almost certain to ask you how you found out.

One reason why people were not content to realize that the unconscious was a hypothesis which was immensely useful is that in this Western world of ours, with its vast success from technology, it has become extremely important for one's feeling of personal prestige that he shall discriminate the reasonable and rational; and in case he finds himself doing anything in which he might be thought to be unreasonable or irrational, he just devotes, oh, almost any necessary portion of the rest of his life to demonstrating that he was both reasonable and rational. So, as I say, since it is one of the great and specious values of this Western world of ours to look upon the reasonable and the rational as very dignified compared with all the rest of the things that can be said about behavior, it isn't enough to have hit upon a splendid hypothesis and arranged a great many experiments and observations to demonstrate that the hypothesis is not just an intellectual convenience but actually gives a sort of common explanatory pattern for many things which can be observed once there is something postulated to fill the discontinuity. Instead of that, one proceeds to make the unconscious—that not susceptible to direct experience—full of reasonable irrationalities and irrational reasonablenesses, and so on, and thereby, I believe, makes oneself magnificently and completely a clown.

Even in the comparatively simple realm of the nonliving some people have long since learned to avoid explanations that offer no possibility of any operational validation, explanations that cannot be converted into any type of act or experiment that will prove whether they are right or wrong, or whether they are to some extent right or to some extent wrong. Physics, for example, has found that it could get itself into wonderful entanglements as long as there was no way of discovering quite what it was talking about. But if, on the other hand, before uttering, giving voice, it thought, "Well, now how could one do something to demonstrate whether this term is empty or, at least likely, full of reference to the world"—as soon as that attitude was developed, physics began to make remarkable sense in its newly expanded world of atomic physics, in which the good old rules did not apply; rules on which we were educated and on which most technology, other than electronics, is based. As I say, once this world of the quantum had been discovered, a great deal of abstruse nonsense was taught, and finally compelled physicists to realize that if they couldn't devise some operation that had a bearing on their concept, they had best be quiet. That is really quite a good rule, I think, in our very much more complicated, much more treacherous field in which prejudice and wisdom are almost indistinguishable—unless of course the wisdom is in you and the prejudice in someone else. In the world of people, explanations are very easily obtained for almost any act of any person. All you have to do is say, "And why did you do that?" and he rattles like a machine gun with great streams of words—verbal statements;

and if you go away, he is apt to use streams of words in a letter to complete the demonstration of how unutterably easily he deceives himself into feeling that he knows what he is doing, which is apparently all that most people need in order to feel comfortable. But for the study either of the actions of groups of people or of the interrelation of groups of people— or even of what I will ultimately say is as purely hypothetical as the unconscious individual personality, if you can guess how to study it—it just doesn't do to ignore this fabulous world of verbal statements which seem to do so much and have actually done so much harm to human life and human thinking, although inexplicably mixed in with being the basis of the great evolution which is human civilization and all the sciences and technologies that there are.

There would be none of all this without this particular potentiality for making articulate noises and for recognizing phonemal areas in those noises, in other words, learning very early in life to discriminate when a certain part of a continuously varying frequency passes from the "ah" to the "ă"[*a* as in *a*dd] phoneme so that you catch the word even though some people's frequencies for "ă" are within a few cycles per second of other people's frequencies for "ah." These we call phonemal stations in sound, and they characterize each language. There are phonemal stations covering the whole range of audible frequencies, I guess, and each language has only a comparatively small number of them—which is why you have to work so hard to make some of the Chinese noises and even some of the German noises, if you weren't educated to them in childhood. This potentiality for learning these exquisite discriminations of a really very complex field, the field of audible sound, and for reproducing them with dependable accuracy; and the potentiality for learning a vast number of combinations of these things which make up words, and for learning a fairly complicated system of rules for sticking them together so as to give the impression of past, present, future, action or rest, order, and so on—these potentialities and the evolution of language have underlaid a great deal of the exceedingly distinguished part of human performance.

So I want to have a good deal to say in the course of time on words. I want to invite your attention to the common experience that you have all undergone and that you are imposing on your children—and know that everybody else is imposing on his children—and to the efforts which not only parents impose on their children but are very anxious indeed to have certain surrogates, in the shape of schoolteachers, and so on, impose on their children: the education of the young to competent use of the language so that, as the parent often says, you can say what you mean, more generally so that what you say can be understood by people of comparable education who happen to speak the same tongue. Now, this takes the learning of not only those things I have mentioned but also of a very large vocabulary, and quite a precise grasp of the principles of grammar; some at least of the rudiments of rhetoric; and, if you expect to move in polite society, speech etiquette—a thing commonly ignored by scientists. Even on back wards in mental hospitals there is a kind of etiquette: there are people who do not speak to each other but who none the less stay silent until the other fellow is through speaking, whereupon they talk to themselves for a while. Moreover, if you are going to be smart, you must also be able to keep up with speech fashions or even, in the case of some slang, speech fads. Now, this is a big job, as each of you can remember when you think how much of your schooling was devoted to English and its various divisions and what not.

I don't suppose anyone in the audience is a deaf-mute, and so I have to ask you to realize that in talking about speech I am using speech—or at least verbal behavior—a fact which is terribly important not only in its own right, but also because a good grasp on the ideas which I am attempting to express about verbal behavior in its role in the development of personality is applicable to many other aspects of the acculturation, or of the socialization of the young. It is easy to see it in speech. It is easy to talk about it in speech. It is notoriously easy to talk about talk. It is somewhat more difficult to talk about toilet habits, and so on, particularly to mixed audiences.

So I will have to leave to you the throwing of inferential bridges from the general consideration that I give to verbal behavior to all the other things which are necessary in order that you will be respected by the people that you want to respect you. And I will ask you to realize that what I have said about getting the child to talk so that he will be understood is a pressing necessity on all parents, with respect to this whole gamut of socialized performances. Their child must be acceptable to some other children. He must be regarded as a decent person, must grow into a decent person.

He must be able to get his just deserts because he knows how to go after them, and so on, and so forth. It is an imperative necessity which parents cannot escape feeling, however wretchedly they and others may discharge the responsibility. It is this urgent pressure to try to get your offspring something like a fair chance in the world as it is realized to be that makes the acculturation or socialization of the human young—almost from the cradle way into the twentieth year—a more or less continuous task, interrupted only when they are safely tucked in bed, or supposed to be safely tucked in bed. And the amount of things that go on during this period can be explored at your leisure the rest of your life, with illumination on the problem of interpersonal relations every time you see a new aspect of the process of socializing the young.

This is a function of the complexity of the social order in which we live. So far as I know, there is no reason to believe that anywhere at any time thus far has there appeared a system of institutions, emphatically right ways of doing things, traditions, prevailing prejudices, fashions, and so on, which have been, from the standpoint of reason, unitary; that is, explicable as a series of deductions and inferences from a central proposition, or internally consistent and congruent. Always the systems of social organization, civilizations, cultures, whatever you wish to call them, have grown in an erratic fashion, in sporadically emerging directions, and under disparate and often conflicting influences, so that they become a wonderful congeries having anything but a common central principle. And the outcome of that is that even if a child were born with the mature genius of Einstein, or of any of the other great figures of human history, he would still have to learn the culture, because it is not capable of being understood; that is, you cannot develop insight into it, you cannot see how it necessarily hangs together because it doesn't necessarily hang together—it falls apart. So the child is subjected to a simply tremendous amount of rote learning, and rote learning—which is one of the beloved terms, I believe, of the educator—is another term for sublimation, a conception that is beloved at least of a few psychiatrists, and I really want to get it beloved by many more of you before the evening is over because the poor term has fallen into some disrepute. Its origin was peculiar. It, I believe, was borrowed from chemistry in which it referred to how sulphur gets from one place to the other under the influence of heat. You know, it doesn't go through all the performances that water does, but you begin to see it disappearing from one place and crystallizing somewhere else. This is called sublimation. Well, sublimation was gathered from chemistry, as so many words are, and applied to a somewhat obscure process by which low and unworthy human motives sort of move mysteriously to a higher level. Once one saw that there was something in this queer notion and began to look at it, it wasn't necessary to raid chemistry or even to feel mysterious about it. The thing is essentially quite easy to state, and may I assure you that the definition that I give is subject to operational control. If a person is possessed of a motive which, as the parents feel and therefore presently he himself feels, endangers his acceptance by the society to which he should be welcome; then if some way or other he can be led to find a partial satisfaction for this motive by some worthy type of activity—play, or what have you—and if this happens without his noticing it, he has sublimated the unworthy motive. And this works beautifully unless the motive demands something so strongly that so charming a solution won't work. And so this vast rote learning of culture is the general instance of which sublimation as seen in psychiatry is a special instance by which the victim without knowing it finds a socially acceptable, more complicated way of living; and that is how rote memory comes to work. It satisfies more or less something given, but it follows socially approved patterns.

And so, actually, the thing which distinguishes the human being from the human animal is the incorporation in the poor human animal of vast amounts of culture, of socially meaningful rather than biologically meaningful entities, which exert very powerful influence on all subsequent performances of the creature. This process begins in practically identical shape with a rather cute sort of solution that some people find for some problems; namely, they just without noticing it find something estimable to do which gives them considerable satisfaction. Now, the operational attack on sublimation—this is a digression—is that if you tell people how they can sublimate, they can't sublimate. In other words, the unwitting part of it—the fact that it is not run through consciousness—is what makes it work and gives a very strong hint of what a vast bunch of abilities we have which do not manifest as such if the contents of consciousness are involved; that doesn't prove anything about the unconscious but it does prove something about the capabilities of the human being. Well, I tell you that human beings are human animals that have been filled with culture—socialized, if you like the word—in which process they move from the biological realm into the world of people. Do not permit yourself to think that because they started as animals, clearly members of the biological realm no matter how immature, and although their bodies and their abilities mature at a more or less specified rate, and although there is parallel development through the shape of experience, trial-and-error learning, and this and that—all of which can be seen in a dog, a horse, or various other animals—don't permit yourself to think that the animal can be discovered after it has been modified by the incorporation of culture: it is no longer there. It is not a business of a social personality being pinned on or spread over a human animal. It is an initially animal human developing into what the term "human" properly applies to—a person.

And this statement implies one thing which I have to state specifically, although the implication is reached by several steps which I have no time to get into. While the many aspects of the physicochemical world are necessary environment for every animal—oxygen being one—culture, social organization, such things as language, formulated ideas, and so on, are an indispensable and equally absolutely necessary part of the environment of the human being, of the person. It is for that reason that we can see and can easily document in many cases the deterioration of the outstandingly human, of the more highly socialized aspects of the person, when he is subjected to isolation and does not have in him the capacity to provide a very active cultural interchange because he is dealing with imaginary or ideal persons. Even in the case of the person well equipped with these possibilities for supplying a great deal out of the richness of his past, nonetheless his end state after a year or so of separation from the channels of mediate communication, the radio, and so on, is by no means as estimable as was his state at the beginning; so the absolutely necessary element of a cultural world with which active interchange is maintained and in which functional activity is carried on is just as necessary to the person as are oxygen, water, foodstuffs. And this business of becoming a human being, which is the great preoccupation of one's parents and teachers and the more or less full-time job of each one of us over a good many years, is an exceedingly important part of each of us, and has an enormous amount to do with civilization and the intricate systems of institutions which are always associated everywhere in history with the appearance of performances of human size, of life size, you might say. Throughout all of this process, a very great part of the refinements of the social order is presented through systems of verbal reference, vocal behavior, graphic behavior, and so on, pertaining to words.

Now, let me run over briefly this particular aspect of the general process of becoming a human being, which is manifested in the early years of life: The transfer from the manifestations of potentialities to learn phonemes and words, and even rough grammatical structures, to the capacity to use language to communicate information and misinformation. All children and for that matter, I believe, all the young of all the species on the face of the earth enjoy, whatever that means, playing with their abilities. As the young mature, these abilities become manifest in play activities and are obviously pleasant to manifest in that way. And so, before it is possible for a child to articulate syllables, there is a playing with the phonemal stations which the child has finally been able to hit on in the babbling and cooing business. There follows the picking up of some syllables, and sooner or later every child falls upon the syllable "ma"; and if there is a slight tendency to perseveration so that it becomes "ma-ma," then truly the child discovers that there is something that he had not previously suspected: namely, magic in this noise-making apparatus of his, because very significant people begin to rally around and do things, and they don't hurt—quite the contrary, they are pleasant. I suppose that that little experience is the beginning of what to most people seems to be a lifelong feeling that there is nothing about them that is as powerful as the noises they make with their mouths. But anyway, it will not be very long before this child has a whole flock of articulate noises more or less strung together as words; and those words, which will be the delight of Grandma and the satisfaction of Mama, and perhaps even a source of mild satisfaction to Papa, will have very little to do indeed with those words as they will be in that person ten years later. The words as they originally come along are happy accidents of maturation and combination of hearing and motor impulse—and vast bunches of potentialities that I couldn't name if I had time to. Especially we see in the case of "ma-ma"—where almost anything might have been said but that happened to be and it causes commotion among the great significant environment—that this obviously represents some personal power. This is one of the most remarkable performances thus far observed. And so "ma-ma" is of course not the name of a creature that runs around offering breasts and rattles: "mama" pertains much more to the general feeling of force, magic, and so on. And I suppose it comes to everyone as a bit of a letdown to discover that "Ma-ma" is the thing that this creature feels is its proper appellation, and it is only because the creature responds to that name that all this wonderful appearance of magic was called out.

The transfer from the feeling of power in this combination of noise to the realization that it is a pet name for the maternal relative is a transfer from the realm of the autistic or wholly personal, almost animal meaning, to the impersonal, social, conventional, or, as we like to say, consensually validated meaning of the word, and to the realm of scientific discourse, and I hope often to the realm of common speech. One's experience in using words has been observed with such care that one has finally learned how to create in the hearer's mind something remotely resembling what one hoped he would think of. Now, that takes a lot of experimenting, a great deal of observation, many corrections, solemn exhortations, rewards and punishments, and, as can be demonstrated in the case of almost everyone, applies only to a large working vocabulary. In addition to that, there is perhaps twice as large a collection of words in an additional vocabulary that isn't used very much, the meanings of which would come as a mild shock to a lexicographer, and a few words in a very personal vocabulary which are definitely retained in an autistic state—they are a secret language which will be expressed only obscurely in a very intimate relationship. Now, so far as there remain autistic words, those words would be fragments of the culture, torn from it, and kept as magic possessions of, let us say, an animal, and that is not what I am dealing with. In so far as a great deal of consensual validation has gone on and one can make noises which are more or less exactly communicative to a hearer who knows the language, the words have been stripped of as much as possible of the accidents of their personal history in you, and it is by that process that they come to be so peculiarly impersonal, just as if, you see, you hadn't learned them with the greatest care, having a wealth of meaning to your original words, and gradually sorting out that which was relevant from that which was irrelevant to the purposes of verbal communication.

Now, a great deal of life runs through this process. It starts out defined by the more or less accidental occurrence of something. One experiences, observes, formulates—after perhaps naming, symbolizing—and subsequently thinks about, that is, analyzes, and perhaps finally gets insight into or thoroughly understands the relationship of various parts of this complex experience, has information about it; but it is more or less a unique performance. And then, because of the way we live, the equipment we have, the tendencies we mature, and so on, and perhaps the necessities to which we are subjected by others, we want to talk about this; and as we first discuss anything new in our experience—as you may be able to observe from day to day, however mature you are—we don't make awfully good sense; and now and then we have the unpleasant experience in the act of telling somebody about it of discovering that we don't know what we are talking about, even though it is our experience.

The point is that the process of consensual validation running here before our eyes calls in an illusion, an illusory person, in the sense of a critic, more or less like what we think the hearer is. We observe what goes on in him when we make this string of words or say this sentence, and it isn't satisfactory; and so we feel that it is an inadequate statement, and therefore, of course, it doesn't communicate even to us as hearers what we are trying to say. So we look again at our experience, and we consider, from the standpoint of illusory critics, and so on: How can the thing be made to communicate? How can I tell somebody about this? And we finally, if we are fairly clever, get the answer. Once we have got that, the unique individuality of the experience begins to shrink, it becomes part of the general structure of life, we forget how strikingly novel the experience was and how peculiarly it had fringes which apply only to us— we lose all that in the process of validation.

You might feel that we were impoverished of much of the original richness of life in the process; maybe we are, but we get great richness from social intercourse, the sharing of experience, the growth of understanding, and the benefits of other people's more or less parallel experience, and so on. In fact, the whole richness of civilization is largely due to this very sort of thing. We can't be alone in things and be very clear on what happened *to* us, and we, as I have said already, can't be alone and be very clear even on what is happening *in* us very long—excepting that it gets simpler and simpler, and more primitive and more primitive, and less and less socially acceptable.

Now, in all this process of being socialized and particularly of developing the ability to communicate by verbal behavior, quite a time after little Willie has gotten to talk about "me wanting" bread and jam, little Willie begins to talk about "I"; and when little Willie gets to talking about "I," just the same as when you hear other people talking about "I," you will notice that something is going on that wasn't there when it was "me" that wanted bread; and it is really much more important than when he finally gets around to saying that he is Willie Brown, or something like that. The coming of "I," as a term, is great stuff.

I have now to refer to a type of experience which may or may not exist—I wouldn't know. I believe it exists, but no one seems to have any time to make many observations; and so since it is more or less important from my way of explaining things and since I know that no one can now controvert the idea, I will present it to you for what it is worth. Some way or other—and the less said about that the better—there is a certain direct contagion of disagreeable experience from significant adults to very young children; in fact this continues in some cases far into life and is part of the paraphernalia that is so puzzling about certain mediumistic and certain hypnotic performances. A simple way of referring to this is empathy. Whether empathy exists or not—as I say, take it or leave it—it is demonstrable that there are feeding difficulties when mother is made apprehensive by a telegram, and that it is not communicated by the tone of her voice; so since it occurs and is often noticed by pediatricians, I guess maybe I am in a moderately defensible position. And, the encouragement of the sublimation by the rote learning of a vast part of the social heritage in the very young is by way of approval and disapproval. Approval, so far as I know, very early in life has almost no effect, but in that case no effect is very welcome. You know that a very young child sleeps as much as possible, and so if there is no disturbance, well, I think it is doing what it wants to do.

Disapproval, on the other hand, in so far as there is emphatic linkage between the young and significant older people, is unpleasant, lowers the euphoria, the sense of well-being, interferes with the ease of falling asleep, the ease of taking nourishment, and so forth.

All this type of interference is originally profoundly unconscious in that it is in no sense a pure content of consciousness made up of sensations, conceptions, deductions, and inferences; but it does come ultimately to be clearly connected with disapproving attitudes on the part of others, with other people not being pleased with what we are doing, or not being satisfied with our performances. This early experience is the beginning of what goes on through life as a uniquely significant emotional experience, called by the name of a profoundly important concept in social study and psychiatry—the conception of anxiety. Anxiety begins that way—it is always that way, the product of a great many people who have disapproved. It comes to be represented by abstractions—by imaginary people that one carries around with one, some of them in the shape of ideal statements, some of them actually as almost phenomenologically evident people who disapprove. The disapproval and its effect get to be so subtly effective that a great deal of anxiety which shoos us this way and that, from this and that feeling, emotion, impulse, comes finally to be so smooth-running that very few people have the foggiest notion of what a vast part of their life is influenced by anxiety.

Anxiety is what keeps us from noticing things which would lead us to correct our faults. Anxiety is the thing that makes us hesitate before we spoil our standing with the stranger. Anxiety when it does not work so suavely becomes a psychiatric problem, because then it hashes our most polite utterances to the prospective boss, and causes us to tremble at the most inopportune times. So you see it is only reasonable and very much in keeping with an enormously capable organization, such as the human being, that anxiety becomes a problem only when it doesn't work smoothly, and that the anxiety which has had to be grasped as a fundamental factor in understanding interpersonal relations is by no means an anxiety attack, a feeling of hollow in the stomach, and so on. Much, much more frequently it manifests as what I have called selective inattention, by which I mean you just miss all sorts of things which would cause you embarrassment, or in many cases, great profit to notice. It is the means by which you stay as you are, in spite of the efforts of worthy psychiatrists, clergymen, and others to help you mend your ways. You don't hear, you don't see, you don't feel, you don't observe, you don't think, you don't this, and you don't that, all by the very suave manipulation of the contents of consciousness by anxiety—or, if you must get lots of words in your statements, by the threat of anxiety, which still is anxiety. This very great extent of the effects of disapproval and the disturbance of euphoria by the significant people in early life—the people who are tremendously interested in getting you socialized—is what makes the concept of anxiety so crucially important in understanding all sorts of things.

The part of the personality[1] which is central in the experience of anxiety we call the "self." It is concerned with avoiding the supposedly distressing—which is often illuminating—with the exclusion from awareness of certain types of very humiliating recollections, and correspondingly the failure of the development of insight from experience. It maintains selective inattention.

Now, the "self" is not coterminous with the ego of the old ego psychologist, or the ego of Freud, or the superego of Freud, or anything except what I will say—which incidentally I believe is a very simple statement of practically universal experience. The self is the content of consciousness at all times when one is thoroughly comfortable about one's self-respect, the prestige that one enjoys among one's fellows, and the respect and deference which they pay one. Under those estimable circumstances there is no anxiety; the self is the whole works; everything else in life runs smoothly without disturbing us the least bit. And it is when any of these things begin to go a little haywire, when we tend to remember a humiliating experience which would disturb our self-esteem, when somebody says something derogatory about us in our hearing or to our face, when somebody snubs us, showing the very antithesis of deference, and when somebody shows up our stupidities, thereby impairing our prestige—it is at those times that anxiety is very apt to manifest itself; but, again, it is apt to be overlooked because it is so generally followed by anger. Anger is much more comfortable to experience than anxiety and, in fact, has much the relation of "I" to "me"; anger is much more powerful and reassuring than anxiety, which is the antithesis of power, which is threat and danger. Anger, however, is supposed to intimidate the other fellow, and at least it obscures the damage to our self-esteem, at least temporarily. And so we say that the self is a system within a personality, built up from innumerable experiences from early life, the central notion of which is that we satisfy the people that matter to us and therefore satisfy ourselves, and are spared the experience of anxiety.

We can say that the operations by which all these things are done—in contradistinction to taking food, getting sexual satisfaction, and sleep, and other delightful things—the operations which maintain our prestige and self-respect which are dependent upon the respect of others for us and the deference they pay us, we call security operations. Security operations are things which we might say are herded down a narrow path by selective inattention. In other words, we don't learn them as fast as we might; we never seem to learn how unimportant they are in many circumstances where they get in our way. They are the things that always have the inside track with denizens of this best of possible variants on the Western culture, the most insecure culture I know— our American people. Well, security operations are the things that don't change much, that have the focus of attention, in and out of season, if there is the least chance of feeling anxious. And the security operations are in many cases assertive, starting out with "I"—and "I" in its most powerful fashion. Sometimes the security operations are more subtle— in fact there are always quite subtle security operations in a person of ordinary abilities—but they interfere with all sorts of grasps on the universe, grasps which would in essence show that the regard in which a person holds us is defined by the past experience of that person and his actual capacity to know what we were doing, which in some cases is very low, that the prestige we did or did not get had little bearing on the prestige which we might get for this particular act six weeks later, that all this vast to-do which in early childhood and the juvenile era is practically necessary to survive the distress of the parents is most ancient baggage that could very well be replaced with a few streamlined pieces that made a great deal of sense in the interpersonal world in which we have our being.

As I say, the self does not "learn" very readily because anxiety is just so busy and so effective at choking off inquiries where there is any little risk of loss of face with one's self or others. And the operations to maintain this prestige and feeling of security, freedom from anxiety, are of such crucial importance from the cradle, I mean actually from the very early months of childhood, somewhere around two months onward, that the content of consciousness pertaining to the pursuit of satisfaction and the enjoyment of life is at best marginal. It is one's prestige, one's status, the importance which people feel one is entitled to, the respect that one can expect from people—and even their envy, which becomes precious in that it gives a certain illusion that one has prestige—that dominate awareness. These things are so focal in interpersonal relations of our day and age that the almost unassailable conviction develops, partly based on the lack of information of our parents and others, that each of us, as defined by the animal organism that we were at birth, are unique, isolated individuals in the human world, as our bodies are—very figuratively—unique and individual in the biological world.

Now, I started out by suggesting that the interrelations, interdependence, interpenetration, and so on, of the biological world is very striking. Yet, no one will quarrel with the separation as an instrument for study, for thought, and so on, of organism and environment. And if you are human biologists, I am perfectly willing for you to talk about individual specimens of man. And in so far as you see material objects, I am perfectly willing to agree that you see people walking around individually, moving from hither to yon in geography, and even persisting from now to then in duration; but that does not explain much of anything about the distinctively human. It doesn't even explain very much about the performance of my thoroughly domesticated cocker spaniels. What the biological organism does is interesting and wonderful. What the personality does, which can be observed and studied only in relations between personalities or among personalities, is truly and terribly marvelous, and is human, and is the function of creatures living in indissoluble contact with the world of culture and of people. In that field it is preposterous to talk about individuals and to go on deceiving oneself with the idea of uniqueness, of single entity, of simple, central being.

So it has come about that there has developed this conception of interpersonal relations as the field of study of those parts of the social sciences concerned with the behavior of people and as the field of study of psychiatry. In so far as difficulties in living are the subject of psychiatry, we must study the processes of living in which the difficulties are manifested, since otherwise we can't really sort out what is "difficulty" and what is perhaps novel genius; we really do have to study interpersonal relations to know what we are talking about when we talk about difficulties in living. As I say, the conceptual system has grown up which finds its subject matter not in the study of personality, which is beyond reach, but in the study of that which can be observed; namely, interpersonal relations. And when that viewpoint is applied, then one of the greatest difficulties encountered in bringing about favorable change is this almost inescapable illusion that there is a perduring, unique, simple existent self, called variously "me" or "I," and in some strange fashion, the patient's, or the subject person's private property.

Progress begins, life unfolds, and interpersonal relations improve—life can become simple and delightful only at the expense of this deeply ingrained illusion and the parallel conviction that that which has sensations must under all conceivable circumstances be the "same" as that which has tenderness and love—tenderness and love being as obviously communal, involving two personalities, as anything known to man can be.

And so let me say very simply that in so far as you will care to check over these various incomplete sketches that I have made on a vast field and will not dismiss what you heard me say as a misunderstanding, you will find that it makes no sense to think of ourselves as "individual," "separate," capable of anything like definitive description in isolation, that the notion is just beside the point. No great progress in this field of study can be made until it is realized that the field of observation is what people do with each other, what they can communicate to each other about what they do with each other. When that is done, no such thing as the durable, unique, individual personality is ever clearly justified. For all I know every human being has as many personalities as he has interpersonal relations; and as a great many of our interpersonal relations are actual operations with imaginary people—that is, in no sense materially embodied people—and as they may have the same or greater validity and importance in life as have our operations with many materially embodied people like the clerks in the corner store, you can see that even though "the illusion of personal individuality" sounds quite lunatic when first heard, there is at least food for thought in it.

DISCUSSION

(*A question regarding the concept of the unconscious.*)

I tried to say nothing about the unconscious except to suggest that it was not phenomenologically describable. I don't use the conception particularly, certainly didn't in this paper, never do in work with patients or in teaching because so far as I know it is very useful for theory, but there are some other expressions that are perhaps more communicative to other people. But I might say what I could imagine to be true of that which is perhaps properly called the conceptual unconscious, because it fills the discontinuities present in conscious life: I would say that it includes much that has been conscious but is preverbal, subverbal, if you please; a great deal that has never been attended to and therefore may have been or may not have been on the margins of awareness; and certainly some experience of the person which has not received any representation within what we call his consciousness or his awareness, including a great development of process which has simply been sidetracked in the process of socialization but which manifests, in various ways, as remnants of previous endowment, previous experience, and previous behavior.

In dealing with patients and in attempting to follow the course of psychotherapeutic endeavor by others, the big problem seems to be to elude the interventions of what I have called the self-system—which is not coterminous with awareness but which is certainly the most emphatic and conspicuous and troublesome influence *on* awareness. You might contrast the self-system with the rest of the personality system, always realizing that I am talking about a hypothesis to explain what happens. I don't know that I have any use for anything except what can be observed. But what can be observed by an acute observer in his relations with another person is something quite different from what that other person, at least initially, can observe; and much of it can be accounted for by reference to processes which are not ordinarily noted, some of them so glaringly obvious that one literally is justified in positing a process like *selective inattention* by which I mean that we always overlook certain obvious things which would be awkward if we noticed them.

(A question asking, in effect, Can we not say that there is a justifiably characterizable self in each person we deal with, which might be called the "real" self?)

It is, I believe, a statistically demonstrable fact that the interpersonal relations of any person, even though he feels very full of the conviction of his individuality, are under ordinary circumstances rather strikingly restricted in variety, freedom you might say. Such a person is very much more apt to do the same sort of thing with a number of people than to do very different things with each one of that number. Furthermore, even more striking are the observable performances in which he will persistently misfunction with certain people in characterizable ways, despite the most incongruous objective data—of which, of course, *he* is unaware. It is a notorious fact about personality problems that people act *as if* someone else were present when he is not, as the result of interpersonal configurations which are irrelevant to the other person's concern, and do this in a recurrent fashion without any great difference in pattern. These various factors are so striking, in interpersonal relations, that it is perfectly easy and for many purposes very practical to speak of the structure of the character of the person.

All these are, I believe, correct statements of observable data. But when it comes to attempting to form a general theory on which to approach explanations of everything that happens to one in one's intercourse with others, and all the variety of things that occur in particularly purposed interpersonal relations such as the psychotherapeutic situation, then it is just as easy to notice that the person maintains quite as many of what you ordinarily call imaginary relationships as he does of those that have the peculiar virtue of objective reference. A person, for example, may be said, with considerable justification, to act toward his wife as he did toward his mother. Now, it is true that there are many differences in detail, but the general patterns of emotional relationship of conscious versus unnoticed motivation, of intended versus experienced acts, are very much those that the person first developed in manifest behavior with his mother; and it is quite useful to think of his experience of that mother as interpenetrating the experience of the wife and, in fact, frequently completely suppressing any individualization of or any attention to the characterization of the wife. That is the more difficult part of this conception but it is quite useful in the sense that it can be made to make sense in many of the maneuvers of interpersonal relations that have effect; whereas operations on any other set of assumptions that explains the same phenomena, raise very considerable theoretical difficulties. In other words, it is a matter of what is most generally useful as a theoretical point of departure.

And now to come to the more specific question: Are we not entirely justified—however much we have respect for the fictions which masquerade as human individuals—in realizing that there is a justifiably characterizable self in each person that we deal with?

I myself have come gradually to find that unnecessary, whether that be some serious misunderstanding of mine or an insight remains, of course, for others to determine. You know that is true of the evolution of most hypotheses.

One listens, for example, in psychotherapy to a great number of revealing communications, hoping and generally finding finally that the thing has been reviewed very simply in a very small context; and then you run up the flag of hope, and so on, and go hammer and tongs to seeing what can be made of this very simple series of statements which the other fellow won't forget while you are trying to make your point clear. Now, it is decidedly easier to explain this great difficulty on the, you might say, individual-less type of hypothesis than on any other that I have yet dealt with.

(*A question regarding the lability of behavior in the human being and in animals, posing whether humanness—a quality produced by the effect of the cultural, interpersonal environment upon the lability of the human animal—can exist outside a culture and therefore whether a sense of self within the person is possible apart from the culture.*)

You raise a wonderful field of comparative study. Contrary to what would be nice and simple to say at this point, we have pretty convincing evidence of the lability of patterns of behavior in characterizable environments, down as low as certain of the rats; for example, it is known that one of the Florida species of rats can be moved from the state of full-fledged wildness to complete domestication in five generations. This is a very interesting observation of a quite remarkably primitive mammal taking on adjustive habits to utterly novel sets of necessity.

But man is the only animal, if you will understand the locution, that ceases to be an animal in the most significant respect when he becomes a person, and to be a person it is necessary that one live in the world of persons and personal entities, and personal organization, and so on, which we ordinarily call the social order or the world of culture. And in so far as a person is separated from the world of culture, he begins to deteriorate in his attributes as a person. His interpersonal relations, after a period of isolation, are distinctly degenerated from the development of refinement and elaboration which they showed at the start, and while it doesn't work quite as rapidly as separation from the physico-chemical universe and oxygen, still it is a move in the same direction explicable on the same basis. Human potentialities are suited to the building up of the person; and when the person is built, he is something else than was implied or given in the human animal at birth. How would you describe that in terms of the Florida rat? You might say that the potentialities of man—in contrast to those of the rat—are almost infinitely labile, even though there is a very rigid, or a pretty rigid, system of maturation. Even that system of maturation gets less and less rigid the further one goes from birth; thus puberty, the appearance of lust in the human, the furthest very dramatic maturation from birth, is much more susceptible of disturbance in its timing than other maturation of things that come earlier. Even internists recognize the condition of delayed puberty; it happens to coincide statistically very closely with what I as a psychiatrist describe as a schizoid type of interpersonal relations. Both the latter and the former, I believe, are explicable as the result of what are ordinarily called strongly repressive influences applied much earlier in life to operations and thought pertaining to the genital regions and genital acts. So here what would certainly be described as purely interpersonal influences, interpersonal manifestations of cultural views, and so on, have a marked effect on the maturation rate of what is much more inherently of the animal than of the person.

(A question regarding the permissibility of thinking in terms of the individual.)

We have, thus far, I believe, thought in terms of the individual, which is certainly a demonstration of the possibility. The point, rather, I think, is on the utility. I have been at some pains not to deny you the privilege of going on in your convictions, but to suggest to you that there is another view that may—well, if nothing else, permit considerable technological advance, or technical advance as we call it psychiatry, and may even be useful as a new orientation for certain types of social investigation. I also tried to say at the beginning that for certain purposes it is certainly very useful to separate organism and environment, particularly, for example, if one is talking about colonies of paramecia, but I think that perhaps there are biologists who think of the paramecium as a particular part of the world showing certain remarkable features of organization in functional activity, but ceasing very suddenly to manifest those if separated from certain parts of the universe which do not manifest those peculiarities of organization in functional activity. It is all perfectly well, if you wish, to limit your personality to the skin over your bones and adnexa, but my notion is not what can be done or what should be done; it is rather a suggestion of a system of reference which seems to eliminate a great many terms, conceptions, perplexities, and to provide some fairly simple operations that seem to bear up pretty well—and which also is extraordinarily unwelcome from the standpoint of our educational training.

My son has to be to many a mother or father something thoroughly unique, almost pricelessly different from anyone else; and with that background it is not difficult to realize that when everything else fails one, membership in that family, which makes one unique and distinguishes one on the basis of the very early valuation, would be a treasured possession. I am talking not so much as to what we are to deny our fellow men or our colleagues, but only in favor of a conceptual system which I believe is defensible and useful.

Notes

[1] When I speak of "parts of personality," it must be understood that "personality" is a hypothesis, so this is a hypothetical part of a hypothesis.

Gordon W. Allport

THE OPEN SYSTEM IN PERSONALITY THEORY

*Gordon Allport was born in Indiana in 1897 and attended Harvard University where he acquired his doctorate in psychology in 1922. He also studied in Berlin, Hamburg, and Cambridge, England. He was one of the figures in the interdisciplinary movement at Harvard and was instrumental in the founding of the Department of Social Relations at Harvard, where he still teaches. He has written a great many books, some of them being:*The Nature of Prejudice, Becoming, The Psychology of Rumor, Personality: A Psychological Interpretation, *and* The Individual and His Religion.

The congruence of behavior and the importance of conscious motives lead Allport naturally to an emphasis upon those phenomena often represented under the terms self and ego. According to Allport man is much more a creature of the present than of the past. He prefers to use the term "functional autonomy" in this respect. Although Allport accepts the importance and inevitability of experimental psychology he has serious reservations about the success of its efforts. His work is more in the field of the psychology of social issues than in the laboratory of experimental psychology. He has done significant work on the nature of prejudice and in the psychology of international relations. Allport sees a discontinuity between normal and abnormal. He considers psychoanalysis as somewhat effective in the treatment of abnormal behavior, but he believes that it is of little value in any attempt to interpret normal behavior. The essay included here represents Allport's views on the place and nature of personality theory.

THE OPEN SYSTEM IN PERSONALITY THEORY*

Our profession progresses in fits and starts, largely under the spur of fashion. The average duration of our fashions I

* This essay was written by invitation of Division 8 (the Division of Personality and Social Psychology) of the American Psy-

estimate to be about ten years. McDougall's instinct theory held sway from 1908 to approximately 1920. Watsonian behaviorism dominated the scene for the next decade. Then habit hierarchies took command, then field theory—and now phenomenology. We never seem to solve our problems or exhaust our concepts; we only grow tired of them.

Presently it is fashionable to investigate such phenomena as response-set, coding, sensory deprivation, and person perception, and to talk in terms of system theory—a topic to which we shall soon return. Ten years ago, fashion called for group dynamics, Guttman scales, and research on the unsavory qualities of the authoritarian personality. Twenty years ago it was frustration aggression, Thurstone scales, and national morale. Nowadays we watch with some consternation the partial eclipse of psychoanalysis by existentialism. And so it goes. Fortunately, most surges of fashion leave a rich residue of gain.

Fashions have their amusing and their serious sides. We can smile at the way bearded problems receive tonsorial transformation. Having tired of "suggestibility," we adopt the new hairdo known as "persuasibility." Modern ethnology excites us, and we are not troubled by the recollection that a century ago John Stuart Mill staked down the term to designate the new science of human character. We like the neurological concept of "gating," conveniently forgetting that American functionalism always stood firm for the dominance of general mental sets over specific. Reinforcement appeals to us but not the age-long debate over hedonism. The problem of freedom we brush aside in favor of "choice points." We avoid the body-mind problem but are in fashion when we talk about "brain models." Old wine, we find, tastes better from new bottles.

The serious side of the matter enters when we and our students forget that the wine is indeed old. Picking up a recent number of the *Journal of Abnormal and Social Psychology,* I discover that the twenty-one articles written by American psychologists confine 90 per cent of their references to publications of the past ten years, although most of the problems they investigate have gray beards. In the same issue of the *Journal,* three European authors locate 50 per

chological Association. It was delivered at the fourteenth annual meeting of the Division in Cincinnati in September, 1959, and appeared in the *Journal of Abnormal and Social Psychology* (1960).

cent of their references prior to 1949. What this proves I do not know, except that European authors were not born yesterday. Is it any wonder that our graduate students reading our journals conclude that literature more than a decade old has no merit and can be safely disregarded? At a recent doctoral examination the candidate was asked what his thesis on physiological and psychological conditions of stress had to do with the body-mind problem. He confessed he had never heard of the problem. An undergraduate said that all he knew about Thomas Hobbes was that he sank with the *Leviathan* when it hit an iceberg in 1912.

A Psycholinguistic Trifle

Our windows are pretty much shuttered toward the past, but we rightly rejoice in our growth since World War II. Among the many happy developments is rejuvenation in the field of psycholinguistics. (Even here, however, I cannot refrain from pointing out that the much-discussed Whorfian hypothesis was old stuff in the days of Wundt, Jespersen, and Sapir.) Be that as it may, I shall introduce my discussion of open systems in personality theory by a crude Whorfian analysis of our own vocabulary. My research (aided by the kind assistance of Stanley Plog) is too cursory to warrant attempting a detailed report.

What we did, in brief, was to study the frequency of the prefixes *re-* and *pro-* in psychological language. Our hypothesis was that *re-* compounds, connoting as they do again-ness, passivity, being pushed or maneuvered, would be far more common than *pro-* compounds connoting futurity, intention, forward thrust. Our sample consisted of the indexes of the *Psychological Abstracts* at five-year intervals over the past thirty years; also, all terms employing these prefixes in Hinsie and Shatzky's *Psychiatric Dictionary* and in English and English's *Psychological Dictonary*. In addition, we made a random sampling of pages in five current psychological journals. Combining these sources, it turns out that *re-* compounds are nearly five times as numerous as *pro-* compounds.

But, of course, not every compound is relevant to our purpose. Terms like *reference, relationship, reticular, report* do not have the connotation we seek; nor do terms like *probability, process* and *propaganda.* Our point is more clearly seen when we note that the term *reaction* or *reactive* occurs hundreds of times, while the term *proaction* or *proactive* occurs only once—and that in English's *Dictionary*, in spite of the fact that Harry Murray has made an effort to introduce the word into psychological usage.

But even if we attempt a more strict coding of this lexical material, accepting only those terms that clearly imply reaction and response on one side and proaction or the progressive programming of behavior on the other, we find the ratio still is approximately 5:1. In other words, our vocabulary is five times richer in terms like *reaction, response, reinforcement, reflex, respondent, retroaction, recognition, regression, repression, reminiscence* than in terms like *production, proceeding, proficiency, problem-solving, propriate,* and *programming*. So much for the number of different words available. The disproportion is more striking when we note that the four terms *reflex, reaction, response,* and *retention* together are used one hundred times more frequently than any single *pro-* compound except *problem-solving* and *projective* —and this latter term, I submit, is ordinarily used only in the sense of reactivity.

The weakness of the study is evident. Not all terms connoting spontaneous, future-oriented behavior begin with *pro*. One thinks of *expectancy, intention, purpose*. But neither do all terms connoting passive responding or backward reference in time begin with *re*. One thinks of *coding, traces, input-output* and the like. But, while our analysis leaves much to be desired, it prepares the way for our critique of personality theory in terms of systems. The connecting link is the question whether we have the verbal, and therefore the conceptual, tools to build a science of change, growth, futurity, and potential; or whether our available technical lexicon tends to tie us to a science of response, reaction, and regression. Our available vocabulary points to personality development from the past up to now, more readily than to its development from here on out into the future.

The Concept of System

Until a generation or so ago, science, including psychology, was preoccupied with what might be called "disorganized complexity." Natural scientists explored this fragment and that fragment of nature; psychologists explored this fragment and that fragment of experience and behavior. The problem of interrelatedness, though recognized, was not made a topic for direct inquiry.

What is called system theory today—at least in psychology—is the outgrowth of the relatively new organismic conception reflected in the work of Von Bertalanffy and Goldstein and in certain aspects of Gestalt psychology. It opposes simple reaction theories, where a virtual automaton is seen to respond discretely to stimuli as though they were pennies in the slot. Interest in system theory is increasing in psychology, though perhaps not so fast as in other sciences.

Now, a system—any system—is defined merely as *a complex of elements in mutual interaction*. Bridgman, as might be expected of an operationist, includes a hint of method in his definition. He writes that a system is "an isolated enclosure in which all measurements that can be made of what goes on in the system are in some way correlated."[1]

Systems may be classified as *closed* or *open*. A closed system is defined as one that admits no matter from outside itself and is therefore subject to entropy according to the second law of thermodynamics. While some outside energies, such as change in temperature and wind, may play upon a closed system, it has no restorative properties and no transactions with its environment, so that like a decaying bridge it sinks into thermodynamic equilibrium.

Some authors, such as Von Bertalanffy,[2] Brunswik[3] and Pumpian-Mindlin,[4] have said or implied that certain theories of psychology and of personality operate with the conception of closed systems. But in my opinion these critics press their point too far. We had better leave closed systems to the realm of physics where they belong (although even here it is a question whether Einstein's formula for the release of matter into energy does not finally demonstrate the futility of positing a closed system even in physics). In any event it is best to admit that all living organisms partake of the character of open systems. I doubt that we shall find any advocate of a truly closed system in the whole range of personality theory. At the same time, current theories do differ widely in the amount of openness they ascribe to the personality system.

THE OPEN SYSTEM IN PERSONALITY THEORY

If we comb definitions of open systems, we can piece together four criteria: (1) There are intake and output of both matter and energy. (2) There are the achievement and maintenance of steady (homeostatic) states, so that the intrusion of outer energy will not seriously disrupt internal form and order. (3) There is generally an increase of order over time, owing to an increase in complexity and differentiation of parts. (4) Finally, at least at the human level, there is more than mere intake and output of matter and energy; there is extensive transactional commerce with the environment.[5]

While all of our theories view personality as an open system in some sense, they can be fairly well classified according to the varying emphasis they place upon each of these criteria and according to how many of the criteria they admit.

CRITERION I

Consider the first criterion: material and energy exchange. Stimulus-response theory in its purest form concentrates on this criterion to the virtual exclusion of all the others. It says, in effect, that a stimulus enters and a response is emitted. There is, of course, machinery for summation, storage, and delay, but the output is broadly commensurate with the intake. We need study only the two poles of stimulus and response with a minimum of concern for intervening processes. Methodological positivism goes one step further, saying, in effect, that we do not need the concept of personality at all. We focus attention on our own measurable manipulations of input and on the measurable manipulations of output. Personality thus evaporates in a mist of method.

CRITERION 2

The requirement of steady states for open systems is so widely admitted in personality theory that it needs little discussion. To satisfy needs, to reduce tension and to maintain equilibrium—this comprises, in most theories, the basic formula of personality dynamics. Some authors, such as Stagner[6] and Mowrer, regard this formula as logically fitting in with Cannon's[7] account of homeostasis.[8] Man's intricate adjustive behavior is simply an extension of the principle involved in temperature regulation, balance of blood volume, sugar content, and the like, in the face of environmental change. It is true that Toch and Hastorf warn against overextending the concept of homeostasis in personality theory.[9] I myself doubt that Cannon would approve the extension, for to him the value of homeostasis lay in its capacity to free man for what he called "the priceless unessentials" of life.[10] When biological equilibrium is attained, the priceless unessentials take over and constitute the major part of human activity. Be that as it may, most current theories clearly regard personality as a *modus operandi* for restoring a steady state.

Psychoanalytic theories are of this order. According to Freud, the ego strives to establish balance among the three "tyrants"—id, superego, and outer environment. Likewise, the so-called mechanisms of ego defense are essentially maintainers of a steady state. Even a neurosis has the same basic adjustive function.[11]

To sum up: Most current theories of personality take full account of two of the requirements of an open system. They allow interchange of matter and energy, and they recognize the tendency of organisms to maintain an orderly arrangement of elements in a steady state. Thus they emphasize stability rather than growth, permanence rather than change, "uncertainty reduction" (information theory) and "coding" (cognitive theory) rather than creativity. In short, they emphasize *being* rather than *becoming*. Hence, most personality theories are biologistic in the sense that they ascribe to personality only the two features of an open system that are clearly present in all living organisms.

There are, however, two additional criteria, sometimes mentioned but seldom stressed by biologists themselves, and similarly neglected in much current personality theory.

TRANSATLANTIC PERSPECTIVE

Before examining Criterion 3, which calls attention to the tendency of open systems to enhance their degree of order, let us glimpse our present theoretical situation in cross-cultural perspective. In this country our special field of study has come to be called "behavioral science" (a label now firmly stuck to us with the glue of the Ford millions). The very flavor of this term suggests that we are occupied with semiclosed systems. By his very name the behavioral scientist seems committed to study man more in terms of behavior than in terms of experience; more in terms of mathematical space and clock time than in terms of existential space and time; more in terms of response than of programming; more in terms of tension reduction than of tension enhancement; more in terms of reaction than of proaction.

Now let us leap our cultural stockade for a moment and listen to a bit of ancient Hindu wisdom. Most men, the Hindus say, have four central desires. To some extent, though only roughly, they correspond to the developmental stages of life. The first desire is for *pleasure*—a condition fully and extensively recognized in our Western theories of tension reduction, reinforcement, libido, and needs. The second desire is for *success*— likewise fully recognized and studied in our investigations of power, status, leadership, masculinity, and need-achievement. The third desire is to do one's duty and discharge one's responsibility. (It was Bismarck, not a Hindu, who said, "We are not in this world for pleasure but to do our damned duty.") Here our Western work begins to fade out: except for some pale investigations of parental punishment in relation to the development of childhood conscience, we have little to offer on the "duty motive." Conscience we tend to regard as a reactive response to internalized punishment, thus confusing the past "must" of learning with the "ought" involved in programming our future.[12] Finally, the Hindus tell us that for many people all these three motives pall, and they then seek intensely for a grade of understanding—for a philosophical or religious meaning—that will liberate them from pleasure, success, and duty.[13] (Need I point out that most Western personality theories treat the religious aspiration in reactive terms—as an escape device, no different in kind from suicide, alcoholism, and neurosis?)

Now we retrace our steps from India to modern Vienna and encounter the existentialist school of logotherapy. Its founder, Viktor Frankl, emphasizes above all the central place of *duty* and *meaning*, the same two motives that the Hindus place highest in their hierarchy of desire. Frankl reached his position after a long and agonizing incarceration in Nazi concentration camps, where, with other prisoners, he found himself stripped to naked existence.[14] In such extremity, what does a person need and want? Pleasure and success are out of the question. One wants to know the meaning of his suffering and to learn how, as a responsible being, he should acquit himself. Should he commit suicide? If so, why; if not, why not? The search for meaning becomes supreme.

Frankl is aware that his painfully achieved theory of motivation departs widely from most American theory, and he points out the implication of this fact for psychotherapy. He specifically criticizes the principle of homeostasis as implying that personality is a quasi-closed system.[15] To cater to the internal adjustments of a neurotic, or to assume that he will regain health by reshuffling his memories, defenses, or conditioned reflexes, is ordinarily self-defeating. In many cases of neurosis, only a total breakthrough to new horizons will turn the trick.

Neither Hindu psychology nor logotherapy underestimates the role of pleasure and success in personality. Nor would Frankl abandon the hard-won gains reflected in psychoanalytic theory and need-theory. He says merely that in studying or treating a person we often find these essentially homeostatic formulations inadequate. A man normally wants to know the whys and wherefores. No other biological system does so; man stands alone in that he possesses a degree of openness surpassing that of any other living system.

CRITERION 3

Returning now to our main argument, we encounter a not inconsiderable array of theories that emphasize the tendency of human personality to go beyond steady states and to strive for an enhancement and elaboration of internal order, even at the cost of considerable disequilibrium.

I cannot examine all of these or name all the relevant authors. One could start with McDougall's proactive sentiment of self-regard, which he viewed as organizing all behavior through a kind of "forward memory" (to use Gooddy's apt term).[16] Not too dissimilar is the stress that Combs and Snygg place on the enhancement of the phenomenal field. We may add Goldstein's conception of self-actualization as tending to enhance order in personality, as well as Maslow's theory of *growth motives* that supplement *deficiency motives*. One thinks of Jung's principle of individuation leading toward the achievement of a self—a goal never actually completed. Some theories, those of Bartlett and Cantril among them, put primary stress on the "pursuit of meaning." Certain developments in post-Freudian "ego psychology" belong here.[17] So, too, does existentialism, with its recognition of the need for meaning and of the values of commitment. (The brain surgeon Harvey Cushing was speaking of open systems when he said, "The only way to endure life is to have a task to complete.") No doubt we should add Woodworth's recent advocacy of the "behavior primacy" theory as opposed to the "need" theory, Robert White's emphasis on "competence," and Erikson's "search for identity."

These theories are by no means identical. The differences between them merit prolonged debate. I lump them here simply because all seem to me to recognize the third criterion of open systems—namely, the tendency of such systems to enhance their degree of order and become something more than they now are.

We all know the objection to theories of this type. Method-ologists with a taste for miniature and fractionated systems complain that they do not lead to "testable propositions."[18] The challenge is valuable in so far as it calls for an expansion of research ingenuity. But the complaint is ill-advised if it demands that we return to quasi-closed systems simply be-cause they are more "researchable" and elegant. Our task is to study what *is*, not merely what is immediately convenient.

CRITERION 4

Now for our fourth and last criterion. Virtually all the theories I have mentioned up to now conceive of personality as something integumented, as residing within the skin. There are theorists (Kurt Lewin, Martin Buber, Gardner Murphy, and others) who challenge this view, considering it too closed. Murphy says that we overstress the separation of man from the context of his living. Hebb has interpreted ex-periments on sensory deprivation as demonstrations of the constant dependence of inner stability on the flow of environ-mental stimulation.[19] Why Western thought makes such a razor-sharp distinction between the person and all else is an interesting problem. Probably the personalistic emphasis in Judeo-Christian religion is an initial factor; and as Murphy has pointed out,[20] the industrial and commercial revolutions further accentuated the role of individuality. Buddhist phi-losophy, by contrast, regards the individual, society, and nature as forming the tripod of human existence. The individ-ual as such does not stick out like a raw digit. He blends with nature, and he blends with society. It is only the merger that can be profitably studied.

Western theorists, for the most part, hold the integumented view of the personality system. I myself do so. Others, rebel-ling against the setting of self over against the world, have produced theories of personality written in terms of social in-teraction, role relations, situationism, or some variety of field theory. Still other writers, such as Talcott Parsons[21] and F. H. Allport,[22] have admitted the validity of both the integu-mented personality system and systems of social interaction, and have spent much effort in harmonizing the two types of system thus conceived.

This problem, without doubt, is the knottiest issue in contemporary social science. It is the issue that, up to now, has prevented us from agreeing on the proper way to reconcile psychological and sociocultural science.

In this matter my own position is on the conservative side. It is the duty of psychology, I think, to study the person-system, meaning thereby the attitudes, abilities, traits, trends, motives, and pathology of the individual—his cognitive styles, his sentiments, his individual moral nature, and their interrelations. The justification is twofold: (1) There is a persistent though changing person-system in time, clearly delimited by birth and death. (2) We are immediately aware of the functioning of this system. Our knowledge of it, though imperfect, is direct, whereas our knowledge of all other outside systems, including social systems, is deflected and often distorted by their necessary incorporation into our own apperceptions.

At the same time, our work is incomplete unless we admit that each person possesses a *range* of abilities, attitudes, and motives, which will be evoked by the different environments and situations he encounters. Hence we need to understand cultural, class, and family constellations and traditions in order to know the schemata the person has probably interiorized in the course of his learning. But I hasten to warn that the study of cultural, class, family, or any other social system does not automatically illumine the person-system, for we have to know whether the individual has accepted, rejected, or remained uninfluenced by the social system in question. The fact that one plays the role of, say, teacher, salesman, or father is less important for the study of his personality than to know whether he likes or dislikes, and how he defines, the role. But, unless we are students of sociocultural systems, we shall never know what it is the person is accepting, rejecting, or redefining.

The provisional solution I would offer is the following: the personality theorist should be so well trained in social science that he can view the behavior of an individual as fitting any system of interaction; that is, he should be able to cast this behavior properly in the culture where it occurs, in its situational context and in terms of role theory and field theory. At the same time he should not lose sight—as some theorists do—of the fact that there is an internal and subjective patterning of all these contextual acts. A traveler who moves from culture to culture, from situation to situation, is none the less a single person; and within him one will find the nexus, the patterning, of the diverse experiences and memberships that constitute his personality.

Thus, I myself would not go so far as to advocate that personality be defined in terms of interaction, culture, or roles. Attempts to do so seem to me to smudge the concept of personality and to represent a surrender of the psychologist's special assignment as a scientist. Let him be acquainted with all systems of interaction, but let him return always to the point where such systems converge and intersect and are patterned—in the single individual.

Hence, we accept the fourth (transactional) criterion of the open system, but with the firm warning that it must not be applied with so much enthusiasm that we lose the personality system altogether.

GENERAL SYSTEMS THEORY

There are those who see hope for the unification of science in what James Miller has called *general behavior systems theory*.[23] This approach seeks formal identities between physical systems, the cell, the organ, the personality, small groups, the species, and society. Critics—for example, Buck[24] —complain that all this is feeble analogizing, that formal identities probably do not exist, and that attempts to express analogies in terms of mathematical models result only in the vaguest generalities. As I see it, the danger in attempting to unify science in this manner lies in the inevitable approach from below—that is, in terms of physical and biological science. Closed systems or systems only partly open become our model; and if we are not careful, human personality in all its fullness is taken captive into some autistic paradise of methodology.

Besides neglecting the criteria of enhanced organization and transaction, general systems theory has an added defect. The human person is, after all, the observer and interpreter of systems. This awkward fact has recently been haunting the founder of the operational movement, P. W. Bridgman.[25] Can we as scientists live subjectively within our system and at the same time take a valid objective view thereof?

Some years ago Elkin published the case of "Harry Holzer," and invited thirty-nine specialists to offer their conceptualizations.[26] As might be expected, many different conceptualizations resulted. No theorist was able entirely to divest the case of his own preconceptions. Each read the objective system in terms of the subjective. Our theories of personality—all of them—reflect the temperament of the author fully as much as the personality of *alter*.

This sad specter of observer contamination should not, I think, discourage us from the search for objectively valid theory. Truth, as the philosopher Charles Peirce has said, is the opinion that is fated to be ultimately agreed to by all who investigate. My point is that the opinion fated to be ultimately agreed to by all who investigate is not likely to be reached through a premature application of general systems theory or through devotion to any one partially closed theory. Theories of open systems hold more promise, though at present they are not in agreement among themselves. But somewhere, sometime, I hope and believe, we shall establish a theory of the nature of personality that all wise men who investigate, including psychologists, will eventually accept.

SOME EXAMPLES

In the meantime, I suggest that we regard all sharp controversies in personality theory as probably arising from the two opposed points of view: the quasi-closed and the fully open.

The principle of reinforcement, to take one example, is commonly regarded as the cement that stamps in a response, as the glue that fixes personality at the level of past deeds. An open system interpretation is very different. Feigl, for instance, has pointed out that reinforcement works primarily in a prospective sense.[27] It is only from a *recognition* of consequences (not from the consequences themselves) that the human individual binds the past to the future and resolves to avoid punishment and to seek rewards in similar circumstances—provided, of course, that it is consonant with his interests and values to do so. Here we no longer assume that reinforcement stamps in; it is taken as one factor among many to be considered in the programming of future action.[28] What a wide difference it makes whether we regard personality as a quasi-closed or an open system!

The issue has its parallels in neurophysiology. How open is the nervous system? We know it is of a complexity so formidable that we have only an inkling as to how complex it may be. Yet one thing is certain: high-level gating often controls and steers lower-level processes. While we cannot tell exactly what we mean by "higher levels," they surely involve ideational schemata, intentions and generic personality trends. They are instruments for programming, not merely for reacting. In the future we may confidently expect that the neurophysiology of programming and the psychology of proaction will draw together. Until they do so, it is wise to hold lightly our self-closing metaphors of sow bug, switchboard, giant computor, and hydraulic pump.

Finally, an example from motivation theory. Some years ago I argued that motives may become functionally autonomous of their origins. (And one lives to regret one's brashness.)

Whatever its shortcomings, the concept of functional autonomy succeeds in viewing personality as an open and changing system. As might be expected, criticism has come chiefly from those who prefer to view the personality system as quasi-closed. Some critics say that I am dealing only with occasional cases where the extinction of a habit system has failed to occur. This criticism, of course, begs the question, for the precise point at issue is: Why do some habit systems fail to extinguish when no longer reinforced? And why do some habit systems that were once instrumental get refashioned into interests and values having a motivational push?

The common counterargument holds that "secondary reinforcement" somehow miraculously sustains all the central desires of a mature person. The scientific ardor of Pasteur, the religio-political zeal of Gandhi and, for that matter, Aunt Sally's devotion to her needlework are explained by hypothetical cross-conditioning, which somehow substitutes for the primary reinforcement of primary drives. What is significant for our purposes is that these critics prefer the concept of secondary reinforcement, not because it is clearer, but because it holds our thinking within the frame of a quasi-closed (reactive) system.

Now is not the time to reargue the matter, but I can at least hint at my present views. I would say first that the concept of functional autonomy has relevance even at the level of quasi-closed systems. There are now so many indications concerning feedback mechanisms, cortical self-stimulation, self-organizing systems, and the like,[29] that I believe we cannot deny the existence of self-sustaining circuit mechanisms, which we can lump together under the rubric *perseverative functional autonomy*.

But the major significance of the concept lies in a different direction, and presupposes the view that personality is a wide-open system seeking progressively new levels of order and transaction. While drive motives remain fairly constant throughout life, existential motives do not. It is the very nature of an open system to achieve progressive levels of order through change in cognitive and motivational structure. Since in this case the causation is systematic, we cannot hope to account for functional autonomy in terms of specific reinforcements. This condition I would call *propriate functional autonomy*.

Both perseverative and propriate autonomy are, I think, indispensable conceptions. The one applies to the relatively closed part-systems within personality; the other, to the continuously evolving structure of the whole.

A last example. It is characteristic of the quasi-closed system outlook that it is heavily nomothetic: it seeks similarities among all personality systems—or, as in general-behavior-systems theory, among *all* systems. If, however, we elect the open-system view, we find ourselves forced in part toward the idiographic outlook. For now the vital question becomes: What makes the system hang together in any one person?[30] Let me repeat this question, for it is the one that more than any other has haunted me over the years: *What makes the system cohere in any one person?* That this problem is pivotal, urgent, and relatively neglected will be recognized by open-system theorists, even while it is downgraded and evaded by those who prefer their systems semi-closed.

FINAL WORD

If this essay has seemed polemical, I can only plead that personality theory lives by controversy. In this country we are fortunate that no single party line shackles our speculations. We are free to pursue any and all assumptions concerning the nature of man. The penalty we pay is that, for the present, we cannot expect personality *theory* to be cumulative—although, fortunately, to some extent personality *research* can be.

Theories, we know, are ideally derived from axioms—or, if axioms are lacking (as in our field), from assumptions. But our assumptions regarding the nature of man range from the Adlerian to the Zilborgian, from the Lockean to the Liebnitzian, from the Freudian to the Hullian, from the cybernetic to the existentialist. Some of us model man after the pigeon;

others view his potentialities as many-splendored. And there is no agreement in sight.

Nils Bohr's principle of complementarity contains a lesson for us. He showed that if we study the position of a particle, we do not at the same time study its momentum. Applied to our own work, the principle tells us that if we focus on reaction, we do not simultaneously study proaction; if we measure one trait, we do not fix our attention on pattern; if we tackle a subsystem, we lose the whole; if we pursue the whole, we overlook the part-functioning. For the single investigator, there seems to be no escape from this limitation. Our only hope is to overcome it by a complementarity of investigators and of theorists.

While I myself am partisan for the open system, I would shut no doors. (Some of my best friends are quasi-closed systematists.) If I argue for the open system, I plead more strongly for the open mind. Our condemnation is reserved for that peculiar slavery to fashion which says that conventionality alone makes for scientific respectability. We still have much to learn from our creative fumblings with the open system. Among our students, I trust, there will be many adventurers.

NOTES

[1] P. W. Bridgman, *The Way Things Are*, Cambridge, Harvard University Press, 1959, p. 188.

[2] L. Von Bertalanffy, "Theoretical Models in Biology and Psychology," in D. Krech and G. S. Klein (eds.), *Theoretical Models and Personality Theory*, Durham, N.C., Duke University Press, 1952.

[3] E. Brunswik, "The Conceptual Framework of Psychology," *International Encyclopedia of Unified Science*, Chicago, University of Chicago Press, 1955, Vol. I, No. 10.

[4] E. Pumpian-Mindlin, "Propositions Concerning Energetic-Economic Aspects of Libido Theory," *Ann. N.Y. Acad. Sci.*, 1959, 76:1038-52.

[5] Von Bertalanffy's definition explicitly recognizes the first two of these criteria as present in all living organisms. A living organism, he says, is "an open system which continually gives up matter to the outer world and takes in matter from it, but which maintains itself in this continuous exchange in a steady state, or approaches such steady state in its variations in time" (*Problems of Life* [trans. of *Das biologische Weltbild*, 1949], New York, Wiley, 1952, p. 125). But elsewhere in this author's writing we

find recognition of the additional criteria (*ibid.*, p. 145; "Theoretical Models and Personality Theory," *op. cit.*, p. 34).

6 R. Stagner, "Homeostasis as a Unifying Concept in Personality Theory," *Psychol. Rev.*, 1951, 58:5-17.

7 W. B. Cannon, *The Wisdom of the Body*, New York, Norton, 1932.

8 In a recent review ("A Cognitive Theory of Dynamics" [review of R. S. Woodworth, *Dynamics of Behavior*], *Contemp. Psychol.*, 1959, 4:129-33), H. S. Mowrer strongly defends the homeostatic theory. He is distressed that the dean of American psychologists, Robert Woodworth (*Dynamics of Behavior*, New York, Holt, 1958), has taken a firm stand against the "need-primacy" theory in favor of what he calls the "behavior-primacy" theory. With the detailed merits of the argument we are not here concerned. What concerns us at the moment is that the issue has been sharply joined. Need-primacy, which Mowrer calls a "homeostatic" theory, does not go beyond our first two criteria for an open system. Woodworth, by insisting that contact with and mastery of the environment constitute a pervasive principle of motivation, recognizes the additional criteria.

9 H. H. Toch and A. H. Hastorf, "Homeostasis in Psychology," *Psychiatry*, 1955, 18:81-91.

10 W. B. Cannon, *op. cit.*, p. 323.

11 When we speak of the "function" of a neurosis, we are reminded of the many theories of "functionalism" current in psychology and social science. Granted that the label, as Merton has shown (R. K. Merton, *Social Theory and Social Structure*, rev. ed., Glencoe, Ill., The Free Press, 1957, Chap. 1.), is a wide one, still we may safely say that the emphasis of functionalism is always on the usefulness of an activity in maintaining the steady state of a personality or social or cultural system. In short, "functional" theories stress maintenance of present direction, allowing little room or none at all for departure and change.

12 G. W. Allport, *Becoming: Basic Considerations for a Psychology of Personality*, New Haven, Yale University Press, 1955, pp. 68-74.

13 H. Smith, *The Religions of Man*, New York, Harper, 1958; New York, Mentor, 1959.

14 V. E. Frankl, *From Death-Camp to Existentialism*, Boston, Beacon, 1959.

15 V. E. Frankl, "Das homöestatische Prinzip und die dynamische Psychologie," Z. *Psychoth. Med. Psychol.*, 1959, 9:41-47.

16 W. Gooddy, "Two Directions of Memory," *J. Indiv. Psychol.*, 1959, 15: 83-88.

17 Pumpian-Mindlin (*op. cit.*, p. 1051) writes, "The focus of clinical psychoanalysis on ego psychology is a direct result of the change from a closed system to an open one."

[18] Cf. T. B. Roby, "An Opinion on the Construction of Behavior Theory," *Amer. Psychologist*, 1959, 14:127-34.

[19] D. O. Hebb, "The Mammal and His Environment," *Amer. J. Psychiat.*, 1955, 111:826-31; reprinted in E. E. Maccoby, T. M. Newcomb, E. L. Hartley (eds.), *Readings in Social Psychology*, New York, Holt, 1958, pp. 335-41.

[20] G. Murphy, *Human Potentialities*, New York, Basic Books: 1958, p. 297.

[21] T. Parsons, *The Social System*, Glencoe, Ill., The Free Press, 1951.

[22] F. H. Allport, *Theories of Personality and the Concept of Structure*, New York, Wiley, 1955.

[23] J. G. Miller, "Toward a General Theory for the Behavioral Sciences," *Amer. Psychologist*, 1955, 10:513-31.

[24] R. C. Buck, "On the logic of General Behavior Systems Theory," in H. Feigl and M. Scriven (eds.), *Minnesota Studies in the Philosophy of Science*, Vol. I, 1956.

[25] *Op. cit.*

[26] F. Elkin, "Specialists Interpret the Case of Harry Holzer," *J. Abnorm. Soc. Psychol.*, 1947, 42:99-111.

[27] H. Feigl, "Philosophical Embarrassments of Psychology," *Amer. Psychologist*, 1959, 14:117.

[28] G. W. Allport, "Effect: A Secondary Principle of Learning," *Psychol. Rev.*, 1946, 53:335-47.

[29] Cf. D. O. Hebb, *The Organization of Behavior*, New York, Wiley, 1949; J. Olds and P. Milner, "Positive Reinforcement Produced by Electrical Stimulation of Septal Area and Other Regions of Rat Brain," *J. Comp. Physio. Psychol.*, 1954, 47:419-27; H. T. Chang, "The Repetitive Discharge of Cortico-thalamic Reverberating Circuit," *J. Neurophysiol.*, 1950, 13:235-57.

[30] Cf. J. G. Taylor, "Experimental Design: A Clack for Intellectual Sterility," *Brit. J. Psychol.*, 1958, 49:106-16.

Carl Rogers

SIGNIFICANT ASPECTS OF CLIENT-CENTERED THERAPY

Carl Rogers was born in Illinois in 1892. After graduating from the University of Wisconsin in 1924, he attended Union Theological Seminary in New York. He transferred later to Teachers College and was introduced to clinical psychology. In 1931 he received a doctorate from Columbia University. In 1940 he was appointed professor of psychology at Ohio State University, and it was during that time that he published his well-known book Counseling and Psychotherapy. *In 1945 Rogers joined the faculty of the University of Chicago and became executive secretary of the Counseling Center.*

In Carl Rogers' theory of personality one detects influences of Combs, Goldstein, Maslow, and Sullivan. The principal elements of his theory are the following: 1) the organism that is the total individual, 2) the phenomenal field that is the totality of experience, and 3) the self that is a differentiated portion of the phenomenal field and consists of a pattern of conscious perceptions and values of the "I" or "me."

The formulation of a personality theory has undoubtedly helped Rogers in his psychoanalytic practice. In contrast to many psychoanalysts' suspicions as to the veracity of what a person says and their continuous search for the hidden meaning behind the patient's words, Rogers believes that self-reports are truly useful as direct sources of information about the person. Personality, according to Rogers, is revealed in what the person says about himself. The main feature of Rogers' theory is his "self-as-object," which is very much a part of the conscious experience of the person. Unconscious motivation, as one might gather, plays hardly any role in Rogers' thinking and theories. Rogers' contribution to personality theory lies mainly in the formulation of the phenomenal self.

SIGNIFICANT ASPECTS OF
CLIENT-CENTERED THERAPY*

In planning to address this group, I have considered and discarded several possible topics. I was tempted to describe the process of nondirective therapy and the counselor techniques and procedures which seem most useful in bringing about this process. But much of this material is now in writing. My own book on counseling and psychotherapy contains much of the basic material, and my recent more popular book on counseling with returning servicemen tends to supplement it. The philosophy of the client-centered approach and its application to work with children is persuasively presented by Allen. The application to counseling of industrial employees is discussed in the volume by Cantor. Curran has now published in book form one of the several research studies which are throwing new light on both process and procedure. Axline is publishing a book on play and group therapy. Snyder is bringing out a book of cases. So it seems unnecessary to come a long distance to summarize material which is, or soon will be, obtainable in written form.

Another tempting possibility, particularly in this setting, was to discuss some of the roots from which the client-centered approach has sprung. It would have been interesting to show how in its concepts of repression and release, in its stress upon catharsis and insight, it has many roots in Freudian thinking, and to acknowledge that indebtedness. Such an analysis could also have shown that in its concept of the individual's ability to organize his own experience there is an even deeper indebtedness to the work of Rank, Taft, and Allen. In its stress upon objective research, the subjecting of fluid attitudes to scientific investigation, the willingness to submit all hypotheses to a verification or disproof by research methods, the debt is obviously to the whole field of American psychology, with its genius for scientific methodology. It could also have been pointed out that although everyone in the clinical field has been heavily exposed to the eclectic "team" approach to therapy of the child guidance movement, and the somewhat similar eclecticism of the Adolf Meyers—Hopkins school of thought, these

* Paper given at a seminar of the staffs of the Menninger Clinic and the Topeka Veterans' Hospital, Topeka, Kansas, May 15, 1946.

eclectic viewpoints have perhaps not been so fruitful in therapy and that little from these sources has been retained in the nondirective approach. It might also have been pointed out that in its basic trend away from guiding and directing the client, the nondirective approach is deeply rooted in practical clinical experience, and is in accord with the experience of most clinical workers, so much so that one of the commonest reactions of experienced therapists is, "You have crystallized and put into words something that I have been groping toward in my own experience for a long time."

Such an analysis, such a tracing of root ideas, needs to be made, but I doubt my own ability to make it. I am also doubtful that anyone who is deeply concerned with a new development knows with any degree of accuracy where his ideas came from.

Consequently I am, in this presentation, adopting a third pathway. While I shall bring in a brief description of process and procedure, and while I shall acknowledge in a general way our indebtedness to many root sources, and shall recognize the many common elements shared by client-centered therapy and other approaches, I believe it will be to our mutual advantage if I stress primarily those aspects in which nondirective therapy differs most sharply and deeply from other therapeutic procedures. I hope to point out some of the basically significant ways in which the client-centered viewpoint differs from others, not only in its present principles but in the wider divergencies which are implied by the projection of its central principles.

THE PREDICTABLE PROCESS OF CLIENT-CENTERED THERAPY

The first of the three distinctive elements of client-centered therapy to which I wish to call your attention is the predictability of the therapeutic process in this approach. We find, both clinically and statistically, that a predictable pattern of therapeutic development takes place. The assurance which we feel about this was brought home to me recently when I played a recorded first interview for the graduate students in our practicum immediately after it was recorded, pointing out the characteristic aspects, and agreeing to play later interviews for them to let them see the later phases of the counseling process. The fact that I knew with assurance what the later pattern would be before it had occurred only struck me as I thought about the incident. We have become clinically so accustomed to this predictable quality that we take it for granted. Perhaps a brief summarized description of this therapeutic process will indicate those elements of which we feel sure.

It may be said that we now know how to initiate a complex and predictable chain of events in dealing with the maladjusted individual, a chain of events which is therapeutic, and which operates effectively in problem situations of the most diverse type. This predictable chain of events may come about through the use of language, as in counseling, through symbolic language, as in play therapy, through disguised language as in drama or puppet therapy. It is effective in dealing with individual stations, and also in small group situations.

It is possible to state with some exactness the conditions which must be met in order to initiate and carry through this releasing therapeutic experience. Below are listed in brief form the conditions which seem to be necessary, and the therapeutic results which occur.

This experience which releases the growth forces within the individual will come about in most cases if the following elements are present:

1. If the counselor operates on the principle that the individual is basically responsible for himself, and is willing for the individual to keep that responsibility.

2. If the counselor operates on the principle that the client has a strong drive to become mature, socially adjusted, independent, productive, and relies on this force, not on his own powers, for therapeutic change.

3. If the counselor creates a warm and permissive atmosphere in which the individual is free to bring out any attitudes and feelings which he may have, no matter how unconventional, absurd, or contradictory these attitudes may be. The client is as free to withhold expression as he is to give expression to his feelings.

4. If the limits which are set are simple limits set on behavior, and not limits set on attitudes. (This applies mostly to children. The child may not be permitted to break a window or leave the room, but he is free to feel like breaking a window, and the feeling is fully accepted. The adult client may not be permitted more than an hour for an interview, but there is full acceptance of his desire to claim more time.)

5. If the therapist uses only those procedures and tech-

niques in the interview which convey his deep understanding of the emotionalized attitudes expressed and his acceptance of them. This understanding is perhaps best conveyed by a sensitive reflection and clarification of the client's attitudes. The counselor's acceptance involves neither approval nor disapproval.

6. If the counselor refrains from any expression or action which is contrary to the preceding principles. This means refraining from questioning, probing, blame, interpretation, advice, suggestion, persuasion, reassurance.

If these conditions are met, then it may be said with assurance that in the great majority of cases the following results will take place.

1. The client will express deep and motivating attitudes.

2. The client will explore his own attitudes and reactions more fully than he has previously done and will come to be aware of aspects of his attitudes which he has previously denied.

3. He will arrive at a clearer conscious realization of his motivating attitudes and will accept himself more completely. This realization and this acceptance will include attitudes previously denied. He may or may not verbalize this clearer conscious understanding of himself and his behavior.

4. In the light of his clearer perception of himself he will choose, on his own initiative and on his own responsibility, new goals which are more satisfying than his maladjusted goals.

5. He will choose to behave in a different fashion in order to reach these goals, and this new behavior will be in the direction of greater psychological growth and maturity. It will also be more spontaneous, and less tense, more in harmony with social needs of others, will represent a more realistic and more comfortable adjustment to life. It will be more integrated than his former behavior. It will be a step forward in the life of the individual.

The best scientific description of this process is that supplied by Snyder. Analyzing a number of cases with strictly objective research techniques, Snyder has discovered that the development in these cases is roughly parallel, that the initial phase of catharsis is replaced by a phase in which insight becomes the most significant element, and this in turn by a phase marked by the increase in positive choice and action. Clinically we know that sometimes this process is relatively shallow, involving primarily a fresh reorientation to an immediate problem, and in other instances so deep as to involve a complete reorientation of personality. It is recognizably the same process whether it involves a girl who is unhappy in a dormitory and is able in three interviews to see something of her childishness and dependence, and to take steps in a mature direction, or whether it involves a young man who is on the edge of a schizophrenic break, and who in thirty interviews works out deep insights in relation to his desire for his father's death, and his possessive and incestuous impulses toward his mother, and who not only takes new steps but rebuilds his whole personality in the process. Whether shallow or deep, it is basically the same.

We are coming to recognize with assurance characteristic aspects of each phase of the process. We know that the catharsis involves a gradual and more complete expression of emotionalized attitudes. We know that characteristically the conversation goes from superficial problems and attitudes to deeper problems and attitudes. We know that this process of exploration gradually unearths relevant attitudes which have been denied to consciousness.

We recognize too that the process of achieving insight is likely to involve more adequate facing of reality as it exists within the self, as well as external reality; that it involves the relating of problems to each other, the perception of patterns of behavior; that it involves the acceptance of hitherto denied elements of the self, and a reformulating of the self-concept; and that it involves the making of new plans.

In the final phase we know that the choice of new ways of behaving will be in conformity with the newly organized concept of the self; that first steps in putting these plans into action will be small but symbolic; that the individual will feel only a minimum degree of confidence that he can put his plans into effect; that later steps implement more and more completely the new concept of self, and that this process continues beyond the conclusion of the therapeutic interviews.

If these statements seem to contain too much assurance, to sound "too good to be true," I can only say that for many of them we now have research backing, and that as rapidly as possible we are developing our research to bring all phases of the precess under objective scrutiny. Those of us working clinically with client-centered therapy regard this predictability as a settled characteristic, even though we recognize that additional research will be necessary to fill out the picture more completely.

It is the implication of this predictability which is startling. Whenever, in science, a predictable process has been discovered, it has been found possible to use it as a starting point for a whole chain of discoveries. We regard this as not only entirely possible, but inevitable, with regard to this predictable process in therapy. Hence, we regard this orderly and predictable nature of nondirective therapy as one of its most distinctive and significant points of difference from other approaches. Its importance lies not only in the fact that it is a present difference, but in the fact that it points toward a sharply different future, in which scientific exploration of this known chain of events should lead to many new discoveries, developments, and applications.

THE DISCOVERY OF THE CAPACITY OF THE CLIENT

Naturally, the question is raised, What is the reason for this predictability in a type of therapeutic procedure in which the therapist serves only a catalytic function? Basically the reason for the predictability of the therapeutic process lies in the discovery—and I use that word intentionally—that within the client reside constructive forces whose strength and uniformity have been either entirely unrecognized or grossly underestimated. It is the clearcut and disciplined reliance by the therapist upon those forces within the client which seems to account for the orderliness of the therapeutic process and its consistency from one client to the next.

I mentioned that I regarded this as a discovery. I would like to amplify that statement. We have known for centuries that catharsis and emotional release were helpful. Many new methods have been and are being developed to bring about release, but the principle is not new. Likewise, we have known since Freud's time that insight, if it is accepted and assimilated by the client, is therapeutic. The principle is not new. Likewise we have realized that revised action patterns, new ways of behaving, may come about as a result of insight. The principle is not new.

But we have not known or recognized that in most if not all individuals there exist growth forces, tendencies toward self-actualization, which may act as the sole motivation for therapy. We have not realized that under suitable psychological conditions these forces bring about emotional release in those areas and at those rates which are most beneficial to the individual. These forces drive the individual to explore his own attitudes and his relationship to reality, and to explore these areas effectively. We have not realized that the individual is capable of exploring his attitudes and feelings, including those which have been denied to consciousness, at a rate which does not cause panic, and to the depth required for comfortable adjustment. The individual is capable of discovering and perceiving, truly and spontaneously, the interrelationships between his own attitudes, and the relationship of himself to reality. The individual has the capacity and the strength to devise, quite unguided, the steps which will lead him to a more mature and more comfortable relationship to his reality. It is the gradual and increasing recognition of these capacities within the individual by the client-centered therapist that rates, I believe, the term "discovery." All of these capacities I have described are released in the individual if a suitable psychological atmosphere is provided.

There has, of course, been lip service paid to the strength of the client, and the need of utilizing the urge toward independence which exists in the client. Psychiatrists, analysts, and especially social caseworkers have stressed this point. Yet it is clear from what is said, and even more clear from the case material cited, that this confidence is a very limited confidence. It is a confidence that the client can take over, if guided by the expert; a confidence that the client can assimilate insight if it is first given to him by the expert, can make choices providing guidance is given at crucial points. It is, in short, the same sort of attitude which the mother has toward the adolescent, that she believes in his capacity to make his own decisions and guide his own life, providing he takes the directions of which she approves.

This is very evident in the latest book on psychoanalysis by Alexander and French. Although many of the former views and practices of psychoanalysis are discarded, and the procedures are far more nearly in line with those of non-directive therapy, it is still the therapist who is definitely in control. He gives the insights; he is ready to guide at crucial points. Thus while the authors state that the aim of the therapist is to free the patient to develop his capacities, and to increase his ability to satisfy his needs in ways acceptable to himself and society; and while they speak of the basic conflict between competition and cooperation as one which the individual must settle for himself; and speak of the integration of new insight as a normal function of the ego, it is clear when they speak of procedures that they have no confidence that the client has the capacity to do any of these things. For in practice:

As soon as the therapist takes the more active role we advocate, systematic planning becomes imperative. In addition to the original decision as to the particular sort of strategy to be employed in the treatment of any case, we recommend the conscious use of various techniques in a flexible manner, shifting tactics to fit the particular needs of the moment. Among these modifications of the standard technique are: using not only the method of free association but interviews of a more direct character, manipulating the frequency of the interviews, giving directives to the patient concerning his daily life, employing interruptions of long or short duration in preparation for ending the treatment, regulating the transference relationship to meet the specific needs of the case, and making use of real-life experiences as an integral part of therapy.[1]

At least this leaves no doubt as to whether it is the client's or the therapist's hour; it is clearly the latter. The capacities which the client is to develop are clearly not to be developed in the therapeutic sessions.

The client-centered therapist stands at an opposite pole, both theoretically and practically. He has learned that the constructive forces in the individual can be trusted, and that the more deeply they are relied upon, the more deeply they are released. He has come to build his procedures upon these hypotheses, which are rapidly becoming established as facts: that the client knows the areas of concern which he is ready to explore; that the client is the best judge as to the most desirable frequency of interviews; that the client can lead the way more efficiently than the therapist into deeper concerns; that the client will protect himself from panic by ceasing to explore an area which is becoming too painful; that the client can and will uncover all the repressed elements which it is necessary to uncover in order to build a comfortable adjustment; that the client can achieve for himself far truer and more sensitive and accurate insights than can possibly be given to him; that the client is capable of translating these insights into constructive behavior which weighs his own needs and desires realistically against the demands of society; that the client knows when therapy is completed and he is ready to cope with life independently. Only one condition is necessary for all these forces to be released, and that is the proper psychological atmosphere between client and therapist.

Our case records and increasingly our research bear out these statements. One might suppose that there would be a generally favorable reaction to this discovery, since it amounts in effect to tapping great reservoirs of hitherto little-used energy. Quite the contrary is true, however, in professional groups. There is no other aspect of client-centered therapy which comes under such vigorous attack. It seems to be genuinely disturbing to many professional people to entertain the thought that this client upon whom they have been exercising their professional skill actually knows more about his inner psychological self than they can possibly know, and that he possesses constructive strengths which make the constructive push by the therapist seem puny indeed by comparison. The willingness fully to accept this strength of the client, with all the reorientation of therapeutic procedure which it implies, is one of the ways in which client-centered therapy differs most sharply from other therapeutic approaches.

THE CLIENT-CENTERED NATURE OF THE THERAPEUTIC RELATIONSHIP

The third distinctive feature of this type of therapy is the character of the relationship between therapist and client. Unlike other therapies in which the skills of the therapist are to be exercised upon the client, in this approach the skills of the therapist are focused upon creating a psychological atmosphere in which the client can work. If the counselor can create a relationship permeated by warmth, understanding, safety from any type of attack, no matter how trivial, and basic acceptance of the person as he is, then the client will drop his natural defensiveness and use the situation. As we have puzzled over the characteristics of a successful therapeutic relationship, we have come to feel that the sense of communication is very important. If the client feels that he is actually communicating his present attitudes, superficial, confused, or conflicted as they may be, and that his communication is understood rather than evaluated in any way, then he is freed to communicate more deeply. A relationship in which the client thus feels that he is communicating is almost certain to be fruitful.

All of this means a drastic reorganization in the counselor's thinking, particularly if he has previously utilized other approaches. He gradually learns that the statement that the time is to be "the client's hour" means just that, and that his biggest task is to make it more and more deeply true.

Perhaps something of the characteristics of the relationship may be suggested by excerpts from a paper written by a young minister who has spent several months learning client-centered counseling procedures:

Because the client-centered, nondirective counseling approach has been rather carefully defined and clearly illustrated, it gives the "*Illusion of Simplicity.*" The technique seems deceptively easy to master. Then you begin to practice. A word is wrong here and there. You don't quite reflect feeling, but reflect content instead. It is difficult to handle questions; you are tempted to interpret. Nothing seems so serious that further practice won't correct it. Perhaps you are having trouble playing two roles—that of minister and that of counselor. Bring up the question in class and the matter is solved again with a deceptive ease. But these apparently minor errors and a certain woodenness of response seem exceedingly persistent.

Only gradually does it dawn that if the technique is true it demands a feeling of warmth. You begin to feel that the attitude is the thing. Every little word is not so important if you have the correct accepting and permissive attitude toward the client. So you bear down on the permissiveness and acceptance. You *will* permiss and accept and reflect the client, if it kills you!

But you still have those troublesome questions from the client. He simply doesn't know the next step. He asks you to give him a hint, some possibilities, after all you are expected to know something, else why is he here? As a minister, you ought to have some convictions about what people should believe, how they should act. As a counselor, you should know something about removing this obstacle—you ought to have the equivalent of the surgeon's knife and use it. Then you begin to wonder. The technique is good, *but* . . . does it go *far* enough? does it really work on clients? is it *right* to leave a person helpless, when you might show him the way out?

Here it seems to me is the crucial point. "Narrow is the gate" and hard the path from here on. No one else can give satisfying answers and even the instructors seem frustrating because they appear not to be helpful in your specific case. For here is demanded of you what no other person can do or point out—and that is to rigorously scrutinize yourself and your attitudes towards others. Do you believe that all people truly have a creative potential in them? That each person is a unique individual and that he alone can work out his own individuality? Or do you really believe that some persons are of "negative value" and others are weak and must be led and taught by "wiser," "stronger" people.

You begin to see that there is nothing compartmentalized about this method of counseling. It is not just counseling, because it demands the most exhaustive, penetrating, and comprehensive consistency. In other methods you can shape tools, pick them up for use when you will. But when genuine acceptance and permissiveness are your tools it requires nothing less than the whole complete personality. And to grow oneself is the most demanding of all.

He goes on to discuss the notion that the counselor must be restrained and "self-denying." He concludes that this is a mistaken notion:

Instead of demanding less of the counselor's personality in the situation, client-centered counseling in some ways demands more. It demands discipline, not restraint. It calls for the utmost in sensitivity, appreciative awareness, channeled and disciplined. It demands that the counselor put all he has of these precious qualities into the situation, but in a disciplined, refined manner. It is restraint only in the sense that the counselor does not express himself in certain areas that he may use himself in others.

Even this is deceptive, however. It is not so much restraint in any area as it is a focusing, sensitizing one's energies and personality in the direction of an appreciative and understanding attitude.

As time has gone by we have come to put increasing stress upon the "client-centeredness" of the relationship, because it is more effective the more completely the counselor concentrates upon trying to understand the client *as the client seems to himself.* As I look back upon some of our earlier published cases—the case of Herbert Bryan in my book, or Snyder's case of Mr. M.—I realize that we have gradually dropped the vestiges of subtle directiveness which are all too evident in those cases. We have come to recognize that if we can provide understanding of the way the client seems to himself at this moment, he can do the rest. The therapist must lay aside his preoccupation with diagnosis and his diagnostic shrewdness, must discard his tendency to make professional evaluations, must cease his endeavors to formulate an accurate prognosis, must give up the temptation subtly to guide the individual, and must concentrate on one purpose only: that of providing deep understanding and acceptance of the attitudes consciously held at this moment by the client as he explores step by step into the dangerous areas which he has been denying to consciousness.

I trust it is evident from this description that this type of relationship can exist only if the counselor is deeply and genuinely able to adopt these attitudes. Client-centered counseling, if it is to be effective, cannot be a trick or a tool. It is not a subtle way of guiding the client while pretending to let him guide himself. To be effective, it must be genuine. It is this sensitive and sincere "client-centeredness" in the therapeutic relationship that I regard as the third characteristic of nondirective therapy which sets it distinctively apart from other approaches.

SOME IMPLICATIONS

Although the client-centered approach had its origin purely within the limits of the psychological clinic, it is proving to have implications, often of a startling nature, for very diverse fields of effort. I should like to suggest a few of these present and potential implications.

In the field of psychotherapy itself, it leads to conclusions that seem distinctly heretical. It appears evident that training and practice in therapy should probably precede training in the field of diagnosis. Diagnostic knowledge and skill is not necessary for good therapy, a statement which sounds like blasphemy to many, and if the professional worker, whether psychiatrist, psychologist, or caseworker, received training in therapy first he would learn psychological dynamics in a

ımic fashion, and would acquire a professional
ᵧ and willingness to learn from his client which is
today all too rare.

The viewpoint appears to have implications for medicine.
It has fascinated me to observe that when a prominent
allergist began to use client-centered therapy for the treatment of nonspecific allergies, he found not only very good
therapeutic results, but the experience began to affect his
whole medical practice. It has gradually meant the reorganization of his office procedure. He has given his nurses a new
type of training in understanding the patient. He has decided
to have all medical histories taken by a nonmedical person
trained in nondirective techniques, in order to get a true
picture of the client's feelings and attitudes toward himself
and his health, uncluttered by the bias and diagnostic evaluation which is almost inevitable when a medical person takes
the history and unintentionally distorts the material by his
premature judgments. He has found these histories much
more helpful to the physicians than those taken by physicians.

The client-centered viewpoint has already been shown
to have significant implications for the field of survey inter-
viewing and public-opinion study. Use of such techniques by
Likert, Lazarsfeld, and others has meant the elimination of
much of the factor of bias in such studies.

This approach has also, we believe, deep implications for
the handling of social and group conflicts, as I have pointed
out in another paper.[2] Our work in applying a client-centered
viewpoint to group therapy situations, while still in its early
stages, leads us to feel that a significant clue to the constructive solution of interpersonal and intercultural frictions in the
group may be in our hands. Application of these procedures
to staff groups, to interracial groups, to groups with personal
problems and tensions, is under way.

In the field of education, too, the client-centered approach
is finding significant application. The work of Cantor, a
description of which will soon be published, is outstanding
in this connection, but a number of teachers are finding that
these methods, designed for therapy, produce a new type
of educational process, an independent learning which is
highly desirable, and even a reorientation of individual direction which is very similar to the results of individual or
group therapy.

Even in the realm of our philosophical orientation, the

client-centered approach has its deep implications. I should like to indicate this by quoting briefly from a previous paper:

As we examine and try to evaluate our clinical experience with client-centered therapy, the phenomenon of the reorganization of attitudes and the redirection of behavior by the individual assumes greater and greater importance. This phenomenon seems to find inadequate explanation in terms of the determinism which is the predominant philosophical background of most psychological work. The capacity of the individual to reorganize his attitudes and behavior in ways not determined by external factors nor by previous elements in his own experience, but determined by his own insight into those factors, is an impressive capacity. It involves a basic spontaneity which we have been loath to admit into our scientific thinking.

The clinical experience could be summarized by saying that the behavior of the human organism may be determined by the influences to which it has been exposed, *but it may also be determined by the creative and integrative insight of the organism itself.* This ability of the person to discover new meaning in the forces which impinge upon him and in the past experiences which have been controlling him, and the ability to alter consciously his behavior in the light of this new meaning, have a profound significance for our thinking which has not been fully realized. We need to revise the philosophical basis of our work to a point where it can admit that forces exist within the individual which can exercise a spontaneous and significant influence upon behavior which is not predictable through knowledge of prior influences and conditionings. The forces released through a catalytic process of therapy are not adequately accounted for by a knowledge of the individual's previous conditionings, but only if we grant the presence of a spontaneous force within the organism which has the capacity of integration and redirection. This capacity for volitional control is a force which we must take into account in any psychological equation.[3]

So we find an approach which began merely as a way of dealing with problems of human maladjustment forcing us into a revaluation of our basic philosophical concepts.

SUMMARY

I hope that throughout this paper I have managed to convey what is my own conviction: that what we now know or think we know about a client-centered approach is only a beginning, only the opening of a door beyond which we are beginning to see some very challenging roads, some fields rich with opportunity. It is the facts of our clinical and research experience which keep pointing forward into new and exciting possibilities. Yet whatever the future may hold, it appears already clear that we are dealing with materials of a new and significant nature, which demand the most open-minded and thorough exploration. If our present formulations of those facts are correct, then we would say that some important elements already stand out; that certain basic attitudes and skills can create a psychological atmosphere which releases, frees, and utilizes deep strengths in the client; that these strengths and capacities are more sensitive and more rugged than hitherto supposed; and that they are released in an orderly and predictable process which may prove as significant a basic fact in social science as some of the laws and predictable processes in the physical sciences.

NOTES

[1] F. Alexander and T. French, *Psychoanalytic Therapy*, New York, Ronald Press, 1946.

[2] C. R. Rogers, *Counseling and Psychotherapy*, New York, Houghton Mifflin Co., 1942.

[3] C. R. Rogers, "The Implications of Nondirective Therapy for the Handling of Social Conflicts," paper given to a seminar of the Bureau of Intercultural Education, New York City, Feb. 18, 1946.

REFERENCES

Allen, F., *Psychotherapy with Children*, New York, Norton, 1942.

Cantor, N., *Employee Counseling*, New York, McGraw-Hill, 1950.

Cantor, N., "The Dynamics of Learning" (unpublished MSS), University of Buffalo, 1943.

Curran, C. A., *Personality Factors in Counseling*, New York, Grune and Stratton, 1945.

Rank, O., *Will Therapy*, New York, Alfred A. Knopf, 1936.

Rogers, C. R., "Counseling," *Review of Educational Research*, April, 1945 (Vol. 15), pp. 155–163.

Rogers, C. R., and J. L. Wallen, *Counseling with Returned Servicemen*, New York, McGraw-Hill, 1946.

Snyder, W. U., "An Investigation of the Nature of Non-Directive Psychotherapy," *Journal of General Psychology*, Vol. 33 (1945), pp. 193–223.

Taft, J., *The Dynamics of Therapy in a Controlled Relationship*, New York, Macmillan, 1933.

Henry A. Murray

SOME PROPOSALS FOR A THEORY
OF PERSONALITY

*Henry Murray was born in New York on May 13, 1893,
and majored in history at Harvard. He received an M.A. in
biology from Columbia University, and Cambridge University awared him a Ph.D. in biochemistry in 1927. It was during his stay at Cambridge that Murray became interested in
psychology, and he became an instructor in psychology at
Harvard in 1927. He has been affiliated with Harvard ever
since. He was one of the charter members of the Boston Psychoanalytic Society, and in 1935 he completed his training
in psychoanalysis under Franz Alexander and Hans Sachs.
Murray was associated with the Harvard Psychological Clinic
and his* Explorations in Personality *illustrates in detail the
depth of that association. In 1950 he became Professor of
Clinical Psychology in the Department of Social Relations
and established the Psychological Clinic Annex in 1949,
where he and others conducted further studies of personality.*

*Murray's views on the structure of personality have been
decisively influenced by psychoanalytic theory. However, it
is mostly in the representation of man's striving, seeking, desire, wishing, and willing that Murray's contributions to psychological theory have been most distinctive. His position is
primarily one of a motivational psychology. Murray himself
states that "the most important thing to discover about an individual is the superordinate directionality (or directionali-
ties) of his activities, whether mental, verbal, or physical."
This interest in directionality has led Murray to the formulation of the most complex and sharply delineated system of
motivational constructs in the contemporary psychological
scene. Murray's theories have been most useful to those students who are engaged in the classification of human behavior. His influence upon the current methods or procedures
for assessing personality has been profound. The following
essay is taken from his classic work* Explorations in Personality.

SOME PROPOSALS FOR A THEORY OF PERSONALITY

Since psychology deals only with motion—processes occurring in time—none of its proper formulations can be static. They all must be dynamic in the larger meaning of this term. Within recent years, however, "dynamic" has come to be used in a special sense: to designate a psychology which accepts as prevailingly fundamental the goal-directed (adaptive) character of behavior and attempts to discover and formulate the internal as well as the external factors which determine it. In so far as this psychology emphasizes facts which for a long time have been and still are generally overlooked by academic investigators, it represents a protest against current scientific preoccupations. And since the occurrences which the specialized professor has omitted in his scheme of things are the very ones which the laity believe to be "most truly psychological," the dynamicist must first perform the tedious and uninviting task of reiterating common sense. Thus he comes on the stage in the guise of a protesting and perhaps somewhat sentimental amateur.

The history of dynamic organismal psychology is a long one if one takes into account all speculations that refer to impelling forces, passions, appetites, or instincts. But only lately have attempts been made to bring such conceptions systematically within the domain of science. We discover tentative signs in the functionalism of Dewey and Angell with its emphasis upon the organization of means with reference to a comprehensive end, in Ach's "determining tendency," and in James's notion of instinct, but not until we come to McDougall[1] do we find a conscientious attempt to develop the dynamic hypothesis. Since then, some of the animal psychologists, notably Tolman,[2] and Stone,[3] have worked with an objectively defined "drive" which is strictly in accord with dynamical principles, and Lewin,[4] representing the Gestalt school of psychology, has made "need" basic to his system of personality. But the theory of drive or need has not been systematically developed by the latter investigators, their interest in external determinants of behavior being predominant.

Outside the universities, the medical psychologists—and here we may, without serious omissions, start with Freud[5]—have for five decades been constructing a quintessentially dynamic theory. For this theory the academic psychologists, with the exception of McDougall, found themselves entirely unprepared. The psychoanalysts not only presented facts which had never entered the academic man's field of observation or thought, but they used a novel nomenclature to designate certain obscure forces which they thought it necessary to conceptualize in order to account for their findings. McDougall and the analysts have been kept apart by numerous differences, but in respect to their fundamental dynamical assumptions they belong together.

The theory to be outlined here is an attempt at a dynamic scheme. It has been guided partly by the analysts (Freud, Jung, Adler), partly by McDougall and by Lewin, and partly by our subjects—whose actions so frequently corrected our preconceptions.

PRIMARY PROPOSITIONS

1. The objects of study are individual organisms, not aggregates of organisms.

2. The organism is from the beginning a whole, from which the parts are derived by self-differentiation. The whole and its parts are mutually related; the whole being as essential to an understanding of the parts as the parts are to an understanding of the whole. (This is a statement of the *organismal* theory.[6]) Theoretically it should be possible to formulate for any moment the "wholeness" of an organism; or, in other words, to state in what respect it is acting as a unit.

3. The organism is characterized from the beginning by rhythms of activity and rest, which are largely determined by internal factors. The organism is not an inert body that merely responds to external stimulation. Hence the psychologist must study and find a way of representing the changing "states" of the organism.

4. The organism consists of an infinitely complex series of temporally related activities extending from birth to death. Because of the meaningful connection of sequences, the life cycle of a single individual should be taken as a unit, the *long unit* for psychology. It is feasible to study the organism during one episode of its existence, but it should be recognized that this is but an arbitrarily selected part of the whole. The history of the organism *is* the organism. This proposition calls for biographical studies.

5. Since, at every moment, an organism is within an en-

vironment which largely determines its behavior, and since the environment changes—sometimes with radical abruptness—the conduct of an individual cannot be formulated without a characterization of each confronting situation, physical and social. It is important to define the environment since two organisms may behave differently only because they are, by chance, encountering different conditions. It is considered that two organisms are dissimilar if they give the same response but only to different situations as well as if they give different responses to the same situation. Also, different inner states of the same organism can be inferred when responses to similar external conditions are different. Finally, the assimilations and integrations that occur in an organism are determined to a large extent by the nature of its closely previous, as well as by its more distantly previous, environments. In other words, what an organism knows or believes is, in some measure, a product of formerly encountered situations. Thus, much of what is now *inside* the organism was once *outside*. For these reasons, the organism and its milieu must be considered together, a single creature-environment interaction being a convenient short unit for psychology. A *long unit*—an individual life—can be most clearly formulated as a succession of related *short units*, or *episodes*.

6. The stimulus situation (S.S.) is that part of the total environment to which the creature attends and reacts. It can rarely be described significantly as an aggregate of discrete sense impressions. The organism usually responds to patterned meaningful wholes, as the Gestalt school of psychology has emphasized:

The effect on a man of a series of unorganized verbal sounds or of language that he does not understand is very different from the effect of words organized into meaningful sentences that he does understand (or thinks he understands). It is the meaning of the words which has potency, rather than the physical sounds per se. This is proved by the fact that the same effect can be produced by quite different sounds: by another tongue that is understood by the subject.

In crudely formulating an episode it is dynamically pertinent and convenient to classify the S.S. according to the kind of effect—facilitating or obstructing—it is exerting or could exert upon the organism. Such a tendency or "potency" in the environment may be called a *press*. For example, a press may be nourishing or coercing or injuring or chilling or befriending or restraining or amusing or belittling to the organism. It can be said that a press is a temporal Gestalt of stimuli which usually appears in the guise of a *threat of harm* or *promise of benefit* to the organism. It seems that organisms quite naturally "classify" the objects of their world in this way: "This hurts," "That is sweet," "This comforts," "That lacks support."

7. The reactions of the organism to its environment usually exhibit a *unitary trend*. This is the necessary concomitant of behavior co-ordination, since co-ordination implies organization of activity in a *certain direction*, that is, toward the achievement of an effect, one or more. Without organization there can be no unified trends, and without unified trends there can be no effects, and without effects there can be no enduring organism. Divided it perishes, united it survives. The existence of organisms depends upon the fact that the vast majority of trends are "adaptive" : they serve to restore an equilibrium that has been disturbed, or to avoid an injury, or to attain objects which are of benefit to development. Thus, much of overt behavior is, like the activity of the internal organs, survivalistically purposeful.

8. A specimen of adaptive behavior can be analyzed into the bodily movements as such, and the effect achieved by these movements. We have found it convenient to use a special term, *actone*, to describe a pattern of bodily movements per se, abstracted from its effect. To produce an effect which furthers the well-being of the organism a consecutive series of subeffects must usually be achieved, each subeffect being due to the operation of a relatively simple actone. Thus, simple actones and their subeffects are connected in such a way that a certain trend is promoted. It is the trend which exhibits the unity of the organism. The unity is not an instantaneous fact, for it may only be discovered by observing the progress of action over a period of time. The trend is achieved by the bodily processes, but it cannot be distinguished by studying the bodily processes in isolation.

This proposition beongs to the organismal theory of reality. It is in disagreement with the common practice of studying a fraction of the organism's response and neglecting the trend of which it is a part. One who limits himself to the observation of the bodily movements, as such, resembles the sufferer from semantic aphasia:

In semantic aphasia, the full significance of words and phrases is lost. Separately, each word or each detail of a drawing can be understood, but the general significance escapes; an act is executed upon command, though the purpose of it is not understood. Reading and writing are possible as well as numeration, the correct use of numbers; but the appreciation of arithmetical processes is defective. . . . A general conception cannot be formulated, but details can be enumerated [Henri Piéron][7]

9. A behavioral trend may be attributed to a hypothetical force (a drive, need, or propensity) within the organism. The proper way of conceptualizing this force is a matter of debate. It seems that it is a force which (if uninhibited) promotes activity which (if competent) brings about a situation that is opposite (as regards its relevant properties) to the one that aroused it. Frequently, an innumerable number of subneeds (producing subeffects) are temporally organized so as to promote the course of a major need. (The concept of need or drive will be more fully developed later.)

10. Though the organism frequently seeks for a certain press—in which case the press is, for a time, expectantly imaged—more frequently the press meets the organism and incites a drive. Thus, the simplest formula for a period of complex behavior is a particular press-need combination. Such a combination may be called a *thema*.[8] A *thema* may be defined as the dynamical structure of a simple *episode*, a single creature-environment interaction. In other words, the endurance of a certain kind of *press* in conjunction with a certain kind of *need* defines the duration of a single *episode*, the latter being a convenient molar unit for psychology to handle. Simple episodes (each with a simple thema) may relatedly succeed each other to constitute a *complex episode* (with its *complex thema*). The biography of a man may be portrayed abstractly as an historic route of themas (compare a musical score). Since there are a limited number of important drives and a limited number of important press, there are a greater (but still limited) number of important themas. Just as chemists now find it scientifically profitable to describe a hundred thousand or more organic compounds, psychologists some day may be inclined to observe and formulate the more important behavioral compounds.

11. Each drive reaction to a press has a fortune that may be measured in degrees of realization ("gratification").

Whether an episode terminates in gratification or frustration (success or failure) is often decisive in determining the direction of an organism's development. Success and failure are also of major importance in establishing the "status" of an organism in its community.

12. In the organism the passage of time is marked by rhythms of assimilation, differentiation, and integration. The environment changes. Success and failure produce their effects. There is learning and there is maturation. Thus new and previously precluded combinations come into being, and with the perishing of each moment the organism is left a different creature, never to repeat itself exactly. No moment or epoch is typical of the whole. Life is an irreversible sequence of nonidentical events. Some of these changes, however, occur in a predictable, lawful manner. There are orderly rhythms and progressions which are functions of the seasons, of age, of sex, of established cultural practices, and so forth. There is the "eternal return" ("spiral evolution"). These phenomena make biography imperative.

13. Though the psychologist is unable to find identities among the episodes of an organism's life, he can perceive uniformities. For an individual displays a tendency to react in a similar way to similar situations, and increasingly so with age. Thus there is sameness (consistency) as well as change (variability), and because of it an organism may be roughly depicted by listing the most recurrent themas, or, with more abstraction, by listing the most recurrent drives or traits.

14. Repetitions and consistencies are due in part to the fact that impressions of situations leave enduring "traces" (a concept for an hypothetical process) in the organism, which may be reactivated by the appearance of situations that resemble them; and because of the connections of these evoked traces with particular reaction systems, the organism is apt to respond to new situations as it did to former ones (redintegration). Some of the past is always alive in the present. For this reason the study of infancy is particularly important. The experiences of early life not only constitute in themselves a significant temporal segment of the creature's history, but they may exercise a marked effect upon the course of development. In some measure they "explain" succeeding events. ("The child is father to the man.")

15. The progressive differentiations and integrations that occur with age and experience are, for the most part, refinements in stimulus discrimination and press discrimination and

improvements in actonal effectiveness. Specific signs become connected with specific modes of conduct, and certain aptitudes (abilities) are developed. This is important because the fortune of drives, and thus the status of the individual, is dependent in large measure upon the learning of differentiated skills.

In early life the sequences of movement are mostly unrelated. Trends are not persistent and disco-ordination is the rule. Opposing drives and attitudes succeed each other without apparent friction. With age, however, conflict comes and after conflict resolution, synthesis, and creative integration. ("Life is creation"—Claude Bernard) Action patterns are co-ordinated, enduring purposes arise and values are made to harmonize. Thus, the history of dilemmas and how, if ever, they were solved are matters of importance for psychology.

16. Since in the higher forms of life the impressions from the external world and from the body that are responsible for conditioning and memory are received, integrated, and conserved in the brain, and since all complex adaptive behavior is evidently co-ordinated by excitations in the brain, the unity of the organism's development and behavior can be explained only by referring to organizations occurring in this region. It is brain processes, rather than those in the rest of the body, which are of special interest to the psychologist. At present, they cannot be directly and objectively recorded but they must be inferred in order to account for what happens. A need or drive is just one of these hypothetical processes. Since, by definition, it is a process which follows a stimulus and precedes the actonal response, it must be located in the brain.

17. It may prove convenient to refer to the mutually dependent processes that constitute dominant configurations in the brain as *regnant* processes; and, further, to designate the totality of such processes occurring during a single moment (a unitary temporal segment of brain processes) as a *regnancy*.[9] According to this conception regnancies correspond to the processes of highest metabolic rate in the gradient which Child[10] has described in lower organisms. It may be considered that regnancies are functionally at the summit of a hierarchy of subregnancies in the body. Thus, to a certain extent the regnant need dominates the organism:

The activities of the nerve-cells and muscle-cells are necessary conditions of the whole action, but they are not in any full sense its cause. They enable the action to be carried out, and they limit at the same time the possibilities of the action. . . . Putting the matter in another way, a knowledge of the nature of muscular and nervous action would not enable us fully to interpret behavior.[11]

We distinguished in general the *modes of action* of higher and lower unities—from the mode of action of the organism as a whole down to the modes of action of those parts of the cell which, like the chromosomes, show a certain measure of independence and individuality. We came to the conclusion that the modes of action of the subordinate unities condition, both in a positive and a negative sense, the modes of action of the higher unities. Being integrated into the activity of the whole they render possible the vital manifestation of these activities by imposing on them a particular form.[12]

Occurrences in the external world or in the body that have no effect upon regnancies do not fall within the proper domain of psychology.

18. Regnant processes are, without doubt, mutually dependent. A change in one function changes all the others and these, in turn, modify the first. Hence, events must be interpreted in terms of the many interacting forces and their relations, not ascribed to single causes. And since the parts of a person cannot be dissected physically from each other, and since they act together, ideally they should all be estimated simultaneously. This, unfortunately, is not at present possible. Much of what has been discovered by other methods at other times has to be inferred.

19. According to one version of the double-aspect theory —seemingly the most fruitful working hypothesis for a psychologist—the constituents of regnancies in man are capable of achieving consciousness (self-consciousness), though not all of them at once. The amount of introspective self-consciousness is a function of age, emotional state, attitude, type of personality, and so forth. Since through speech a person may learn to describe and communicate his impression of mental occurrences (the subjective aspect of regnant events) he can, if he wishes, impart considerable information about the processes which the psychologist attempts to conceptualize.

20. During a single moment only some of the regnant

processes have the attribute of consciousness. Hence, to explain fully a conscious event as well as a behavioral event the psychologist must take account of more variables than were present in consciousness at the time. Consequently, *looking at the matter from the viewpoint of introspective awareness,* it is necessary to postulate unconscious regnant processes. An unconscious process is something that must be conceptualized as regnant even though the S[13] is unable to report its occurrence.

21. It seems that it is more convenient at present in formulating regnant processes to use a terminology derived from subjective experience. None of the available physicochemical concepts are adequate. It should be understood, however, that every psychological term refers to some hypothetical, though hardly imaginable, physical variable, or to some combination of such variables. Perhaps some day the physiologists will discover the physical nature of regnant processes and the proper way to conceptualize them; but this achievement is not something to be expected in the near future, since an adequate formulation must include all major subjective experiences: expectations, intentions, creative thought, and so forth. Tolman,[14] however, has already shown that many of the necessary variables can be operationally defined in terms of overt behavioral indices.

It is not only more convenient and fruitful at present to use subjective terminology (perception, apperception, imagination, emotion, affection, intellection, conation), but even if in the future it becomes expedient for science to use another consonant terminology it will not be possible to dispense with terms that have subjective significance; for these constitute data of primary importance to most human beings. The need to describe and explain varieties of inner experience decided the original, and, I predict, will establish the final orientation of psychology.

22. One may suppose that regnancies vary in respect to the number, relevance, and organization of the processes involved, and that, as Janet supposes, a certain amount of integrative energy or force is required to unify the different parts. Regnancies become disjunctive in fatigue, reverie, and sleep, as well as during conflict, violent emotion, and insanity. The chief indices of differentiated conjunctive regnancies are these: alertness, nicety of perceptual and apperceptual discrimination, long endurance of a trend of complex action,

increasingly effective changes of actone, rapidity of learning, coherence, relevance and concentration of thought, absence of conflict, introspective awareness, and self-criticism.

23. Because of the position of regnancies at the summit of the hierarchy of controlling centers in the body, and because of certain institutions established in the brain which influence the regnancies, the latter (constituting as they do the personality) must be distinguished from the rest of the body. The rest of the body is as much outside the personality as the environment is outside personality. Thus, we may study the effects of illness, drugs, endocrine activity, and other somatic changes upon the personality in the same fashion as we study the changes produced by hot climate, strict discipline, or warfare. In this sense, regnant processes stand between an inner and an outer world.

24. There is continuous interaction between regnancies and other processes in the body. For the chemical constitution of the blood and lymph, as well as a great variety of centripetal nervous impulses originating in the viscera, have a marked effect on personality. Indeed, they may change it almost completely. The personality, in turn, can affect the body by exciting or inhibiting skeletal muscles, or through the power of evoked traces (images) can excite the autonomic nervous system and thereby modify the physiology of organs (compare autonomic neuroses). The personality can also vary the diet it gives the body; it can train it to stand long periods of intense exercise, drive it to a point of utter exhaustion, indulge it with ease, and allow it to accumulate pounds of fat, poison it with drugs, bring it in contact with virulent bacteria, inhibit many of its cravings, mortify it or destroy it by suicide. The relations between a personality and its body are matters of importance to a dynamicist.

25. *Time-binding.* Man is a "time-binding"[15] organism; which is a way of saying that, by conserving some of the past and anticipating some of the future, a human being can, to a significant degree, make his behavior accord with events that have happened as well as those that are to come. Man is not a mere creature of the moment, at the beck and call of any stimulus or drive. What he does is related not only to the settled past but also to shadowy preconceptions of what lies ahead. Years in advance he makes preparations to observe an eclipse of the sun from a distant island in the South Pacific and, lo, when the moment comes he is there to record the event. With the same confidence another man prepares to

meet his god. Man lives in an inner world of expected press (pessimistic or optimistic), and the psychologist must take cognizance of them if he wishes to understand his conduct or his moods, his buoyancies, disappointments, resignations. Time-binding makes for continuity of purpose.

NOTES

[1] W. McDougall, *Introduction to Social Psychology*, London, 1908; *Outline of Psychology*, New York, 1923.

[2] E. C. Tolman, *Purposive Behavior in Animals and Men*, New York, 1932.

[3] C. P. Stone, "Sexual Drive," Chapter XVIII, in *Sex and Internal Secretions*, ed. by Edgar Allen, Baltimore, 1932.

[4] K. Lewin, *A Dynamic Theory of Personality*, New York, 1935.

[5] S. Freud, *Collected Papers* (4 vols.), International Psychoanalytical Library, London, 1924–25; *A General Introduction to Psychoanalysis*, New York, 1920; *New Introductory Lectures on Psychoanalysis*, New York, 1933.

[6] Here the wording has been taken from E. S. Russell (*Form and Function*, London, 1916; *The Interpretation of Development and Heredity*, Oxford, 1930) who has stated most admirably the organismal viewpoint elaborated by W. E. Ritter (*The Unity of the Organism*, Boston, 1919) and others.

[7] Quoted from Alfred Korzybski, *Science and Sanity*. Lancaster, Pa., 1933, p. 19.

[8] I am indebted to Mrs. Eleanor C. Jones for this term.

[9] The term "regnancy" was suggested to me by Mrs. Eleanor C. Jones.

[10] C. M. Child, *Senescence and Rejuvenescence*, Chicago, 1915.

[11] E. S. Russell, *The Interpretation of Development and Heredity*, Oxford, 1930, p. 186.

[12] *Ibid.*, p. 280.

[13] "S" stands for "subject" (the organism of our concern).

[14] E. C. Tolman, *Purposive Behavior in Animals and Men*.

[15] Alfred Korzybski, *Manhood of Humanity*, New York, 1921.

Kurt Lewin

A DYNAMIC THEORY OF PERSONALITY

Kurt Lewin is considered by many of his contemporaries as one of the most brilliant figures in contemporary psychology. He was born in Prussia in 1890 and attended the Universities of Freiberg, Munich, and Berlin, the latter awarding him a doctorate in 1914. In 1926 he was appointed professor of psychology at the University of Berlin. When Hitler came to power, he emigrated to the United States and taught at Cornell and the University of Iowa. In 1945 Lewin became affiliated with The Massachusetts Institute of Technology. He died in 1947.

Lewin's first and most significant contribution to personality theory is the application of field theory to psychology. Field theory is not a new system of psychology, but a set of concepts by means of which one can represent psychological reality. Some of the principal elements of his field theory can be described as follows: 1) behavior is a function of the field which exists at the time the behavior occurs, 2) analysis starts with the situation as a whole from which are differentiated the component parts, 3) the concrete person in a concrete situation can be represented mathematically. Lewin defines field as "the totality of coexisting facts which are conceived of as mutually interdependent." Lewin has applied his concepts of field theory to a number of psychological and sociological phenomena, such as infant and child behavior, feeble-mindedness, adolescence, national character differences, and group dynamics.

A DYNAMIC THEORY OF PERSONALITY

THE CONFLICT BETWEEN ARISTOTELIAN AND GALILEIAN MODES OF THOUGHT IN CONTEMPORARY PSYCHOLOGY

In the discussion of several urgent problems of current experimental and theoretical psychology I propose to review the development of the concepts of physics, and particularly the transition from the Aristotelian to the Galileian mode of thought. My purpose is not historical; rather do I believe that certain questions, of considerable importance in the reconstruction of concepts in present-day psychology, may be clarified and more precisely stated through such a comparison, which provides a view beyond the difficulties of the day.

I do not intend to infer by deduction from the history of physics what psychology ought to do. I am not of the opinion that there is only one empirical science, namely, physics; and the question whether psychology, as a part of biology, is reducible to physics or is an independent science may here be left open.

Since we are starting from the point of view of the researcher, we shall, in our contrast of Aristotelian and Galileian concept formation, be less concerned with personal nuances of theory in Galileo and Aristotle than with certain ponderable differences in the modes of thought that determined the actual research of the medieval Aristotelians and of the post-Galileian physicists. Whether some particular investigator had previously shown the later sort of thinking in respect to some special point or whether some very modern speculations of the relativity theory should accord in some way with Aristotle's is irrelevant in the present connection.

In order to provide a special setting for the theoretical treatment of the dynamic problems, I shall consider first the general characteristics of Aristotelian and Galileian physics and of modern psychology.

GENERAL CHARACTER OF THE TWO MODES OF THOUGHT

In Physics

If one asks what the most characteristic difference between "modern" post-Galileian and Aristotelian physics is, one receives, as a rule, the following reply, which has had an important influence upon the scientific ideals of the psychologist: The concepts of Aristotelian physics were anthropomorphic and inexact. Modern physics, on the contrary, is quantitatively exact, and pure mathematical, functional relations now occupy the place of former anthropomorphic explanations. These have given to physics that abstract appearance in which modern physicists are accustomed to take special pride.

This view of the development of physics is, to be sure,

pertinent. But if one fixes one's attention less upon the style of the concepts employed and more upon their actual functions as instruments for understanding the world, these differences appear to be of a secondary nature, consequences of a deep-lying difference in the conception of the relation between the world and the task of research.

ARISTOTELIAN CONCEPTS

Their Valuative Character. As in all sciences, the detachment of physics from the universal matrix of philosophy and practice was only gradually achieved. Aristotelian physics is full of concepts which today are considered not only as specifically biological but also as preeminently valuative concepts. It abounds in specifically normative concepts taken from ethics, which occupy a place between valuative and nonvaluative concepts: the highest forms of motions are circular and rectilinear, and they occur only in heavenly movements, those of the stars; the earthly sublunar world is endowed with motion of inferior types. There are similar valuative differences between causes: on one side there are the good or, so to speak, authorized forces of a body which come from its tendency toward perfection ($\tau\acute{\epsilon}\lambda o\varsigma$), and on the other side the disturbances due to chance and to the opposing forces ($\beta\acute{\iota}\alpha$) of other bodies.

This kind of classification in terms of values plays an extraordinarily important part in medieval physics. It classes together many things with very slight or unimportant relation, and separates things that objectively are closely and importantly related.

It seems obvious to me that this extremely "anthropomorphic" mode of thought plays a large role in psychology, even to the present day. Like the distinction between earthly and heavenly, the no less valuative distinction between "normal" and "pathological" has for a long time sharply differentiated two fields of psychological fact and thus separated the phenomena which are fundamentally most nearly related.

No less important is the fact that value concepts completely dominate the conceptual setting of the special problems, or have done so until very recently. Thus, not till lately has psychology begun to investigate the structural (Gestalt) relations concerned in perception, thus replacing the concept of optical illusion, a concept which, derived not from psychological but from epistemological categories, unwarrantedly lumps together all these "illusions" and sets them apart from the other phenomena of psychological optics. Psychology speaks of the "errors" of children, of "practice," of "forgetting," thus classifying whole groups of processes according to the value of their products, instead of according to the nature of the psychological processes involved. Psychology is, to be sure, beyond classifying events *only* on the basis of value when it speaks of disturbances, of inferiority and superiority in development, or of the quality of performance on a test. On all sides there are tendencies to attack actual psychological processes. But there can hardly be any doubt that we stand now only at the beginning of this stage, that the same transitional concepts that we have seen in the Aristotelian physics to lie between the valuative and the nonvaluative are characteristic of such antitheses as intelligence and feeble-mindedness or drive and will. The detachment of the conceptual structure of psychology from the utilitarian concepts of pedagogy, medicine, and ethics is only partly achieved.

It is quite possible, indeed I hold it to be probable, that the utility or performance concepts, such as a "true" cognition versus an "error," may later acquire a legitimate sense. If that is the case, however, an "illusion" will have to be characterized not epistemologically but biologically.

Abstract Classification. When the Galileian and post-Galileian physics disposed of the distinction between heavenly and earthly and thereby extended the field of natural law enormously, it was not due solely to the exclusion of value concepts, but also to a changed interpretation of classification. For Aristotelian physics the membership of an object in a given class was of critical importance, because for Aristotle the class defined the essence or essential nature of the object, and thus determined its behavior in both positive and negative respects.

This classification often took the form of paired opposites, such as cold and warm, dry and moist, and compared with present-day classification had a rigid, absolute character. In modern quantitative physics dichotomous classifications have been entirely replaced by continuous gradations. Substantial concepts have been replaced by functional concepts.[1]

Here also it is not difficult to point out the analogous stage of development in contemporary psychology. The separation of intelligence, memory, and impulse bears throughout the characteristic stamp of Aristotelian classification; and in some fields, for example, in the analysis of feelings (pleasantness and unpleasantness) or of temperaments[2] or of drives,[3] such dichotomous classifications as Aristotle's are even today of great significance. Only gradually do these classifications lose their importance and yield to a conception which seeks to derive the same laws for all these fields, and to classify the whole field on the basis of other, essentially functional, differences.

The Concept of Law. Aristotle's classes are abstractly defined as the sum total of those characteristics which a group of objects have in common. This circumstance is not merely a characteristic of Aristotle's logic, but largely determines his conception of *lawfulness* and *chance*, which seems to me so important to the problems of contemporary psychology as to require closer examination.

For Aristotle those things are lawful, conceptually intelligible, which occur *without exception*. Also—and this he emphasizes particularly—those are lawful which occur *frequently*. Excluded from the class of the conceptually intelligible as mere chance are those things which occur only *once*, individual events as such. Actually, since the behavior of a thing is determined by its essential nature, and this essential nature is exactly the abstractly defined class (that is, the sum total of the common characteristics of a whole group of objects), it follows that each event, as a particular event, is chance, undetermined. For in these Aristotelian classes individual differences disappear.

The real source of this conception may lie in the fact that for Aristotelian physics not all physical processes possess the lawful character ascribed to them by post-Galileian physics. To the young science of physics the universe it investigated appeared to contain as much that was chaotic as that which was lawful. The lawfulness, the intelligibility of physical processes was still narrowly limited. It was really present only in certain processes, for example, the courses of the stars, but by no means in all the transitory events of the earth. Just as for other young sciences, it was still a question for physics, whether physical processes were subject to law and if so how far. And this circumstance exercised its full effect on the formation of physical concepts, even though in philosophical principle the idea of general lawfulness already existed. In post-Galileian physics, with the elimination of the distinction between lawful and chance events, the necessity also disappeared of proving that the process under consideration was lawful. For Aristotelian physics, on the contrary, it was necessary to have criteria to decide whether or not a given event was of the lawful variety. Indeed, the regularity with which similar events occurred in nature was used essentially as such a criterion. Only such events, as the celestial, which the course of history proves to be regular, or at least frequent, are subject to law; and only in so far as they are frequent, and hence more than individual events, are they conceptually intelligible. In other words, the ambition of science to understand the complex, chaotic, and unintelligible world, its faith in the ultimate decipherability of this world, were limited to such events as were certified by repetition in the course of history to possess a certain persistence and stability.

In this connection it must not be forgotten that Aristotle's emphasis on frequency (as a further basis for lawfulness, besides absolute regularity) represents, relative to his predecessors, a tendency toward the extension and concrete application of the principle of lawfulness. The "empiricist," Aristotle, insists that not only the regular but also the frequent is lawful. Of course, this only makes clearer his antithesis of individuality and law, for the individual event as such still lies outside the pale of the lawful, and hence, in a certain sense, outside the task of science. Lawfulness remains limited to cases in which events recur and classes (in Aristotle's abstract sense) reveal the essential nature of the events.

This attitude toward the problem of lawfulness in nature, which dominated medieval physics and from which even the opponents of Aristotelian physics, such as Bruno and Bacon, escaped only gradually, had important consequences in several respects.

As will be clear from the preceding text, this concept of lawfulness had throughout a quasi-statistical character. Lawfulness was considered as equivalent to the highest degree of generality, as that which occurs very often in the same way, as the extreme case of regularity, and hence as the perfect antithesis of the infrequent or of the particular event. The statistical determination of the concept of lawfulness is still clearly marked in Bacon, as when he tries to decide through his *tabula praesentia* whether a given association of properties is real (essential) or fortuitous. Thus he ascertains, for example, the numerical frequency of the cases in which the properties warm and dry are associated in everyday life.

Less mathematically exact, indeed, but no less clear is this statistical way of thinking in the whole body of Aristotelian physics.

At the same time—and this is one of the most important consequences of the Aristotelian conception—regularity or particularity was understood entirely in *historical* terms.

The complete freedom from exceptions, the "always" which is found also in the later conceptions of physical lawfulness, still has here its original connections with the frequency with which similar cases have occurred in the actual, historical course of events in the everyday world. A crude example will make this clearer: light objects, under the conditions of everyday life, relatively frequently go up; heavy objects usually go down. The flame of the fire, at any rate under the conditions known to Aristotle, almost always goes upward. It is these frequency rules, within the limits of the climate, mode of life, et cetera, familiar to Aristotle, that determine the nature and tendency to be ascribed to each class of objects and lead in the present instance to the conclusion that flames and light bodies have a tendency upward.

Aristotelian concept formation has yet another immediate relation to the geographically-historically given, in which it resembles, as do the valuative concepts mentioned above, the thinking of primitive man and of children.

When primitive man uses different words for "walking," depending upon its direction, north or south, or upon the sex of the walker, or upon whether the latter is going into or out of a house,[4] he is employing a reference to the historical situation that is quite similar to the putatively absolute descriptions (upward or downward) of Aristotle, the real significance of which is a sort of geographic characterization, a place definition relative to the earth's surface.[5]

The original connection of the concepts with the "actuality," in the special sense of the given historic-geographic circumstances, is perhaps the most important feature of Aristotelian physics. It is from this almost more even than from its teleology that his physics gets its general anthropomorphic character. Even in the minute particulars of theorizing and in the actual conduct of research, it is always evident not only that physical and normative concepts are still undifferentiated but also that the formulation of problems and the concepts that we would today distinguish, on the one hand, as historic[6] and, on the other, as nonhistoric or systematic are inextricably interwoven. (Incidentally, an analogous confusion exists in the early stages of other sciences, for example, in economics.)

From these conceptions also the attitude of Aristotelian physics toward lawfulness takes a new direction. So long as lawfulness remained limited to such processes as occurred repeatedly in the same way, it is evident not only that the young physics still lacked the courage to extend the principle to all physical phenomena but also that the concept of lawfulness still had a fundamentally historic, a temporally particular significance. Stress was laid not upon the general validity which modern physics understands by lawfulness, but upon the events in the historically given world which displayed the required stability. The highest degree of lawfulness, beyond mere frequency, was characterized by the idea of always, eternal ($\dot{a}\epsilon\dot{\iota}$ as against $\dot{\epsilon}\pi\iota$ τὸ πολύ). That is, the stretch of historic time for which constancy was assumed was extended to eternity. General validity of law was not yet clearly distinguished from eternity of process. Only permanence, or at least frequent repetition, was proof of more than momentary validity. Even here in the idea of eternity, which seems to transcend the historical, the connection with immediate historic actuality is still obvious, and this close connection was characteristic of the "empiricist" Aristotle's method and concepts.

Not only in physics but in other sciences—for example, in economics and biology—it can be clearly seen how in certain early stages the tendency to empiricism, to the collection and ordering of facts, carries with it a tendency to historical concept formation, to excessive valuation of the historical.

GALILEIAN PHYSICS

From the point of view of this sort of empiricism, the concept formation of Galileian and post-Galileian physics must seem curious and even paradoxical.

As remarked above, the use of mathematical tools and the tendency to exactness, important as they are, cannot be considered the real substance of the difference between Aristotelian and Galileian physics. It is indeed quite possible to recast in mathematical form the essential content of, for example, the dynamic ideas of Aristotelian physics (see page 209). It is conceivable that the development of physics could have taken the form of a mathematical rendition of Aristotelian concepts such as is actually taking place in psychology today. In reality, however, there were only traces of such a tendency, such as Bacon's quasi-statistical methods, mentioned above. The main development took another direction, and proved to be a change of content rather than a mere change of form.

The same considerations apply to the exactness of the new physics. It must not be forgotten that in Galileo's time there were no clocks of the sort we have today, that these first became possible through the knowledge of dynamics founded upon Galileo's work.[7] Even the methods of measurement used by Faraday in the early investigations of electricity show how little exactness, in the current sense of precision to such and such a decimal place, had to do with these critical stages in the development of physics.

The real sources of the tendency to quantification lie somewhat deeper; namely, in a new conception by the physicist of the nature of the physical world, in an extension of the demands of physics upon itself in the task of understanding the world, and in an increased faith in the possibility of their fulfillment. These are radical and far-reaching changes in the fundamental ideas of physics, and the tendency to quantification is simply one of their expressions.

Homogenization. The outlook of a Bruno, a Kepler, or a Galileo is determined by the idea of a comprehensive, all-embracing unity of the physical world. The same law governs the courses of the stars, the falling of stones, and the flight of birds. This homogenization of the physical world with respect to the validity of law deprives the division of physical objects into rigid, abstractly defined classes of the critical significance it had for Aristotelian physics, in which membership in a certain conceptual class was considered to determine the physical nature of an object.

Closely related to this is the loss in importance of logical dichotomies and conceptual antitheses. Their places are taken by more and more fluid transitions, by gradations which deprive the dichotomies of their antithetical character and represent in logical form a transition stage between the class concept and the series concept.[8]

Genetic Concepts. This dissolution of the sharp antitheses of rigid classes was greatly accelerated by the coeval transition to an essentially functional way of thinking, to the use of conditional-genetic concepts. For Aristotle the immediate perceptible appearance, that which present-day biology terms the *phenotype,* was hardly distinguished from the properties that determine the object's dynamic relations. The fact, for example, that light objects relatively frequently go upward sufficed for him to ascribe to them an upward tendency. With the differentiation of phenotype from *genotype* or, more generally, of descriptive from conditional-genetic[9] concepts and the shifting of emphasis to the latter, many old class distinctions lost their significance. The orbits of the planets, the free falling of a stone, the movement of a body on an inclined plane, the oscillation of a pendulum, which if classified according to their phenotypes would fall into quite different, indeed into antithetical classes, prove to be simply various expressions of the same law.

Concreteness. The increased emphasis upon the quantitative which seems to lend to modern physics a formal and abstract character is not derived from any tendency to logical formality. Rather, the tendency to a full description of the concrete actuality, even that of the particular case, was influential, a circumstance which should be especially emphasized in connection with present-day psychology. The particular object in all departments of science not only is determined in kind and thereby qualitatively, but it possesses each of its properties in a special intensity or to a definite degree. So long as one regards as important and conceptually intelligible only such properties of an object as are common to a whole group of objects, the individual differences of degree remain without scientific relevance, for in the abstractly defined classes these differences more or less disappear. With the mounting aspirations of research toward an understanding of actual events and particular cases, the task of describing the differences of degree that characterized individual cases had necessarily to increase in importance, and finally required actual quantitative determination.

It was the increased desire, and also the increased ability, to comprehend concrete particular cases, and to comprehend them fully, which, together with the idea of the homogeneity of the physical world and that of the continuity of the properties of its objects, constituted the main impulse to the increasing quantification of physics.

Paradoxes of the New Empiricism. This tendency toward the closest possible contact with actuality, which today is usually regarded as characteristic and ascribed to an antispeculative tendency, led to a mode of concept formation diametrically opposed to that of Aristotle, and, surprisingly enough, involved also the direct antithesis of his "empiricism."

The Aristotelian concepts show, as we have seen above, an immediate reference to the historically given reality and to the actual course of events. This immediate reference to the historically given is lacking in modern physics. The fact, so decisively important for Aristotelian concepts, that a certain process occurred only once or was very frequently or invariably repeated in the course of history, is practically irrelevant to the most essential questions of modern physics.[10] This circumstance is considered fortuitous or merely historical.

The law of falling bodies, for example, does not assert that bodies very frequently fall downward. It does not assert that the event to which the formula $s - \frac{1}{2}gt^2$ applies, the "free and unimpeded fall" of a body, occurs regularly or even frequently in the actual history of the world. Whether the event described by the law occurs rarely or often has nothing to do with the law. Indeed, in a certain sense, the law refers only to cases that are never realized, or only approximately realized, in the actual course of events. Only in experiment, that is, under artificially constructed conditions, do cases occur which approximate the event with which the law is concerned. The propositions of modern physics, which are often considered to be antispeculative and empirical, unquestionably have in comparison with Aristotelian empiricism a much less empirical, a much more constructive character than the Aristotelian concepts based immediately upon historical actuality.

IN PSYCHOLOGY

Here we are confronted by questions which, as problems of actual research and of theory, have strongly influenced the development of psychology and which constitute the most fundamental grounds of its present crisis.

The concepts of psychology, at least in certain decisive respects, are thoroughly Aristotelian in their actual content, even though in many respects their form of presentation has been somewhat civilized, so to speak. The present struggles and theoretical difficulties of psychology resemble in many ways, even in their particulars, the difficulties which culminated in the conquest over Aristotelian ways of thinking in physics.

Fortuitousness of the Individual Case. The concept formation of psychology is dominated, just as was that of Aristotelian physics, by the question of regularity in the sense of frequency. This is obvious in its immediate attitude toward particular phenomena as well as in its attitude toward lawfulness. If, for example, one shows a film of a concrete incident in the behavior of a certain child, the first question of the psychologist usually is, "Do all children do that, or is it at least common?" And if one must answer this question in the negative, the behavior involved loses for that psychologist all or almost all claim to scientific interest. To pay attention to such an "exceptional case" seems to him a scientifically unimportant bit of folly.

The real attitude of the investigator toward particular events and the problem of individuality is perhaps more clearly expressed in this actual behavior than in many theories. The individual event seems to him fortuitous, unimportant, scientifically indifferent. It may, however, be some extraordinary event, some tremendous experience, something that has critically determined the destiny of the person involved, or the appearance of an historically significant personality. In such a case it is customary to emphasize the "mystical" character of all individuality and originality, comprehensible only to "intuition," or at least not to science.

Both of these attitudes toward the particular event lead to the same conclusion: that that which does not occur repeatedly lies outside the realm of the comprehensible.

Lawfulness as Frequency. The esteem in which frequency is held in present-day psychology is due to the fact that it is still considered a question whether, and if so how far, the psychical world is lawful, just as in Aristotelian physics this esteem was due to a similar uncertainty about lawfulness in the physical world. It is not necessary here to describe at length the vicissitudes of the thesis of the lawfulness of the psychic in philosophical discussion. It is sufficient to recall that even at present there are many tendencies to limit the operation of law to certain "lower" spheres of psychical events. For us it is more important to note that the field which is considered lawful, not in principle, but in the actual research of psychology—even of experimental psychology—has been extended only very gradually. If psychology has only very gradually and hesitantly pushed beyond the bounds of sensory psychology into the fields of will and affect, it is certainly due not only to technical difficulties but mainly to the fact that in this field actual repetition, a recurrence of the same event, is not to be expected. And this repetition remains, as it did for Aristotle, to a large extent the basis for the assumption of the lawfulness or intelligibility of an event.

As a matter of fact, any psychology that does not recognize lawfulness as inherent in the nature of the psychical, and hence in all psychical processes, even those occurring only once, must have criteria to decide, like Aristotelian physics, whether or not it has in any given case to deal with lawful phenomena. And, again, just as in Aristotelian physics, frequency of recurrence is taken as such a criterion. It is evidence of the depth and momentum of this connection (between repetition and lawfulness) that it is even used to define experiment, a scientific instrument which, if it is not directly opposed to the concepts of Aristotelian physics, has at least become significant only in relatively modern times.[11] Even for Wundt repetition inhered in the concept of experiment. Only in recent years has psychology begun to give up this requirement, which withholds a large field of the psychical from experimental investigation.

But even more important perhaps than the restriction of experimental investigation is the fact that this extravagant valuation of repetition (that is, considering frequency as the criterion and expression of lawfulness) dominates the formation of the concepts of psychology, particularly in its younger branches.

Just as occurs in Aristotelian physics, contemporary child psychology regards as characteristic of a given age, and the psychology of emotion as characteristic of a given expression, that which a group of individual cases have in common. This abstract Aristotelian conception of the class determines the kind and dominates the procedure of classification.

Class and Essence. Present-day child psychology and affect psychology also exemplify clearly the Aristotelian habit of considering the abstractly defined classes as the essential nature of the particular object and hence as an explanation of its behavior. Whatever is common to children of a given age is set up as the fundamental character of that age. The fact that three-year-old children are quite often negative is considered evidence that negativism is inherent in the nature of three-year-olds, and the concept of a negativistic age or stage is then regarded as an explanation (though perhaps not a complete one) for the appearance of negativism in a given particular case!

Quite analogously, the concept of drives—for example, the hunger drive or the maternal instinct—is nothing more than the abstract selection of the features common to a group of acts that are of relatively frequent occurrence. This abstraction is set up as the essential reality of the behavior and is then in turn used to explain the frequent occurrence of the instinctive behavior, for example, of the care of infant progeny. Most of the explanations of expression, of character, and of temperament are in a similar state. Here, as in a great many other fundamental concepts, such as that of ability, talent, and similar concepts employed by the intelligence testers, present-day psychology is really reduced to explanation in terms of Aristotelian essences, a sort of explanation which has long been attacked as faculty psychology and as circular explanation, but for which no other way of thinking has been substituted.

Statistics. The classificatory character of its concepts and the emphasis on frequency are indicated methodologically by the commanding significance of statistics in contemporary psychology. The statistical procedure, at least in its commonest application in psychology, is the most striking expression of this Aristotelian mode of thinking. In order to exhibit the common features of a given group of facts, the average is calculated. This average acquires a representative value, and is used to characterize (as mental age) the properties of "the" two-year-old child. Outwardly, there is a difference between contemporary psychology, which works so much with numbers and curves, and the Aristotelian physics. But this difference, characteristically enough, is much more a difference in the technique of execution than in the actual content of the concepts involved. Essentially, the statistical way of thinking, which is a necessary consequence of Aristotelian concepts, is also evident in Aristotelian physics, as we have already seen. The difference is that, owing to the extraordinary development of mathematics and of general scientific method, the statistical procedure of psychology is clearer and more articulate.

All the efforts of psychology in recent years toward exactness and precision have been in the direction of refinement and extension of its statistical methods. These efforts are quite justified in so far as they indicate a determination to achieve an adequate comprehension of the full reality of mental life. But they are really founded, at least in part, on the ambition to demonstrate the scientific status of psychology by using as much mathematics as possible and by pushing all calculations to the last possible decimal place.

This formal extension of the method has not changed the underlying concepts in the slightest: they are still thoroughly Aristotelian. Indeed, the mathematical formulation of the method only consolidates and extends the domination of the underlying concepts. It unquestionably makes it more difficult to see the real character of the concepts and hence to supplant them with others; and this is a difficulty with which Galileian physics did not have to contend, inasmuch as the Aristotelian mode of thought was not then so intrenched and obscured in mathematics (see page 203).

Limits of Knowledge. Exceptions. Lawfulness is believed to be related to regularity and is considered the antithesis of the individual case. (In terms of the current formula, lawfulness is conceived as a correlation approaching $r = \pm 1$.) So far as the psychologist agrees at all to the validity of psychological propositions, he regards them as only regularly valid, and his acceptance of them takes such a form that one remains aware of a certain distinction between mere regularity and full lawfulness; and he ascribes to biological and, above all, to psychological propositions (in contrast to physical) only regularity. Or else lawfulness is believed to be only the extreme case of regularity,[12] in which case all differences (between lawfulness and regularity) disappear in principle while the necessity of determining the degree of regularity still remains.

The fact that lawfulness and individuality are considered antitheses has two sorts of effect on actual research. It signifies in the first place a limitation of research. It makes it appear hopeless to try to understand the real, unique, course of an emotion or the actual structure of a particular individual's personality. It thus reduces one to a treatment of these problems in terms of mere averages, as exemplified by tests and questionnaires. Anyone to whom these methods appear inadequate usually encounters a weary skepticism or else a maudlin appreciation of individuality and the doctrine that this field, from which the recurrence of similar cases in sufficient numbers is excluded, is inaccessible to scientific comprehension and requires instead sympathetic intuition. In both cases the field is withdrawn from experimental investigation, for qualitative properties are considered as the direct opposite of lawfulness. The manner in which this view is continually and repeatedly advanced in the discussion of experimental psychology resembles, even to its particulars, the arguments against which Galileian physics had to struggle. How, it was urged at that time, can one try to embrace in a single law of motion such qualitatively different phenomena as the movements of the stars, the flying of leaves in the wind, the flight of birds, and the rolling of a stone downhill? But the opposition of law and individual corresponded so well with the Aristotelian conception and with the primitive mode of thinking which constituted the philosophy of everyday life that it appears often enough in the writings of the physicists themselves, not, however, in their physics but in their philosophy.[13]

The conviction that it is impossible wholly to comprehend the individual case as such implies, in addition to this limitation, a certain laxity of research: it is satisfied with setting forth mere regularities. The demands of psychology upon the stringency of its propositions go no farther than to require a validity "in general" or "on the average" or "as a rule." The "complexity" and "transitory nature" of life processes make it unreasonable, it is said, to require complete, exceptionless, validity. According to the old saw that "the exception proves the rule," *psychology does not regard exceptions as counterarguments so long as their frequency is not too great.*

The attitude of psychology toward the concept of lawfulness also shows clearly and strikingly the Aristotelian character of its mode of thought. It is founded on a very meager confidence in the lawfulness of psychological events, and has for the investigator the added charm of not requiring too high a standard of validity in his propositions or in his proofs of them.

Historic-Geographic Concepts. For the view of the nature of lawfulness and for the emphasis upon repetition which we have seen to be characteristic of Aristotelian physics, in addition to the motives which we have just mentioned, the immediate reference to the concerned actuality in the historic-geographic sense was fundamental. Likewise—and this is evidence of the intimacy in which these modes of thought are related—present-day psychology is largely dominated by the same immediate reference to the historic-geographic datum. The historical bent of psychological concepts is again not always immediately obvious as such, but is bound up with nonhistoric, systematic concepts, and undifferentiated from them. This quasi-historical set forms, in my opinion, the central point for the understanding and criticism of this mode of concept formation.

Although we have criticized the statistical mode of thought, the particular formulas used are not ultimately important to the questions under discussion. It is not the fact that an arithmetic mean is taken, that one adds and divides, that is the object of the present critique. These operations will certainly continue to be used extensively in the future of psychology. The critical point is not that statistical methods are applied, but how they are applied and, especially, what cases are combined into groups.

In contemporary psychology the reference to the historic-geographic datum and the dependence of the conclusions upon frequency of actual occurrence are striking. Indeed, so far as immediate reference to the historic datum is concerned, the way in which the nature of the one-, two-, or three-year-old child is arrived at through the calculation of statistical averages corresponds exactly to Bacon's collection of the given cases of dryness in his *tabulae praesentiae*. To be sure, there is a certain very crude concession made in such averages to the requirements of nonhistoric concepts: patently pathological cases, and sometimes even cases in which an unusual environment is concerned, are usually excluded. Apart from this consideration, the exclusion of the most extreme abnormalities, the determination of the cases to be placed in a statistical group is essentially on historic-geographic grounds. For a group defined in historic-geographic terms, perhaps the one-year-old children of Vienna or New York in the year 1928, averages are calculated which are doubtless of the greatest significance to the historian or to the practical school man, but which do not lose their dependence upon the accidents of the historic-geographic given even though one go on to an average of the children of Germany, of Europe, or of the whole world, or of a decade instead of a year. *Such an extension of the geographic and historic basis does not do away with the specific dependence of this concept upon the frequency with which the individual cases occur within historically-geographically defined fields.*

Mention should have been made earlier of that refinement of statistics which is founded upon a restriction of the historic-geographic basis, such as a consideration of the one-year-old children of a proletarian quarter of Berlin in the first years after the [Great] War. Such groupings usually are based on the qualitative individuality of the concrete cases as well as upon historic-geographic definitions. But even such limitations really contradict the spirit of statistics founded on frequency. Even they signify methodologically a certain shift to the concrete particulars. Incidentally, one must not forget that even in the extreme case of such refinement, perhaps in the statistical investigation of the only child, the actual definition is in terms of historic-geographic or at best of sociological categories; that is, according to criteria which combine into a single group cases that psychologically are very different or even antithetical. Such statistical investigations are consequently unable as a rule to give an explanation of the dynamics of the processes involved.

The immediate reference to the historically given actuality which is characteristic of Aristotelian concept formation is evident also in the discussion of experiment and nearness to life conditions. Certainly one may justly criticize the simple reaction experiments, the beginnings of the experimental psychology of the will, or the experiments of reflexology on the ground of their wide divergence from the conditions of life. But this divergence is based in large part upon the tendency to investigate such processes as do not present the individual peculiarities of the particular case but which, as "simple elements" (perhaps the simplest movements), are common to all behavior, or which occur, so to speak, in everything. In contrast to the foregoing, approximation to life conditions is often demanded of, for example, the psychology of will. By this is usually meant that it should investigate those cases, impossible to produce experimentally, in which the most important decisions of life are made. And here also we are confronted by an orientation toward the historically significant. It is a requirement which, if transferred to physics, would mean that it would be incorrect to study hydrodynamics in the laboratory; one must rather investigate the largest rivers in the world. Two points, then, stand out: in the field of theory and law, the high valuation of the historically important and disdain of the ordinary; in the field of experiment, the choice of processes which occur frequently (or are common to many events). Both are indicative in like measure of that Aristotelian mixing of historical and systematic questions which carries with it for the systematic the connection with the abstract classes and the neglect of the full reality of the concrete case.

GALILEIAN CONCEPT FORMATION

Opposed to Aristotelian concept formation, which I have sought briefly to characterize, there is now evident in psychology a development which appears occasionally in radical or apparently radical tendencies, more usually in little half steps, sometimes falling into error (especially when it tries most exactly to follow the example of physics), but which on the whole seems clearly and irresistibly to be pushing on to modifications that may ultimately mean nothing less than a transition from Aristotelian to Galileian concept formation.

No Value Concepts. No Dichotomies. Unification of Fields. The most important general circumstances which paved the way for Galileian concepts in physics are clearly and distinctly to be seen in present-day psychology.

The conquest over *valuative*, anthropomorphic classifications of phenomena on bases other than the nature of the mental process itself (see page 198) is not by any means complete, but in many fields, especially in sensory psychology, at least the chief difficulties are past.

As in physics, the grouping of events and objects into paired opposites and similar logical dichotomies is being replaced by groupings with the aid of serial concepts which permit of continuous variation, partly owing simply to wider experience and the recognition that transition stages are always present.

This has gone furthest in sensory psychology, especially in psychological optics and acoustics, and lately also in the domain of smell. But the tendency toward this change is also evident in other fields, for example, in that of feeling.

Freud's doctrine especially—and this is one of its greatest services—has contributed largely to the abolition of the boundary between the normal and the pathological, the ordinary and the unusual, and hereby furthered the *homogenization* (see page 204) of all the fields of psychology. This process is certainly still far from complete, but it is entirely comparable to that introduced in modern physics by which heavenly and earthly processes were united.

Also in child and animal psychology the necessity is gradually disappearing of choosing between two alternatives—regarding the child as a little adult and the animal as an undeveloped inferior human, or trying to establish an unbridgeable gap between the child and adult, animal and man. This homogenization is becoming continually clearer in all fields, and it is not a purely philosophical insistence upon some sort of abstract fundamental unity but influences concrete research in which differences are fully preserved.

Unconditional General Validity of Psychological Laws. The clearest and most important expression of increasing homogeneity, besides the transition from class to serial concepts, is the fact that the validity of particular psychological laws is no longer limited to particular fields, as it was once limited to the normal human adult on the ground that anything might be expected of psychopathics or of geniuses, or that in such cases the same laws do not hold. It is coming to be realized that every psychological law must hold without exception.

In actual content, this transition to the concept of strict exceptionless lawfulness signifies at once the same final and all-embracing homogenization and harmonization of the whole field that gave to Galileian physics its intoxicating feeling of infinite breadth, because it does not, like the abstract class concepts, level out the rich variety of the world and because a single law embraces the whole field.

Tendencies toward a homogeneity based upon the exceptionless validity of its laws have become evident in psychology only very recently, but they open up an extraordinarily wide perspective.[14]

The investigation of the laws of structure—particularly the experimental investigation of wholes—has shown that the same laws hold not only within different fields of psychological optics but also in audition and in sensory psychology in general. This in itself constitutes a large step in the progress toward homogeneity.

Further, the laws of optical figures and of intellectual insight have turned out to be closely related. Important and similar laws have been discovered in the experimental investigation of behavioral wholes, of will processes, and of psychological needs. In the fields of memory and expression, psychological development appears to be analogous. In short, the thesis of the general validity of psychological laws has very recently become so much more concrete, particular laws have shown such capacity for fruitful application to fields that at first were qualitatively completely separated, that the thesis of the homogeneity of psychic life in respect to its laws gains tremendously in vigor and is destroying the boundaries of the old separated fields.[15]

Mounting Ambitions. Methodologically also the thesis of the exceptionless validity of psychological laws has a far-reaching significance. It leads to an extraordinary increase in the demands made upon proof. It is no longer possible to take exceptions lightly. They do not in any way "prove the rule," but on the contrary are completely valid disproofs, even though they are rare, indeed, so long as one single exception is demonstrable. The thesis of general validity permits of no exceptions in the entire realm of the psychic, whether of child or adult, whether in normal or pathological psychology.

On the other hand, the thesis of exceptionless validity in psychological laws makes available to investigation, especially to experiment, such processes as do not frequently recur in the same form, as, for example, certain affective processes.

From the Average to the Pure Case. A clear appreciation of this circumstance is still by no means habitual in psychology. Indeed, from the earlier, Aristotelian point of view the new procedure may even seem to conceal the fundamental contradiction we have mentioned above. One declares that one wants to comprehend the full concrete reality in a higher degree than is possible with Aristotelian concepts and yet considers this reality in its actual historical course and its given geographical setting as really accidental. The general validity, for example, of the law of movement on an inclined plane is not established by taking the average of as many cases as possible of real stones actually rolling down hills, and then considering this average as the most probable case.[16] It is based rather upon the frictionless rolling of an ideal sphere down an absolutely straight and hard plane, that is, upon a process that even the laboratory can only approximate and which is most improbable in daily life. One declares that one is striving for general validity and concreteness, yet uses a method which, from the point of view of the preceding epoch, disregards the historically given facts and depends entirely upon individual accidents, indeed upon the most pronounced exceptions.

How physics arrives at this procedure, which strikes the Aristotelian views of contemporary psychology as doubly paradoxical, begins to become intelligible when one envisages the necessary methodological consequences of the change in the ideas of the extent of lawfulness. When lawfulness is no longer limited to cases which occur regularly or frequently but is characteristic of every physical event, the necessity disappears of demonstrating the lawfulness of an event by some special criterion, such as its frequency of occurrence. Even a particular case is then assumed, without more ado, to be lawful. Historical rarity is no disproof, historical regularity no proof, of lawfulness. For the concept of lawfulness has been quite detached from that of regularity; the concept of the complete absence of exceptions to law is strictly separated from that of historical constancy (the "forever" of Aristotle).[17]

Further, the content of a law cannot then be determined by the calculation of averages of historically given cases. For Aristotle the nature of a thing was expressed by the characteristics common to the historically given cases. Galileian concepts, on the contrary, which regard historical frequency as accident, must also consider it a matter of chance which properties one arrives at by taking averages of historical cases. If the concrete event is to be comprehended and the thesis of lawfulness without exception is to be not merely a philosophical maxim but determinative of the mode of actual research, there must be another possibility of penetrating the nature of an event, some way other than that of ignoring all individual peculiarities of concrete cases. The solution of this problem may be obtained only by the elucidation of the paradoxical procedures of Galileian method through a consideration of the problems of dynamics.

DYNAMICS

CHANGES IN THE FUNDAMENTAL DYNAMIC CONCEPTS OF PHYSICS

The dynamic problems of physics were really foreign to the Aristotelian mode of thought. The fact that dynamic problems had throughout such great significance for Galileian physics permits us to regard dynamics as a characteristic consequence of the Galileian mode of thought.[18] As always, it involved not merely a superficial shift of interest, but a change in the content of the theories. Even Aristotle emphasized "becoming," as compared with his predecessors. It is perhaps more correct to say that in the Aristotelian concepts statics and dynamics are not yet differentiated. This is due especially to certain fundamental assumptions.

TELEOLOGY AND PHYSICAL VECTORS

A leading characteristic of Aristotelian dynamics is the fact that it explained events by means of concepts which we today perceive to be specifically biological or psychological: *every object tends, so far as not prevented by other objects, toward perfection,* toward the realization of its own nature. This nature is for Aristotle, as we have already seen, that which is common to the class of the object. So it comes about that the class for him is at the same time the concept and the goal (τέλός) of an object.

This teleological theory of physical events does not show only that biology and physics are not yet separated. It indicates also that the dynamics of Aristotelian physics resembles in essential points the animistic and artificial mode of thought of primitive man, which views all movement as life and makes artificial manufacture the prototype of existence. For, in the case of manufactured things, the maker's idea of the object is, in one sense, both the cause and the goal of the event.

Further, for Aristotelian concepts the *cause* of a physical event was very closely related to psychological "drives": the object strives toward a certain goal; so far as movement is concerned, it tends toward the place appropriate to its nature. Thus heavy objects strive downward, the heavier the more strongly, while light objects strive upward.

It is customary to dismiss these Aristotelian physical concepts by calling them anthropomorphic. But perhaps it would be better, when we consider that the same fundamental dynamic ideas are today completely dominant in psychology and biology, to examine the actual content of the Aristotelian theses as far as possible independently of the style of their presentation.

It is customary to say that teleology assumes a direction of events toward a goal, which causal explanation does not recognize, and to see in this the most essential difference between teleological and causal explanation. But this sort of view is inadequate, for the causal explanation of modern physics uses directed quantities, mathematically described vectors. Physical force, which is defined as "the cause of a physical change," is considered a directed, vectorial factor. In the employment of vectorial factors as the foundation of dynamics there is thus no difference between the modern and the Aristotelian view.

The real difference lies rather in the fact that *the kind and direction of the physical vectors in Aristotelian dynamics are completely determined in advance by the nature of the object concerned.* In modern physics, on the contrary, *the existence of a physical vector always depends upon the mutual relations of several physical facts*, especially upon the relation of the object to its environment.[19]

SIGNIFICANCE OF THE WHOLE SITUATION IN ARISTOTELIAN AND GALILEIAN DYNAMICS

For Aristotelian concepts, the environment plays a part only in so far as it may give rise to "disturbances," forced modifications of the processes which follow from the nature of the object concerned. The vectors which determine an object's movements are completely determined by the object. That is, they do not depend upon the relation of the object to the environment, and they belong to that object once for all, irrespective of its surroundings at any given time. The tendency of light bodies to go up resided in the bodies themselves; the downward tendency of heavy objects was seated in those objects. In modern physics, on the contrary, not only is the upward tendency of a lighter body derived from the relation of this body to its environment, but the weight itself of the body depends upon such a relation.

This decisive revolution comes to clear expression in Galileo's classic investigations of the law of falling bodies. The mere fact that he did not investigate the heavy body itself, but the process of "free falling or movement on an inclined plane," signifies a transition to concepts which can be defined only by reference to a certain sort of situation (namely, the presence of a plane with a certain inclination or of an unimpeded vertical extent of space through which to fall). The idea of investigating free falling, which is too rapid for satisfactory observation, by resorting to the slower movement upon an inclined plane presupposes that the dynamics of the event is no longer related to the isolated object as such, but is seen to be dependent upon the whole situation in which the event occurs.

Galileo's procedure, in fact, includes a penetrating investigation of precisely the situation factors. The slope of the inclined plane, that is, the proportion of height to length, is defined. The list of situations involved (free falling, movement on an inclined plane, and horizontal movement) is exhausted and, through the varying of the inclination, classified. The dependence of the essential features of the event (for example, its velocity) upon the essential properties of the situation (the slope of the plane) becomes the conceptual and methodological center of importance.

This view of dynamics does not mean that the nature of the object becomes insignificant. The properties and structure of the object involved remain important also for the Galileian theory of dynamics. But the situation assumes as much importance as the object. *Only by the concrete whole which comprises the object and the situation are the vectors which determine the dynamics of the event defined.*

In carrying out this view, Galileian physics tried to characterize the individuality of the total situation concerned as concretely and accurately as possible. This is an exact reversal of Aristotelian principles. The dependence of an event upon the situation in which it occurs means for the Aristotelian mode of thought, which wants to ascertain the general by seeking out the like features of many cases, nothing more than a disturbing force. The changing situations appear as something fortuitous that disturbs and obscures the essential nature. It was therefore valid and customary to exclude the influence of the situation as far as possible, to abstract from the situation, in order to understand the essential nature of the object and the direction of its goal.

GETTING RID OF THE HISTORICAL BENT

The actual investigation of this sort of vectors obviously presupposes that the processes involved occur with a certain regularity or frequency (see page 201). For otherwise an exclusion of the differences of the situation would leave no similarities. If one starts from the fundamental concepts of Aristotelian dynamics, the investigation of the dynamics of a process must be more difficult—one might think here of emotion in psychology—the more it depends upon the nature of the situation concerned. The single event becomes thereby unlawful in principle because there is no way of investigating its dynamics.

The Galileian method of determining the dynamics of a process is directly opposed to this procedure. Since the dynamics of the process depends not only upon the object but also, primarily, upon the situation, it would be nonsensical to try to obtain general laws of processes by excluding the influence of the situations as far as possible. It becomes silly to bring in as many different situations as possible and regard only those factors as generally valid that are observed under all circumstances, in any and every situation. It must, on the contrary, become important to comprehend the whole situation involved, with all its characteristics, as precisely as possible.

The step from particular case to law, from "this" event to "such" an event, no longer requires the confirmation by historical regularity that is characteristic of the Aristotelian mode of thought. This step to the general is automatically and immediately given by the principle of the exceptionless lawfulness of physical events.[20] What is now important to the investigation of dynamics is not to abstract from the situation, but to hunt out those situations in which the determinative factors of the total dynamic structure are most clearly, distinctly, and purely to be discerned. *Instead of a reference to the abstract average of as many historically given cases as possible, there is a reference to the full concreteness of the particular situations.*

We cannot here examine in great detail why not all situations are equally useful for the investigation of dynamics, why certain situations possess a methodological advantage, and why as far as possible these are experimentally set up. Only one circumstance, which seems to me very seldom to be correctly viewed and which has given rise to misunderstandings that have had serious consequences for psychology, requires elucidation.

We have seen above how Galileian concepts separated the previously undifferentiated questions of the historical course of events on one side and of the laws of events on the other. They renounced in systematic problems the immediate reference to the historic-geographic datum. That the procedure instituted does not, as might at first appear, contradict the empirical tendency toward the comprehension of the full reality may already be clear from our last consideration: the Aristotelian immediate relation to the historically regular and its average really means giving up the attempt to understand the particular, always situation-conditioned event. When this immediate relation is completely abandoned, when the place of historic-geographic constancy is taken by the position of the particular in the whole situation, and when (as in experimental method) it is just the same whether the situation is frequent and permanent or rare and transitory, only then does it become possible to undertake the task of understanding the real, always ultimately unique, event.

THE MEANING OF THE PROCESS DIFFERENTIAL

Methodologically there may seem to result here another theoretical difficulty which can perhaps be better elucidated

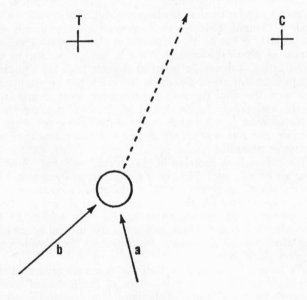

Figure 1.

by a simple example than by general discussion. In order that the essentials may be more easily seen, I choose an example not from familiar physics but from problematical psychology. If one attempt to trace the behavior of a child to psychical field forces, among other things—the justification for this thesis is not here under discussion—the following objection might easily be raised. A child stands before two attractive objects (say a toy *T* and a piece of chocolate *C*), which are in different places (see Figure 1). According to this hypothesis, then, there exist field forces in these directions (*a* and *b*). The proportional strength of the forces is indifferent, and it does not matter whether the physical law of the parallelogram of forces is applicable to psychical field forces or not. So far, then, as a resultant of these two forces is formed, it must take a direction (*r*) which leads neither to *T* nor to *C*. The child would then, so one might easily conclude according to this theory, reach neither *T* nor *C*.[21]

In reality such a conclusion would be too hasty, for even if the vector should have the direction *r* at the moment of starting, that does not mean that the actual process permanently retains this direction. Instead, *the whole situation changes with the process*, thus changing also, in both strength and direction, the vectors that at each moment determine the dynamics. Even if one assumes the parallelogram of forces and in addition a constant internal situation in the child, the actual process, because of this changing in the situation, will always finally bring the child to one or the other of the attractive objects (Figure 2).[22]

What I would like to exhibit by this example is this: If one tries to deduce the dynamics of a process, particularly the vectors which direct it, from the actual event, one is compelled to resort to process differentials. In our example, one can regard only the process of the first moment, not the whole course, as the immediate expression of the vector present in the beginning of the situation.

The well-known fact that all, or at least most, physical laws are differential laws[23] does not seem to me, as is often supposed, to prove that physics endeavors to analyze everything into the smallest "elements" and to consider these elements in the most perfect possible isolation. It proceeds rather from the circumstance that physics since Galileo no longer regards the historic course of a process as the immediate expression of the vectors determinative of its dynamics. For Aristotle, the fact that the movement showed a certain total course was proof of the existence of a tendency to that course, for example, toward a perfect circular movement. Galileian concepts, on the contrary, even in the course of a particular

process, separate the quasi-historical from the factors determining the dynamics. They refer to the whole situation in its
full concrete individuality, to the state of the situation at
every moment of time.

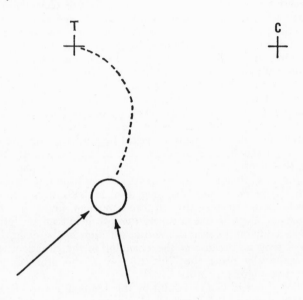

Figure 2.

Further, for Galileian concepts, the forces, the physical
vectors which control the situation, are proved by the resulting process. However, it is valid to exclude the quasi-historical in order to get the pure process, and therefore necessary
to comprehend the type of process by recourse to the process
differential, because only in the latter, and hence unmixed,
is it expressed. This recourse to the process differential thus
arises not, as is usually supposed, from a tendency to reduce
all events to their "ultimate elements," but as a not immediately obvious complementary expression of the tendency
to derive the dynamics from the relation of the concrete particular to the concrete whole situation and to ascertain as
purely and as unmixed with historic factors as possible the
type of event with which this total situation is dynamically
related.

Experimentally also it is important to construct such situations as will actually yield this pure event, or at least permit of its conceptual reconstruction.

METHODOLOGICAL

It remains to examine more closely the logical and methodological consequences of this mode of thought. Since law and individual are no longer antitheses, nothing prevents relying for proof upon historically unusual, rare, and transitory events, such as most physical experiments are. It becomes clear why it is very illuminating, for systematic concepts, to produce such cases, even if not exactly for the sake of their rarity itself.

The tendency to comprehend the actual situation as fully and concretely as possible, even in its individual peculiarities, makes the most precise possible qualitative and quantitative determination necessary and profitable. But it must not be forgotten that only this task, and not numerical precision for its own sake, gives any point or meaning to exactness.

Some of the most essential services to knowledge of the quantitative, and in general of the mathematical, mode of representation are (1) the possibility of using continuous transitions instead of dichotomies in characterization, thereby greatly refining description, and (2) the fact that with such functional concepts it is possible to go from the particular to the general without losing the particular in the general and thereby making impossible the return from the general to the particular.

Finally, reference should be made to the method of approximation in the description of objects and situations, in which the continuous, functional mode of thought is manifest.

FUNDAMENTAL DYNAMIC CONCEPTS IN PSYCHOLOGY

The dynamic concepts of psychology today are still thoroughly Aristotelian,[24] and indeed the same internal relations and motives seem to me here displayed, even to the details.

ARISTOTELIAN IDEAS: INDEPENDENCE OF THE SITUATION; INSTINCT

In content, which is easiest to exhibit and indeed hardly requires exposition, psychological dynamics agrees most completely with Aristotelian concepts: it is teleology in the Aristotelian sense. The traditional mistake of regarding causal explanation as an explanation without the use of directed forces has notably retarded the progress of dynamics, since psychological dynamics, like physical, cannot be understood without the use of vector concepts. It is not the fact that directed quantities are employed in psychological dynamics that gives it its Aristotelian character, but the fact that the process is ascribed to vectors connected with the object of investigation, for example, with the particular person, and *relatively independent of the situation.*

The concept of instinct in its classical form is perhaps the most striking example of this. The instincts are the sum of those vectors conditioned by predispositions which it is thought must be ascribed to an individual. The instincts are determined essentially by finding out what actions occur most frequently or regularly in the *actual life* of the individual or of a group of like individuals. That which is *common* to these frequent acts (for example, food getting, fighting, mutual aid) is regarded as the *essence* or essential nature of the processes. Again, completely in the Aristotelian sense, these abstract class concepts are set up as at once the goal and the cause of the process. And indeed the instincts obtained in this way, as averages of historical actuality, are regarded as the more fundamental the more abstract the class concept is and the more various the cases of which the average is taken. It is thought that in this way, and only in this way, those "accidents" inherent in the particular case and in the concrete situation can be overcome. For the aim that still completely dominates the procedure of psychology in large fields is founded upon its effort to free itself of the connection to specific situations.

INTRINSIC DIFFICULTIES AND UNLAWFULNESS

The whole difference between the Aristotelian and Galileian modes of thought becomes clear as soon as one sees what consequences, for a strict Galileian view of the concept of law, follow from this close and fixed connection of the instinct to the individual "in itself." In that case the instinct (for example, the maternal) must operate continually without interruption; just as the explanation of negativism by the "nature" of the three-year-old child entails for Galileian concepts the consequence that all three-year-old children must be negative the whole day long, twenty-four hours out of the twenty-four.

The general Aristotelian set of psychology is able to dodge these consequences. It is satisfied, even for proof of the existence of the vectors which should explain the behavior, to depend upon the concept of regularity. In this way it avoids the necessity of supposing the vector to be existent in every situation. On the basis of the strict concept of law it is possible to disprove the hypothesis, for example, of the existence of a certain instinct by demonstrating its nonexistence in given concrete cases. Aristotelian concepts do not have to fear such disproofs, inasmuch as they can answer all references to concrete particular cases by falling back on mere statistical validity.

Of course, these concepts are thereby also unable to explain the occurrence of a particular case, and by this is meant not the behavior of an abstractly defined "average child," but, for example, the behavior of a certain child at a certain moment.

The Aristotelian bent of psychological dynamics thus not only implies a limitation of explanation to such cases as occur frequently enough to provide a basis for abstracting from the situation, but leaves literally any possibility open in any particular case, even of frequent events.

ATTEMPTS AT SELF-CORRECTION: THE AVERAGE SITUATION

The intrinsic difficulties for dynamics which the Aristotelian mode of thought brings with it, namely, the danger of destroying the explanatory value of the theory by the exclusion of the situation, are constantly to be observed in contemporary psychology and lead to the most singular hybrid methods and to attempts to include the concept of the situation somehow. This becomes especially clear in the attempts at quantitative determination. When, for example, the question is raised and an attempt made to decide experimentally how the strengths of various drives in rats (perhaps hunger, thirst, sex, and mother love) compare with each other, such a question (which corresponds to asking in physics which is stronger, gravitation or electromotive force) has meaning only if these vectors are ascribed entirely to the rat and regarded as practically independent of the concrete whole situation, independent of the condition of the rat and its environment at the moment. Such a fixed connection is, of course, ultimately untenable, and one is compelled at least in part to abandon this way of thinking. Thus the first step in this direction consists in taking account of the *momentary condition of the drive* with regard to its state of satiation: the various possible degrees of strength of the several drives are ascertained, and their maximal strengths are compared.

It is true, of course, that the Aristotelian attitude is really only slightly ameliorated thereby. The curve expresses the statistical average of a large number of cases, which is not binding for an individual case; and, above all, this mode of thought applies the vector independently of the structure of the situation.

To be sure, it is not denied that the situation essentially determines the instinctive behavior in the actual particular case, but in these problems, as in the question of the child's spontaneous behavior in the baby tests, it is evident that no more is demanded of a law than a behavioral average. The law thus applies to an average situation. It is forgotten that there just is no such thing as an "average situation" any more than an average child.

Practically, if not in principle, the reference to the concept of an "optimal" situation goes somewhat further. But even here the concrete structure of the situation remains indeterminate: only a maximum of results in a certain direction is required.

In none of these concepts, however, are the two fundamental faults of the Aristotelian mode of thought eliminated: the vectors determining the dynamics of the process are still attributed to the isolated object, independently of the concrete whole situation; and only very slight demands are made upon the validity of psychological principles and the comprehension of the concrete actuality of the individual single process.

This holds true even for the concepts immediately concerned with the significance of the situation. As mentioned before, the question at the center of the discussion of the situation is, quite in the Aristotelian sense, how far the situation can hinder (or facilitate). The situation is even considered as a constant object and the question is discussed: Which is more important, heredity or environment? Thus again, on the basis of a concept of situation gotten by abstraction, a dynamic problem is treated in a form which has none but a statistical historical meaning. The heredity or environment discussion also shows, even in its particulars, how completely these concepts separate object and situation and derive the dynamics from the isolated object itself.

The role of the situation in all these concepts may perhaps be best exhibited by reference to certain changes in painting. In medieval painting at first there was, in general, no environment, but only an empty (often a golden) background. Even when gradually an environment did appear it usually consisted in nothing more than presenting, beside the one person, other persons and objects. Thus the picture was at best an assembling of separate persons in which each had really a separate existence.

Only later did the space itself exist in the painting: it became a whole situation. At the same time this situation as a whole became dominant, and each separate part, so far indeed as separate parts still remain, is what it is (for example, in such an extreme as Rembrandt) only in and through the whole situation.

BEGINNINGS OF A GALILEIAN MODE OF THOUGHT

Opposed to these Aristotelian fundamental ideas of dynamics there are now signs in psychology of the beginnings of a Galileian mode of thought. In this respect the concepts of sensory psychology are farthest advanced.

At first, even in sensory psychology, explanations referred to isolated single perceptions, even to single isolated elements of these perceptions. The developments of recent years have brought about, at first slowly but then more radically, a revolution in the fundamental dynamic ideas by showing that the dynamics of the processes are to be deduced, not from the single elements of the perception, but from its whole structure. For it is impossible by a consideration of the elements to define what is meant by *figure* in the broader sense of the word. Rather, the whole dynamics of sensory psychological processes depends upon the ground[25] and beyond it upon the structure of the whole surrounding field. The dynamics of perception is not to be understood by the abstract Aristotelian method of excluding all fortuitous situations, but this principle is penetrating today all the fields of sensory psychology—only by *the establishment of a form of definite structure in a definite sort of environment.*

Recently the same fundamental ideas of dynamics have been extended beyond the special field of perception and applied in the fields of higher mental processes, in the psychology of instinct, will, emotion, and expression, and in genetic psychology. The sterility, for example, of the always circular discussion of heredity or environment and the impossibility of carrying through the division, based upon this discussion, of the characteristics of the individual begin to show that there is something radically wrong with their fundamental assumptions. A mode of thought is becoming evident, even though only gradually, which, corresponding somewhat to the biological concept of phenotype and genotype, tries to determine the predisposition, not by excluding so far as possible the influence of the environment, but by accepting in the concept of disposition its necessary reference to a group of concretely defined situations.

Thus in the psychological fields most fundamental to the whole behavior of living things the transition seems inevitable to a Galileian view of dynamics, which derives all its vectors not from single isolated objects, but from the mutual relations of the factors in the concrete whole situation, that is, essentially, from the momentary condition of the individual and the structure of the psychological situation. *The dynamics of the processes is always to be derived from the relation of the concrete individual to the concrete situation*, and, so far as internal forces are concerned, from the mutual relations of the various functional systems that make up the individual.

The carrying out of this principle requires, to be sure, the completion of a task that at present is only begun: namely, the providing of a workable representation of a concrete psychological situation according to its individual characteristics and its associated functional properties, and of the concrete structure of the psychological person and its internal dynamic facts. Perhaps the circumstance that a technique for such a concrete representation, not simply of the physical but of the psychological situation, cannot be accomplished without the help of topology, the youngest branch of mathematics, has contributed to keeping psychological dynamics, in the most important fields of psychology, in the Aristotelian mode of thought. But more important than these technical questions may be the general substantial and philosophical presuppositions: too meager scientific courage in the question of the lawfulness of the psychical, too slight demands upon the validity of psychological laws, and the tendency, which goes hand in hand with this leaning toward mere regularity, to specifically historic-geographic concepts.

The accidents of historical processes are not overcome by excluding the changing situations from systematic consideration, but only by taking the fullest account of the individual nature of the concrete case. *It depends upon keeping in mind that general validity of the law and concreteness of the individual case are not antitheses, and that reference to the totality of the concrete whole situation must take the place of reference to the largest possible historical collection of frequent repetitions.* This means methodologically that the importance of a case, and its validity as proof, cannot be evaluated by the frequency of its occurrence. Finally, it means for psychology, as it did for physics, a transition from an abstract classificatory procedure to an essentially concrete constructive method.

That psychology at present is not far from the time when the dominance of Aristotelian concepts will be replaced by that of the Galileian mode of thought seems to me indicated also by a more external question of psychological investigation.

It is one of the characteristic signs of the speculative early stage of all sciences that schools, representative of different systems, oppose each other in a way and to an extent that is unknown, for example, in contemporary physics. When a difference of hypotheses occurs in contemporary physics there still remains a common basis that is foreign to the schools of the speculative stage. This is only an external sign of the fact that the concepts of that field have introduced a method that permits step-by-step approximation to understanding. Thereby results a continuous progress of the science which is constantly more narrowly limiting the consequences for the whole structure of differences between various physical theories.

There seems to me much to indicate that even the development of the schools in contemporary psychology is bringing about a transition to a similar sort of constant development, not only in sensory psychology but throughout the entire field.

NOTES

[1] E. Cassirer, *Substanzbegriff und Funktionsbegriff, Untersuchungen über die Grundfragen der Erkenntniskritik*, Berlin, B. Cassirer, 1910.

2 R. Sommer, "Ueber Persönlichkeitstypen," *Ber. Kong. f. exper. Psychol.*, 1925.

3 Lewin, *Die Entwicklung der experimentellen Willenspsychologie und die Psychotherapie*, Leipzig, S. Hirzel, 1929.

4 L. Lévy-Bruhl, *La Mentalité primitive*, Paris, Alcan, 1922; 5th ed., 1927.

5 In the following pages we shall frequently have to use the term "historic-geographic." This is not in common usage, but it seems to me inaccurate to contrast historic and systematic questions. The real opposition is between "type" (of object, process, situation) and "occurrence." And for concepts that deal with occurrence, the reference to absolute geographic space co-ordinates is just as characteristic as that to absolute time co-ordinates by means of dates. At the same time, the concept of the geographic should be understood in such a general sense as to refer to juxtaposition, correlative to historical succession, and as to be applicable to psychical events.

6 There is no term at present in general use to designate non-historic problem formulations. I here employ the term "systematic," meaning thereby, not "ordered," but collectively nonhistoric problems and laws such as those which form the bulk of present-day physics (see p. 206).

7 E. Mach, *Die Mechanik in ihrer Entwicklung*, Leipzig, 1921.

8 E. Cassirer, *op. cit.*

9 Lewin, *Gesetz und Experiment in der Psychologie*, Berlin-Schlachtensee, Weltkreisverlag, 1927.

10 So far as it is not immediately concerned with an actual "History of the Heavens and the Earth" or a geography.

11 The Greeks, of course, *knew* of experiment.

12 As is well known, the concept of possible exceptions and the merely statistical validity of laws has very recently been revived in physical discussion. Even if this view should finally be adopted, it would not in any way mean a return to Aristotelian concepts. It suffices here to point out that, even in that event, it would not involve setting apart within the physical world a class of events on the basis of its degree of lawfulness, but the whole physical universe would be subject only to a statistical lawfulness. On the relation of this statistical view to the problem of precision of measurement, see Lewin, *Gesetz und Experiment in der Psychologie*.

13 To avoid misunderstanding, the following should be emphasized: When we criticize the opposition of individual and law, as is customary in psychology, it does not mean that we are unaware of the complex problems of the concept of individuality.

14 The association psychology contains an attempt at this sort of homogeneity, and it has really been of essential service in this direction. Similarly, in our time reflexology and behaviorism have contributed to the homogenization of man and animal and of

bodily and mental. But the Aristotelian view of lawfulness as regularity (without which it would have been impossible to support the law of association) brought this attempt to nothing. Consequently, the experimental association psychology, in its attempt at the end of the nineteenth century to derive the whole mental life from a single law, displayed the circular and at the same time abstract character that is typical of the speculative early stages of a science, and of Aristotelian class concepts.

Indeed, it seems almost as if, because of the great importance of frequency and repetition for Aristotelian methodological concepts, the law of association was designed to make use of these as the actual content of psychological principles, inasmuch as frequent repetition is regarded as the most important cause of mental phenomena.

[15] For this section compare especially M. Wertheimer, "Untersuchungen zur lehre von der Gestalt, II," *Psychol. Forsch.*, 1923, 4, 301–350; W. Köhler, *Gestalt Psychology*, New York, Liveright, 1929; K. Koffka, *The Growth of the Mind: An Introduction to Child Psychology* (trans. by R. M. Ogden), New York, Harcourt, Brace; London, Kegan Paul, 1924 (2d ed., 1928); and Lewin, *Vorsatz, Wille und Bedürfnis, mit Vorbemerkungen über die psychischen Kräfte und Energien und die Struktur der Seele*, Berlin, Springer, 1926. A review of the special researches is found in W. Köhler, "Gestaltprobleme und Anfänge einer Gestalttheorie," *Jahresber. d. ges. Physiol.*, 1924.

[16] In psychology it is asserted, often with special emphasis, that one obtains, perhaps from the construction of baby tests, a representation of the "general human," because those processes are selected which occur most frequently in the child's daily life. Then one may expect with sufficient probability that the child will spontaneously display similar behavior in the test.

[17] The contrast between Aristotelian and Galileian views of lawfulness and the difference in their methods may be briefly tabulated as follows:

	FOR ARISTOTLE	FOR GALILEO
1. The regular is	lawful	lawful
The frequent is	lawful	lawful
The individual case is	chance	lawful
2. Criteria of lawfulness are	regularity frequency	not required
3. That which is common to the historically occurring cases is	an expression of the nature of the thing	an accident, only historically conditioned

[18] E. Mach, *The Science of Mechanics* (Eng. trans.), 2d ed., rev., Chicago, 1902.

[19] Naturally this applies also to internal causes, which involve the mutual relation of the parts of a physical system.

[20] It is impossible here to go more fully into the problem of induction. (Cf. Lewin, *Gesetz und Experiment in der Psychologie*.)

[21] I am neglecting here the possibility that one of the field forces entirely disappears.

[22] Even if the distances of the attractive objects and the strength of their attractions were equal, the resulting conflict situation would lead to the same result, owing to the lability of the equilibrium.

[23] H. Poincaré, *La Science et l'hypothèse*, Paris, 1916.

[24] The same holds, incidentally, for biology, which I cannot here especially examine, although I regard psychology in general as a field of biology.

[25] E. Rubin, *Visuellwahrgenommene* Figuren, Copenhagen, Gyldenalske, 1921.

Kurt Goldstein

ON THE STRUCTURE OF PERSONALITY

Kurt Goldstein was born in Upper Silesia, now a part of Poland, in 1878. He received his medical training at the University of Breslau in 1903. In 1930 he was appointed to the University of Berlin as professor of neurology and psychiatry. In 1933 he went to Amsterdam where he completed his most important book The Organism. *He came to the United States in 1935 and was affiliated with the New York Psychiatric Institute and was appointed clinical professor of neurology at Columbia University. He gave the William James lectures at Harvard, which were published in 1940 under the title* Human Nature in the Light of Psychopathology. *The essay which follows is a chapter from this book.*

Goldstein has had considerable influence upon the thinking of contemporary psychologists, since he is the foremost exponent of organismic theory. Some psychologists have tried to link him with Gestalt psychology, a link which Goldstein himself has denied. Organism stems from the attempt by contemporary psychologists to bring body and mind together again. It has found expression in the work of Adolf Meyer, in the new medical orientation of psychosomatics, and in the fundamental work of Coghill on the development of the nervous system in relation to behavior. In psychology, organismic theory has been developed by Kantor, Wheeler, Hilgard, Werner, Murphy, and Rogers. Organismic psychology has undoubtedly borrowed quite a few concepts from Gestalt psychology.

As a result of Goldstein's observations of brain-injured soldiers during the World War I and some of his earlier studies of speech disturbances, Goldstein decided that any particular symptom displayed by a patient could be understood only as a manifestation of the total organism. In effect, mind and body are not separate entities, and the organism is a single unity. What happens to a part affects the whole. Organization is the natural state of the organism, disorganization is pathological and is usually brought about by a threatening environment. Goldstein believed that the individual is motivated by one sovereign drive rather than by a plurality of drives. He used the name of self-actualization or self-realization for this sovereign motive.

ON THE STRUCTURE OF PERSONALITY

Our analysis has disclosed some characteristic trends in the structure of the organism. We have seen the specific significance of the abstract attitude for human behavior, the relation between abstract and concrete behavior, and the role both play in human life. We have familiarized ourselves with the character of conscious and nonconscious events and the way they influence each other. We have become acquainted with some of the general rules that determine the human being's coming to terms with the outer world. We have learned that man is a being who does not merely strive for self-preservation but is impelled to manifest spontaneity and creativeness, that man has the capacity of separating himself from the world and of experiencing the world as a separate entity in time and space. All these features we have inferred from the changes which patients with brain injuries show as a result of the loss of various capacities.

In attempting to understand human behavior, however, we cannot content ourselves with these results so long as we are unable to determine the qualitative structure of the individual human organism in which reactions in a given situation are ultimately rooted. It will be remembered that in all our discussions we had to refer back to the potentialities of the organism as basic for all its activities. We arrived at the conclusion that the drive which sets the organism going is nothing but the forces which arise from its tendency to actualize itself as fully as possible in terms of its potentialities. But what are the potentialities of a given individual?

In making definite general statements about human potentialities we must be mindful of the fact that any such general statements are abstractions from what has been observed in individuals and that we have learned nothing about how to investigate these potentialities. Unquestionably, we have to go back to concrete findings as offered by the isolating methods. But how, among the innumerable observable phenomena, shall we discriminate between those which really correspond to the nature of the individual and those which are only more or less accidental reactions produced by the method that has been used? To decide this question we are in need of a criterion. We are faced here with a problem which lies at the center of modern psychology, the problem of how to characterize personality.

Although for a time the study of personality was neglected to a marked degree by psychology, scholars are now at work in many places trying to find a way to comprehend it. I cannot describe these various attempts here, but those who wish to become thoroughly acquainted with the complexity of this problem and the multiplicity of the attempts to attack it will find Gordon W. Allport's *Personality: A Psychological Interpretation* an excellent guide. (In addition to giving an admirable critical review of the research methods in this field, the book presents a conception of Allport's own which is well worth following up.)

We can assume that those factors belong essentially to an organism which guarantees its existence. There is no question that, in spite of its changing in time and under varying conditions, an organism remains to a certain degree the same. Notwithstanding all the fluctuations of the behavior of a human being in varying situations, and the unfolding and decline that occur in the course of his life, the individual organism maintains a relative constancy. If this were not the case, the individual would not experience himself as himself, nor would the observer be able to identify a given organism as such. It would not even be possible to talk about a definite organism.

This is not the place to elaborate on the highly specialized and subtle controversies that center around the question of specificity versus consistency of traits, nor to reiterate the difficulties which the advocates of specificity have encountered and the criticisms which have been presented recently in various publications. I prefer to take another route. I should like to contribute to the discussion by drawing evidence in favor of consistency from a kind of material which is not so well known but through which biology can supplement psychology.

Consistency appears in pathology in a special form, in the abnormally ordered behavior of the patient. It is true that we have to deal here with a pathologically exaggerated phenomenon, but, as we have explained above, the tendency to ordered behavior belongs to the normal organism as well.

Consequently, in their content observable activities during ordered behavior can be considered as reflecting essential capacities belonging to the individual concerned.

If we consider an organism first in the usual atomistic way, as composed of parts, members, and organs, and then in its natural behavior, we find that in the latter case many kinds of behavior which on the grounds of the first consideration can be conceived of as possible are not actually realized. Instead, a definite selective range of kinds of behavior exists. These we shall classify as "preferred" behavior. To avoid possible misunderstanding it should be pointed out that this term does not imply any conscious awareness or choice of a special way of performing; it is merely descriptive of the observable type of behavior. The way in which the organism actually experiences this state of preferred behavior we shall describe later.

To illustrate the phenomenon we have ample choice in the various fields of pathological human behavior, normal human behavior, and animal behavior. To mention one example in animal life, we know that a cat, when dropped, always lands on its feet. In spite of differing environmental situations it always returns to an optimally balanced position, and this we call the preferred position. If we turn the head of a cat toward one side we find an immediate compensation for this abnormal position, a turning back to the old position. Or, if this is prevented, the posture of the rest of the body changes until a definite total position is again achieved. Thus, within a certain range, the animal has the capacity of adapting itself to differing environmental situations through specific positions of the body. Certain definite positions and actions belong to the various activities of the animal—sitting, eating, sleeping, and so on. The number of possible positions and performances becomes much larger in the higher animals, and especially in man. But even in human beings the possible positions and other modes of behavior by no means correspond in number to the organization of the members concerned, and to the quantitative variability of the environmental situation, as it appears in the usual analytical investigation.

The phenomena to which I wish to point first can be easily observed. Anyone can make the pertinent observations. If a person points to a place that lies more or less to the side, he does not always execute the pointing movement of the arm in the same manner. If the object at which he is pointing is slightly to the side, say to the right, he points only with his extended arm, without moving the rest of the body, in such a way that the angle between arm and the frontal plane of the body is obtuse, about 130° to 140°. If the object at which he is pointing lies more nearly in front of him, then the arm is no longer moved alone, but the trunk too is moved somewhat, toward the other side (the left), so that the pointing arm still forms approximately the same angle with the frontal plane of the body as before. If the object pointed at lies further to the side—say to the extreme right—then the body turns so far to the right that, when the subject points, the angle between the frontal plane and the arm is again essentially the same as before. Of course, it is possible to behave differently; for example, one can point forward while the body remains fixed. But this is not the natural way. In the pointing movement, then, the organism seems to have the tendency to prefer a definite relation between the positions of arm and trunk, and does not conform to the varying environmental demands, although this could very well be done by changing the relation between the arm and trunk positions. To take another example, if one asks a person who is standing to describe a circle, one type of individual usually describes a circle of medium size in a frontal plane parallel to the line of the body, using the index finger of the right hand, the arm being half flexed at the elbow. Larger circles and circles in other positions, possibly executed with the extended arm, seem unnatural and uncomfortable to such persons, who naïvely proceed in the manner we have described. When the trunk is bent forward, however, it is natural for this type to describe the circle in a horizontal plane. One might think the horizontal circle simply the result of the movement of the arm in the same relationship to the upper part of the body as before, and due only to the change in bodily position. If this were true, we should have a circle in an oblique plane; actually, however, it is in the horizontal plane. In this position, apparently, the circle in the horizontal plane corresponds to the preferred behavior. Accurate analysis shows that the manner of describing the circle is unequivocally determined by the *total* situation of the subject. In "total situation" the factor of the subject's attitude toward the task is included; consequently the circle is not made by all subjects in the same way. In a specific situation, however, each one makes it in a specific way which he prefers, quite naïvely, to all other possible ways.

Through this simple experiment one can detect some characteristic properties of individuals belonging to different types of personality. In the one type the objectifying attitude prevails. This type prefers to describe a small circle in an almost frontal parallel plane. Another type is more subjective and has a prevailing motor attitude. This type describes a large circle with extended arm, with excessive movement in the shoulder joint; actually, the subject does not describe a true circle, but moves his arm around in a circular fashion, for which an excessive excursion is most natural. These variations in the execution of the circle reveal differences between men and women, between persons of different character, vocations, and so on. But each person has his own preferred way of performing, and it is this that is essential for the point under discussion.

If one who is accustomed to hold his head somewhat obliquely is forced to hold it straight, it requires a special effort, and, in addition, after a certain time the head will return into the usual, "normal" position, unless the subject prevents this by continuously paying attention to the position of his head. If, in going to sleep, one assumes a variety of positions, one will very soon take a certain position which leads naturally to falling asleep. Much wakefulness is due simply to the fact that one is prevented by some circumstance from assuming this natural position. If we trace the causes for the assumption of such positions, we find a great variety of bodily and psychological factors, but they are almost always fixed for a given individual.

In abnormal persons such phenomena can be observed even better than in normal persons. We have stressed the fact that in our patients we are dealing with states of disintegration or decreased differentiation of personality. The reduced and narrowed personality of the patient is cut off from many events in the outer world which the normal person experiences; it is confined to a more limited order, as is shown by the tendency to abnormal orderliness as a means of avoiding catastrophes. In an organism thus reduced to a simpler form of organization and to a shrunken range of activities, preferred behavior comes strikingly to the foreground, and it ought therefore to be easier to discover its qualitative characteristics.

There are two further circumstances which bring preferred behavior to the foreground in abnormal persons. A normal person, because of his capacity for abstraction and voluntary action, is able to execute tasks in a not so preferred condition and to maintain a not preferred behavior. In addition, he is not restricted to the type of preferred behavior we have been discussing; he is capable also of preferred performances on a higher level, which correspond to his higher level of performance in general. The abnormal person is either wholly incapable of this, or less capable of it, because of his lack of the capacity for abstraction. As a consequence, he is subject in a higher degree to preferred behavior. This is manifest in the fact that a patient who is asked to execute a movement in an uncomfortable position invariably shifts into a more comfortable one unless his attention is concentrated entirely on the task demanded of him. To prevent such concentration it usually suffices to have him carry out the movement with closed eyes. We find then that, even against his will, and usually without his knowledge, he assumes the preferred position. The second circumstance is as follows. In normal persons preferred performances have a certain range of variability within which a performance is still adequate. In abnormal persons this realm is narrowed and the preferred performances are restricted to more rigid positions and to more fixed relations between positions. Thus, for example, in a patient with a disturbance of the left frontal lobe, the preferred position of the head is a slight tilting to the right. This is his natural position. If the examiner brings the head into a straight position or tilts it to the left or even further to the right, the head returns, without the subject's knowledge, into the natural position, where it ultimately will remain. The same thing happens if the patient himself intentionally holds his head in an abnormal position and then pays no further attention to it. A normal person can hold his head in a position that is to a certain degree oblique without discomfort and without having an irresistible tendency to bring the head back to its normal position. The patient is forced to bring his head back.

What we have said about these simple motor actions is valid for all other performances. Every individual reveals preferences not only in the motor sphere, in walking, standing, sitting, eating, and so on, but in the sensory and intellectual processes, in the realm of feeling and voluntary activities. The perceptual field offers some interesting examples. When angles between 30° and 150° are presented optically, not all the steps of the differential threshold are experienced as equal. What we recognize primarily are acute, obtuse, and right angles. (The knowledge of these facts we owe especially to the investigations of Max Wertheimer and other Gestalt psychologists.) These are the preferred impressions around which all others are grouped. Each of the preferred impressions has its range. An angle of 93°, for instance, appears as a poor right angle, deviating somehow from the preferred impression, and does not give the impression of uniqueness. In tachystoscopic experiments it is the circle which is easiest to recognize; polygonal figures are perceived as circles. The circle is also preferred tactually. In the common field of vision there is a preference for the square, for certain curves, symmetry against asymmetry, the vertical against a somewhat oblique line, and so on. Corresponding phenomena are found in the field of tones. The fourth and the fifth are preferred. Small deviations leave perception relatively unaffected. Larger deviations are experienced as an impurity of the fifth (as a bad fifth, et cetera), without one's always being able to say in which direction the deviation occurs.

In pathology the assimilation of an oblique line to a vertical is particularly instructive. The line presented may deviate considerably from the objective vertical and still be experienced as a vertical. This becomes especially apparent when a patient sees the line as a vertical irrespective of whether it deviates to the right or to the left. When I showed one of my patients a stick one foot long at a distance of two yards, first in a vertical position and then in a ten-degree inclination to the left or to the right, he did not notice the difference, but saw only a vertical rod. (Correspondingly, a stick that deviated by ten degrees from the horizontal was always seen as horizontal. Only in deviations above ten degrees did the patient see that the stick was oblique.) When the stick was turned from the vertical into the oblique position he did not see the change until the stick reached the region where he could experience deviations.

The usual explanation of these phenomena, even in normal persons, as being the effects of past experience, habit, training, et cetera, has proved invalid. For material on the subject I may refer here to the numerous experiments in Gestalt psychology and to many published observations in pathology.

Performances under preferred conditions show two characteristics: (1) They represent the most exact execution of the required task under the circumstances given; for example, pointing in the preferred realm is much more exact than elsewhere; (2) they are executed with a feeling of comfort and ease, of fitness and adequacy. Natural performances under not-preferred conditions are experienced as disagreeable, unsatisfactory, unnatural.

As I have explained elsewhere, observation shows that preferred performances are determined not only by the processes in the area where we observe them but also by the condition of the rest of the organism. On the basis of many facts reported elsewhere, I reached the conclusion that preferred behavior in one field always means preferred behavior on the part of the whole organism; the tendency toward preferred behavior is an expression of the fact that the organism constantly seeks a situation in which it can perform at its best and with optimal comfort. Preferred performances are the performances which correspond best to the capacities of the organism. Thus observation of such performances may serve as a means of finding out the capacities—the constants —of the organization and functioning of the individual. The problem of research on personality can thus be substantiated. We are only at the beginning of this kind of quest. Consequently, our discussion will have to deal more with possible methods of procedure in this new field than with a comprehensive survey of facts.

For our purposes we should have to explore an individual by exposing him to a variety of tasks in the fields of perception, motor performance, memory, thinking, and so on; in every instance we must seek to determine what are for him the preferred ways of execution. These consist not only of the actual patterns of the performance as determined from observed overt behavior but include the preferred mediums of execution, as, for instance, retention through the medium of visualization or through the medium of kinesthetic representation. For every task there is an objective optimal manner of adequate execution, and for every individual there is a certain range of possible variations within the realm of his preferences. Consequently, we may call the preferred way of execution a constant of the individual. Ultimately these constants are basic traits of the constitutional and character make-up of the individual. Wherever the individual does his best, notwithstanding the fact that another solution may be more adequate in the light of the objective optimal execution, we are dealing with a constant. Here we face a number of interesting psychological problems and educational implications upon which I can only touch in passing. Very likely the question of individual aptitudes—perhaps even the problem of intelligence—ought to be oriented by the measure to which objective adequacy and the subjective preferred way of performing approach each other.

In all these investigations, of course, we have to be mindful of certain positive and negative criteria.

1. No matter what the behavioral field in which we may test an individual, we are justified in speaking of a constant only when and if other pertinent tests show that, concomitantly with the execution in that field, the rest of the organism is in *ordered* condition; for example, definite behavior in a sensory field can be called constant only when we ascertain that, among other things, blood pressure, respiration, pulse rate, threshold of reflexes, et cetera, correspond to the norm of the individual, which is to be determined for each field in the way just described.

2. If a required task falls outside the realm of the preferred ways that are peculiar to an individual, the corresponding capacity is wanting in a greater or less degree. In such a case we have to vary the methods of examination until the subject is able to cope with the task in some way that he finds natural. For example, an individual is subjected to a task for the execution of which visual memory is a prerequisite (for example, he is asked to memorize a complicated path). Now we find that, if we try to impose the use of visual imagery, his general state becomes disturbed. But if we allow him to choose another means of coping with the task —for instance, memorizing by verbalization instead of visualization—then he may perform fairly well, and his general condition will remain undisturbed. He will verbalize, for example, in this way: "First I have to turn left, then go a hundred feet straight ahead, then turn to the right," and so on. The result is not, of course, so successful as it would be through visualization, which is better adapted to this particular task, but it is precisely because of this that the performance is so revealing to us. It indicates the patient's lack of capacity in the visual field and brings to light his preference for memorizing by language; another person may have another preference, drawing upon kinesthetic memory, for example. Thus this method may be instrumental in discovering the constants in individuals in certain types of performances.

3. The preferred and ordered behavioral forms (constants) are not identical in all the performances of an in-

dividual. On the contrary, the individual responds to every type of task in a special way. This is determined by the organism's tendency to come to terms with the requirements of the outer world in the best possible condition of the whole. This can be attained by various means in various tasks. Consequently, constants have to be determined through the discovery of the *types of task* which the individual can perform most successfully, as evidenced in his preferences. Of course, the circumstances under which a task is presented also have an influence in that they elicit differing preferred ways. But by varying and controlling these circumstances we can find out under what conditions an individual performs best and which of his preferred ways represents a true constant. For example, if a person is faced with a task under conditions which prescribe different speeds of execution, he may execute this task adequately within a certain range of speed but fail when other speeds are demanded. Now we can define his constant on the basis of the knowledge we have gained by introducing controlled circumstantial variables.

The constant in the temporal course of processes must be regarded as particularly characteristic of individuality. The important role of the specific temporal sequence of processes for the ordered activity of the normal organism can be seen in the fact that many pathological phenomena may be regarded as being predominantly the expression of changes in the normal temporal course. This is shown not only by the analysis of symptoms but also by investigations with time-measuring methods (for example, chronaxie and electro-encephalography). Every human being has his own rhythm. This rhythm manifests itself in various temporal measures in various performances, but in any given performance it is always in the same measure. A performance is normal only when an individual can accomplish it in the rhythm that is natural to him for this performance. This holds true for psychological events like emotion or thought processes or acts of will; it is also the case in physiological processes, like the beating of the heart and respiration, and in physicochemical processes. All these time constants indicate particular characteristics of the personality.

From my experience to date I believe that we are justified in selecting a number of factors as guiding for the determination of constants. We have pointed out that each person prefers a definite medium for the performance of certain tasks —for instance, a definite sense modality or the motor apparatus or speech; all this is indicative of certain constants. The preference for a concrete or an abstract approach falls under the same aspect.

But we must be careful not to relapse into the old notion of visual, auditory, motor, and other types. The preference for a certain sensory medium in one field involves certain characteristics of behavior in fields other than the preferred one. These characteristics are not necessarily the same and may be of different natures although they are dependent upon preferences in other fields. They are ultimately embedded and rooted in a definite interactional organization of the personality as a whole. And we must inquire about the qualitative nature of this interaction. For example, if a person is preinclined to the concrete attitude, his behavior is very often accompanied by less emphasis on verbalization and language than is the case in the person preinclined to the abstract. In turn, the latter will fail to regard many details in his environment which do not elicit a language response. Again, the person with a tendency toward the abstract leans toward personalized emotional contacts with others; the person with a tendency toward the concrete is more given to objective realities in social contacts. I mention these examples in order to illustrate two points: (1) that preferred ways in one field influence and shape preferred ways in other fields; (2) that this influence does not occur by direct causation, nor does it manifest itself by uniform phenotypic symptoms, but rather indirectly, by way of the functional organization of the whole. The usual test approach fails here to consider the peculiar interactional dependence of all behavioral fields upon the personality structure as a whole. This complex relation remains to be explored and defined before we can draw conclusions from results in tests which are based on the erroneous premise that any capacity is a factor of *uniform* manifestation in *all* the activities of an individual. Obviously, all this has a bearing upon the much-discussed problem of types, as, for instance, the introvert-extrovert problem.

It is true that as yet we do not know very much about the determinants of the functional relation between a preferred performance in one field and performances in other fields. Pathology, however, has adduced empirical evidence to the effect that changes of constants in one field are accompanied by changes in other fields, so that we may reasonably infer from this material the functional interdependence we have suggested above.

Only on the basis of the knowledge of the structural interrelation between preferred performances in various fields can the problem of what are called types be treated in a reasonable way. In the last few decades an immense literature has accumulated on the subject, and certainly there are groups of individuals who are so similar with respect to some traits, and so different from other individuals, that it seems very reasonable to consider them as belonging together to a special class, as being a type.

In accordance with differing approaches toward the understanding of human behavior, attempts have been made to define these groups in various ways. Plato's metaphysical division of the human soul into three parts we meet again in Bain's classification of men as "mentals," "men of action," and "vitals." The theoretical, economic, social, and political types of Spranger represent the expression of another still more philosophical approach. Physical features form the basis for the creation of anthropological types marked by differences of skull, hair, color, and so on. Impressed by differences in temperament or, more recently, by differences in the functions of the endocrine glands, some investigators have distinguished the melancholic, the choleric, the phlegmatic, and the sanguine types. An interest in the constitutional habit was the basis for the well-known types of Kretschmer which have achieved significance in psychiatry. From the psychological standpoint, types have been discriminated on the basis of the special development of single senses (the auditive type, the visual type, et cetera. Finally there should be mentioned the much-discussed distinction of types according to differences in the individual's general attitude to the world, the introverted and extroverted types.

In all these hypotheses there is certainly something which we feel to be true. Notwithstanding this, all these attempts must be considered failures, even if they happen to be useful for some practical purpose. The never-ending discussion about the correctness of these distinctions shows this only too clearly. The cause of the failure seems to me to be grounded in the same methodological error as the failure of the reflex theory. Single phenomena are taken as essential factors either because of their accidentally coming into the foreground or because of theoretical prejudice. If one considers such single factors as the basis of personality, then one easily yields to the impression that individuals are merely examples of types characterized by these factors. This procedure is wrong, however, in its selection of the determining factors, and does injustice to the nature of individuality. The error in selection could be avoided if the factors were determined by the methods we used in establishing the preferred behavior of the individual. And such a procedure alone would do justice to the nature of individuality. Under these circumstances individuals would never appear as mere examples of types. We could, of course, use the concept of types as a means of sorting the immense variety of individuals for practical purposes. Then it might be useful in several respects. It might serve to reveal the significance of some attributes within the organization of an individual, to reveal the special character which an individual may have through the predominance of such an attribute. Further, the better knowledge of similarities and differences in individuals might help us to understand why some are fitted to get along with one another, others not. Finally, the concept of types, which has frequently been utilized for stressing differences between groups, might be extremely useful in demonstrating factors of similarity.

In connection with the question of the functional relation between those factors of personality which we call preferred, I should like to suggest that factor analysis might offer an appropriate method of approach. Factor analysis tries to discover the factors on the basis of which personality can be understood. If it were possible to determine with this instrument the performances that are preferred (in the sense in which we have defined the term), then we might hope to discover by objective mathematical methods some consistent traits of personality. But this cannot be attained through a comparative investigation of a great number of subjects by means of standardized tests. How can we tell whether we grasp the essential factors with these tests? Methodologically this would be possible only if we could study the tested group under conditions which represent an ordered state for each individual within the group. This presupposes, however, that we are acquainted with the nature of each person in that group; and so we are brought back to the individual as our point of departure. Factor analysis may have value as a technique if it is applied fruitfully to the individual proper, where the major determinants of preferred performances and their structural interrelation within the whole personality may become susceptible of mathematical representation.

The methods which till now we have considered instrumental for determining the basic constants of an individual are more or less confined to a cross-sectional aspect of his *present* behavioral state, but there can be no doubt that we ought to include the temporal aspect of his total behavior— that is, the course of life and the biographical span of the personality explored. In other words, the biographical method, or "anamnesis," as we call it in medicine, is an indispensable supplementary source of information. It can furnish a distinction between the factors which make for ordered or disordered behavior, between genuine constants and the more casual phenotypic reaction patterns, habits, and so on. Only on the basis of information regarding the course of the individual's life can we really identify unequivocally the constants in question, by recognizing their consistency and persistence in the pattern of that person's development.

I am, of course, well aware of a question which probably has beset the mind of the reader since I began to outline the importance of preferred behavior. In what way are the individual's constants influenced and modified by *experience,* and in what way do they in turn shape and mold the experiences of the individual? In attempting to answer this question, we must first of all recognize the ultimate consequence which follows from the conception of preferred behavior. If there are any constants at all, then they must operate as selective and accentuating factors upon the experiences of the individual and the stimuli by which he is affected.

In order to appreciate this rule we must recall the result of our discussion of the problem of drives. It will be remembered that we came to the conclusion that the only drive or basic tendency of the organism is to actualize itself according to its potentialities in the highest possible degree. This is possible only if the organism is faced with situations it can cope with. From what we have learned about the behavior of our patients we know that, if the patient is faced with environmental conditions with which his changed personality cannot come to terms, then he is either not touched at all or he responds with a catastrophic reaction. He can exist—that is, actualize his capacities—only if he finds a new milieu that is appropriate to his capacities. Only then can he act in an orderly way, and only then can his powers of recognition, attention, memory, and learning be at their best.

These facts offer us the key to our question regarding the relation between preferred performances and experience in the normal person. The experiences a person has, or is able to assimilate or acquire, hinge upon his capacities, and these we can infer from his preferred ways of behavior. Only if given the opportunity to realize himself in these ways will he be in an ordered state, which is the basis of good performance; in other words, the more the demands made upon him correspond to his preferred ways of behaving, the more nearly perfect will his achievements be. Of course, these preferred ways of behaving have a determinable range of variation and should not be treated as fixed and rigid patterns. The experienceable environmental segments may vary within certain limits according to this range of variability. And it is this scale of variability which has to be carefully studied and weighed by the investigator of the mutual interdependence of preferred behavior and environmental demands. In order to determine and secure the best possible performances of an individual, and in order to develop his manifold potentialities to their full capacity, we have to know the extent of this interdependence. In pathology this fact is quite obvious. We have acquainted ourselves with the rule that patients have catastrophic reactions, and that their intact performance fields are also reduced, if the demands of the outer world exceed the scope of their impaired capacities. Such a diminution of capacity for performance also takes place if the demands are too low, and the capacities which remain are not called upon and utilized to their full extent. Then a shrinkage of the patient's milieu and personality sets in which is greater than the actual impairment would entail.

From this it follows that, if we wish to prompt the development of an organism in the way best suited to its potentialities, our demands must be neither too low nor too high. The measure of the commensurate degree is to be found in the organism's range of preferred ways of behaving.

We have tried to qualify the relation between the demands of the outer world and the development of the capacities of an individual. With this in mind we can also understand the far-reaching influence of a given milieu upon the actualization of the individual's potentialities. Wherever a person grows up, his environment is of a specific nature, and this provides the cultural and social contents of his developmental socialization; that is, the determination of the specific character of the potentialities of any individual is oriented by the contents of his milieu. This relation between the individual and his environment has implications for a number of much-discussed problems, such, for instance, as questions having to do with learning and education, with racial differences, and with differences in the development of societies and culture. These problems seem to pertain to quite diverse topics, but in my opinion they all go back ultimately to one question —namely, How can the individual actualize himself in the world in the way that best corresponds to his capacities?

I should like to comment briefly on my views on the solution of the problem of differences in character between the inhabitants of different countries and states and between races. These differences stand out most strikingly if, under the influence of a bias, we push single properties into the foreground as chief characteristics and compare the groups or races as to such properties. If we do this, we see only the differences, and are inclined to overrate them in a way that does not at all correspond to the facts. This fallacious procedure is the mainspring of all personal national and racial prejudice and one of the chief causes of much of the suffering and distress in the world. Fundamentally, this state of affairs is the result of a lack or a falsification of knowledge, and of a corruption of science, which lends pseudoscientific arguments and pretended justification to all kinds of abominable actions.

The importance of enlightenment in this field cannot be overstated. It cannot be said often enough that individuals, peoples, races, can actualize themselves without harming each other, that this can be accomplished only by an adequate organization of group life, and that, moreover, the life of any group is guaranteed only in an organization which guarantees the existence of other groups as well. The search for innate factors of any kind which can account for racial differences has been vain, and it is not surprising that this is so. The empirical evidence adduced and the painstaking analysis undertaken by Boas, Klineberg, and others, have shown that all the varieties of race and culture which have been attributed to inborn, unchangeable factors are as a matter of fact culturally and socially determined. Even such differences as those in pigmentation and other constitutional properties do not alter the fact that all men are endowed with equal inherent potentialities. All individual differences granted—and, in fact, precisely because of the vast variety of existing individual differences—we know that no race possesses traits by which it can be distinguished intrinsically from other races. The fact that there is great diversity of traits of personality in all races and groups, and that it traverses the boundaries of every population and sector of the globe, proves that all the phenomena which are common to a group or race are not reducible to common inborn personality traits in that group.

Our biological point of view, especially our notion of preferred behavior, would seem to contradict these statements. Therefore I must re-emphasize the postulate that the range of variability in the preferred ways of human behavior has to be considered as the deciding factor in the variety of social and cultural patterns. Within the interactional relation of environment and organism the members of any group will actualize their potentialities according to the peculiarities of their environment, adapting themselves to its natural and social demands. The problem of differences in society and culture is basically similar to the problem of personality, as far as the contents of life, conflicts and demands, are concerned. Here, too, we cannot draw artificial dividing lines in the true unitary pattern of life in which the person and his environment are interwoven, and we have therefore to reject the doctrines of the extreme environmentalist, as well as those of the extreme believer in heredity. How the relation between individual and society presents itself from our standpoint we shall see later.

On the basis of the relationship we have tried to establish between the range of variability in preferred behavior and the diversity of cultural products, we come to noteworthy conclusions: (1) Our assertion that man as a species is endowed with potentialities which are basically equal is confirmed by the fact that, different from ours as modes of life and thought among primitive peoples are, there is no doubt in the minds of competent anthropologists that, if we transplant a member of such a group into our society, he can be trained to think in our terms; this holds particularly, of course, with regard to children. (2) The importance of the relationship between capacities and environment for ordered behavior may again be ascertained by the study of abnormal persons. In contrast with normal persons, they are so rigidly bound to a definite environment that they perish if this environmental setting is changed in a way not adequate to their preserved potentialities. This pathological fact teaches us something with regard to the adjustment of the normal person to changes of environment. The variability of which we have spoken has a certain limit. If the changes imposed upon an individual or group go beyond the limits of possible adjustmental variations, or if, in other words, the demands of the outer world exceed the range of adequacy for the individual, then catastrophe occurs and the organism can no longer function in orderly fashion. I think this rule may offer us a key to the understanding of certain disorders in individual behavior as well as in the functioning of a society. For example, many a disturbance has been found in the development of children who are left-handed, and who have been forced into right-handedness, in which the disorder appears in fields totally different from the sphere of left- or right-handedness, so that only a scrutinizing analysis can reveal the cause. . . . (3) There is a third aspect in the relation of preferred behavior and environment. It will be recalled that when we turned our attention to the problem of how experience influences preferred behavior, and vice versa, we stressed the fact that the preferred tendencies of an individual operate as selective and accentuating factors upon his experience. It may not seem obvious, but close reflection suggests that there is an intimate relation between the preferred modes of behavior of the individual and the psychological motivations of his conduct, contact with others, likes and dislikes, and attitudes toward life.

Just as we have agreed with Woodworth that habits once formed may achieve a motivational impulse, so we may assume that the drive to actualize one's potentialities also operates as a motivating force in one's emotional valuations in accordance with one's preferred ways of acting.

Gardner Murphy

AFFECT AND PERCEPTUAL LEARNING

Gardner Murphy was born in 1895 in Chillicothe, Ohio. He studied at Harvard, Yale, and Columbia. Columbia awarded him a Ph.D. in 1923, and he taught at Columbia and was also chairman of the Department of Psychology at the City College of New York. In 1952 he was appointed director of research at the Menninger Foundation in Topeka, Kansas. His main publications include Personality: A Biosocial Approach to Origins and Structure, General Psychology, Experimental Social Psychology, *and* Historical Introduction to Modern Psychology.

Murphy's personality theory is very eclectic, as he himself states: "We have used jointly, or even simultaneously, the Gestalt doctrine of insight, the psychoanalytic principles regarding psychodynamics, especially unconscious drives, and the associationist doctrines regarding the gradual forging of mental connections, transfer of training, summation and dissociation."

Murphy believes that the basic components of personality are the physiological dispositions that arise from underlying genetic and embryological dispositions, canalizations that are formed early in life, the conditioned responses that are deeply ingrained through repeated enforcement processes, and the cognitive and perceptual habits that are the joint product of canalization and conditioning. Murphy is especially interested in theories of motivation, and he believes that interests that occur in the artistic and manual areas are the direct result of tensions in specific regions of the body. Thus music appreciation and a love of wrestling are actually organic traits according to Murphy. This part of Murphy's motivational theory is far-reaching. What other theories might call "acquired" or "learned" may be in actual fact organic traits. It is Murphy's general position that the biosocial viewpoint of personality is in effect a genetic theory of personality, and his major efforts are devoted to formulating comprehensive hypotheses regarding the way in which personality develops.

AFFECT AND PERCEPTUAL LEARNING

A question directed to a group of modern psychologists regarding the role of affect (or the physiological substrate of affect) in perception might elicit the following responses: (*a*) Affect cannot influence perception. (*b*) Affect can intensify or weaken the perceptual response (for example, through a mechanism like that of dynamogenesis or intersensory processes). It may intensify, or prolong, or consolidate the percept. It may prevent the perceptual structure from changing (this is sometimes called rigidity), or it may make it more labile, but it may not directly alter perceptual structure. (*c*) Affect can intensify or weaken certain aspects of a perceptual response, as in some of the "perceptual defense" studies. (*d*) Affect can intensify or weaken certain aspects of a perceptual response in such a way as to influence later perceptual responses, for example, it can result in perceptual learning. The present paper explores some of the issues related to the last of these possibilities.

I

It is interesting to note the unfinished debate (compare Socrates versus the Sophists, and the Gibsons [4] versus Postman [15]) between those who assert and those who deny that the development of perception must move toward realistic contact with the environment. But in view of the fact that in everyday life, and in our laboratories, our hopes and fears lead to appearances that are notoriously deceptive, it seems to the present writer a little odd that affect does not enter into these discussions of perceptual development (or rather, I should say that affect is not officially included among the factors influencing the perceptual act).

This becomes still more strange when one notes that "set," "hypothesis," "attitude," "mood," and "value" are almost universally agreed upon as influencing perception. When one focuses on these processes so as to see them at close range, they are seldom affect-free. And the influences which they exert are, so far as I know, universally conceded to last on into subsequent perceptual responses, as has long been clear, especially since the time of Rubin (23).

The issue here is not whether perception moves toward greater *realism* or toward *better organized* structure, or toward finer differentiation and fuller integration. Space precludes discussion of these and many other possibilities. The present paper presupposes that the types of perceptual learning described by the Gibsons exist. Rather, the aim is solely to explore the rather neglected but very pressing issue regarding the role of affect in perception and in perceptual learning. The only aspect of affectivity considered here is the pleasantness-unpleasantness dimension.

II

In exploring the possibility that affect may alter the emphasis, or dominance relations, within a perceptual act, the following seem to be some of the more easily identifiable processes: (a) the percept may be so structured as to reveal emphasis upon a component which has been associated with positive hedonic tone (autistic perception, that is, a drive-satisfying type); (b) the percept may be so structured as to cope with a difficult or challenging environment by emphasizing a component associated with negative tone, or, in any event, with components acting as a threat, requiring an "alerting" response. It will be noted that "alerting" likewise operates in the service of a "pleasure principle" by warding off that which might cause distress. It constitutes a roundabout way to pleasure (as in "secondary process thinking" in psychoanalysis); (c) a percept may be so structured as to be more satisfying, for example, more interesting in its own right, not because it represents the environmental possibilities to be more favorable than they actually are, but through the greater satisfaction that comes from grasping more fully, rather than less fully, the nature of the stimulus. Here belongs, for example, the aesthetic satisfaction of hearing a full orchestration rather than a few tuneful bits of symphonic music. Perhaps we should add, here, the satisfaction of being independent, not being suggestible, and so on, but the case for satisfaction in making contact with reality remains. (d) A percept may become rigid through a circular-response mechanism (remotely reminiscent of causalgia, or fingers clutched about a live wire). The relation of such rigidity to repetition compulsion may be worth exploring. In many instances, however, the rigidity is not a simple reflex, but expresses a fear of giving up the percept, lest we be lost. This is especially evident when one cannot give up a rigid self-image, through fear of disorientation or of having nothing left to cling to. The clinically-minded reader will think of many other categories. (e) A percept may be consolidated in such a way as to hurt the perceiver, through the mechanism described by Freud as masochism; the punishment gives satisfaction.

Most (if not all) of these mechanisms, whatever their ultimate form, are most easily conceptualized in hedonistic terms; they all seek pleasure or release from stress. The emphasis of the present paper is on pursuing just *one* of the present possibilities, namely, the possibility wherein perceptual learning is of a simple, directly pleasure-seeking type, in which the perceptual structure is so organized as to accent or emphasize those components which directly give pleasure. At a later time I hope to be able to do more justice to those instances in which the emphasis is carried so far that something gets *left out*, and consequently there are distortion, evasion, misinterpretation.

In earlier studies some of us (8, 25) have used Rubin's terminology of "figure and ground" to describe the emphasis or dominance factor within a perceptual whole. This use may or may not be advisable. In the present paper the concept of "emphasis," as used by Tolman (30) and Muenzinger (13) will be used, and an attempt made to suggest that we are basically dealing with the same thing as "dominance," as used by Razran (18), or "regnancy" as used by Murray (14). That particular form of dominance known as "figure and ground" will be noted only when the situation resembles that of Rubin.

I suggest two hypotheses: (*a*) subject to exceptions to be noted later, perceptual structure changes in such fashion as to give *emphasis* to that which is pleasant, in contrast to that which is unpleasant or affectively neutral; (*b*) many such changes are *cumulative*; constituting a form of perceptual learning. This means that directional modifications in cognitive structure are made as a result of affective factors. This would bring us rather closely into line with Chein's (10) definition of autism as "the movement of cognitive processes in the direction of need satisfaction." It is suggested that positive affect not only plays a vital role in the *modification* of perceptual responses but also that it is a clue to some forms of perceptual learning.

Postponing for the present the detailed discussion of negatively toned components in the perceptual field, the hypotheses mean that, given two or more aspects of a perceptual whole and repeatedly associating one of these with positive affect, will tend, when these various perceptual aspects are simultaneously presented, to lead the dominant role to be taken by that which has been associated with positive affect.

We assume, of course, that our learner, if awake, is actively forming these associations; shifting his attention; interested in this detail, bored with that one; and making such sense as he can out of his situation. Perception is an integrative process or act rather than an unselective intake of stimuli. What we are concerned with here is rather a specific empirical relation between the various aspects of the perceptual whole, namely, the apparent fact that positive affect (pleasantness) may serve to modify a perceptual response by accentuating some aspects of it.

III

While my purpose is not chiefly historical, I should like to give a few illustrations of recent efforts to cope with this problem. Woodworth (32) has pointed out that we should regularly recognize an affective factor in learning and should describe this as "reënforcement of perception," rather than reinforcement of an *act*. In the course of experiments in salivary conditioning, Razran (20) showed that paintings which had one affective status for a given hungry subject took on a different aspect (apparently because of a new accent on some features and the loss of accent on other features) as a result of a food stimulus paired with them. Sanford (24) demonstrated that the meaning of photographs as indicating objects related to food was altered by periods of food deprivation. Schafer and Murphy (25) devised a simple situation involving two caricatured faces, one face associated with a reward, the other with a punishment, and showed that when the two faces were presented together, the one that had been previously "rewarded" took on the dominant role. This experiment, when repeated in a modified form by Rock and Fleck (22), gave nonconfirmatory results; but Jackson (8) has repeated both the Schafer-Murphy and the Rock-Fleck experiments, and showed that among other things the field within which such modifications are to be induced must be small and compact, the Schafer effect being easy to reproduce when the Schafer technique is used. Incidentally, one of the most interesting things in the Jackson study was the evidence for intra-individual consistency. Those subjects who showed this effect more plainly with one pair of faces tended to show it likewise with another pair of faces. Smith and Hochberg (28) have shown that the Schafer effect can be reproduced without using reward; they utilized electric shock as punishment and found that the shock had a tendency to prevent the shocked aspect from appearing as figure. This raises the old question of whether the absence of punishment is in itself a "reward."

Yet in the huge welter of experiments and communications appearing in the "New Look" psychology and the complex issue of the role of affect and impulse upon perceptual and other cognitive structures, I am not aware that much is known about the specific way in which the perceptual field is altered by affect. It is true that much has been written about perceptual defense. But in perceptual defense we have a process of exclusion, and the actual dominance relations within the perceptual field are not investigated.

IV

I should like first to stress the importance of *instability* in perceptual structure, if modification is to occur. In attempting a preliminary answer to this question, James Simpson, in helping me with this paper, has suggested a diagrammatic way (Table 1) in which to show a hypothetical course of perceptual development under the influence of various needs and through the utilization of rewards (stimuli bearing positive affect). In Table 1 we are to imagine our hypothetical subject as presented tachistoscopically with a complex visual schema including the numbers 1—4—9 embedded in other material. The first response is one of curiosity, which in the light of the work of Harlow and his associates (5) I should like to call both a cognitive and an affective response, and a social response to the experimenter. The experienced affect is perhaps at first a slight anxiety with mixed feeling tone. The perceptual response is the number sequence 1—4—9, an undistorted percept. The subject at this time makes no overt response because the initial percept is unstable and fleeting. We proceed to a second presentation. There is a need to achieve, as the subject warms up to the task, and also a persisting need to solve the problem and to make a social response to the experimenter. This mixture of pleasant and unpleasant components will be a factor in unsteadying the percept, and there are variations around the 1—4—9 response. For example, in this instance the instability leads to the addition of an additional number 2, since 1—4—9—2 is one of the overlearned stock number combinations available near

TABLE 1

HYPOTHETICAL COURSE OF PERCEPTUAL DEVELOPMENT UNDER THE INFLUENCE OF VARIOUS NEEDS AND THROUGH UTILIZATION OF REWARDS (STIMULI BEARING POSITIVE AFFECT)

AMBIGUOUS TACHISTOSCOPIC STIMULUS	SEQUENCE IN TRIAL 1	NEED PATTERN (CONSCIOUS AND UNCONSCIOUS)	PREDOMINANT AFFECT (KIND/AMOUNT)	PERCEPTUAL RESPONSES	OVERT RESPONSES
X1X4X9X	1st	Cognitive: (curiosity) Social: (experimenter)	Anxiety, Unpleasant and Pleasant/Minimal	149 (undistorted percept)	None
	2nd	Achievement and Cognitive (solve problem) Social: (experimenter)	Pleasant and Unpleasant/Moderate	1492 (cognitive distortion)	None
	3rd	Sex and Social (girl friend)	Erotic: Pleasant/Strong	5-1492 (affective distortion)	None
	4th	Achievement and Cognitive (solve problem) Social: (experimenter)	Pleasant/Moderate	149 (cognitive correction)	"149" (correct solution)
					(Subject receives $ reward)
	IN SUBSEQUENT TRIALS:				
X1X4X9X	1st	Acquisition (money) Achievement (solution) Social: (experimenter)	Pleasant/Moderate	149 (learned interpretation)	"149" (correct solution)

to consciousness and to the effector response system. On the third presentation, however, a slight shift of internal conditions causes our subject to remember his girl friend with considerable delight in thinking of a coming date, and her telephone number 5—1492 is perceived. Still, however, there is no overt response. On the fourth presentation, the cognitive and achievement and social factors remain. There is a pleasant lingering affect. The reality trend has swung again slightly into the ascendant and the cognitive response 1—4—9 is now called for and uttered, and the subject receives a reward. In subsequent trials the first thing to be noted is the re-inforcement effect of the reward and the further structuring of the response 1—4—9. Similar sequences can be devised for other patterns.

Our interest is in the question: Where and how does the reward get in its work? The issue which seems to me to call for attention is the fact that initially there are *unstable* perceptual responses which permit modifications—sometimes only a shift in dominance relations, sometimes so gross and heavy an accent on one detail that other aspects of reality are missed, and there is distortion or error. It is by virtue of the momentary instability of the perceptual system that the reward can exert its influence. Doubtless my own autistic distortions are responsible for any assigning importance to these issues; but I should like to raise a series of questions upon which clarification may perhaps be achieved through the critique, controversy, and experimentation that may be stimulated.

V

Suppose we ask ourselves now just *how* can an unstable perceptual response system be *modified*? It may be modified either through changes in the world of outer stimulation or through changes inside the organism. Under the former head, absolute or relative increases or decreases in the intensity of the stimuli may alter the perceptual field. Some aspects of the field may be muted, or may even be eliminated. Other aspects, therefore, may be relatively or indeed absolutely emphasized. This is what we mean by an alteration in the relative emphasis in various parts of the field. Secondly, it is my thesis that stimulation from within the organism (for example, from various internal sources, including neural and endocrine sources) may at any time accent or mute some aspects of the perceptual field. It is suggested that affective processes, whatever their physiology, or however well we may learn to gauge their presence by the galvanometer or other instruments, should regularly exert some influence. The influence might be of a purely intersensory type, as a color may change appearance during the action of a sound or tactual stimulation; but at any rate, it is hard to see how affective processes could be so isolated from the functions of the organism as to exert no influence at all on the perceptual response system. Granting the great importance of the structural properties of the environmental stimulus and the structural properties of the responding organism, affectivity nevertheless appears to involve a continuous input of stimulation, resulting in facilitation or inhibition. A commonplace illustration is the fact that we are so delighted with something that we do not notice an imperfect detail, or are so angry that we "look for trouble." We must therefore ask more precisely about the processes that might lead affectively toned material to take a dominant place in perceptual structure.

Let us note some relations of affectivity to body movement (the following are commonplace evolutionary assumptions; compare, for example, Holt, 6): Movement toward and movement away from objects are present even in unicellular animals. As organization becomes more complex, the means of locomotion and of contact and avoidance become more complex, but the basic differentiation between "movement toward" and "movement away from" remains. Let us assume that primitive awareness, when once it begins, involves some capacity to differentiate stimulus objects from their contexts. Moreover, in so far as we note that primitive behavior is oriented positively toward some elements in the environment and negatively toward others, let us assume that there are primitive impulsions toward and away from objects. From the present viewpoint, these primitive impulsions toward and away from objects may involve affects. Positive hedonic tone may appear at the level of experience when we are approaching an object and getting more and more contact with it. Some objects are biologically beneficent. *In the long run, from an evolutionary point of view, we should expect positive movement to occur in the case of those objects which it is "good for" the organism to possess. By the same logic, there is a primitive basis for positive affect; positive affect is the subjective aspect of approach behavior.*

The types of biologically determined perceptual responses that we have been assuming are of course enormously elaborated by the learning process, and in particular by the education of human beings in the world of symbols. Objects that are at first devoid of great affect (words, gestures, coins, et cetera) come to carry enormous affective freight, and one's seeing and hearing may be influenced by the *meaning* of the symbol, that is, the symbol may take on a dominant role because of what it stands for. But it is not clear that the basic functioning of *affect* could be altered by this fact. Indeed, this fact seems to point to our human dependence on abstract or remote objects by virtue of their linkage, in our life history, with more concrete and immediate goals. The dominance relations within a perceptual field may indeed be determined largely by very remote, subtle, and complicated acquired meanings of the components of the field. But the hypothesis is offered that however the affective character of these components of the field arises, their affective character influences their dominance relations.

When, therefore, at the level of direct satisfactions of biological needs, objects begin to stimulate the individual, there is a tendency for the perceptual response to the satisfying object to become more and more prominent. Primitive movements of approach are therefore accompanied by primitive positive hedonic tone. Perceptual responses to objects that are pleasant tend to move into prominent positions in the perceptual structure.

It is agreed that expectancy and hypothesis testing are fundamental in perceptual learning. But why does expectancy in relation to the pleasant become dominant at times over expectancy in relation to the neutral or the unpleasant? Perhaps part of the problem is the means-end relationship; that is, we look for trouble if this helps us to *avoid* trouble. But if we are simply functioning at a fantasy level, or if, in a post-test series, we are simply ruminating on the good, bad, and indifferent things through which we have passed, there is no means-end service accomplished by expectancy related to the neutral or the unpleasant, and the pleasure principle can operate.

From an organism's general evolutionary position, response to the "good" and to the "dominant" in the environment are often identical. We must not miss the good things that are available. Expectancy leads to sensitization. But carry-over of this good-expecting attitude can be very disruptive of adjustment; when these attitudes carry over into situations in which life is rigged against us, we get into trouble with reality, since perception has to be basically a reality-oriented process. It is for this very reason that perceptual responses become rather deeply ingrained, and it is for this very reason that there is a danger that perception will miscarry at times and lead us to expect the good even where it is not there. We know at heart, as Ulysses did, that we have to be lashed to the mast, or the sirens and the lotus-eaters will get us.

From this standpoint it is believed logical to conclude that during continuous or repeated stimulation, pleasant things tend to receive more and more emphasis in any unstable perceptual field. I cannot here discuss the question whether such hedonic factors in learning operate in essentially the same way at this primitive level and also at the level of such complex phenomena as self-defense, self-justification, and the intrinsically satisfying process of rational planning. Razran (18, 19), among others, has amassed much evidence that there are levels of learning. I have, however, indicated (page 256) where my bias lies, namely, in the belief that a pleasure principle enters into much that at first sight seems free of it; it seems to me that the perceptual field is structured by the satisfactions of the social and cognitive worlds, for example, through the satisfactions which thinking subjects necessarily confront through the joys and the vicissitudes of the thought process itself. I cannot, therefore, find an area where hedonistic perceptual theory cannot apply.[1]

Positive affect will be present whenever we are carrying forward evolutionarily given goal-seeking activities. The satisfactions, of course, may be aroused either directly by the goal or by objects associated or conditioned to the goal, and the process may be quite complex, as in being gratified through money or honorific letters after one's name. The hypothesis entertained is that any aspect of a perceptual field which is signalized in this fashion by gratification is likely to be the conscious aspect of a goal-seeking activity. Moreover, in the light of the general theory of dominance in the theory of conditioning, response to that which is *most* gratifying will tend to have the highest position in the dominance hierarchy. The greater the satisfaction, therefore, the greater the movement, during successive encounters with a situation, toward the apex of the dominance hierarchy.

If we now ask by what process a component in a perceptual whole can be reinforced by the sheer presence of affect, we may tentatively restate the problem as one ultimately involving the dominance relations which may perhaps hold, not only in conditioning, but in all psychological events, as shown in Figure 1. From Razran's extensive analysis (18) it appears that conditioning does not simultaneously attach S_1 to R_2 and S_2 to R_1; the dominance relation is expressed in the fact (ordinarily, at least) that one of these possibilities is realized, not both.

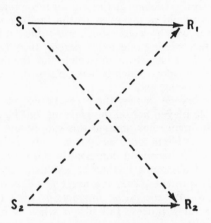

Figure 1. Dominance relations

Let us at the same time use the Birch-Bitterman (2) concept of "sensory integration." Sensory integration (as well as disintegration or loss of connection) goes on continuously. If the question be raised, "How can such integration be achieved by an affective component?" our reply is that the affective component often betrays the dominance relations at work in the response system, which as we have seen is both an *affective* and an *overt* behavior system. For example, when you say, "Tell me what you see," the subjects in the experiments cited above moved in the direction of emphasizing that aspect of the field which had previously been associated with reward. Sensory integration takes one form through the action of affect, and simultaneously excludes other forms. The results of such association should be cumulative, as are the effects of most types of learning involving simple association; and the experimental data, as in the Schafer-Murphy and Jackson experiments, confirm this view.

VI

Under the very simple conditions described so far, it is sufficient to say that that which is not satisfying is that which is shoved to one side. Perhaps the biological process of escaping or shoving to one side is the basis for the phenomena of negative affect. The turning away or rejection of an experience at the conscious level corresponds, from the present viewpoint, to the biological turning away or rejection of the object. This would apply even to the Smith and Hochberg experiment in which electric shock was sufficient basis for the associated face's being rejected. I suggest that the perceptual field takes on a structure in which the dominant role is played by that aspect which is being pursued, and ground by that which is being fled.

But, as everyone knows, there are important instances of dominant role played *not by the pleasant, but by the unpleasant*. Charles Snyder has phrased this simply and well: "How is an organism able to move *away* from a given object without that object's first becoming dominant in the perceptual field?" A problem that cannot further be avoided! Obviously, the whole of the present thesis, if correct at all, can apply only to a *trend during successive interactions with the environment*, not with a process full blown when it first appears. It is only with experience, if ever, that structure becomes stabilized in a satisfying way. Perception is often unstable, wobbly, during the learning. Moreover, the unpleasant is at times dominant *both at the time of its first appearance and after the achievement of stable structure*.

I have indeed taken on a rather large problem when stating that that which is associated with unpleasantness is among the things tending to become nondominant. In some situations that which is most frustrating is actually most likely to be observed. This is analogous, of course, as already noted, to the "emphasizing" (or alerting) effect. It is often touch and go whether we shall *face* or *avoid* a threat stimulus. Since in this paper I am not allowing myself to dilate upon all the conditions (expectancy, masochism, et cetera) that might lead to such a result, I will oversimplify by referring to the asymmetrical ∪ curves which have sometimes resulted from studies of "recall of pleasant and unpleasant experiences" (11, 12; compare also 16). These curves, ideally taking perhaps such a form as is shown in Figure 2, may represent simultaneously the advantage of pleasant over unpleasant, and the advantage of strong over weak affect. *Severely unpleasant* alerting situations can take precedence over *mildly pleasant* situations. That which becomes dominant may be that which is very annoying rather than that which is mildly pleasant. Indeed, I gladly agree that there are many instances analogous to the phenomenon of trauma, in which the alerting affect may have consequences far *more* marked than those of positive affect. Various types of ∪ curves would therefore be appropriate to depict the situation. This means that we must include a dimension of sheer *intensity* along with our affectivity dimension. And, to be logical, we must again say that the unpleasant gets into the picture in proportion to its intensity, and because it is ultimately a means to the pleasant.

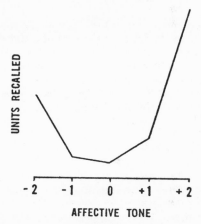

Figure 2.   Advantage of pleasant over unpleasant, and strong over weak affect

In the recent studies by Dulaney (3) and Pustell (17) another dimension of the punishment situation is stressed. Dulaney appears to have shown that when one of four tachistoscopically presented figures is severely shocked, and S learns to avoid *reporting* that this one "stands out" among the rest, he also learns to avoid *perceiving* that this one "stands out"; the result appears to be experimental as well as behavioral. But in Pustell's parallel study in which the shock comes so quickly after the stimulus that S *cannot avoid it*, many Ss (notably the males) develop "vigilance" (lowering of thresholds for the critical stimulus) rather than defense.

Such studies may help us to understand the omnipresent importance of *set* in perceptual learning. Set can either lower a perceptual threshold or raise it. The question is why we are sometimes set for the pleasant, or, as in the vigilance experiments, why we are set for the unpleasant. Maybe because we can thus better *use* the pleasant or thus *get away* from the unpleasant. From such a viewpoint, needs and readinesses are the same thing. The conflict between hypothesis and need psychology disappears.

The discussion of the conditions governing the dominance of the unpleasant could lead into all outdoors, and I must call a halt. But let me emphasize once again that the present approach recognizes that the unpleasant often can, and does, become dominant.

VII

It is time now to look at those issues, among the ones presented, that can be decided by experiment. The following questions must be answered in the course of any investigation dealing with these issues:

Under what conditions does the "Schafer effect" (perceptual learning process resulting from dominance of the pleasant) appear?

1. In which sensory modalities?
2. Does it appear when reward alone is used, or only when reward and punishment are combined?
3. At what levels of awareness does it appear?

a. For example, does it appear when affectively toned stimuli are presented below their usual (sensory) threshold value?

b. Does it appear when affective material is supraliminal, but no explicit connection is formed by S between affect and the rest of the perceptual field?

c. Does it appear *only* when an explicit connection is formed?

d. Does it appear *only* when the connection is verbalized?

e. Does it appear *only* when there is ego involvement in forming the connection?

4. What is the role of frequency, intensity, vividness in such learning?

5. What is the role of extinction (and of consolidation) when rewards and punishments are removed?

6. Does this kind of approach have any utility at all when the satisfactions come chiefly from events inside the person— as related, for example, to self-respect? How is the reappraisal of oneself during psychotherapy related to the simplest figure-ground dynamics?

7. Last, but by no means least, what is the relation of *extrinsic* rewards and punishments to the *intrinsic* satisfactions which come directly from clear, internally consistent, well-oriented perception, and the frustrations which come from confused, bewildered, internally inconsistent perception? If there is such a thing as joy in discovery, there is such a thing as joy in the sheer use of the perceptual apparatus, and this must be carefully distinguished from the delights of autistic distortion, if for no other reason than that at a later time we shall have to compare the satisfaction of reality seeking with the satisfaction of reality evasion.

The experiments about to be described comprise a group of interlocking studies in the visual, tactual, and auditory modalities, utilizing adult subjects who can, when desirable, take part in all of the various experiments and in other experiments and clinical studies at the Menninger Foundation.[2]

I will sketch here a few of the studies which my associates and I are carrying out in the attempt to test such hypotheses as these and to develop methods suited to the definition of affect and its role in perceptual learning.

After Jackson's repetition of the Schafer-Murphy experiment, one of the more obviously pressing needs was to ascertain whether similar results could be achieved in other modalities. After a large number of pilot studies introducing variations in the basic design of the Schafer study, we finally decided to stick as literally as possible to the bare outline of the Schafer method, but to use the auditory and tactual modalities. In the auditory field the technique finally developed was to tape-record two voices, each reading prose material (from Rachel Carson's *The Sea Around Us*); to present in planned haphazard order the materials read by one voice and by the other; then in the test series to present by tape recording a conglomerate of the two—that is, both voices on the same tape—and ascertain to which voice the subject made his perceptual response (he could not hear both at once). These investigations by Fred and Charles Snyder (29) have indicated that an auditory version of the Schafer effect is feasible: the subjects tend to hear those materials which were associated with monetary rewards in competition with those associated with monetary punishments.

In the investigation of tactual figure-ground effects by Teodoro Ayllon and Robert Sommer (1), ceramic plaques were used, with a deep irregular contour line vertically down the middle. In the training series, the subject traced the groove with his gloved right index finger, while looking at a right-pointing face painted to the left of the groove or a left-pointing face painted to the right of the groove, and simply learned the names of these faces while receiving electric shock for one face and no shock for the other. (The absence of shock appears to be a reward, but this controversial question will have to be studied much more fully at a later time.) In the *test* series, the subject, now blindfolded, moved his gloved finger down the groove, which (except for set-breaking figures) was always the same. Here there was a trend to perceive the nonshocked face (a "defense" reaction in accordance with the autism principle) when the unpleasantness of the shock was rated by S as "slight."

When, however, the shock was at a level reported to be "moderate" or "severe," there was a significant tendency toward "alerting," that is, to perceive the *shocked* face. Further studies with both auditory and tactual figure-ground effects are being carried forward, with emphasis upon three problems: first, the problem of *generalization*, when new material is used that has something in common with the material on which training has already been carried out; second, the "extinction" of freshly acquired perceptual habits; and third the defense and "alerting" responses at different levels of unpleasantness. Several other half-finished studies of perceptual dominance are under way, designed to answer some of the questions stated on pages 268-69.

We have also been interested in the use of the Ames techniques (9), especially with reference to the questions: Can the perceptual distortions or misinterpretations investigated by the Ames methods be reduced or eliminated to some degree by the use of affective factors related to certain cues? Can the unlearning of such misinterpretations be facilitated by a process through which distortion is punished and correct perception apprehended? James Simpson (26) selected the aniseikonic-lens situation as one serviceable for such studies. He has apparently established the fact that positive and negative affect, induced, respectively, by music and a ratchet sound, operate to accentuate or weaken the distortion effects of the very complex visual field which the aniseikonic lenses present, so that acceptance or rejection of the usual aniseikonic effects is differentially facilitated. In so far as the test situation, after music and ratchet sound have been discontinued, presented the subject with a complex and conflicting set of cues for space perception, we may say, by a somewhat forced use of language, that this was also a study of the influence of affect upon figure-ground organization. It is probably better, however, to avoid such linguistic forcing, and simply to say that the interpretation of the cue structure depended upon affects which had been aroused in the earlier (learning) situation.

Perhaps it is worth while to say still once again that we do not believe that "autism" effects are universally demonstrable. We do not believe that affect is the only factor in perceptual learning. We do not believe that affect operates in the same way in all persons. We do not believe that age, sex, and cultural factors can be ignored. Indeed, the structure of the affective life, person for person, has proved to be a major problem to cope with in such studies. We find, for example, that certain effects are relatively easily obtained with naïve subjects, but in general very uncharacteristic of subjects who understand such experiments and introduce problems and hypotheses of their own regarding the processes at work. As would be suspected on the basis of the material reported by Razran (20), the perceptual changes belong at a certain level of learning, and characterize particular types of orientation to a task. Our question is not: Why do our colleagues resist extensions of the evidence for autistic phenomena? but simply: *Under what conditions* does the Schafer effect appear?

VIII

Indeed, working as we do in a clinical atmosphere, side by side with those whose concern is with the endless richness of differences in human needs and cognitive patterns, and working with the "perception team" of George Klein, Riley Gardner, Philip Holzman, and Herbert Schlesinger, we have been constantly alerted to the problem of individuality. While our chief concern is with the general laws stated above, this does not mean that individual differences can be ignored. We have no choice, for facts about individuality leap at us and upon us. We shall attempt, then, to show that the reality of individual differences does not invalidate our belief that general laws are our first problem.

The fact seems to be that among subjects in most such experiments—young adults of little more than average sophistication—there are always a few who appear consistently to move "in the unexpected direction." Long ago, Razran (19) pointed out that some of his subjects in simple adult human conditioning situations moved in the expected direction "like Pavlov's dogs," that some did not condition, while others conditioned "in the unexpected direction." Others of the New Look investigators have, of course, been finding this sort of thing. We are inclined to think that the following problems take shape in consequence of this face: (a) Some of the "rewards and punishments" as seen from the experimenter's point of view are simply not rewards and punishments for the particular subjects. To expect such "rewards and punishments" to have exceptionless consequences would be like expecting a color-blind man to respond in a normal way to a rainbow. In Jackson's study, those Ss who admitted feelings about the money rewards and punishments showed a very marked tendency to move in the rewarded direction, while those who denied feelings about the money showed a tendency to move in the opposite direction. (b) Some of the rewards and punishments are not at that point on the U curve to which we assigned them. They are either intensely gratifying, bring in ego involvements—"see how smart I am," et cetera—or they serve as threats and challenges, as alerting stimuli which may bring negative affect when we expect positive, et cetera. "What is he trying to do?" "Is he one of these psychologists that always has a trap for you?" Or, most commonly, "What is the point of this shoving money at me and taking it away?" All these considerations mean that even money, which is the most ancient and general of human inventions designed to provide something that has a dependable affective value throughout a community and can be standardized on a hedonistic basis as something that one strives to win and hates to lose, does not induce affect of dependable uniformity. If we can find rewards and punishments that will better serve the purpose, we shall be glad to use them; indeed, we have interesting results using unpleasant tones, electric shock, mild frustrations in carrying out intellectual tasks, and other annoying stimuli, as well as music stimuli, empirically "calibrated" for affect.

In general, however, we are inclined to believe that it does not make a great deal of difference what positive and negative stimulation we use, provided that the affect is fairly uniform. Under these conditions we appear to be dealing not with genuine exceptions with reference to affectivity in connection with perceptual dominance, but rather with the fact that sometimes no affectivity is present, and sometimes the affectivity which we assumed to be present was replaced in some subjects by a different kind of affect. If such affective categories are empirically determined, they must be freshly tried out through "cross validation."

Cross validation of this sort is feasible. It is at present our impression that those subjects who move in the direction of punishment in some experiments tend to do so in other such experiments to a degree greater than would be expected by chance alone; we seem to encounter the recognizable "negative" personality. The data seem, however, to indicate that the exceptions are cases where quantitative and qualitative differences between subjects result in different affects being invoked and necessarily different consequences involved. A needed experiment from the point of view of sound, clear generalization is one in which the subject has no chance to develop these negative responses because he never clearly apprehends the components in the situation that are being rewarded and punished, and therefore cannot effectively defend himself against them. Some of our experiments seem to offer the possibility of achieving this purpose. But we agree that our experiments are *very far indeed* from offering adequate explanation of individual differences, or the reasons for them.

Another related issue: To what degree are our results attributable to the training of our subject in certain habits of attending? The question is related to the problem of whether results of these sorts can be due to distraction. Neither in the training series nor in the test series are the data adequate regarding the deployment of the subject's attention. We are exploring the question of whether the whole Schafer effect can be conceptualized as the "conditioning of attention." Another urgently needed branch of experimentation, in which we are following the suggestions of J. E. Hochberg, is one in which the subject's perceptual learning reaches a point at which he cannot, despite great effort, perceive what has been punished, or cannot avoid seeing what has been rewarded.

We hope of course, that such experiments will enable us to understand better the nature of perceptual dynamics, the nature of the learning process, the nature of autism, and some of the possibilities for educational and clinical application.

It looks to us at this time as if Woodworth were right and as if we were reinforcing perception. This would enable us to take the four decades of research by Thorndike and his students, and gratefully utilize them to the full, simply noting that it was probably not the peripheral act, but the central process that was rewarded and punished in all these studies. In the same way we can take the massive materials of Hull and Skinner and gratefully note that they can without violence be interpreted as reinforcement of perception. Indeed, I suspect that Neal Miller's experiments will soon be leading to the same conclusion. For example, he and his associates (21) have directly excited affectivity through electrical stimulation of the brain stem, apparently finding that this serves very well as a motive. From this point it is only one step to the point in which some types of brain stem stimulation may be used as "rewards" without any peripheral tension reduction.

We are working here with a very simple form of perceptual learning. There are others. We make no squatter claims. With Tolman (31) we are sure that "there is more than one kind of learning." But we suspect that that garden variety of learning that offers the classical basis for our vast system of social rewards and punishments is a matter of instilling in the individual a new way of perceiving the environment. Some things, originally neutral, he comes to see as desirable; others, originally neutral, he comes to see as undesirable. The affect may range from abject horror to the mystic's sense of unutterable joys, and the connections formed may range from the simplest nonsense-syllable kind of connection to the profoundest creative integration. Through all this, I believe, runs a central theme: The perceptual field comes to take on a structure in which the acceptable, the good, the satisfying, tends to take the dominant position. Some will think that this is too lowly, too primitive a view of human nature. I cannot see it that way. Socrates in the dialogue of the *Gorgias* said he was persuaded that all men alike seek joy, and that the difference between a noble man and a base man lay not in the operation of this simple principle, but in the wisdom which showed the noble man that virtue brought the greatest joy. It is not by rejecting man's ineradicable earthy quest of joy, but by understanding it and its consequences that the science of man may be helpful to man.

NOTES

[1] It would be of interest to see whether the language of *drive reduction* (and of anxiety reduction) could state all these things better. I am inhibited in attempting this myself, as I often find it difficult, in my own case and in that of others, to be sure about drives (and anxieties), while pleasantness and unpleasantness usually remain easily identified.

[2] This investigation was supported by a research grant, M-715 (C), from the National Institute of Mental Health, of the National Institutes of Health, Public Health Service.

REFERENCES

1. Ayllon, T., and R. Sommer, "Autism, Emphasis, and Figure-Ground Perception," *J. Psychol.*, in press.

2. Birch, H. E., and M. E. Bitterman, "Sensory Integration and Cognitive Theory," *Psychol. Rev.*, 1951, **58**, 355–361.

3. Dulany, D. E., Jr., "Avoidance Learning of Perceptual Defense and Vigilance," unpublished doctor's dissertation, University of Michigan, 1954.

4. Gibson, J. J., and Eleanor J. Gibson, "Perceptual Learning: Differentiation or Enrichment?" *Psychol. Rev.*, 1955, **62**, 32–41.

5. Harlow, H. F., Margaret K. Harlow, and D. R. Meyer, "Learning Motivated by a Manipulation Drive," *J. Exp. Psychol.*, 1950, **40**, 228–234.

6. Holt, E. B., *Animal Drive and the Learning Process*, New York, Holt, 1931.

7. Hull, C. L., *Principles of Behavior*, New York, Appleton-Century, 1943.

8. Jackson, D. N., "A Further Examination of the Role of Autism in a Visual Figure-Ground Relationship," *J. Psychol.*, 1954, **38**, 339–357.

9. Kilpatrick, F. P., *Human Behavior from the Transactional Viewpoint*, Hanover: Inst. for Assoc. Research, 1952.

10. Levine, R., I. Chein, and G. Murphy, "The Relation of the

Intensity of a Need to the Amount of Perceptual Distortion: A Preliminary Report," *J. Psychol.*, 1942, 13, 282–293.

11. Meltzer, H., "The Present Status of Experimental Studies on the Relationship of Feeling to Memory," *Psychol. Rev.*, 1930, 37, 124–139.

12. Meltzer, H., "Individual Differences in Forgetting Pleasant and Unpleasant Experiences," *J. Educ. Psychol.*, 1930, 21, 399–409.

13. Muenzinger, K. F., "Motivation in Learning: I. Electric Shock for Correct Response in the Visual Discrimination Habit," *J. Comp. Psychol.*, 1934, 17, 267–277.

14. Murray, H. A., *Explorations in Personality*, New York, Oxford, 1938.

15. Postman, L., "Association Theory and Perceptual Learning," *Psychol. Rev.*, 1955, 62, 438–446.

16. Postman, L., and G. Murphy, "The Factor of Attitude in Associative Memory," *J. Exp. Psychol.*, 1943, 33, 228–238.

17. Pustell, E., "Cue and Dive Aspects of Anxiety in Relation to Perceptual Vigilance and Defense," unpublished doctor's dissertation, University of Michigan, 1954.

18. Razran, G. H. S., "Conditioned Responses: An Experimental Study and a Theoretical Analysis," *Arch. Psychol.*, 1935, No. 191.

19. Razran, G. H. S., "Attitudinal Control of Human Conditioning," *J. Psychol.*, 1936, 2, 327–337.

20. Razran, G. H. S., "Conditioning and Perception," *Psychol. Rev.*, 1955, 62, 83–95.

21. Roberts, W. W., N. E. Miller, and J. M. R. Delgado, "Motivation of Learning by Electrical Stimulation in the Diencephalon," *Amer. Psychologist*, 1954, 9, 456–457 (abstract).

22. Rock, I., and F. S. Fleck, "A Re-examination of the Effect of Monetary Reward and Punishment in Figure-Ground Perception," *J. Exp. Psychol.*, 1950, 40, 766–776.

23. Rubin, E., *Visuell Wahrgenommene Figuren*, Copenhagen, Gyldendolska, 1921.

24. Sanford, R. N., "The Effects of Abstinence from Food upon Imaginal Processes: A Preliminary Experiment," *J. Psychol.*, 1937, 3, 145–159.

25. Schafer, R., and G. Murphy, "The Role of Autism in a Visual Figure-Ground Relationship," *J. Exp. Psychol.*, 1943, 32, 335–343.

26. Simpson, J. E., "The Influence of Auditory Stimulation on Aniseikonic Perception," *J. Psychol.*, in press.

27. Skinner, B. F., *The Behavior of Organisms*, New York, Appleton-Century, 1938.

28. Smith, D. E., and J. E. Hochberg, "The Effect of 'Punishment' (electric shock) on Figure-Ground Perception," *J. Psychol.*, 1954, 38, 83–87.

29. Snyder, F., and C. Snyder, "The Effect of Monetary Reward and Punishment on Auditory Perception," *J. Psychol.*, in press.

30. Tolman, E. C., *Purposive Behavior in Animals and Men,* New York, Century, 1932.

31. Tolman, E. C., "There Is More Than One Kind of Learning," *Psychol. Rev.,* 1949, **56,** 144–155.

32. Woodworth, R. S., "Reënforcement of Perception," *Amer. J. Psychol.,* 1947, **60,** 119–124.

William H. Sheldon

CONSTITUTIONAL FACTORS
IN PERSONALITY

William Sheldon was born in 1899 in Warwick, Rhode Island. In 1926 he received a Ph.D. in psychology from the University of Chicago, and in 1933 he was awarded a medical degree by the same university. In 1936 he went to the University of Chicago as a professor of psychology. In 1938 he moved to Harvard, and in 1947 he accepted the position of Director of the Constitution Laboratory, College of Physicians and Surgeons, Columbia University, where he has remained. Sheldon's writings represent an attempt to identify and describe the major structural components of the human body, which he does in his book The Varieties of Human Physique *and in* The Varieties of Temperament. *In the field of constitutional psychology he is clearly indebted to two predecessors, Kretschmer and Viola. His medical training is clearly reflected in his concern for biological and hereditary factors in behavior.*

Sheldon's personality theory is a vigoruos defense of the crucial importance of the physical structure of the body as the primary *determinant of behavior. In emphasizing the physique and its measurement there is the strong conviction that biological-hereditary factors are of immense importance in determining behavior and a strong belief that the riddle of the human organism can be unraveled only with the aid of increased understanding of these factors.*

The essay reprinted here is probably Sheldon's best and most concise statement of the nature of constitutional psychology.

CONSTITUTIONAL FACTORS IN PERSONALITY

In medicine it is common to hear an experienced clinician make such an observation as this: The patient *looks like* one of those who are susceptible to cancer, or to ulcer, or to infantile paralysis. But when pressed for a detailed explanation the cautious clinician generally declines to specify the signs which led him to his intuition.

Through the ages there have always been a few—physicians as well as others—who are less cautious in the rationalization of their subjective impressions of people, and these less cautious ones have from time to time devised "systems" of various sorts for diagnosing and judging men. Such systems have for the most part been scientifically sterile, for they have rarely been associated with any experimental or validating program. Yet in many of them some truth or usefulness must have resided, if viability is at all a criterion of either.

One of the most conspicuous threads in the intellectual history of the past 2,500 years is the persistent recurrence of certain fundamentally similar assumptions concerning the relationship betwen physical and mental characteristics. Since the time of Hippocrates, and probably long before him, systems for the analysis of personality and character have risen, flourished for a time, and disappeared. Usually the enthusiasm of one generation has withered under the scrutiny of the next, but the underlying idea of a systematic connection between physique, temperament, and immunity or susceptibility to various (constitutional) diseases has persisted.

In this essay we shall first review our heritage of constitutional thought, and then examine briefly a modern attempt to reduce the problem of constitution to workable dimensions.

A GENERAL HISTORICAL ORIENTATION

Hippocrates, about 425 B.C., described two antithetical physical types, which he called the *habitus apoplecticus* (thick, strong, muscular) and the *habitus phthisicus* (delicate, linear, weak). The former he found particularly susceptible to apoplexy, and the latter, especially susceptible to tuberculosis (*phthisis*). He describes the two "types" as different both temperamentally and physically. Throughout the succeeding centuries various more or less similar typologies have flourished, some of them, like that of Hippocrates, resting on a simple dichotomy of polar variants, and some depending on a trichotomy instead of a dichotomy.

During the nineteenth century in particular, several reincarnations of the early typologies were brought forth. Most of these were variations of the more modern French threefold typology which describes a *digestive, muscular,* and *respiratory-cerebral* type (Rostan, 1828). Of the present-day examples of this family of typologies the best known is that of the German psychiatrist Kretschmer.

Between the time of Hippocrates and the late eighteenth century there are, so far as we know, no attacks on the problem of constitutional description which can be said to contribute materially to the modern effort in that direction. There are discursive references to types, but no consistent efforts even to establish typologies. The nineteenth and early twentieth centuries, however, are the golden age of typologies, and a short review of the principal constitutional literature of this period is first in order. We shall do well at least to glance at the French, Italian, German, American-British, and psychoanalytic developments, although in the space available we can, of course, do full justice to none of these.

THE FRENCH TYPOLOGIES

During the early nineteenth century the French literary and scientific influence was already waning rapidly, but several French writers of this period contributed to the development of a threefold typology which is now most closely associated with the names of Rostan (1828) and the German, Kretschmer, who revived it nearly one hundred years later. The approach (of the entire French group) is literary and anecdotally observational rather than systematically scientific. There is rich, shrewd insight, based both on clinical and general observation, but there is no attempt to cross the difficult barrier which intervenes between an intelligently generalized insight and the objective structuralization of a taxonomy.

To the French probably belongs most of the credit for the formulation of the threefold typology which we now associate more with German than with French names. Rostan's descriptions of the *digestive* type (which Kretschmer has called pyknic), of the *muscular* type (athletic), and of the two subtypes which Rostan called *respiratory* and *cerebral* (asthenic or athletic-asthenic to Kretschmer) are classic. Yet Rostan made little "scientific" contribution, in the sense in which we use that term. He elaborated and in a literary sense sharpened certain rather universal concepts which had been taken for granted both by himself and by a long line of predecessors. Neither Rostan nor any other of the French group made what could be called a serious attempt to translate the ancient intuitions into the quantitative language of modern science.

In the midnineteenth century, and even as late as the present day, many schools of phrenology, physiognomy, and character reading have flourished. Nearly all of these trace their genealogy back to the French influence. Many of them are attributed to Gall and Spurzheim, two French anatomists who were contemporary with Rostan. Both of these men made notable contributions in the field of brain anatomy, but Spurzheim in particular became interested during his later years in the problem of brain localization, and in the question of general human typologies. He developed a system of personality analysis based in part on skull configuration.

History has shown that such ideas are dangerous when put prematurely before a public, without norms, controls, and quantitative procedures. Many later opportunists have made stock of the speculations of Gall and Spurzheim, in some cases distorting their ideas to provide a rationalization for "systems" of phrenology which approach the miraculous.

THE ITALIAN CONTRIBUTION

Next to the French, a group of Italian anthropologists and clinicians of the late nineteenth and early twentieth centuries have pioneered most actively in the constitutional field. It was this group who first seemed to feel the impact of the new scientific spirit as applied to the constitutional sphere of interest. Darwin, Huxley, Spencer, and their followers in and out of England had prepared the ground, and the idea of applying measuremental, statistical methods to problems of human life was growing in men's minds. To the Italians belongs the credit of the first vigorous attempt to make use of anthropometry in defining constitutional differences. At Padua, about 1885, Di Giovanni founded a school of clinical anthropology. He standardized many of the now common anthropometric techniques—methods of measuring precisely various parts of the body.

Viola, a pupil of De Giovanni, developed what he called the morphological index. This is really an index measuring the linearity (as compared with the mass) of a human body. It is derived by adding the length of an arm to the length of a leg, and dividing the resulting sum by a number arrived at by multiplying together eight trunk measurements (one of them used twice). Thus a person with a high morphological index is *microsplanchnic* (small-bodied), while the *megalosplanchnic* (large-bodied) individual has a low morphological index. The microsplanchnics are people with small trunks and relatively long limbs. The megalosplanchnics (or macrosplanchnics) have large, heavy bodies and relatively short limbs. The former represent the old *phthisic habitus* of Hippocrates, the latter, the *habitus apoplecticus*. It is the ancient dichotomy in new (this time anthropometric) clothing.

Viola thus brought quantification into one aspect of the constitutional problem. He was able to measure one variable which seemed to him important and meaningful. He believed that the microsplanchnic is a *hyperevolute* and relatively intelligent type of human being, in contrast with the *hypoevolute* characteristics and relatively low intelligence which he associated with macrosplanchny. In several studies carried on by followers of Viola, low positive correlations were found between microsplanchny and intelligence test scores. Naccarati (1921) reported a correlation of $+ .36$ between these two variables for a group of 75 Columbia University students. But this finding was exceptional. Several other investigators failed to find such a relationship. In one study of 450 University of Chicago students (Sheldon, 1927), the correlation between microsplanchny and intelligence test scores was $+ .14$.

No discussion of the constitutional problem can fairly omit mention of Lombroso, who worked and wrote during the closing decades of the nineteenth century and into the twentieth century. He stands as a man of great genius, possibly of the greatest genius, in the constitutional field. Although he never developed a system of physical or mental classification, and never laid any particular claim to scientific objectivity in his methods, the scope and penetration of his insights were gigantic. From youth he trained himself to watch and to study man, and as he put it, "to observe relationships." Also, he was a prodigious reader. He held the chair of Legal Medicine at the University of Turin.

Lombroso is remembered principally for his theory of atavistic retrogression, which offers one explanation for the phenomena of criminality and degeneracy. In criminals he observed signs of "throwback" to remote ancestors. His extensive writings constitute reading which is both entertaining and instructive, but since he made no pretense of establishing a system of scientific objectivity his work has been an easy target for representatives of what might be called the school of impatient criticism.

Probably the present consensus of opinion would be that Di Giovanni, Viola, and later Pende (1928) have made a contribution of lasting importance in their procedures of anthropometric quantification. Also, they may fairly be said to have been the first to demonstrate a statistically supported relationship between a general morphological variable and a psychological variable. Their work has constituted a stimulus to much of the American research in the field.

THE GERMAN CONTRIBUTION

Beneke (1878), a German pathologist, deserves a share of the credit for whatever may have been accomplished by modern constitutional studies. He recorded precise measurements upon the internal organs of persons who had succumbed to various maladies, and kept systematic records of his work. In his theoretical conception he followed in substance the French threefold classification of types (Rostan), although he changed the terminology. At first he used the terminology of another German (Carus, 1852), calling the first type (French *digestive*) the *phlegmatic* type; the second (French *muscular*) the *athletic* type; and the third group of subtypes (French subtypes *respiratory* and *cerebral*) the *asthenic* and *cerebral* types respectively.

In 1878 Beneke published a monograph on pathological anomalies associated with constitutional variation, and suggested for the three constitutional types the following names: *rachitic*, *carcinomatous*, and *scrofulous-phthisical*. As the names imply, Beneke associated rickets with the first type, cancer with the second, and tuberculosis and scrofula with the third.

Here then was one of the first documented modern contributions to constitutional medicine. Unfortunately Beneke, like the Italians, made no attempt to establish norms for physical variation *at large*, or to develop a basic taxonomy aimed at isolating and describing *components* of physique. He merely collected isolated anthropometric measurements and reported them as such, or rather as averages, and then added the verbal typology as something of an afterthought.

Beneke's third (*scrofulous-phthisical*) type is once more the old *phthisic habitus* of Hippocrates, but his other two "types" present somewhat newer concepts. The idea of a cancer type (carcinomatous) appears here for the first time, so far as the writer is aware. Beneke found that the majority of people dying from cancer were of heavy, muscular make-up, corresponding to the old muscular type of the French, or to the athletic type of Carus. This is a lead which may yet be of value in constitutional medicine, and it may be added that our own preliminary studies have tended to confirm it. That is to say, the component which we now call *mesomorphy* (see page 296) appears to be one factor showing a positive relationship with cancer. The "rachitic type" seems to be more vague, and is probably a mixture of the old French digestive and cerebral types, or of what we now call *endomorphy* and *ectomorphy*.

In the work of the German psychiatrist Kretschmer we find a revival of the French typology just about as Rostan defined it, except that Kretschmer has substituted one more new term (*pyknic* instead of *digestive*) for the first type, and he has taken over the older terms *athletic* and *asthenic* for the other two general types (later he substituted the term *leptosomic* for *asthenic*). Also, he has added the idea of dysplastic or incompatible mixtures of types, so that he really has four designative groups, pyknics, athletics, asthenics, and dysplastics.

Kretschmer has made at least four contributions to the constitutional field, exclusive of the work of some hundreds of his followers and associates. First he has revived the typology concept in what had previously been its most highly developed form. He redefined and sharpened it and for the first time made it widely and popularly available, thus stimulating a vast amount of work in the field. Moreover, he has kept this work alive during a period when the tide of academic attitude and fashion has seemed to run strongly against him.

Second, he added for the first time the idea of dysplasia, or mixture of types. This represents a long stride in constitutional research, for it leads quite naturally to another step— the idea of continuous distributions and measurable elemental components *instead* of types. This last step, however, Kretschmer never has taken. He is still engaged in a Laocoön-like struggle with his types, and consequently has never found a dimensional frame of reference in which to establish norms for an attack on *general* problems.

Third, he demonstrated a statistical relationship between physical constitution and two psychiatric entities. This work has been repeated in many clinics, and the majority of the reports confirm (at least in a measure) Kretschmer's findings that the asthenic physique predisposes toward schizoid psychopathology while the massive (pyknic) physique predisposes toward the more vigorously expressive (manic-depressive or circular) forms of psychopathology.

Fourth, Kretschmer has extended the type concept beyond morphology to include temperament. Working from the point of view of a psychiatrist, and therefore dealing mainly with psychopathology, he has described with what even his severest critics call penetrative insight, a dichotomy of temperamental types which he associates respectively with schizoid and circular characteristics manifest in everyday behavior.

His *Physique and Character*, translated into English in 1925, presents all four of these basic ideas. The work has been harshly criticized, but in some quarters it has been warmly defended. The least that can be said for Kretschmer is that he has given impetus to constitutional research. The worst that his critics have said of him is that his generalizations are not supported by a sufficiently rigorous method.

Kretschmer has not quite escaped from the "type approach." His conception of polar types implies a kind of multimodal distribution of both physical and temperamental patterns which is not true to life. There are not three kinds of physique, or of temperament. There is unquestionably a continuous (although multidimensional) distribution of both. Failure to grasp the idea of varying *components* (instead of types), and the consequent effort to describe the variations of human morphology without the aid of a device for scaling structural variables, have left Kretschmer's work singularly open to attack.

Several other typologies which are more strictly psychological, rather than constitutional, have originated among the modern German-speaking group. . . .

THE AMERICAN AND BRITISH DEVELOPMENTS

On both sides of the Atlantic, the contributions of the English-speaking people to the constitutional field have been rather isolated and eclectic. There has been but little suggestion of a focus or "school" of constitutional research either in England or America. Numerous individuals here and there have attacked the problem, however. These investigators have for the most part contented themselves with attempting to correlate anthropometric measurements or indices with isolated fragments of conscious behavior (psychological test scores, attitudes, and the like). Such studies have failed to penetrate to the heart of the problem. The assumption seems too often to have been implicit that a direct correlation should be found between segmental fragments of the physical or constitutional pattern and isolated behavioral fragments like specific motor skills, general information, verbal attitudes, and so on.

Significant correlations between such remote variables are not to be found, however, and should never have been expected. To seek them is to ignore the obvious complexity of human personality, and the multiplication of futile studies of this nature has tended not only to discourage research in an already difficult field, but also to discount in some quarters the good sense of psychologists. We have gradually learned that in order to reach the heart of the constitutional problem, it is necessary (1) to deal with integrated personality patterns rather than with isolated segments of structure and behavior, and (2) to contrive to measure elemental components ("first-order" components, see page 300) at those levels of personality at which we choose to work. When the physical and mental expressions of personality are viewed as expressions of primary, first-order components, significant enough relationships are found to emerge (see page 302).

In England, Havelock Ellis was fond of calling himself, facetiously, a "criminal anthropologist." In *The Criminal* (1890) he summarized and pointed the then already controversial doctrine that a close relationship existed between criminality and constitutional (or more accurately, degenerative and atavistic) factors. His point of view and methods of supporting it are very similar to those of Lombroso. Ellis added no original researches, except of an anecdotal and literary nature. He wrote at a time when the tide of reaction against generalization drawn from anecdotal material was rising. He was swept away by this tide, so far as his anthropology is concerned, although he later applied the same methods to the study of sexuality with greater resultant acclaim.

Goring's *The English Convict* (1913) is the best-known British contribution to the constitutional field. Goring took precise anthropometric measurements on a large sampling of English convicts, and demonstrated convincingly the statistical untenability of Lombroso's more or less unguarded assumptions concerning relationships between specific bodily (especially head and facial) measurements and specific criminal tendencies. Goring wote as the timely champion of hardheaded skepticism, and his carefully elaborated study dealt a lethal blow to that kind of (anecdotal) science of which Lombroso and Ellis were probably terminal representatives.

By many modern students of the biological and psychological sciences, Goring's work has been taken as a conclusive discrediting of the entire constitutional approach. Yet Goring did not deal with any systematized description of constitutional patterning, but only with isolated anthropometric measurements and indices which were handled as if they were discrete entities. To try to relate such data to the complex psychological and sociological behavior of an individual is much like asking a dismembered finger to point or a dismembered brain to think.

Constitutional research in America has consisted chiefly of isolated reports pursuing correlations between anthropometric and psychological "fragments" of personality. During the nineteen twenties in particular, a host of such studies were reported, nearly all of them yielding either very low correlations, or none at all, between mental and physical measurements. Paterson in *Physique and Intellect* (1930) presented an exhaustive, pessimistic summary of these studies and sounded what was accepted as a death knell to the whole question, so far as academic psychology was concerned. However, the Kretschmerian influence was just then beginning to be felt in this country, and a good deal of support for Kretschmer's findings was being brought forward in other countries, particularly by Krasusky (1927), Ssucharewa (1928), Willemse (1932), Enke (1933), and Stevenson (1939).

There have been a number of American reports on the correlation between Kretschmer's types and psychiatric or psychological data, and the majority of these have tended to confirm his general thesis, at least in part. Among the better known of the more or less confirmatory Kretschmerian studies are those of Wertheimer and Hesketh (1926), Shaw (1925), Burchard (1936), Campbell (1932), and Garvey (1933). These workers found correlations of some degree between the Kretschmer types and psychotic classifications. On the other hand, Klineberg, Asch, and Block (1934) attempted to correlate Kretschmerian ratings of type with various mental tests and similar psychological data, and found only extremely low correlation. Similarly, Cabot (1938) made a careful analysis of the relation of schoolteachers' ratings on bodily build to various psychological and temperamental traits in a group of school children. He, too, reported virtually negative results. Mohr and Gundlach (1927) had reported nearly the same finding for a group of Illinois convicts, although they found a few significantly positive correlations between physical type and tests of temperament. For an excellent further summary of the specific researches on this question, see Cabot's monograph (1938, pp. 10–22).

The American experiments with Kretschmer's typology might be summarized about as follows: (1) The descriptions of the physical types and the criteria for their recognition were found to be confusing and unsatisfactory. In fact, it was soon made evident that types as such do not exist. (2) Yet in a number of instances where investigators sidestepped this stumbling block, accepting what may possibly be called *the spirit rather than the letter* of Kretschmer's claims, and proceeding to grade physiques according to their manifest general tendencies—in a considerable number of such instances significant positive correlations were found between physical tendency and psychotic tendency. (3) However, no American students, using Kretschmer's technique as he presented it, have been able to demonstrate significant relationships between physical type and temperamental or normal psychological characteristics.

Another, perhaps stronger impetus to constitutional thinking in this country has come from the practice of medicine. During the past two decades there has been an increasingly articulate emphasis in the medical schools upon the point of view that the physiological organism must be considered as an integrated unit which reacts as a whole, not in parts. This emphasis has been especially noticeable in the teaching of psychiatry, and in endocrinology. The words "constitution" and "constitutional factors" are now heard frequently in the clinics, although they are ordinarily used without more specific meaning than a vague designative reference to the *general fact* that hereditary, innate, or very deepseated and relatively permanent individual differences must exist. However, the prevalent use of the term "constitution" in medicine seems to indicate at least that the need for a method of constitutional analysis is being strongly felt.

Tucker and Lessa (1940) have published a good summary

of the rather bewildering mass of medical and anthropological literature which bears in one way or another on the problem of relating constitutional factors to clinical symptoms and procedures. Their paper includes a comprehensive bibliography and brings into relief the long groping of clinicians for a meaningful taxonomy of elemental constitutional factors.

From the physical anthropologists themselves has come little to help the psychologist and the clinician in their efforts to deal with constitution. The complaint is usually made that the anthropologist measures for the sake of measuring. Even when the measurements are applied to the classification of "races," the psychologist protests that with "race" he is left with a psychologically meaningless variable. But not all anthropological studies are devoid of constitutional interest.

The anthropologist Hooton (*Crime and the Man,* 1939) carried out a variant of the unaided anthropometric attack. In a survey of criminal and noncriminal population, he found certain statistically tenable anthropometric differences which appear to establish a degree of association between bodily build and type of crime. Since his criteria of bodily build depend almost entirely on stature and weight, and since we know that people of the same height and weight actually vary greatly in bodily build or somatotype (see page 296), Hooton's findings may be of greater importance than appears on the surface. If with such a tool alone he found a valid positive relationship, a more discriminative classification of physical constitution might, as Hooton indicates, open the way to a still more important contribution in the field of criminology.

THE CONSTITUTIONAL IMPLICATIONS OF THE PSYCHOANALYTIC MOVEMENT

Psychoanalysis, if literally interpreted, is a rather ambitious undertaking. The psychoanalysts attempt to penetrate deeply into the motivating mechanisms lying behind consciousness. One of their most insistent claims has been that of the discovery of a close relationship between physical and mental processes. They speak sometimes of "psychogenic factors affecting the organism" and sometimes of "somatogenic factors affecting the mind." In either case a step is taken toward recognition of the inevitability of substituting the conception of a continuum for the rudimentary dichotomy of mind and body.

Among the psychoanalysts, Franz Alexander of Chicago (1935) has taken the lead in emphasizing the proposition that any system of analysis aimed at comprehension of *a fragment* of personality (such as the conscious processes, for example) must in the end deal with *the total personality,* inclusive of both mental and physical processes, if it is not to fail in its purpose. Traditionally, psychoanalysis attempts to reach an understanding of the whole individual through a deep penetration "from the top," that is to say, through something suggesting a small incision made in consciousness itself. By free association, dream analysis, and the like, the analysts have found that it is possible to penetrate to remarkably obscure, deep-lying characteristics of the individual.

Alexander and some others have felt that when once a systematic description of physical and physiological variation becomes available, couched in terms of concepts which have common roots (common components, possibly) with a similarly systematic description of psychological variables, the way will be open to a more effective attack on the general problem of analysis. Analysis might then become not merely *psycho*analysis, but general, *constitutional* analysis, or total analysis. The descriptive adjective is unimportant, so long as it refers to a process by which the analyst directs his attack upon more than one level of description. By approaching the individual through both a physical and a psychological attack, the analyst can effect a kind of "pincers movement," and the efficiency of the analytic attack should be enhanced.

In line with this conception Draper (1924) has for the past quarter-century taught a point of view in his Constitution Clinic at the New York Presbyterian Hospital which advocates, ideally at least, a fourfold simultaneous attack on the problem of constitutional analysis. He postulates four "panels" of personality, a morphological, physiological, immunological, and a psychological panel. This is a most useful general conception, and one which has exerted a good influence on a generation of medical students. By way of implementation Draper uses the Freudian psychoanalytic approach to the psychological panel, and has access to the usual clinical approaches to physiology and immunology. On the morphological side he has unfortunately relied heavily upon anthropometric measurements used alone, without a constitutional frame of reference, or without reference to the *general* component factors in morphological differentiation. So used, measurements tend merely to cancel one another out, and only low correlations are found.

The general movement toward integrating psychological and somatic studies has been spreading among the younger generation of psychoanalysts and kindred scientists. In 1939 the new *Journal of Psychosomatic Medicine* was founded. Dunbar (1935), in her *Emotions and Bodily Changes,* wrote a general review aimed at integration of psychoanalytic concepts with recent developments in physiology, endocrinology, metabolism, homeostasis, and in the study of "functional" illness. This book provides a good modern orientation, on the clinical side, for the student of constitutional analysis (see also Chapters 8, 17, 18, and 19).

In summary, for the step of progression from the ancient dichotomy of Hippocrates to the trichotomy with which we are more lately familiar, we are indebted most immediately to a group of French anatomists. Italian anthropologists have played a principal role in the development of anthropometric technique and in a vigorous although rather fruitless attempt to apply it to the problem of constitutional differentiation. Lombroso stands as the classic, probably tragic, example of what happens when a brilliant, active mind tackles the constitutional problem without benefit of a scientifically acceptable basic taxonomy.

In Germany, Beneke made the first real beginning toward constitutional medicine with his systematic, comparative studies of autopsy material, while Kretschmer, with making at least four definable contributions, has become probably the most articulate figure in the modern constitutional approach. He has added a certain scientific respectability to the French typology; he has introduced the idea of dysplasia, and thereby opened the way to a conception of scalable components; he has shown a statistically sound relationship between morphological and psychiatric variables; and he has extended his typological approach into the field of temperamental analysis. In referring thus to Kretschmer, we also include the scores of his collaborators, followers, and friendly critics who have attempted to validate and carry on his work.

England has made but little contribution to this field. Havelock Ellis is closely comparable to Lombroso, and Goring's ponderous labor on criminal anthropology has, in the present writer's opinion, probably achieved more actual harm than good. For by attacking a good problem with inadequate tools, thereby arriving at negative results, he has, in a sense, vaccinated a generation of anthropologists against one of the fields for which anthropology exists. An accusation of sterility can be directed against the work of the physical anthropologists between the time of Goring and Hooton's recent revitalizing of this field. They appear to have incubated all their eggs in the basket of random anthropometry. Eggs so treated do not hatch. Anthropometric measurements, *used merely as such,* will no more tell the story of a physique than would some of the words of a narrative, rearranged at random, tell its story.

In America, psychological, anthropological, and clinical students alike have for more than a generation relied mainly upon unaided anthropometry. This has been relatively a sterile period, but the psychoanalytic and Kretschmerian influences appear to have touched off a revival of interest in a more vital approach. A group of psychoanalytically inclined investigators, led particularly by Alexander, have lately been developing a point of view which postulates the total organism as the primary focus of study. This point of view seems already to have found a warm welcome in some of the clinical centers, although the problem of its adequate implementation still confronts us.

STATEMENT OF THE PRESENT-DAY PROBLEM

The history of the constitutional approach makes it plain that we are still confronted with the existence of a general problem having to do with the definition of the *most basic nature* of individual differences, or with the definition and measurement of *first-order* constitutional differences among people. It is an ancient problem, and many efforts have been made to direct a fruitful attack upon it. Some of these attacks have succeeded in part, but the formulation of a comprehensive constitutional psychology remains a goal of first importance.

Schemes for the classification of morphology, physiology, temperament, and of consciousness itself have not been wanting. The question is, Have any of these systems resulted in the definition and measurement of variables which can be regarded as *basic components* common to the various levels of the expression of personality? Have we yet been able to carry out a crucial test of the relationships between structure and function, or between different levels of personality? Most of the published research on the correlation between physical and mental characteristics has rested on a relatively casual choice of variables. Under such circumstances it is easy to understand why correlations are low or absent. For if measurable relationships between constitutional variables are to be discovered, these variables need to be chosen against some criterion of basic relevance.

Therefore a first step in an investigation which would measure and correlate constitutional factors must be that of isolating and defining first-order variables at different levels of personality. Further, since psychological reactions are processes in which the living individual plays a part as an integrated unit, our efforts to study the relationship between psychological reactions and constitutional factors must not only find a way of analyzing both into their most basic recognizable components, but must then also contrive to work with the *patterning* of these basic components, not merely with the isolated components themselves.

In short, to achieve a constitutional psychology, it is necessary to make peace not only with the need for a factorial analysis, but with a concomitant need for a meaningful synthesis. The two needs are obviously not incompatible. They are complementary, supporting one another like the two slopes of a roof.

An Approach to the Problem—A Summary

Of the many contemporary efforts to systematize a constitutional approach to personality, we shall now examine the one with which the author is naturally most familiar. Beginning with a doctoral thesis in 1924, a constitutional research project has been in progress through more than a decade. Its object has been to lay a skeletal foundation for a constitutional psychology—a psychology of basic individual differences—first by devising a technique for describing human morphology in terms of continuous variables, and second by defining and measuring analogous first-order variables of temperament.

Indispensable collaboration has come from many workers. Dr. S. S. Stevens, of Harvard, has played a particularly indispensable part in systematizing and ordering the philosophical assumptions and mathematical principles underlying the central idea of component analysis.

THE BASIC COMPONENTS OF MORPHOLOGY

The procedures employed in the morphological analysis of human beings have already been described (*The Varieties of Human Physique*, 1940). Having failed to arrive at useful results with anthropometric techniques alone, we came to the conclusion that in order to set up the framework of a morphological taxonomy *ab initio*, it would first be necessary to *scrutinize* a large collection of physiques, and if possible to see them all at one time. Photography not only would make this possible, but also would permit us to see each physique from as many directions at once as we might desire. Accordingly, a procedure was adopted in which the individual is photographed in a standardized posture from the frontal, lateral, and dorsal positions on a single film.

Four thousand college students were photographed in this manner, and later many more who were not college students. When the four thousand cases were assembled so that they could be studied in one place, and could be arranged experimentally in series, it was found that a certain orderliness of nature could be made out by the unaided eye. Certainly there were no "types," but only dimensions of variation.

The first problem was to determine how many dimensions or components of structural variation could be recognized by inspectional examination. The criteria we employed in seeking to discover "primary structural components" were two: (1) Could the entire collection of photographs be arranged in an ascending (or descending) progression of strength of the characteristic under consideration, with agreement between experimenters working independently? (2) In the case of a suspected new component of structural variation, is it, upon examination of the photographs, found to be impossible to define this apparently new component in terms of mixtures, regular or dysplastic, of the other already accepted components?

Application of these two criteria revealed the presence of three primary components of structural variation, and although a set of photographs was virtually worn out by experimental sortings and rearrangements, we were unable to find a fourth structural variant which was not obviously the result of a mixture of these three.

To arrange the entire series of four thousand along each of the three accepted axes of variation was relatively easy, not only for the body as a whole, but also for different regions of the body separately (thus providing a method for the ultimate measurement of dysplasia). The distributions for the body as a whole were then scaled tentatively by the method of equal-appearing intervals, and we had at hand a rough approximation to the general patterning of a continuous tridimensional distribution. This was not yet an objectively defined distribution, but the first step toward meaningful objectification had been taken. We now had a fairly good idea of what it was that needed to be measured, and were ready to make use of anthropometry.

The second problem was to find such anthropometric measurements as would (1) most reliably reflect those obvious differences in physique that our anthroposcopic inspection had already shown to be present, and (2) refine and objectify these differences so that precise allocations of physiques on the tridimensional distribution could be made. Such measurements were selected by trial and error. We found by experiment that the measurements most valuable for the purpose were certain diameters expressed as ratios to stature, and that most of these diameters could be taken with needle-point dividers from the film more accurately (more reliably) than from the living subjects, provided the photographs were perfectly posed.

The question of how many such diameters to use is simply the question of how precisely accurate an allocation is desired. In dealing with groups statistically, we scale the strength of each of the primary components on a seven-point scale. For this purpose a minimum of seventeen diameter measurements is adequate for determining what is called the somatotype. In the detailed analysis of an individual, more precise differentiation may be made by using a greater number of measurements.

In order more readily to determine the somatotype from a series of seventeen measurements, a machine has been constructed into which the measurements may be entered. The manipulation of switches then discloses the correct somatotype. This machine, as at present constructed, may be used for the somatotyping of any male individual in the age range of sixteen to twenty-one.

The somatotype is a series of three numerals, each expressing the approximate strength of one of the primary components in a physique. The first numeral always refers to *endomorphy* (see below), the second to *mesomorphy*, and the third to *ectomorphy*. Thus when a seven-point scale is used, a 7-1-1 is the extreme endomorph, a 1-7-1 is the most extreme mesomorph, and a 1-1-7 the most extreme ectomorph. The 4-4-4 falls at the midpoint (of the scale, not of the frequency distribution) with respect to all three components. Seventy-six different somatotypes have been described, and photographic illustrations of most of them are presented in *The Varieties of Human Physique* (Sheldon, Stevens, and Tucker, 1940).

As these components occur in nature they are complex, continuous variables. The somatotype is an oversimplification which merely serves the purpose of bracketing a physique within certain defined boundaries. When the somatotype is determined, analysis of the physique is of course only begun, but the somatotype provides the basis for a morphological taxonomy which is both comprehensive and statistically manipulable. The bugaboo of types thus disappears in a continuous distribution in which every physique has a place, and the establishment of norms becomes a routine.

When *endomorphy* predominates, the digestive viscera are massive and highly developed, while the somatic structures are relatively weak and undeveloped. Endomorphs are of low specific gravity. They float high in the water. Nutrition may of course vary to some degree independently of the primary components. Endomorphs are usually fat, but they are sometimes seen emaciated. In the latter event they do not change into mesomorphs or ectomorphs any more than a starved spaniel will changed into a mastiff or a collie. They become simply emaciated endomorphs.

When *mesomorphy* predominates, the somatic structures (bone, muscle, and connective tissue) are in the ascendancy. The mesomorphic physique is high in specific gravity and is hard, firm, upright, and relatively strong and tough. Blood vessels are large, especially the arteries. The skin is relatively thick with large pores, and it is heavily reinforced with underlying connective tissue. The hallmark of mesomorphy is uprightness and sturdiness of structure, as the hallmark of endomorphy is softness and sphericity.

Ectomorphy means fragility, linearity, flatness of the chest, and delicacy throughout the body. There is relatively slight development of both the visceral and somatic structures. The ectomorph has long, slender, poorly muscled extremities with delicate, pipestem bones, and he has, relative to his mass, the greatest surface area and hence the greatest sensory exposure to the outside world. He is thus in one sense overly exposed and naked to his world. His nervous system and sensory tissue have relatively poor protection. It might be said that the ectomorph is biologically "extroverted," as the endomorph is biologically "introverted." Psychologically, as we shall see later, these characteristics are usually reversed—the ectomorph is the introvert, the endomorph is *one type* of extrovert. The hallmark of ectomorphy is the stooped posture and hesitant restraint of movement.

The digestive viscera (dominant in endomorphy) are derived principally from the endodermal embryonic layer. The somatic tissues (dominant in mesomorphy) are derived from the mesodermal layer, while the skin and nervous system, which are relatively predominant in ectomorphy, come from the ectodermal embryonic layer.

The anthropometric measurements are standardized for normal or average nutrition, within a particular age range. Therefore those measurements which change with nutritional changes readily detect the under- or over-nourished individual. But apparently no nutritional change can cause the measurements of a person of one somatotype to stimulate those of another somatotype. Nutritional changes are recognized as such by the somatotyping process. When an individual's measurements are posted in the somatotyping machine, the machine indicates where the somatotype lies. If a severe nutritional disturbance is present, the machine does not indicate a false somatotype, but indicates only an unusual aberration from the normal pattern. We have as yet seen no case in which metabolic or nutritional changes led us to the assignment of two different somatotypes for the same individual, although we have somatotyped people from photographs taken at different periods in their (adult) lives when a weight change of as much as one hundred pounds had taken place.

When the relative strength of the three primary components of morphology has been determined, the physical analysis may be said to be anchored. But identification of the somatotype is only a beginning. So many secondary variables still remain to be described that the horizon of individuality seems only to broaden and to recede to greater distance as the techniques of physical description mature to usefulness.

Some of the important secondary variables are dysplasia, gynandromorphy (bisexuality), texture (fineness or coarseness of tissue), aesthetic harmony of structure, secondary local dysplasias or hereditary local patternings of the primary components (often called racial characteristics), pigmentation, distribution of secondary sexual characteristics (gynandromorphic dysplasias and characteristic patterns), hair and hair distribution, and so on. We have tried to standardize the scaling of most of these characteristics just mentioned, but many other important physical variables lie on beyond these. Furthermore the work on secondary factors is for the most part new and incomplete, since none of this work could be done in a meaningful frame of reference until the somatotyping techniques and the norms for the primary components were well established.

THE BASIC COMPONENTS OF TEMPERAMENT

As in the studies of physique, the first problem at this more complex level of personality was to discover and define criteria for a useful basic taxonomy. It was necessary at the beginning to determine what first-order components are present in temperament. The method which has finally yielded fruitful results is a variation on the technique of factor analysis applied to quantitative ratings on a group of traits.

The literature on temperament, and especially on the measurement of extroversion and introversion, contains many hundreds of references to alleged traits of temperamental differentiation. This literature was first combed for differentiative behavioral traits. The trait definitions were then modified and rewritten until they appeared to embrace or to imply all of the specific characteristics mentioned in the literature. A number of trait definitions were added which were drawn from our own clinical and general observation of people, and finally the list was boiled down to exactly fifty traits.

A group of thirty-three young men, mostly graduate students and instructors, were then studied by the writer through the course of a series of weekly analytic interviews extending through a period of one year. These men were finally rated on each of the fifty experimental traits, a seven-point scale being used. The intercorrelations for the fifty traits were then run, and were posted on a correlation chart (See Appendix 4, Sheldon and Stevens, 1942). That is to say, the basic procedure of what is now called factor analysis was carried out. The purpose was to discover whether or not there were any "nuclear clusters" of traits showing positive correlation among themselves and also negative correlation with other nuclear clusters which might be present.

The result was clear-cut. Clusters of the sort just indicated were present, and clearly defined. After some statistical experimenting had been done, two criteria were adopted for qualification of a trait within a nuclear cluster: (1) The trait must show a positive correlation of at least +.60 with each of the other traits already accepted in the cluster, and (2) it must show a negative correlation of at least −.30 with every trait found in any of the other clusters. When the criteria of positive intracorrelation and negative intercorrelation were applied, it was found that three clusters of traits were present in the material. Six traits then defined what was designated as Group 1, seven defined Group 2, and nine defined Group 3. Twenty-two of the original fifty traits had qualified. These twenty-two appear in Table I:

TABLE I

TWENTY-TWO TRAITS ORIGINALLY DEFINING THE THREE PRIMARY TEMPERAMENTAL COMPONENTS

	GROUP 1		GROUP 2		GROUP 3
V-1 *	Relaxation	S-1	Assertive Posture	C-1	Restraint in Posture
V-2	Love of Comfort	S-3	Energetic Characteristic	C-3	Overly Fast Reaction
V-6	Pleasure in Digestion	S-4	Need of Exercise	C-8	Sociophobia
V-10	Dependence on Social Approval	S-7	Directness of Manner	C-9	Inhibited Social Address
V-15	Deep Sleep	S-13	Unrestrained Voice	C-10	Resistance to Habit
V-19	Need of People When Troubled	S-16	Quality of Seeming Older	C-13	Vocal Restraint
		S-19	Need of Action When Troubled	C-15	Poor Sleep Habits
				C-16	Youthful Intentness
				C-19	Need of Solitude When Troubled

* The number before each trait refers to its position in Table II.

This was the beginning of what is called the Scale for Temperament. It now consists of sixty traits, twenty in each

TABLE II

The Scale for Temperament

Name   Date   Photo No.   Scored by

	I VISCEROTONIA	II SOMATOTONIA	III CEREBROTONIA
1.	Relaxation in Posture and Movement	Assertiveness of Posture and Movement	Restraint in Posture and Movement, Tightness
2.	Love of Physical Comfort	Love of Physical Adventure	Physiological Over-Response
3.	Slow Reaction	The Energetic Characteristic	Overly Fast Reactions
4.	Love of Eating	Need and Enjoyment of Exercise	Love of Privacy
5.	Socialization of Eating	Love of Dominating, Lust for Power	Mental Overintensity, Hyperattentionality, Apprehensiveness
6.	Pleasure in Digestion	Love of Risk and Chance	Secretiveness of Feeling, Emotional Restraint
7.	Love of Polite Ceremony	Bold Directness of Manner	Self-Conscious Motility of the Eyes and Face
8.	Sociophilia	Physical Courage for Combat	Sociophobia
9.	Indiscriminate Amiability	Competitive Aggressiveness	Inhibited Social Address
10.	Greed for Affection and Approval	Psychological Callousness	Resistance to Habit, and Poor Routinizing
11.	Orientation to People	Claustrophobia	Agoraphobia
12.	Evenness of Emotional Flow	Ruthlessness, Freedom from Squeamishness	Unpredictability of Attitude
13.	Tolerance	The Unrestrained Voice	Vocal Restraint, and General Restraint of Noise
14.	Complacency	Spartan Indifference to Pain	Hypersensitivity to Pain
15.	Deep Sleep	General Noisiness	Poor Sleep Habits, Chronic Fatigue
16.	The Untempered Characteristic	Overmaturity of Appearance	Youthful Intentness of Manner and Appearance
17.	Smooth, Easy Communication of Feeling, Extroversion of Viscerotonia	Horizontal Mental Cleavage, Extroversion of Somatotonia	Vertical Mental Cleavage, Introversion
18.	Relaxation and Sociophilia Under Alcohol	Assertiveness and Aggression Under Alcohol	Resistance to Alcohol and to Other Depressant Drugs
19.	Need of People When Troubled	Need of Action When Troubled	Need of Solitude When Troubled
20.	Orientation Toward Childhood and Family Relationships	Orientation Toward Goals and Activities of Youth	Orientation Toward the Later Periods of Life

* The thirty traits with brackets constitute collectively the short form of the scale.

group. The additional thirty-eight items were added as rapidly as traits meeting the criteria could be discovered and tested—a tedious process, since each individual used as a subject was analyzed through a period of at least one year. The scale in its present form is shown in Table II.

Names have been given to the three correlated groups of traits. *Viscerotonia*, the first component, in its extreme manifestation is characterized by general relaxation, love of comfort, sociability, conviviality, gluttony for food, for people, and for affection. The viscerotonic extremes are people who "suck hard at the breast of mother earth" and love physical proximity with others. The motivational organization is dominated by the gut and by the function of anabolism. The personality seems to center around the viscera. The digestive tract is king, and its welfare appears to define the primary purpose of life.

Somatotonia, the second component, is roughly a predominance of muscular activity and of vigorous bodily assertiveness. The motivational organization seems dominated by the soma. These people have vigor and push. The executive department of their internal economy is strongly vested in their somatic muscular systems. Action and power define life's primary purpose.

Cerebrotonia, the third component, is roughly a predominance of the element of restraint, inhibition, and of the desire for concealment. These people shrink away from sociality as from too strong a light. They "repress" somatic and visceral expression, are hyperattentional, and sedulously avoid attracting attention to themselves. Their behavior seems dominated by the inhibitory and attentional functions of the cerebrum, and their motivational hierarchy appears to define an antithesis to both of the other extremes.

CONCERNING THE RELATIONSHIP BETWEEN PHYSIQUE AND TEMPERAMENT

We have been less interested in the statistical relationship between physique and temperament than in the problem of standardizing a procedure for the general (physical and temperamental) analysis of the individual. The project may be regarded as in one sense an effort to make a contribution to the theory and technique of psychoanalysis. Constitutional psychology and Freudian analysis are, as we see it, something like upward and downward extensions, respectively, of a continuum. The Freudians start with consciousness and go as far (down) as they can. We start with the solid bone and flesh of the individual and go as far (up) as we can. The two procedures need to be carried on conjointly, and indeed in certain cases where the two analyses have been so conducted, excellent results have obtained.

The correlation between physique and temperament is, however, an interesting by-product of constitutional analysis. In a study extending over a period of five years, we have been able to analyze two hundred cases, both morphologically and temperamentally. The intracorrelations among the three primary components at each level, and the intercorrelations between the two levels are shown in Table III.

TABLE III

INTRACORRELATIONS AND INTERCORRELATIONS AMONG THE PRIMARY COMPONENTS

	VISCERO-TONIA	MESO-MORPHY	SOMATO-TONIA	ECTO-MORPHY	CEREBRO-TONIA
Endomorphy ..	+.79	—.29	—.29	—.41	—.32
Viscerotonia ..		—.23	—.34	—.41	—.37
Mesomorphy ..			+.82	—.63	—.58
Somatotonia ..				—.53	—.62
Ectomorphy ..					+.83

The correlations between the same components at the two levels, morphological and temperamental, are seen to be of the order of +.81 (endomorphy-viscerotonia, +.79; mesomorphy-somatotonia, +.82; and ectomorphy-cerebrotonia, +.83). These correlations are higher than we had previously expected, and they contradict the current academic supposition that physical constitution plays only a small part in motivation and temperament. However, this common supposition can hardly be regarded as founded upon any convincing evidence, since there have been no previous studies which attempted to break down both physical and temperamental factors into comparable component elements.

In any event the correlation between the two levels is by no means perfect, and we have found that from the point of view of individual analysis it is the disagreements or inconsistencies between the physical and temperamental patterns that are most valuable in throwing light on motivation.

Roughly, we find at least four general factors at work in the development of a personality: (1) The amount of the endowment; (2) the quality of the endowment; (3) the mixture of the components, or their order of predominance; and (4) the dyscrasias, or incompatibilities, between morphology and manifest temperament. Of the latter, there are several subvarieties, the most important being those cases in which the temperamental manifestation reverses a relationship of dominance between two of the morphological components. Beyond these general factors there are many secondary variables which can be measured with a greater or less degree of reliability, once the analysis of the primary components is made secure. Such factors as peripheral and central concentration of strength, endowment of sexuality, and gynandrophrenia (mental bisexuality) appear to play an important part, and these factors are closely related to the primary morphological components.

CONCLUSION

Comparable primary components of morphology and of manifest temperament can be identified and can be quantitatively measured. The relationship between these two levels of personality appears to be a closer one than has generally been supposed. Description of people in terms of the primary components, and in terms of other secondary components which are more or less related to them, offers the framework for a basic taxonomy of individual differences, and provides an orientation upon which constitutional analysis or psychoanalysis can be conducted. With further standardization, the methods of constitutional analysis appear also to offer promise of usefulness in attacking the problems of practical human genetics, and those of isolating and controlling the so-called constitutional diseases, such as cancer, ulcer, epilepsy, tuberculosis, and hereditary mental afflictions. In the field of constitutional medicine the frustrating obstacle has been lack of a taxonomy of individual differences adequate for comparative classifications of patients. In the component approach may lie the basis upon which such a taxonomy can be standardized.

BIBLIOGRAPHY

ALEXANDER, F. 1935. *The Psychoanalysis of the Total Personality* (trans. by B. Glueck & B. D. Lewin), New York, Nervous & Mental Diseases Publ.

————. 1936. *The Medical Value of Psychoanalysis*, New York, Norton.

BAKWIN, H., and R. M. BAKWIN. 1929. "Types of Body Build in Infants," *Amer. J. Dis. Child.*, 37, 461–472.

BARDEEN, C.R. 1920. "The Height, Weight Index of Build in Relation to Linear and Volumetric Proportion, etc.," *Contr. Embryol., Carneg. Instn.*, 46, 483–552.

BAUER, J. 1924. *Die konstitutionelle Disposition zu inneren Krankheiten*, Berlin, Springer.

BEAN, R. B. 1912. "Morbidity and Morphology," *Johns Hopk. Hosp. Bull.*, 23, 363.

————. 1923. "The Two European Types," *Amer. J. Anat.*, 31, 359.

BENEDETTI, P. 1931. "Das Problem der Disposition zur Krebskrankheit," *Z. menschl. Vererb.-u. KonstLehre*, 16, 261–291.

BENEKE, F. W. 1878. *Die anatomischen Grundlagen der Konstitutionsanomalien des Menschen*, Marburg.

BLEULER, E. 1921. "Körperliche wud geistige Konstitutionen," *Naturwissenschaften*, 9, 753.

BRANDT, W. 1936. "Die biologischen Unterschiede des Pyknikers und des Leptosomen," *Dtsch. med. Wschr.*, 62, 501–502.

BRYANT, J. 1914. "The Carnivorous and Herbivorous Types of Man," *Boston med. surg. J.*, 170, 795; 172, 321; 173, 384.

BURCHARD, E. M. L. 1936. "Physique and Psychosis—An Analysis of the Postulated Relationship Between Bodily Constitution and Mental Disease Syndrome," *Comp. Psychol. Monogr.*, 13, No. 61.

CABOT, P. S. DEQ. 1938. "The Relationship Between Characteristics of Personality and Physique in Adolescents," *Genet. Psychol. Monogr.*, 20, No. 1.

CAMPBELL, J. K. 1932. "The Relation of the Types of Physique to the Types of Mental Diseases," *J. Abnorm. Soc. Psychol.*, 27, 147–151.

CIOCCO, A. 1936a. "Studies on Constitution: III. Somatological Differences Associated with Diseases of the Heart in White Females," *Hum. Biol.*, 8, 38–91.

————. 1936b. The Historical Background of the Modern Study of Constitution," *Bull. Inst. Hist. Med.*, 4, 23–38.

CONNOLLY, C. J. 1939. "Physique in Relation to Psychosis," *Stud. Psychol. Psychiat., Catholic Univ. Amer.*, 4, No. 5.

DAVENPORT, C. B. 1923. "Body Build, Its Development and Inheritance," *Publ. Carnegie Instn.*, No. 329.

DI GIOVANNI, A. 1909. *Clinical Commentaries Deduced from the*

Morphology of the Human Body (trans. by J. J. Eyre.), London and New York, Rebman.

DRAPER, G. 1924. *Human Constitution: A Consideration of Its Relationship to Disease*, Philadelphia and London, Saunders.

DUNBAR, H. F. 1935. *Emotions and Bodily Changes*, New York, Columbia University Press.

ELLIS, H. 1890. *The Criminal*, London, Walter Scott; New York: Scribner's.

ENKE, W. 1933. "The Affectivity of Kretschmer's Constitutional types as Revealed in Psycho-Galvanic Experiments," *Character & Pers.*, 3, 225–233.

FEIGENBAUM, J., and D. HOWAT. 1934. "The Relation Between Physical Constitution and the Incidence of Disease: The Disease Groups Include Peptic Ulcer, Cholecystitis and Diabetes Mellitus," *J. Clin. Invest.*, 13, 121–138.

FREEMAN, W. 1934. "Human Constitution: A Study of the Correlations Between Physical Aspects of the Body and Susceptibility to Certain Diseases," *Ann. Intern. Med.*, 7, 805–811.

GARRETT, H. E., and W. N. KELLOGG. 1928. "The Relation of Physical Constitution to General Intelligence, Social Intelligence and Emotional Stability," *J. Exp. Psychol.*, 11, 113–129.

GARVEY, C. R. 1933. "Comparative Body Build of Manic-Depressives and Schizophrenic Patients," *Psychol. Bull.*, 30, 567–568.

GILDEA, E. F., E. KAHN, and E. B. MAN. 1936. "The Relationship Between Body Build and Serum Lipoids and a Discussion of These Qualities as Pyknophilic and Jeptophilic Factors in the Structure of the Personality," *Amer. J. Psychiat.*, 92, 1247–1260.

GOLDTHWAIT, J. E. 1915. "An Anatomic and Mechanistic Conception of Disease," *Boston Med. Surg. J.*, 172, 881.

GORING, C. 1913. *The English Convict*, London, H. M. Stationery Office.

GRAVES, W. W. 1924. "The Relations of Scapular Types to Problems of Human Heredity, Longevity, Morbidity and Adaptability in General," *Arch. Intern. Med.*, 34, 1–26.

GREULICH, W. W., and H. THOMS. 1939. "Pelvic Type and Its Relationship to Body Build in White Women," *J. Amer. Med. Assn.*, 112, 485–493.

HACKEL, W. 1932. "Pathologisch-anatomische und anthropometrische Studien über Konstitution," *Z. menschl. Vererb.-u. f. KonstLehre*, 16, 63–80.

HARRIS, J. A. 1930. "The Measurement of Man in the Mass," in Harris, Jackson, Paterson, and Scammon, *The Measurement of Man*. Minneapolis, University of Minnesota Press.

HENCKEL, K. O. 1925. "Konstitutionstypen und europäische Rassen," *Klin. Wschr.*, 4, 2145.

HESS, A. F., and S. N. BLACKBERG. 1932. "Constitutional Factors in the Etiology of Rickets," *Amer. J. Physiol.*, 102, 8.

HIPPOCRATES. *On Ancient Medicine: The Genuine Works of Hippocrates* (trans. by F. Adams), New York, Wood.

HNAT, F. 1933. "The Importance of the Study of Human Constitution in the Practice of Medicine," *J. Med. Soc., N. J., 30,* 557–559

HOOTON, E. A. 1939. *Crime and the Man,* Cambridge, Harvard University Press.

JAENSCH, E. 1930. *Eidetic Imagery and Typological Methods of Investigation* (trans. by Oeser), New York, Harcourt, Brace.

KLINEBERG, O., S. E. ASCH, and H. BLOCK. 1934. "An Experimental Study of Constitutional Types," *Genet. Psychol. Monogr., 16,* 145–221.

KRASUSKY, W. S. 1927. "Kretschmers konstitutionele Typen unter den Kindern im Schulalter," *Arch. Kinderheilk.,* 82–83, 22–32.

KRETSCHMER, E. 1921. *Körperbau und Charakter,* Berlin, Springer (trans. from the second German edition as *Physique and Character,* by W. J. H. Sprott), London, Kegan Paul, Trench, Trubner, 1925.

KROGMAN, W. M. 1941. *Bibliography of Human Morphology, 1914–1939,* Chicago, University Chicago Press.

KUGELMAN, I. N. 1935. *Growing Superior Children,* New York, Appleton-Century.

LAVATER, J. C. 1804. Essays on Physiognomy: For the Promotion of the Knowledge and the Love of Mankind (2nd ed., 4 vols.) (trans. by Thomas Holcroft), London, C. Whittingham.

LAYCOCK, T. 1862. "Physiognomical Diagnosis," *Med. Times, London,* Part 1, 1.

LEDERER, R. *Konstitutionspathologie in den medizinischen Specialwissenschaften,* Vol. 1, Berlin, Springer.

LOMBROSO, C. 1889. *L'uomo deliquente* (4th ed.), Torino, Flli. Bocca.

———. 1911. *Crime, Its Causes and Remedies* (trans. by Horton), Boston, Little, Brown.

LUCAS, W. P., and H. B. PRYOR. 1933. "The Body Build Factor in the Basal Metabolism of Children," *Amer. J. Dis. Child.,* Part 1, *46,* 941–948.

MANOUVRIER, L. 1902. "Étude sur les rapports anthropométriques en général et sur les principales proportions du corps," *Mém. Soc. Anthrop. Paris,* Ser. 3, T. 2.

McCLOY, C. H. 1936. "Appraising Physical Status and the Selection of Measurements," *Univ. Ia Stud. Child Welf., 12,* No. 2.

MILLER, E. 1927. *Types of Mind and Body,* New York, Norton.

MILLS, R. W. 1917. "The Relation of Body Habitus to Visceral Form, Position, Tonus and Motility," *Amer. J. Roentgenol., 4,* 155.

MOHR, G. J., and R. H. GUNDLACH. 1927. "The Relation Between Physique and Performance," *J. Exp. Psychol., 10,* 117–157.

NACCARATI, S. 1921. "The Morphologic Aspect of Intelligence," *Arch. Psychol., N.Y.,* No. 45.

PATERSON, D. G. 1930. *Physique and Intellect,* New York, Appleton-Century.

PEARL, R. 1933. *Constitution and Health,* London, Kegan Paul, Trench, Trubner.

PEARL, R., and R. D. PEARL. 1934. "Studies on Human Longevity: VI," *Hum. Biol.,* 6, 98–222.

PEARL, R., A. C. SUTTON, W. T. HOWARD, JR., and M. RIOCH. 1929. "Studies on Constitution: I," *Hum. Biol.,* 1, 10–56.

PEARSON, K. 1906. "Relationship of Intelligence to Size and Shape of the Head and Other Mental and Physical Characters," *Biometrika,* 5, 105–146.

PENDE, N. 1928. *Constitutional Inadequacies* (trans. by S. Naccarati), Philadelphia, Lea & Febiger.

PETERSON, W. F. 1932. "Constitution and Disease," *Physiol. Rev.,* 12, 283–308.

PIGNET. 1901. "Du coefficient de robusticité," *Bull. méd. Paris,* 15, 373–376.

PLATTNER, W. 1934. "Metrische Körperbaudiagnostik," *Z. ges. Neurol. Psychiat.,* 151, 374–404.

RIPPY, E. L. 1936. "Physical Types and Their Relation to Disease," *Dallas Med. J.,* 22, 112–115.

RITALA, A. M. 1935. "Inheritance of Constitution of the Parents by the Newborn Child as Demonstrated by Body Measurements," *Acta Soc. Med. "Duodecim."* (Ser. B, parts 1–3, No. 20), 23, 1–56.

ROSTAN, L. 1828. *Cours élémentaire d'hygiène* (2nd ed., 2 vols.), Paris.

SHAW, F. C. 1924–1925. "A Morphologic Study of the Functional Psychoses," *St. Hosp. Quart., N. Y.,* 10, 413–421.

SHELDON, W. H. 1927a. "Morphological Types and Mental Ability," *J. Person. Res.,* 5, 447–451.

———. 1927b. "Social Traits and Morphological Types," *Person. J.,* 6, No. 1.

———. 1927c. "Ability and Facial Measurements," *Person. J.,* 6, No. 2.

SHELDON, W. H., and S. S. STEVENS. 1942. *The Varieties of Temperament,* New York, Harper.

SHELDON, W. H., S. S. STEVENS, and W. B. TUCKER. 1940. *The Varieties of Human Physique,* New York, Harper.

SIGAUD, C. 1914. *La forme humaine,* Paris, A. Maloine.

SLYE, M. 1927. "Cancer and Heredity," *Ann. Intern. Med.,* 1, 951.

SNYDER, L. H. 1926. "Human Blood Groups: Their Inheritance and Racial Significance," *Amer. J. Phys. Anthrop.,* 9, 233–263.

SOMMERVILLE, R. C. 1924. "Physical, Motor and Sensory Traits," *Arch. Psychol., N. Y.,* 12, 1–108.

SPRANGER, E. 1928. *Types of Men* (trans. by Pigors), Halle, Niemeyer.

SPURZHEIM, J. G. 1833. *Phrenology in Connexion with the Study of Physiognomy,* Boston, Marsh, Capen & Lyon.

SSUCHAREWA, G. E. 1928. "Körperbau, Motorik und Charakter der Oligophrenen, II," *Z. ges. Neurol. Psychiat.,* 114, 22–37.

STERN-PIPER, L. 1923. "Kretschmers psycho-physische Typen und die Rassenformen in Deutschland," *Arch. Psychiat. Nervenkr.,* 67, 569.

STEVENSON, P. H., S. M. SUNG, T. PAI, and R. S. LYMAN. 1937. "Chinese Constitutional Differentiation and Kretschmerian Typology," *Hum. Biol.,* 9, 451–481.

STILLER, B. 1907. *Die asthenische Konstitutionskrankheit,* Stuttgart, F. Enke.

STOCKARD, C. R. 1923. "Human Types and Growth Relations," *Amer. J. Anat.,* 31, 261.

————. 1931. *The Physical Basis of Personality,* New York, Norton.

TODD, T. W. 1930. *Behavior Patterns of the Alimentary Tract,* Beaumont Foundation Lectures, Series No. 9, Baltimore, William & Wilkins.

TREADGOLD, H. A. 1934. "Functional Efficiency and Body-Build in the Young Male Adult," *Lancet,* Part 1, 1377–1382.

TSCHERNING, R. 1923. "Ueber die somatische und psychische Konstitution bei Ulcus ventriculi," *Arch. VerdauKr.,* 31, 351–360.

TSCHERNORUTZKY, M. W. 1931. "Wechselbeziehungen zwischen Funktionseigenschaften und Konstitutionstypus," *Z. menschl. Vererb.-u. KonstLehre,* 15, 134.

TUCKER, W. B., and W. A. LESSA. 1940. "Man: A Constitutional Investigation," *Quart. Rev. Biol.,* 15, 265–289; 411–455.

VAN DER HORST. 1924. "Experimentell-psychologische Untersuchungen zu Kretschmers 'Körperbau und Charakter,'" *Z. ges. Neurol. Psychiat.,* 93, 341–380.

VIOLA, G. 1933. *La costituzione individuale,* Bologna, L. Cappeli.

VOLLMER, H. 1937. "The Shape of the Ear in Relation to Body Constitution," *Arch. Pediat.,* 54, 574–590.

VON ROHDEN, F. 1925. "Ueber Beziehungen zwischen Konstitution und Rasse," *Z. ges. Neurol. Psychiat.,* 98, 255.

WARSTADT, A., and W. A. COLLIER. 1935. "Ueber den angeblichen Zusammenhang von Schizophrenie und Tuberkulose," *Allg. Z. Psychiat.,* 103, 355–365.

WEIDENREICH, F. 1926. *Rasse und Körperbau,* Berlin, Springer.

WEISMAN, S. A. 1938. *Your Chest Should Be Flat* (Foreword by R. E. Scammon), Philadelphia, Lippincott.

WERTHAM, F. 1930. "Progress in Psychiatry: IV. Experimental Type Psychology," *Arch. Neurol. Psychiat., Chicago,* 24, 605–611.

WERTHEIMER, F. I., and F. E. HESKETH. 1926. *The Significance of the Physical Constitution in Mental Disease,* Medical Monographs, Vol. 10, Baltimore, Williams & Wilkins.

WESTPHAL, K. 1931. "The Use of Indices as an Auxiliary Method in the Establishment of Physical Types," *Hum. Biol., 3*, 420–428.

WHEELER, W. M. 1927. "Physiognomy of Insects," *Quart. Rev. Biol., 2*, 1.

WILLEMSE, W. 1932. *Constitution-Types in Delinquency*, New York, Harcourt, Brace.

YOUNG, M. 1933. "A Study of Rheumatic Fever and Asthmatic Children, with Special Reference to Physical Type," *J. Hyg., Camb., 33*, 435.

ZWEIG, H. 1919. "Habitus und Lebensalter," *Z. Angew. Anat., 4*, 255.

Abraham H. Maslow

MOTIVATION AND PERSONALITY: NOTES ON BEING-PSYCHOLOGY

Before assuming his present position as chairman of the Department of Psychology at Brandeis University, Abraham Maslow taught for fourteen years at Brooklyn College. He was Andrew Kay Visiting Fellow at Western Behavioral Sciences Institute, La Jolla, California from 1961–1962. He is the author of three books, Principles of Abnormal Psychology, Motivation and Personality *and* Toward a Psychology of Being, *and of about eighty articles.*

Maslow has aligned himself closely with an organismic, or what he calls a holistic-dynamic, point of view. Maslow condemns psychology for its "pessimistic, negative and limited conception" of man. Psychology, according to Maslow, has dwelled more upon the faults of man than upon his strengths. It has thoroughly explored his sins but neglected his virtues. In effect, Maslow believes that if psychologists study crippled, stunted, and neurotic people they are bound to produce a crippled psychology. Maslow's contribution to the organismic point of view lies mainly in the fact that he preoccupies himself with healthy people rather than with sick ones. Man, he believes, has an inborn nature which is essentially good, and is never evil. When man is bad and wicked, it is only because the environment has made him so. As Maslow himself states: "This inner nature is not strong and overpowering and unmistakable like the instinct of animals. It is weak and delicate and subtle and easily overcome by habit, cultural pressure and wrong attitudes toward it. Even though weak, it never disappears in the normal person, perhaps not even in the sick person. It persists, even though denied, underground."

MOTIVATION AND PERSONALITY:
NOTES ON BEING-PSYCHOLOGY[1]

I. DEFINITION OF BEING-PSYCHOLOGY
  BY ITS SUBJECT MATTER, PROBLEMS, JURISDICTIONS

(COULD ALSO BE CALLED ONTO PSYCHOLOGY
TRANSCENDENTAL PSYCHOLOGY, PSYCHOLOGY OF PERFECTION,
PSYCHOLOGY OF ENDS)

1. Deals with ends (rather than with means or instruments); with end-states, end-experiences (intrinsic satisfactions and enjoyments); with persons insofar as they are ends-in-themselves (sacred, unique, noncomparable, equally valuable with every other person rather than as instruments or means-to-ends); with techniques of making means into ends, of transforming means-activities into end-activities. Deals with objects per se, as they are in their own nature, not insofar as they are self-validating, intrinsically valid, inherently valuable, per se valuable, needing no justification. Here-now states in which the present is experienced fully, per se (as end in itself), and not as repetition of past or prelude to future.

2. Deals with states of finis and of telos; that is, of completion, climax, finality, ending, totality, consummation, finishing (states in which nothing is lacking, nothing more is needed or wanted, no improvement is possible). States of pure happiness, joy, bliss, rapture, ecstasy, fulfillment, realization, states of hopes fulfilled, of problems solved, of wishes granted, of needs gratified, of goals attained, of dreams realized. Already being there; having arrived rather than striving to get there. Peak experiences. States of pure success (transient disappearance of all negation).

2a. Unhappy, tragic states of completion and finality, insofar as they yield B-cognition. States of failure, of hopelessness, of despair, of collapse of defenses, acute failure of value system, acute confrontation with real guilt, can *force* perception of truth and reality (as an end and no longer as a means) in some instances where there is enough strength and courage.

3. States felt to be, perceived to be perfect. Concepts of perfection. Ideals, models, limits, examplars, abstract

definitions. The human being insofar as he potentially is, or can be conceived to be, perfect, ideal, model, authentic, fully human, paradigmatic, godlike, exemplary, or insofar as he has potentialities and vectors in these directions (that is, man as he *might* be, *could* be, or potentially *is* under best conditions; the ideal limits of human development, to which he approaches, but never attains permanently). His Destiny, Fate. These ideal human potentialities extrapolated out from the ideal far goals of psychotherapy, education, family training, end-product of growth, self development, and so on. (See, "Operations that Define B-Values.") Deals with Definition of Core and with defining characteristics of the human being; his nature; his "intrinsic core" or "inner core"; his essence, his presently existing potentialities; his *sine qua nons* (instincts, constitution, biological nature, inherent, intrinsic human nature). This makes possible definition (quantitatively) of "full humanness" or "degree of humanness" or "degree of human diminution." Philosophical Anthropology in European sense. (Differentiate *"sine qua non,"* defining characteristics (which define the concept "humanness"), *from* the exemplar (model, Platonic idea, ideal possibility, perfect idea, hero, template, die). Former is the minimum; latter is the maximum. Latter is pure, static Being which the former tries to Become. Former has very low entrance requirements to the class, for example, human is featherless biped. Also membership is all-or-none, in or out.

4. States of desirelessness, purposelessness, of lack of D-need, of being unmotivated, non-coping, non-striving, of enjoying rewards, of having been satisfied. Profit taking. (Able, therefore, "to leave one's interests, wishes and aims entirely out of sight; thus of entirely renouncing one's own personality for a time, so as to remain pure knowing subject . . . with clear vision of the world"—Schopenhauer.)

4a. States of fearlessness; anxiety-free states. Courage. Unhampered, freely flowing, uninhibited, unchecked human nature.

5. Metamotivation (dynamics of action when all the D-needs, lacks, wants, have been satisfied). Growth-motivation. "Unmotivated" behavior. Expression. Spontaneity.

5a. States and processes of pure (primary and/or integrated) creativeness. Pure here-now activity ("freedom" from past or future insofar as this is possible). Improvisation. Pure fitting of person and situation (problem) to each other, moving toward person-situation fusion as an ideal limit.

6. Descriptive, empirical, clinically or personologically or psychometrically described states of fulfillment of the promise (or destiny, vocation, fate, call), of the self (self-actualization, maturity, the fully evolved person, psychological health, authenticity, attainment of "real self," individuation, the creative personality, identity, real-izing or actual-izing of potentiality).

7. Cognition of Being (B-Cog.) Transactions with extrapsychic reality which are centered upon the nature of that reality rather than upon the nature of, or interests of, the cognizing self. Penetration to the essence of things or persons. Perspicuity.

7a. Conditions under which B-Cognition occurs. Peak experiences. Nadir or desolation experiences. B-Cog. before death. B-Cog. under acute psychotic regression. Thereapeutic insights as B-Cog. Fear and evasion of B-Cog; dangers of B-Cog.

    a. Nature of the percept in B-Cognition. Nature of reality as *described* and as *ideally extrapolated* under B-Cognition, that is, under "best" conditions. Reality conceived to be independent of the perceiver. Reality unabstracted. (See Note on B-Cognition and D-Cognition.)

    b. Nature of the perceiver in B-Cognition, veridical because detached, desireless, unselfish, "disinterested," Taoistic, fearless, here-now (see note on Innocent Perceiving), receptive, humble (not arrogant), without thought of selfish profit, and so on. Ourselves as most efficient perceivers of reality.

8. Transcending time and space. States in which they are forgotten (absorption, focal attention, fascination, peak-experiences, nadir-experiences), irrelevant or hampering or harmful. Cosmos, people, objects, experiences seen insofar as they are timeless, eternal, spaceless, universal, absolute, ideal.

9. The sacred; sublime, ontic, spiritual, transcendent, eternal, infinite, holy, absolute; states of awe; of worship, oblation, and so on. "Religious" states insofar as they

are naturalistic. Everyday world, objects, people seen under the aspect of eternity. Unitive Life. Unitive consciousness. States of fusion of temporal and eternal, of local and universal, of relative and absolute, of fact and value.

10. States of innocence (using child or animal as paradigm) (see B-Cognition) (using mature, wise, self-actualizing person as paradigm). Innocent perceiving (ideally no discrimination of important and unimportant; everything equally probable; everything equally interesting; less differentiation of figure and ground; only rudimentary structuring and differentiation of environment; less means-ends differentiation, as everything tends to be equally valuable in itself; no future, no prognosis, no foreboding, therefore no surprises, apprehensions, disappointments, expectations, predictions, anxieties, rehearsals, preparations, or worries; one thing is as likely to happen as another; non-interfering-receptiveness; acceptance of whatever happens; little choosing, preferring, selecting, discriminating; little discrimination of relevance from irrelevance; little abstraction; wonder). Innocent behaving (spontaneity, expressiveness, impulsiveness; no fear, controls or inhibitions; no guile, no ulterior motives; honesty; fearlessness; purposeless; unplanned, unpremeditated, unrehearsed; humble, not arrogant); no impatience (when future unknown); no impulse to improve world, or reconstruct it. (Innocence overlaps with B-Cognition very much; perhaps they will turn out to be identical in the future.)

11. States tending toward ultimate holism, that is, the whole cosmos, all of reality, seen in a unitary way; insofar as everything is everything else as well, insofar as anything is related to everything; insofar as all of reality is a single thing which we perceive from various angles. Bucke's cosmic consciousness. Fascinated perception of a portion of the world as if it were the whole world. Techniques of seeing something as if it were all there was, for example, in art and photography, cropping, magnification, blowing up, and so on (which cut off object from all its relations, context, imbededness, and so on, and permit it to be seen in itself, absolutely, freshly). Seeing *all* its characteristics rather than abstracting in terms of usefulness, danger, convenience, and so on. The

Being of an object is the whole object; abstracting necessarily sees it from the point of view of means and takes it out of the realm of the per se).

Transcending of separateness, discreteness, mutual exclusiveness, and of law of excluded middle.

12. The observed or extrapolated characteristics (or Values) of Being. (See List of B-Values attached.) The B-realm. The Unitive Consciouness. See attached memo for "The operations that give definition to the B-Values."

13. All states in which dichotomies (polarities, opposites, contradictories) are resolved (transcended, combined, fused, integrated), for example, selfishness and unselfishness, reason and emotion, impulse and control, trust and will, conscious and unconscious, opposed or antagonistic interests, happiness and sadness, tears and laughter, tragic and comic, Appollonian and Dionysian, romantic and classical, and so on. All integrating processes which transform oppositions into synergies, for example, love, art, reason, humor, and so on.

14. All synergic states (in world, society, person, nature, self, and so on). States in which selfishness becomes the same as unselfishness (when by pursuing "selfish ends" I *must* benefit everyone else; and when by being altruistic, I benefit myself, that is, when the dichotomy is resolved and transcended). States of society when virtue pays, that is, when it is rewarded extrinsically as well as intrinsically; when it doesn't cost too much to be virtuous or intelligent or perspicuous or beautiful or honest, and so on. All states which foster and encourage the B-values to be actualized. States in which it is easy to be good. States which discourage resentment, counter-values and counter-morality (hatred and fear of excellence, truth, goodness, beauty, and so on). All states which increase the correlation between the true, the good, the beautiful, and so on, and move them toward their ideal unity with each other.

15. States in which the Human Predicament (Existential Dilemma) is transiently solved, integrated, transcended, or forgotten, for example, peak-experience, B-humor and laughter, the "happy ending," triumph of B-justice, the "good death," B-love, B-art, B-tragedy or comedy, all integrative moments, acts and perceptions, and so on.

II. Collation of the Various Ways in Which the Word
    "Being" Has Been Used In *Toward a Psychology of
    Being*[2]

1. It has been used to refer to the whole cosmos, to every-
    thing that exists, to all of reality. In peak-experiences, in
    states of fascination, of focal attention, attention can
    narrow down to a single object or person which is then
    reacted to "as if" it were the whole of Being, that is, the
    whole of reality. This implies that it is all holistically in-
    terrelated. The only complete and whole thing there is
    is the whole Cosmos. Anything short of that is partial,
    incomplete, shorn away from intrinsic ties and relations
    for the sake of momentary, practical convenience. It
    refers also to Cosmic Consciousness. Also implies hier-
    archical-integration rather than dichotomizing.

2. It refers to the "inner core," the biological nature of the
    individual—his basic needs, capacities, preferences; his
    irreducible nature; the "real self" (Horney); his inher-
    ent, essential, intrinsic nature. Identity. Since "inner
    core" is both species-wide (every baby has the need to
    be loved) and individual (only Mozart was perfectly
    Mozartian), the phrase can mean either "being fully
    human" and/or "being perfectly idiosyncratic."

3. Being can mean "expressing one's nature," rather than
    coping, striving, straining, willing, controlling, interfer-
    ing, commanding (in the sense that a cat is being a cat,
    as contrasted with the sense in which a female imper-
    sonator is being a female, or a stingy person "tries" to be
    generous). It refers to effortless spontaneity (as an in-
    telligent person expresses intelligence, as a baby is baby-
    ish) which permits the deepest, innermost nature to be
    seen in behavior. Since spontaneity is difficult, most
    people can be called the "human impersonators," that
    is, they are "trying" to be what they think is human
    rather than just being what they are. It therefore also
    implies honesty, nakedness, self-disclosure. Most of the
    psychologists who have used it, include (covertly) the
    hidden, not yet sufficiently examined assumption that a
    neurosis is *not* part of the deepest nature, the inner core,
    or the real Being of the person, but is rather a more
    superficial layer of the personality which conceals or
    distorts the *real self*, that is, neurosis is a defense against

real Being, against one's deep, biological nature. "Trying" to be may not be as good as "being" (expressing), but it is also better than *not* trying, that is, hopelessness, not coping, giving up.

4. The Being of any person, animal or thing can mean its "suchness" or its "isness," its raw, concrete nature, its being whatever it phenomenologically and sensuously is, its own particular experiential quality, for example, the redness of the red, the felinity of the cat, the Renoirishness of a Renoir, the particular, peculiar, like-nothing-else sound of the oboe, the unique, idiographic pattern of qualities that now "means" Uriah Heep, Don Quixote, or Abraham Lincoln. Obviously there is no question here of validation, justification, explanation, or meaning. The answer to the question "Why?" is "It just *is* so. This is what it is. It is so because it is so." In this sense, Being is pointless and has no excuse or reason for existing: it just *does* exist.

5. Being can refer to the *concept* "human being," "horse," and so on. Such a concept has defining characteristics, includes and excludes from membership within it by specific operations. For human psychology this has limitation because any person can be seen *either* as a member, or example of, the concept or class "human being," *or* as the sole member of the unique class "Addison J. Sims."

Also, we can use the class concept in two extremely different ways, minimum or maximum. The class can be defined minimally so that practically no one is excluded, for example, human beings are featherless bipeds. This gives us no basis for grading quality or for discriminating among human beings in any way. One is either a member of the class or not a member of the class, either in or out. No other status is possible.

Or else the class can be defined by its perfect examplars (models, heroes, ideal possibilities, Platonic ideas, extrapolations out to ideal limits and possibilities). Hundreds of defining characteristics of perfect humanness could then be listed, and degrees of humanness can then be quantitatively determined by the number of defining characteristics fulfilled (R. Hartman). This usage has many advantages, but its abstract and static quality must be kept in mind. There is a profound difference between describing carefully the best actual human beings I can get (self-actualizing people), none of whom are perfect, and on the other hand, describing the ideal, the perfect, the conceptually pure concept of the exemplar, constructed by extrapolating out ahead from the descriptive data on actual, imperfect people. The *concept* "self-actualizing people" describe not only the people but also the ideal limit which they approach. This should make no difficulty. We are used to blueprints and diagrams of "the" steam engine or automobile, which are certainly never confused with, for example, a photograph of my automobile or your steam engine.

Such a conceptual definition gives the possibility also of distinguishing the essential from the peripheral (accidental, superficial, non-essential). It gives criteria for discriminating the real from the not-real, the true from the false, the necessary from the dispensable or expendable, the eternal and permanent from the passing, the unchanging from the changeable.

6. Being can mean the "end" of developing, growing, and becoming. It refers to the end-product or limit, or goal or *telos* of becoming rather than to its process, as in the following sentence: "In this way, the psychologies of being and of becoming can be reconciled, and the child, simply being himself, can yet move forward and grow." This sounds very much like Aristotle's "final cause," or the telos, the final product, the sense in which the acorn now has within its nature the oak tree which it will become. (This is tricky because it is our tendency to anthropomorphize and say that the acorn is "trying" to grow up. It is not. It is simply "being" an infant. In the same way that Darwin could not use the word "trying" to explain evolution, so also must we avoid this usage. We must explain his growth forward toward his limit as an epiphenomenon of his being, as "blind" by-products of contemporary mechanisms, and processes.)

III. THE B-VALUES (AS DESCRIPTIONS OF THE WORLD PERCEIVED IN PEAK-EXPERIENCES)

The characteristics of being are also the values of being. (Paralleled by the characteristics of fully human people, the preferences of fully human people; the characteristics of selfhood [identity] in peak-experiences; the characteristics of

ideal art; the characteristics of ideal children; the characteristics of ideal mathematical demonstrations, of ideal experiments and theories, of ideal science and knowledge; the far
goals of all ideal [Taoistic, non-interfering] psychotherapies;
the far goals of ideal humanistic education; the far goals and
the expression of some kinds of religion; the characteristics of
the ideally good environment and of the ideally good society).

1. Truth	7a. Necessity
2. Goodness	8. Completion
3. Beauty	9a. Order
4. Wholeness	9. Justice
4a. Dichotomy-	10. Simplicity
transcendence	11. Richness
5. Aliveness, Process	12. Effortlessness
6. Uniqueness	13. Playfulness
7. Perfection	14. Self-Sufficiency.

1. Truth: honesty; reality (nakedness; simplicity; richness; essentiality; oughtness; beauty; pure; clean and
   unadulterated completeness).
2. Goodness (rightness; desirability; oughtness; justice;
   benevolence; honesty); (we love it, are attracted to it,
   approve of it).
3. Beauty (rightness; form; aliveness; simplicity; richness; wholeness; perfection; completion; uniqueness;
   honesty).
4. Wholeness (unity; integration; tendency to oneness;
   interconnectedness; simplicity; organization; structure;
   order, not dissociated; synergy; homonymous and integrative tendencies).
4a. Dichotomy-transcendence (acceptance, resolution, integration, or transcendence of dichotomies, polarities,
   opposites, contradictions); synergy (that is, transformation of oppositions into unities, of antagonists into
   collaborating or mutually enhancing partners).
5. Aliveness (process; not-deadness; spontaneity; self-
   regulation; full-functioning; changing and yet remain-
   ing the same; expressing itself).
6. Uniqueness (idiosyncrasy; individuality; non-compar-
   ability; novelty; quale; suchness; nothing else like it).
7. Perfection (nothing superfluous; nothing lacking; everything in its right place, unimprovable; just-right-

ness; just-so-ness; suitability; justice; completeness; nothing beyond; oughtness).

7a. Necessity (inevitability; it must be *just* that way; not changed in any slightest way; and it is good that it *is* that way).

8. Completion (ending; finality; justice; it's finished; no more changing of the Gestalt; fulfillment; *finis* and *telos*; nothing missing or lacking; totality; fulfillment of destiny; cessation; climax; consummation closure; death before rebirth; cessation and completion of growth and development).

9. Justice (fairness; oughtness; suitability; architectonic quality; necessity; inevitability; disinterestedness; non-partiality).

9a. Order (lawfulness; rightness; nothing superfluous; perfectly arranged).

10. Simplicity (honesty; nakedness; essentiality; abstract, unmistakability; essential skeletal structure; the heart of the matter; bluntness; only that which is necessary; without ornament, nothing extra or superfluous).

11. Richness (differentiation; complexity; intricacy; totality; nothing missing or hidden; all there; "non-importance"; that is, everything is equally important; nothing is unimportant; everything left the way it is, without improving, simplifying, abstracting, rearranging).

12. Effortlessness (ease; lack of strain, striving or difficulty; grace; perfect and beautiful functioning).

13. Playfulness (fun; joy; amusement; gaiety; humor; exuberance; effortlessness).

14. Self-sufficiency (autonomy; independence; not needing anything other than itself in order to be itself; self-determining; environment-transcendence; separateness; living by its own laws; identity).

IV. OPERATIONS WHICH DEFINE THE MEANINGS OF THE B-VALUES IN TESTABLE FORM

1. First seen as described characteristics of self-actualizing (psychologically healthy) people, as reported by themselves and as perceived by investigator and by people close to them (Values 1, 2, 3, 4, 4a, 5, 6, 7, (?), 8, 9, 9a, 10, 11, 12, 13, 14, and also perspicuity, acceptance, ego-transcendence, freshness of cognition, more peak-

experiences, *Gemeinschaftsgefuhl,* B-love, non-striving, B-respect, creativeness$_{sa}$).

2. Seen as preferences, choices, desiderata, values of self-actualizing people, in themselves, in other people, in the world (granted fairly good environmental conditions and fairly good chooser). Some likelihood that many more than self-actualizing people have same, though weaker preferences, needing, however, *very* good environmental conditions and *very* good condition of the chooser. The probability of preference for any and all of the B-values increases with increase in (*a*) psychological health of the chooser. The probability of preference for any and all of the B-values increases with increase in (*a*) psychological health of the chooser, (*b*) synergy of the environment, and (*c*) strength, courage, vigor, self-confidence, and so on of chooser.

   Hypothesis: The B-values are what many (most? all?) people deeply *yearn for* (discoverable in deep therapy).

   Hypothesis: The B-values are ultimate satisfiers, whether or not consciously sought, preferred, or yearned for; that is, bring feelings of perfection, completion, fulfillment, serenity, destiny fulfilled, et cetera. Also in terms of producing good effects (therapeutic and growth), see Chapter 3 in *Toward a Psychology of Being.*

3. Reported to the investigator as characteristics of the world (or as trends toward such characteristics) perceived in the peak-experiences by the peak-experiencers (that is, the way the world looks in the various peak-experiences). These data supported in general by the common reports in the literatures on mystic experience, love experience, esthetic experience, creative experiences, parental and reproductive experiences, intellectual insight, therapeutic insights (not always), athletic sports, bodily experiences (sometimes), and by some aspects of religious writings.

4. Reported to the investigator as characteristics of the self by peak-experiencers ("acute identity-experiences") (all values with possible exception of 9, plus creativeness$_{sa}$; here-now quality; non-striving which may be taken as exemplifying 5, 7, 12; poetic communication).

5. Observed by the investigator as characteristics of the behavior of the peak-experiencers (same as #4 preceding).

6. Same for other B-cognitions when there is sufficient

strength and courage; for example, some foothill-experiences; some nadir and desolation experiences (psychotic regression, confrontation with death, destruction of defenses, illusions or value-systems, tragedy and tragic experiences, failures, confrontation with human predicament or existential dilemma); some intellectual and philosophical insights, constructions and workings through; B-cognition of the past ("embracing the past"). This "operation" or source of data not sufficient in itself; that is, needs other validations. Sometimes supports findings by other operations, sometimes contradicts them.

7. Observed as characteristics of "good" art ("good" so far means "preferred by this investigator"); for example, painting, sculpture, music, dancing, poetry, and other literary arts (all values except 9, and with some exceptions to 7 and 8).

A pilot experiment: Children's non-representational paintings rated by artistic judges on 10-point scale from "most generally esthetic quality" to "least generally esthetic quality," another set of judges rating all these paintings on 10-point scale for "wholeness," another set of judges rating for "aliveness," another set of judges rating for "uniqueness." All four variables correlate positively. *A pilot investigation:* leaves impression that it is possible by examination of paintings or short stories to make a better than chance judgment about the health of the artist.

Testable Hypothesis: That the correlation between beauty, wisdom, and goodness and psychological health increases with age. People in increasing age decades to be rated for health, beauty, goodness and wisdom, each rating by different sets of judges. Correlation should be positive throughout and should be higher for people in the thirties, still higher in the forties, et cetera. So far hypothesis supported by casual observation.

Hypothesis: Rating novels in all fifteen B-values will show that "poor" novels (so rated by judges) are less close to the B-values than "good" novels. Same for "good" music and "poor" music. Non-normative statements are possible also; for example, which painters, which words, what kind of dancing help to heighten or to strengthen or exemplify individuality, honesty, self-sufficiency, or other B-values. Also, which books, poems are preferred by more matured people. How possible is it to use healthy people as "biological assays" (more sensitive and efficient perceivers and choosers of B-values, like canaries in a coal mine)?

8. What little we know about the characteristics of and the determinants of increasing and decreasing psychological health in children of all ages in our culture indicates on the whole that increasing health means movement toward various and perhaps all of the B-values. "Good" external conditions in school, family, and so on, may then be defined as conducive to psychological health or toward the B-values. Phrasing this in terms of testable hypotheses would yield; for example, psychologically healthier children are more honest (beautifull, virtuous, integrated, and so on . . .) than less healthy children, health to be measured by projective tests or behavior samples or psychiatric interview, or absence of classical neurotic symptoms, and so on.

Hypothesis: Psychologically healthier teachers should produce movement toward the B-values in their students, and so on.

Question in non-normative style: Which conditions increase and which decrease integration in children? honesty, beauty, playfulness, self-sufficiency, and so on?

9. "Good" (2) or "elegant" mathematical demonstrations are the ultimate in "simplicity" (10), in abstract truth (1), in perfection and completion and "order" (7, 8, 9). They can be and often are seen as very beautiful (3). Once done, they look easy and *are easy* (12). This move toward, yearning for, love for, admiration for, even in some people need for, perfection, and so on, is roughly paralleled by all machine makers, engineers, production engineers, toolmakers, carpenters, specialists in administration and organization in business, army, and so on. They too show *drang nach* the above B-values. This should be measurable in terms of choices between, for example, an elegantly simple machine, and an unnecessarily complex one, a well-balanced hammer and a clumsily balanced hammer, a "fully" functioning engine and a partially functioning one (5), and so on. Healthier engineers, carpenters, et cetera, should spontaneously demonstrate greater preference for and closeness to the B-values in all their products, which should be more

324 *Varieties of Personality Theory*

preferred, command a higher price, and so on, than the less B-ward products of less developed and evolved engineers, carpenters, and so on. Something similar is probably also true of the "good" experiment, the "good" theory, and for "good" science in general. It is probable that a strong determinant of the use of the word "good" in these contexts is "closer to the B-values" in about the same sense as is true for mathematics.

10. Most (insight, uncovering, non-authoritarian, Taoistic) psychotherapists, of whatever school, when they can be induced to speak of the ultimate goals of psychotherapy will even today, speak of the fully human, authentic, self-actualizing, individuated person or some approximation thereof both in the descriptive sense and in the sense of the ideal, abstract concept. When teased out into sub-details, this usually means some or all of the B-values; for example, honesty (1), good behavior (2), integration (4), spontaneity (5), movement toward fullest development and maturing and harmonizing of potentialities (7, 8, 9), being what one fully is in essence (10), being all that one can be and accepting one's deeper self in all its aspects (11), effortless, easy functioning (12), ability to play and to enjoy (13), independence, autonomy, and self-determination (14). I doubt that any therapist would seriously object to any of these, although some might want to add.

The only massive evidence we have on the actual effects of successful and unsuccessful psychotherapy comes from the Rogers group, and all of it, without exception so far as I am aware, supports or is compatible with the hypothesis that the B-values are the far goal of psychotherapy. This operation, that is, before and after psychotherapy, is available for putting to the test the as yet untested hypothesis that therapy also increases the beauty of the patient and also his sensitiveness to, yearning for, and enjoyment of beauty. A parallel set of hypotheses for humor$_{sa}$, is also testable.

Pilot experiment: Unquantified observation from two-year-long experiments with group therapy; both the college boys and the college girls in general looked more beautiful or handsome both to me and to the participants themselves (and actually became more beautiful, attractive, as measured by the judgment of strangers) because of increased self-love and self-respect and increased pleasure in pleasing the group members (out of increased love for them). In general, if we stress the uncovering aspect of therapy, then whatever it reveals was there already in some sense. Therefore, whatever emerges or is revealed by uncovering therapy is very likely to be constitutionally or temperamentally or genetically intrinsic to the organism; that is, its essence, its deepest reality, is biologically given. That which is dissipated by uncovering therapy is thereby proved to be, or at least indicated to be, *not* in-by or imposed upon the organism. The relevant evidence which indicates that the B-values are strengthened or actualized by uncovering therapy therefore supports the belief that these B-values are attributes or defining characteristics of the deepest, most essential, most intrinsic human nature. This general proportion is quite testable in principle. Rogers' technique of "moving Toward and Away From" in therapy (*A Therapist's View of Personal Goals*, Pendle Hill Pamphlet, 1960) offers a wide range of possibilities of research on what helps movement toward and away from B-values.

11. The far goals of "creative," "humanistic," or "whole person" education, especially non-verbal, art, dance, et cetera, education, overlap very considerably with the B-values, and may turn out to be identical with them, plus all sorts of psychotherapeutic additions which are probably means rather than ends. That is, this kind of education half consciously wants the same kind of research that has been done and will be done on the effects of therapy, and can, therefore, in principle be paralleled with "creative" education. As with therapy, so also with education, can be seen the possibility of winding up with a usable, normative concept; that is, that education is "good" which best "be-ifies" the student; that is, helps him to become more honest, good, beautiful, integrated, and so on. This probably holds true also for higher education, if the acquisition of skills and tools is excluded, or seen only as a means to ultimate B-ends.

12. About the same is true for certain versions of the large theistic and nontheistic religions, and for both the legalistic and mystical versions of each of these. On the whole they propagate; (*a*) a God who is the embodiment of most of the B-values; (*b*) the ideal, religious and Godly man is one who best exemplifies or at least yearns for these same "Godlike" B-values; (*c*) all techniques, cere-

monials, rituals, dogmas can be seen as means toward achieving these ends; (*d*) heaven is the place or state, or time of achievement of these values. Salvation, redemption, conversion, are all acceptances of the truth of the above, and so on. Since these propositions are supported by selected evidence, they need a principle of selection outside themselves; that is, they are compatible with B-psychology, but do not prove it to be true. The literature of religion is a useful storehouse if one knows what to pick and use. As with other propositions above, we may turn things about and offer as theoretical proposition to try out, for example, B-values are definers of "true" of functional, usable, helpful religion. This criterion is probably best satisfied now by a combination of Zen and Tao and Humanism.

13. It is my impression that *most* people move away from B-values under hard or bad environmental conditions that threaten the D-need gratifications; for example, concentration camps, prison camps, starvation, plague, terror, hostility from the environment, abandonment, rootlessness, widespread breakdown of value systems, absence of value systems, hopelessness, et cetera. It is not known why a *few* people under these very same "bad" conditions move toward the B-values. However, both kinds of movement are testable.

Hypothesis: That one useful meaning of "good conditions" is "synergy," defined by Ruth Benedict as "social-institutional conditions which fuse selfishness and unselfishness, by arranging it so that when I pursue 'selfish' gratifications, I automatically help others, and when I try to be altruistic, I automatically reward and gratify myself also; i.e., when the dichotomy or polar opposition between selfishness and altruism is resolved and transcended." Thus the hypotheses: a good society is one in which virtue pays: the more the synergy in a society or sub-group or pair or within a self, the closer we come to the B-values; poor social or environmental conditions are those which set us against each other by making our personal interests antagonistic to each other, or mutually exclusive, or in which the personal gratifications (D-needs) are in short supply so that not all can satisfy their needs, except at the expense of others. Under good conditions, we have to pay little or nothing for being virtuous, for pursuing the B-values, and so on; under good conditions, the virtuous businessman is more successful financially; under good conditions, the successful person is loved rather than hated or feared or resented; under good conditions, admiration is more possible (unmixed with erotization or dominatization, and so on).

14. There is some evidence to indicate that what we call "good" jobs and "good" working conditions on the whole help to move people toward the B-values; for example, people in less desirable jobs value safety and security most, while people in the most desirable jobs most often value highest the possibilities for self-actualization. This is a special case of "good" environmental conditions. Again the possibility is implied here of moving toward nonnormative statements; for example, which work conditions produce greater wholeness, honesty, idiosyncrasy, and so on, thereby replacing the word "good" with the phrase "conducing to the B-values."

15. The hierarchy of basic needs and their order of prepotency was discovered by the operation of a "reconstructive biology," that is, the frustration of which needs produce neurosis. Perhaps one day not too far off we shall have sensitive enough psychological instruments to put to the test the hypothesis that threat to or frustration of any of the B-values produces a kind of pathology or existential illness, or a feeling of human diminution; that is, that they are also "needs" in the above sense (that we yearn for them in order to complete ourselves or become fully human?). At any rate, it is possible now to ask the researchable questions which have not yet been researched, "What are the effects of living in a dishonest world, an evil world, an ugly world, a split, disintegrated world, a dead, static world, a world of clichés and stereotypes, an incomplete, unfinished world, a world without order or justice, an unnecessarily complicated world, an oversimplified, overabstract world, an effortful world, a humorless world, a world without privacy or independence?"

16. I have already pointed out that one usable operational meaning of the "good society" is the degree to which it offers all its members the basic need satisfactions and the possibilities of self-actualization and human fulfill-

ment. To this phrasing can be added the proposition "the good society" (by contrast with the poor society) exemplifies, values, strives for, makes possible the achievement of the B-values. This can also be phrased non-normatively, as we have done above. The abstractly ideal Eupsychia would perfectly achieve the B-values. To what extent is the good society (Eupsychia) the same as the synergic society?

V. How Can B-Love Bring Dis-interest, Neutrality, Detachment, Greater Perspicuity?

When does Love sometimes bring blindness? When does it mean *greater* and when lesser perspicuity?

The point at which a corner is turned is when the love becomes so great and so pure (unambivalent) for the object itself that *its* good is what we want, not what it can do for us; that is, when it passes beyond being means and becomes an end (with our permission). As with the apple tree, for instance; we can love *it* so much that we don't want it to be anything else; we are happy it is as it is. Anything that interferes with it ("butts in"), can do *only* harm and make it *less* an apple tree, or less perfectly living by its own intrinsic, inherent rules. It can look so perfect that we're afraid to touch it for fear of lessening it. Certainly, if it is seen as perfect, there is no possibility of improving it. As a matter of fact, the effort to improve (or decorate, and so on) is itself a proof that the object is seen as less than perfect, that the picture of "perfect development" in the improver's head is conceived by him to be better than the final end of the apple tree itself; that is, he can do better than the apple tree, he knows better; he can shape it better than it can itself. So we feel half-consciously that the dog-improver is not really a dog-lover. The real dog-lover will be enraged by the tail cropping, the ear cropping or shaping, the selective breeding that makes this dog fit a pattern from some magazine, at the cost of making it nervous, sick, sterile, unable to give birth normally, epileptic, et cetera. (And yet such people do call themselves dog-lovers.) Same for people who train dwarf-trees or teach bears to ride a bicycle or chimpanzees to smoke cigarettes.

Real love, then, is (sometimes at least) non-interfering and non-demanding and can delight in the thing itself; therefore, it can gaze at the object without guile, design, or calculation of any selfish kind. This makes for less abstracting (or selecting of parts or attributes or single characteristics of the object), less viewing of less-than-the-whole, less atomizing or dissecting. This is the same as saying that there is less active or procrustean structuring, organizing, shaping, molding, or fitting to theory, or to a preconception; that is, the object remains more whole, more unified, which amounts to saying, more itself. The object is less measured against criteria of relevance or irrelevance, importance or unimportance, figure or ground, useful or useless, dangerous or not dangerous, valuable or valueless, profit or no-profit, good or bad, or other criteria of selfish human perceiving. Also, the object is less apt to be rubricized, classified, or placed in a historical sequence, or seen as simply a member of a class, as a sample, or instance of a type.

This means that all the (unimportant as well as important) aspects or characteristics of (holistic) parts of the object (peripheral as well as central) are more apt to be given equal care or attention, and that *every* part is apt to be delightful and wonderful; B-love, whether of a lover or a baby or a painting or a flower, almost always guarantees this kind of distributed looking-with-care-intense-and-fascinated.

Seen in this holistic context, little flaws are apt to be seen as "cute," charming, endearing, *because* idiosyncratic, because they give character and individuality to the object, because they make it what-it-is-rather-than-something-else, perhaps also *just* because they are unimportant, peripheral, nonessential.

Therefore, the B-lover (B-Cognizer) will see details that will evade the D-lover or non-lover. Also, he will more easily see the per se nature of the object itself, in its own right and in its own style of being. Its own delicate and cartilaginous structure is more likely to be yielded to by receptive looking, which is non-active, non-interfering, less arrogant. That is, its perceived shape is more determined by its own shape when B-cognized than when a structure is imperiously imposed upon it by the perceiver, who will therefore be more likely to be too brusque, too impatient, too much the butcher hacking a carcass apart, for his own appetite, too much the conqueror demanding unconditional surrender, too much the sculptor modeling clay which has no structure of its own.

VI. CHARACTERISTICS OF B-COGNITION AND D-COGNITION
OF THE WORLD[3]

B-COGNITION	D-COGNITION
(1) Seen as whole, as complete, self-sufficient, as unitary. Either Cosmic Consciousness (Bucke), in which whole cosmos is perceived as single thing with oneself belonging in it; or else the person, object, or portion of the world seen is seen as if it were the whole world, that is, rest of world is forgotten. Integrative perceiving of unities. Unity of the world or object perceived.	Seen as part, as incomplete, not self-sufficient, as dependent upon other things.
(2) Exclusively, fully, narrowly attended to; absorption, fascination, focal attention; total attention. Tends to de-differentiate figure and ground. Richness of detail; seen from many sides. Seen with "care," totally, intensely, with complete investment. Totally cathected. Relative importance becomes unimportant; all aspects equally important.	Attended to with simultaneous attention to all cause that is relevant. Sharp figure-ground differentiation. Seen embedded in relationships to all else in world, as part of the world. Rubricized; seen from some aspects only; selective attention and selective inattention to some aspects; seen casually, seen only from some point of view.
(3) No comparing (in Dorothy Lee's sense). Seen per se, in itself, by itself. Not in competition with anything else. Some member of the class (in Hartman's sense).	Placing on a continuum or within a series; comparing, judging, evaluating. Seen as a member of a class, as an instance, a sample.
(4) Human-irrelevant	Relevant to human concerns; for example, What good is it? What can it be used for? Is it good for or dangerous to people? et cetera.

(5) Made richer by repeated experiencing. More and more perceived. "Intra-object richness."

Repeated experiencing impoverishes, reduces richness, makes it less interesting and attractive, takes away its demand-character. Familiarization leads to boredom.

(6) Seen as unneeded, as purposeless, as not desired, as unmotivated perceiving. Perceived as if it had no reference to the needs of the perceiver. Can therefore be seen as independent, in its own right.

Motivated perceiving. Object seen as need-gratifier, as useful or not useful.

(7) Object-centering. Self-forgetful, ego-transcending, unselfish, disinterested. Therefore, it-centered. Identification and fusion of perceiver and perceived. So absorbed and poured into the experience that self disappears, so that whole experience can be organized around the object itself as a centering point or organizing point. Object uncontaminated and unconfused with self. Abnegation of the perceiver.

Organized around ego as a centering point, which means projection of the ego into the percept. Perception not of the object alone but of the object-mixed-with-self-of-the-perceiver.

(8) The object is permitted to be itself. Humble, receptive, passive, choiceless, undemanding. Taoistic, non-interference with the object or percept. Let-be Acceptance.

Active shaping, organizing and selecting by the perceiver. He shifts it, rearranges it. He works at it. This must be more fatiguing than B-cognizing, which probably is fatigue-curing. Trying, striving, effort. Will, control.

(9) Seen as end in itself, Self-validating. Self-justifying. Intrinsically interesting for its own sake. Has intrinsic value.

A means, an instrument, not having self-contained worth but having only exchange-value, or standing for something else, or a ticket to some other place.

(10) Outside time and space. Seen as eternal, universal. "A minute is a day; a day is a minute." Disorientation of perceiver in time and space, not conscious of surroundings. Percept not related to surroundings. A-historical.

In time and space. Temporal. Local. Seen *in* history, and in the physical world.

(11) The characteristics of Being are perceived as Values of Being. See attached memo on B-Values.

D-Values are means-values, that is, usefulness, desirability-undesirability, suitability for a purpose. Evaluations, comparisons, condemnations, approvals, or disapprovals, judgments upon.

(12) Absolute (because timeless and spaceless, because detached from the ground, because taken per se, because rest of world and history all forgotten). This is compatible with the perception of process and shifting, alive organizations *within* the perception—but it is strictly *within* the perception.

Relative to history, to culture, to characterology, to local values, to the interests and needs of man. It is felt to be *passing*. Depends on man for its reality; if man were to disappear, *it* would disappear. Shifting from one syndrome to another as a whole, that is, it is now a bit in this syndrome, now a bit in *that* syndrome.

(13) Resolution of dichotomies, polarities, conflicts. Inconsistencies seen to exist simultaneously and to be sensible and necessary, that is, to be seen as a higher unity or integration, or under a superordinate whole.

Aristotelean logic, that is, separate things seen as dissected and cut off and quite different from each other, mutually exclusive, often with antagonistic interests.

(14) Concretely (*and* abstractly) perceived. All aspects at once. Therefore ineffable (to ordinary language); describable, if at all, by poetry, art, and so on, but even this will

Only abstract, categorized, diagrammatic rubricized, schematized. Classifying. "Reduction to the abstract."

make sense only to one who has already had same experience. Essentially esthetic experience (in Northrop's sense). Non-choosing preferring or selecting. Seen in its suchness (different from the concrete perception of young children, of primitive adults, or of brain-injured people because it co-exists with abstract ability).

(15) The idiographic object; the concrete, unique instance. Classification impossible (except for abstracted aspects) because sole member of its class.

Nomothetic, general, statistical lawfulness.

(16) Increase of dynamic isomorphism between inner and outer worlds. As the essential Being of the world is perceived by the person, so also does he concurrently come closer to his own Being; and vice versa.

Decreased ismorphism.

(17) Object often perceived as sacred, holy, "very special," It "demands" or "calls for" awe, reverence, piety, wonder.

Object "normal," everyday, ordinary, familiar, nothing special, "familiarized away."

(18) World and self often (not always) seen as amusing, playful, comic, funny, absurd, laughable; but also as poignant. Laughter (which is close to tears). Philosophical humor, humor$_{\text{...}}$. World, person, child, and so on, seen as cute, absurd, charming, lovable. May produce

Lesser forms of humor, if seen at all. Serious things quite different from amusing things. Hostile humor, humorlessness. Solemnity.

mixed   laughing-crying.
Fusion   of   comic-tragic
dichotomy.

(19) Non-interchangeable. Not   Interchangeable. Replaceable.
replaceable. No one else
will do.

VII. INNOCENT COGNITION (AS AN ASPECT OF B-COGNITION)

In innocence; that is, to the innocent, everything moves toward becoming equally probable; everything is equally important; everything is equally interesting. The best way to try to understand this is to see it through the eyes of the child. For instance, to the child the word "importance" doesn't mean anything at first. That which catches the eye, anything that glitters or happens to strike the eye by accident is as important as anything else. There seems to be only rudimentary structuring and differentiation of the environment (what comes forward as figure and what recedes into the background as ground).

If one expects nothing, if one has no anticipations or apprehensions, if in a certain sense there is no future, because the child is moving totally "here now," there can be no surprise, no disappointment. One thing is as likely as another to happen. This is "perfect waiting," and spectatorship without any demands that one thing happen rather than another. There is no prognosis. And no prediction means no worry, no anxiety, no apprehension or foreboding. Any child's reaction to pain, for instance, is total, without inhibition, without control of any kind. The whole organism goes into a yell of pain and rage. Partly this can be understood as a concrete reaction to the concrete here-now moment. This is possible because there is no expectation of the future, hence, no preparation for the future, no rehearsal or anticipation. Neither is there any eagerness when the future is unknown ("I can't wait"). There is certainly no impatience.

In the child there is a total, unquestioning acceptance of whatever happens. Since there is also very little memory, very little leaning on the past, there is little tendency in the child to bring the past into the present or into the future. The consequence is that the child is totally here-now, or totally innocent, one could say, or totally without past and future. These are all ways of defining further concrete perception, B-cognition (of the child), and also the occasional B-cognition of the sophisticated adult who has managed to achieve the "second naïveté."

This is all related to my conception of the creative personality as one who is totally here-now, one who lives without the future or past. Another way of saying this is: "The creative person is an innocent." An innocent could be defined as a grown person who can still perceive or think or react like a child. It is this innocence that is recovered in the "second naïveté," or perhaps I will call it the "second innocence" of the wise old man who has managed to recover the ability to be childlike.

Innocence may also be seen as the direct perception of the B-values, as in the H. C. Andersen fable of the child who was able to see that the King had no clothes on, when all the adults had been fooled into thinking so (just as in Asch's experiment).

Innocence on the behavioral side is unselfconscious spontaneity when absorbed or fascinated; that is, lack of self-awareness, which means loss of self or transcendence of it. Then behavior is totally organized by fascination with the interesting world outside the self, which then means "not trying to have an affect on the onlooker," without guile or design, without even being aware that one is an object of scrutiny. The behavior is purely experience and not a means to some interpersonal end.

VIII. Under What Condition and by Which People Are B-Values Chosen or Not Chosen?

The evidence available shows that B-Values are more often chosen by "healthy" people (self-actualizing, mature, productive characters, and so on). Also by a preponderance of the "greatest," most admired, most loved people throughout history. (Is this why they are admired, loved, considered great?)

Animal experimentation on choice shows that strong habits, previous learning, and so on, lowers the biological efficiency, flexibility, adaptability of self-healing choice, for example, in adrenalectomized rats. Experiments with familiarization demonstrate that people will continue to choose and to prefer even the inefficient, the annoying, and the initially nonpreferred if previously forced to choose them over a ten-day period. General experience with human beings supports these findings, for example, in the area of good habits. Clinical experience indicates that this preference for the habitual and familiar is greater and more rigid, compulsive and neurotic in people who are more anxious, timid, rigid, constricted, and so on. Clinical evidence and some experimental evidence indicates that ego-strength, courage, health, and creativeness make more likely in adults and children the choice of the new, the unfamiliar, the unhabitual.

Familiarization in the sense of adaptation also can cut the tendency to choose the B-values. Bad smells cease to smell bad. The shocking tends to cease shocking. Bad conditions are adapted to and not noticed any more, that is, cease to be conscious, even though their bad *effects* may continue without conscious awareness; for example, effects of continued noise or of continued ugliness or of chronically poor food.

Real choice implies equal and simultaneous presentation with the alternatives. For instance, people used to a poorly reproducing phonograph preferred it to a hi-fi phonograph. People used to the hi-fi preferred *that*. But when both groups were exposed to *both* poor and good music reproduction, both groups finally chose the better reproduction of the hi-fi (Eisenberg).

The preponderance of the experimental literature on discrimination shows that it is more efficient when the alternatives are simultaneously present and close together rather than far apart. We may expect that the selection of the more beautiful of two paintings or the more honest of two wines or the more alive of two human beings will be more likely the closer together they are in space and time.

Proposed experiment: if the gamut of qualities is from 1 ("poor" cigars, wine, fabric, cheese, coffee, and so on) to 10 ("good" cigars, wine, and so on) the persons used to level 1 may very well choose 1, if the only alternative choice is at the other extreme, for example, 10. But it is probable that the person will choose 2 rather than 1, 3 rather than 2, and so on, and in this way finally be brought to choose level 10. The alternative choices ought to be within the same realm of discourse, that is, not too far apart. Using this same technique for those who initially prefer the very good wine; that is, giving them a choice between 10 and 9, 9 and 8, 5 and 4, and so on, they will probably continue to choose the higher value.

In the various senses above, uncovering insight therapy can be seen as leading up to a "real choice" process. The ability to make real choice is much greater after successful therapy than it was before; that is, it is constitutionally rather than culturally determined; it is determined by the self rather than by the external or internal "others." The alternatives are conscious rather than unconscious, fear is minimized, and so on. Successful therapy increases the tendency to prefer B-values as well as to exemplify them.

This implies that characterological determinants of choosers must also be held constant or taken into account; for example, learning that the "better" choice (higher in the hierarchy of values, going toward B-values) tastes better by actually tasting it, is more difficult for traumatized, negatively conditioned, or generally neurotic people, for shy, timid people, for narrowed, impoverished, coarcted people, for rigid, stereotyped, conventionalized people, and so on (because they may be afraid to try the experience, or to experience the taste, or may deny the experience, suppress it, repress it, and so on.) This characterological control holds true in principle both for constitutional determinants and for acquired determinants.

Many experiments show that social suggestion, irrational advertising, social pressure, propaganda, have considerable effect against freedom of choice and even freedom of perception; that is, the choices may be misperceived and then mis-chosen. This deleterious effect is greater in conforming than in independent, stronger people. There are clinical and social-psychological reasons for predicting that this effect is greater in younger than in older people. However, all of these effects, and similar ones, from, for example, subliminal conditioning, propaganda, prestige suggestion, or false advertising, subliminal stimuli, covert positive reinforcement, and so on, rest upon blindness, ignorance, lack of insight, concealment, lying, and unawareness of the situation. Most of these effects can be eliminated by making the ignorant chooser consciously aware of the way in which he has been manipulated (Baker-Metznph experiment), that is, of the truth.

Really free choice—in which the inner, intrinsic nature of the chooser is the main determinant—is therefore enhanced by freedom from social pressure, by an independent rather than dependent personality, by chronological maturity, by strength and courage rather than by weakness and fear, and by truth, knowledge, and awareness. Satisfying each of these conditions should increase the percentage of B-choices.

The hierarchy of values, in which the B-values are the "highest" is in part determined by the hierarchy of basic needs, by the pre-potency of deficit-needs over growth-needs, by the prepotency of homeostasis overgrowth, and so on. In general, where there are two lacks to be gratified, the more prepotent, that is, the "lower," is chosen to be gratified. Therefore, an expectable, highly probable preference for B-values rests in principle upon prior gratification of lower, more prepotent values. This generalization generates many predictions; for example, the safety-need-frustrated person will prefer the true to the false, the beautiful to the ugly, the virtuous to the evil, and so on, less often than will the safety-need-gratified person.

This implies a restatement of the age-old problem: In what senses are "higher" pleasures (for example, Beethoven) superior to "lower" pleasures (for example, Elvis Presley)? How can this be *proved* to one "stuck" in the lower pleasures? Can it be taught? Especially can it be taught to one who doesn't want to be taught?

What are the "resistances" to the higher pleasures? The general answer (in addition to all the above considerations) is: The higher pleasures taste (feel) better than the lower ones, for instance, to anyone who can be induced to experience them both. But all the special, experimental conditions above are necessary in order for the person to be able to make a real choice; that is, to be able fully and freely to compare the two tastes. Growth is theoretically possible *only* because the "higher" tastes are better than the "lower" and because the "lower" satisfaction becomes boring. (See Chapter 4 in *Toward a Psychology of Being* for discussion of "growth-through-delight-and-eventual-boredom-with consequent-seeking-for-new-higher-experience.")

Constitutional factors of another type also determine choices and therefore values. Chickens, laboratory rats, farm animals have all been found to vary from birth in efficiency of choice, especially of a good diet; that is, some animals are efficient choosers and some are poor choosers, in a biological sense. That is, these latter poor choosers will sicken or die if left to choose for themselves. The same is reported in an unofficial way for human infants by child psychologists, pediatricians, and so on. All these organisms also vary in the energy with which they will struggle for satisfaction and the overcoming of frustration. In addition, constitution work with human adults shows that the different body types show some difference in choices of satisfactions.

Neurosis is a powerful destroyer of choice-efficiency, preference for B-values, preference for real need-satisfactions, and so on. It is even possible to define psychological ill health by the degree to which that is chosen which is "bad" for the health of the organism, for example, drugs, alcohol, bad diet, bad friends, bad jobs, and so on.

Cultural conditions, in addition to all the obvious effects, are a main determinant of the range of choices possible, for example, of careers, of diet, and so on. Specifically, economic-industrial conditions are also important; for example, large scale, profit-seeking, mass-distribution industry is very good at supplying us with, for example, inexpensive and well-made clothes, and very bad at supplying us with good, unpoisoned foods such as chemical-free bread, insecticide-free beef, hormone-free fowl, and so on.

Therefore, we may expect B-values to be more strongly preferred by: (1) people who are more healthy, matured, (2) older, (3) stronger, more independent, (4) more courageous, (5) more educated, and so on. The conditions which will increase the percentage of choice of B-values are absence of great social pressure, and so on.

All the above can easily be cast in a non-normative form for those who get uneasy over the use of the terms "good" and "bad," "higher" and "lower," and so on, even though these can be defined operationally. For instance, the non-human Martian could ask "When and by whom and under what conditions is truth chosen rather than falsehood, integrated rather than disintegrated, complete rather than incomplete, orderly rather than disorderly?"

Another old question can also be rephrased in this more manageable way: Is man basically good or evil? No matter how we choose to define these words, man turns out to have both good and evil impulses, and to behave in both good and evil ways (of course, this observation doesn't answer the question of which is deeper, more basic, or more instinct-like). For purposes of scientific investigation we had better rephrase this question to read "Under what conditions and when will who choose the B-values?" that is, be "good." What minimizes or maximizes this choice? What kind of society maximizes this choice? What kind of education? Of therapy?

Of family? These questions in turn open up the possibility of asking: "How can we make men 'better'? How can we improve society?"

NOTES

1 These pieces are not yet in final form, nor do they form a complete structure. They build upon the ideas presented in my *Motivation and Personality*, Harper, 1954, and in my *Toward a Psychology of Being*, Van Nostrand, 1962, and carry these ideas further toward their ideal limit. They were written during my tenure as Andrew Kay Visiting Fellow at the Western Behavioral Sciences Institute, La Jolla, California, 1961.

Additional notes on Being-Psychology are available in my *Summer Notes on Social Psychology of Industry and Management*, published by Non-Linear Systems, Delmar, California, 1963.

2 Van Nostrand, 1962.

3 Improved from A. H. Maslow, Chapter 6 of *Toward a Psychology of Being*, Van Nostrand, 1962. See Chapter 7 for characteristics of the B-Cognizer (of the Self) in the peak-experiences. *See also* memo below on Innocence. Some additions from beginning knowledge of nadir experience, tragedy, "desolation experiences," confrontation with death, etc.

John Dollard and Neil Miller

THE LEARNING PROCESS

John Dollard was born in Wisconsin in 1900 and received his Ph.D. in sociology from the University of Chicago in 1931. In 1932 he accepted a post at Yale University and since 1948 has been a professor of psychology and research associate at Yale. He was trained at the Berlin Institute of Psychoanalysis and is a member of the Western New England Psychoanalytic Society. Dollard has written many works in the social sciences ranging from anthropology to psychotherapy. His book Caste and Class in a Southern Town *is regarded a classic in the field of culture and personality analysis. His most recent publication,* Steps in Psychotherapy, *written with Frank Auld and Alice White, includes the detailed description of an individual in treatment.*

Neil Miller was born in Wisconsin in 1909 and received his Ph.D. in psychology from Yale in 1935. During 1935–1936 he was a Social Science Research Council traveling fellow, during which time he secured a training analysis at the Vienna Institute of Psychoanalysis. Since 1950 he has been the James Rowland Angell professor of psychology at Yale. Dollard and Miller have collaborated on several volumes such as Frustration and Aggression, Social Learning and Imitation, Personality and Psychotherapy.

In their approach to personality theory Dollard and Miller show much interest in learning and the process of development. In their thinking, habit, one of the key concepts in the stimulus-response theory, occupies an important role. They are explicit in defining the nature of motivation and they specify in considerable detail the development and elaboration of motives.

THE LEARNING PROCESS

Principles governing significant aspects of the learning process have been formulated as a result of many careful experimental studies. The most important of these principles will be described briefly. For ease in reference, each principle will first be defined and then illustrated before its function is discussed. Since adequate summaries are available elsewhere,[1] no attempt will be made to describe the evidence supporting each of these principles.

EXTINCTION

Reward is essential to the learning of a habit; it is also essential to the maintenance of a habit. When a learned response is repeated without reward, the strength of the tendency to perform that response undergoes a progressive decrease. This decrement is called *experimental extinction,* or, more simply, extinction.

When the little girl, looking for candy, picked up a book and did not find any candy under it, her tendency to pick up the same book again was reduced. In this case, previous training having already established a general habit of not looking in the same place twice in this kind of a situation, one performance of a non-rewarded response usually eliminated it for the rest of that trial. In the absence of previous training, the process of extinction is often much slower. A fisherman who has been rewarded by catching many fish in a certain creek may come back to that creek many times, but if these visits are never again rewarded by securing fish (as a sub-goal with acquired reward value), his visits will gradually become less frequent and less enthusiastic.

The process of extinction should not be confused with forgetting. Forgetting occurs during an interval in which a response is not practiced. Extinction occurs when a response is practiced without reward.

If non-rewarded performances did not weaken the tendency to repeat a habit, maladaptive habits would persist indefinitely. The apparent function of extinction is to eliminate responses which do not lead to reward, so that other responses can occur. Thus, when the little girl did not find candy under the first book, she ceased looking under that book and went on to pick up other books. Non-rewarded responses occur when the innate hierarchy is not adapted to the conditions of the specific environment, when the conditions in the environment change so that a previously rewarded response no longer is adequate, or when a response has previously been rewarded by chance. The effects of extinction tend to correct the results of these conditions.

The process of extinction is usually not immediate but extends over a number of trials. The number of trials required for the complete extinction of a response varies with certain conditions.

Stronger habits are more resistant to extinction than weaker habits. Other things equal, any factor which will produce a stronger habit will increase its resistance to extinction. One such factor is a greater number of rewarded training trials. Thus, a storekeeper is more likely to give up trying to sell a new line of goods if he fails to make sales to a series of customers near the beginning of his experience with these goods than he is if he has the same streak of bad luck after having made many successful sales. Two additional factors producing a stronger habit and hence a greater resistance to extinction are: a stronger drive during training and a greater amount of reward per trial during training.

The resistance to extinction is also influenced by the conditions of extinction. Fewer trials are required to cause the subject to abandon a given response when the drive during extinction is weaker, when there is more effort involved in the responses being extinguished, when the interval between extinction trials is shorter, and when the alternative responses competing with the extinguished response are stronger.

Finally, the rapidity with which a response is abandoned can be influenced by habits established during previous experiences with non-reward in similar situations. Thus, for the child in the experiment with the books, not finding candy under an object was a cue which, during the child's previous life history, had always been associated with non-reward for the response of looking again under the same object during the same trial. Under different circumstances, a fisherman who happens to cast many times in the same pool and then is rewarded by catching a fish on a cast which follows the cue of a previously unsuccessful cast, can learn to try many casts in the same pool.

Acquired drives and acquired rewards are as subject to extinction as is any other form of habit.[2] A little girl acquired a great desire to see a certain guest during a period when he happened to bring the girl presents on his visits to the family. After a number of visits on which the guest did not bring her presents, her desire to see him waned. Similarly, the delicious aroma of foods can lose its ability to whet the appetite of professional cooks; and promises, if not at least sometimes fulfilled, can lose their acquired reward value.

Although the process of extinction may be slowed down by

certain factors, all habits that have to date been carefully investigated in the laboratory have been found to be subject to extinction. Thus, there is reason to believe that seeming exceptions to extinction, such as the examples of so-called functional autonomy cited by G. W. Allport (1937, pp. 190–212), are either cases in which the habit has become so strong that evidence of extinction is hard to notice during the number of non-rewarded repetitions observed, or cases in which the habit is actually being supported periodically by unrecognized conditions of drive and reward. It seems inadvisable to depend on the eternal persistence without reward of crucial responses from one's employer or one's wife.

Many facts about the details of the process of extinction have been demonstrated by careful experiments; its causes are less well understood. In the course of the present investigation an analysis . . . was made of the factors which tend to cause a child to stop crying. This analysis suggests that extinction does not constitute a new principle, but is the result rather of conditions favoring the reward of responses which are incompatible with the response being extinguished.[3]

Crying loudly for a period of time produces strong stimulation from tenseness in the throat, soreness of the throat, and fatigue. The stopping of crying is followed by reduction in the strength of these stimuli. In this way the responses involved in stopping crying are rewarded. With these responses rewarded every time the infant stops, they will gain in dominance unless the effects of this reward are offset by greater rewards for the response of crying. Thus, unless crying is rewarded, the tendency to cry will be progressively weakened by competition with the tendency to stop crying.

In a similar manner, other responses involve an increase in stimulation from muscle tension and fatigue. Stopping these responses produces a reduction in the strength of this stimulation. Thus muscle strain and fatigue are drives constantly motivating the subject to stop the response he is making; escape from muscle strain and fatigue are ever present to reward stopping. Extinction occurs unless the effects of the drive of fatigue and consequent reward for stopping are overridden by the effects of other, stronger drives and rewards. But fatigue, even though overridden by the effects of stronger drives and rewards, will continue to mount during a long series of trials. Thus the motivation to perform the response may be weakened somewhat by increasing competition with fatigue. Experimental evidence indicates that, exactly as would be expected on the basis of this hypothesis, a long series of trials, even though rewarded, may have a transitory effect resembling weak extinction. Pavlov has recognized this phenomenon, which is called "inhibition of reinforcement."[4]

As the strength of the stimulation associated with the response increases, extinction shades over by imperceptible degrees into punishment. As a person continues eating, eventually the hunger drive is reduced to zero. Beyond this point the drive can be reduced no further, and reinforcement ceases. For a while escape from fatigue lurks as a minor reward for stopping the effort involved in eating. Eventually, however, a much stronger drive and reward enter the scene. Stomach distention becomes painful. This pain is reduced by responses of reverse peristalsis, such as belching. The reduction of pain rewards these responses and strengthens their connection to the cue of a full stomach. But even incipient reverse peristalsis tends to be incompatible with the response of eating. Thus, the subject learns to stop eating.[5]

The stronger drive, and hence greater escape-reward, which may be secured through relatively strong punishments produces a more rapid and permanent abandonment of a response than do the weaker and more diffuse rewards presumably involved in extinction. More definite overt evidence of conflict is also usually observed.

In conclusion, mere repetition does not strengthen a habit. Instead, non-rewarded repetitions progressively weaken the strength of the tendency to perform a habit.[6] Usually the tendency to perform a habit does not disappear immediately. The number of trials required for extinction depends on the strength of the habit, on the particular conditions of extinction, and on past experience with non-rewarded trials. Extinction may be caused by the fact that escape from the stimulation of muscle tension and fatigue rewards stopping. Definite punishment can eliminate a habit more quickly than can mere non-reward. The fact of extinction emphasizes the importance of reward.

SPONTANEOUS RECOVERY

The effects of extinction tend to disappear with the passage of time. After a series of unsuccessful expeditions, a fisherman may have abandoned the idea of making any further trips to a particular stream. As time goes on, his tendency to try that stream again gradually recovers from the effects of extinction, so that next month or next year he may take another chance. This tendency for an extinguished habit to reappear after an interval of time during which no non-rewarded trials occur is called *spontaneous recovery*.

The fact of recovery demonstrates that extinction does not destroy the old habit, but merely inhibits it. With the passage of time, the strength of the inhibiting factors produced during extinction is weakened more rapidly than the strength of the original tendency to perform the habit. In this manner, a net gain is produced in the strength of the tendency to perform the habit.

Many carefully controlled experiments have demonstrated that a certain amount of spontaneous recovery is a regular characteristic of extinguished habits. After enough repeated extinctions, however, the habit may become so completely inhibited that it shows little tendency to reappear. Habits which have been disrupted by punishment are much less subject to recovery than habits which have been disrupted by extinction.

Spontaneous recovery follows as a natural deduction from the hypothesis that extinction is the product of stimulation from fatigue. According to this hypothesis, the performance of the response to be extinguished produces increased stimulation from fatigue. Stopping the response is followed by a rewarding reduction in this stimulation. Thus is built up a habit of responding to the fatigue and accompanying cues by stopping. With the passage of time, however, the fatigue will disappear as one of the cues eliciting the responses involved in stopping, and these will consequently be weakened. Released from competition with stopping, the extinguished response will be relatively strengthened, that is, will recover. If stopping has been rewarded strongly and often enough, however, the other cues in the situation may elicit so strong a tendency to stop that recovery from extinction will not be complete.

Even if the hypothesis advanced above to explain extinction and recovery in terms of more basic principles should turn out to be incomplete or false, the facts of extinction and recovery remain and play important roles in the learning process. The function of extinction is to force the subject to try new responses. If any of these responses are rewarded, they will be strengthened to the point where their competition may permanently eliminate the old habit. If none of these new responses is rewarded, however, their extinction plus the recovery of the old response will induce the subject to try the old response again. Recovery is adaptive in those situations in which the absence of reward is only temporary.

GENERALIZATION

The effects of learning in one situation transfer to other situations; the less similar the situation, the less transfer occurs. Stated more exactly, reward for making a specific response to a given pattern of cues strengthens not only the tendency for that pattern of cues to elicit that response but also the tendency for other similar patterns of cues to elicit the same response. The innate tendency for this to occur is called *innate stimulus generalization*. The less similar the cue or pattern of cues, the less the generalization. This is referred to as a *gradient of generalization*.

No two situations are ever completely the same. In the experiment with the little girl, for example, the books were put back into the bookcase in slightly different patterns of unevenness on different trials, and the girl approached the bookcase from different angles. In many other types of learning situations, the variability of the correct cues is considerably greater than in this experiment. Therefore, if the response were completely specific to the pattern of cues associated with its reward, learning would be impossible, for the specific pattern of cues would never repeat itself in exact detail. If the cues eliciting the response were completely generalized, on the other hand, it would also be impossible to learn; the girl could never learn to select a specific book because she would have an equally strong tendency to pick up each of the other books. This dilemma is partially resolved by an innate gradient of generalization, so that there is a stronger tendency to respond to cues in proportion to their similarity to those present in preceding situations in which the response was rewarded. As a solution to this dilemma, the gradient of generalization is supplemented by the process of discrimination and by the mechanism of the acquired equivalence of cues. These will be discussed later.

Examples of generalization are common in everyday experience. A child bitten by one dog is afraid of other animals and more afraid of other dogs than of cats and horses. Natives who have learned to escape punishment by concealing facts from white administrators or missionaries tend to transfer these habits to the anthropologists they meet in the field.

The phenomena of generalization have been studied in detail by Pavlov (1927), Bekhterev (1932), and a host of other subsequent experimenters. Generalization can occur either on the basis of the qualitative similarity of the cues involved, or on the basis of identical elements in the two situations. Perhaps ultimately these are reducible to the same thing.

The gradient of generalization refers to the qualitative differences or cue aspect of stimuli. The *distinctiveness* of a cue is measured by its dissimilarity from other cues in the same situation, so that little generalization occurs from the cue in question to other cues in the situation. Thus the distinctiveness of a cue varies with the other cues that are present. A red book in a row of black books is a more distinctive cue than is the same volume in a row of other red books, because less generalization occurs from red to black than from one shade of red to another.

Once a response has been rewarded in one situation, the function of generalization is to increase the probability that the response will be tried in other like situations. For example, after the response of stopping at a tourist cabin near one town has been rewarded by an exceptionally good, quiet, cheap night's rest, generalization will increase the probability that the individual will try stopping at similar tourist cabins near other towns. If a generalized response is rewarded in the new, but similar, situations, the tendency to perform that response in these situations will be further strengthened.

DISCRIMINATION

If a generalized response is not rewarded, the tendency to perform that response is weakened. By the reward of the response to one pattern of cues and the non-reward or punishment of the response to a somewhat different pattern of cues, a *discrimination* may gradually be established. The process of discrimination tends to correct maladaptive generalizations. It increases the specificity of the cue-response connection.

By being rewarded for stopping at tourist cabins in the West and non-rewarded for stopping at tourist cabins in the East, a person may gradually learn to discriminate between the two situations on the basis of the geographical cue. But the process of learning to discriminate is complicated by the fact that the effects of extinction also generalize. Thus, after being non-rewarded for stopping at a series of tourist cabins in the East, our heroes of the highway may be reluctant to stop at tourist cabins in the West.

The less different the cues in the two situations, the more generalization will be expected to occur, and hence the more difficult it will be to learn discrimination. If the cues are too similar, so much of the effects of reward may generalize from the rewarded cue to the non-rewarded one and so much of the effects of extinction may generalize from the non-rewarded cue to the rewarded one, that it will be impossible to learn a discrimination.

GRADIENT IN THE EFFECTS OF REWARD

Delayed rewards are less effective than immediate rewards. In other words, if a number of different responses are made to a cue and the last of these responses is followed by reward, the connection to the last response will be strengthened the most, and the connection to each of the preceding responses will be strengthened by a progressively smaller amount. Similarly, if a series of responses is made to a series of cues, as when a hungry boy takes off his hat in the hall, dashes through the dining room into the kitchen, opens the icebox, and takes a bite to eat, the connections more remote from the reward are strengthened less than those closer to the reward. In this series, the connection between the sight of the hall closet and the response of hanging up the hat will be strengthened less than the connection between the sight of the icebox door and the response of opening it.

In the experiment performed on the little girl, it was necessary for her to make the response of approaching the bookcase as well as to make the response of selecting a specific book. If the effects of reward were completely specific to the final response performed, picking up the correct book, she would not learn to approach the bookcase and hence would not find the candy. On the other hand, if the effects of reward were completely general, the response of taking out the wrong book would be strengthened just as much as would the response of taking out the correct book, and learning would be impossible. This dilemma is resolved by the *gradient of reward.*[7] The connection between the cue of the sight of the bookcase at a distance and the response of going toward the bookcase is sufficiently strengthened by each reward to cause the little girl to run toward the bookcase faster and more eagerly on successive trials. But the response of picking out the correct book is strengthened more by the reward than are the earlier responses of picking out the wrong books. Thus the response of selecting the correct book eventually crowds out the responses of picking out the preceding wrong books, and the sequence of behavior is shortened. Since it is physically impossible for the girl to take a book from the bookcase before she arrives there, the responses of taking out a book do not crowd out those of running to the bookcase.

The gradient of reward accounts for an increase in tendency to respond, the nearer the goal is approached. Because cue-response connections near the reward are strengthened more than connections remote from the reward, a hungry man on his way to dinner has a tendency to quicken his pace in rounding the last corner on the way home.

The gradient of reward also explains why, after both a longer and a shorter route to the goal have been tried, the shorter route tends to be preferred. A thirsty child learns to secure water from drinking fountains in the park. Approach to a fountain seen nearby is usually followed more immediately by the rewarding goal response of drinking than is approach to a fountain seen at a distance. Thus during a series of trials in which both fountains are approached, the connection between the cue of seeing the near fountain and the response of approaching that fountain is the more firmly established. The response with the stronger connections crowds out the weaker connection; approaching the near fountain becomes dominant in the hierarchy. Similarly, a child will learn to approach that one of two equally distant fountains where fewer people are waiting in line for a drink.

With human subjects who have had the proper social training, symbolic stimuli that have acquired a rewarding value are often used to bridge the gap between the performance of an act and the occurrence of an innate reward. Money or even the thought of making money can be immediately associated with the performance of a task; after an interval, the money can be immediately associated with some primary reward, such as eating. In this way, the decrement which would be expected on the basis of the gradient of reward is markedly lessened Similarly, a parent punishing a child is likely to attempt to eliminate the effects of the time gap between stealing and punishment by a verbal rehearsal of the circumstances of the crime. As would be expected, younger children who have had less training in responding to symbolic stimuli are less affected by such a procedure and hence more influenced by immediacy of reward. Similarly, lower-class individuals who have not been taught to save—that is, have had less opportunity of having the presence of a bank balance immediately associated with primary rewards—are more influenced by immediacy of reward. But even in the cases in which well-established habits of responding to symbolic stimuli help to bridge the gap between the response to a cue and the reward of that response, the gradient of reward is not completely masked; more immediate rewards are regularly more effective than more remote ones.

In summary, the effects of reward are not limited to the particular cue-response sequence which is immediately associated with reward but also strengthen other cue-response connections less immediately associated with reward. This spread of the effects of reward has the function of strengthening the connections to responses comprising the first steps of the sequence leading to reward. It can be greatly facilitated if certain stimuli involved in the sequence acquire a sub-goal, or secondary rewarding value, by repeated association with the primary reward. Nevertheless, the effects of reward taper off in a gradient, so that the connections immediately associated with the reward are strengthened more than remoter connections. This gradient of reward has the function of tending to force the subject to choose the shortest of alternative paths to a goal and to eliminate unnecessary responses from a sequence.

ANTICIPATORY RESPONSE

From the principle of the gradient of reward and from that of generalization, an additional principle can be deduced: namely, that responses near the point of reward tend wherever physically possible to occur before their original time in the response series, that is, to become anticipatory. When the little girl was looking for candy, the response of selecting the correct book moved forward in the series and crowded out the originally prior response of selecting the wrong book. Since the same cue, the bookcase within reach, elicits both responses, it was not necessary for generalization to occur. But the cues from the bookcase were fairly similar at different distances—when it was just beyond reach and when the girl was removing one of the books. Thus, the girl tended to start reaching before she actually arrived at the bookcase.

This tendency for responses to occur before their original point in the rewarded series is an exceedingly important aspect of behavior.[8] Under many circumstances, it is responsible for the crowding out of useless acts in the response sequence; under other circumstances, it produces anticipatory errors. . . . Anticipatory responses may produce stimuli playing an important role in acquired motivation and in reasoning and foresight. At present, the simpler dynamics of anticipatory response will be illustrated.

A child touches a hot radiator. The pain elicits an avoidance response, and the escape from pain rewards this response. Since the sight and muscular feel of the hand approaching the radiator are similar in certain respects to the sight and muscular feel of the hand touching the radiator, the strongly rewarded response of withdrawal will be expected to generalize from the latter situation to the former. After one or more trials, the child will reach out his hand toward the radiator and then withdraw it before touching the radiator. The withdrawal response will become anticipatory; it will occur before that of actually touching the radiator. This is obviously adaptive, since it enables the child to avoid getting burned.

A person at a restaurant orders a delicious steak, sees it, and then eats it. The taste of the steak elicits and rewards salivation. On subsequent occasions, the sight of the steak or even its ordering may elicit salivation before the food has actually entered the mouth.

A person sees a green persimmon, picks it up, and bites into it. The astringent taste evokes the response of puckering the lips and spitting out the fruit. This response is rewarded by a decrease in the extreme bitterness of the taste. Upon subsequent occasions, puckering of the lips and incipient spitting responses are likely to have moved forward in the sequence so that they now occur to the cue of seeing a green persimmon instead of to the cue of tasting it.

In the foregoing examples, the anticipatory aspect of the learned responses was adaptive. The tendency for responses to move forward in a sequence, however, does not depend upon the subject's insight into the adaptive value of the mechanism. That the principle of anticipation functions in a more primitive way than this is indicated most clearly by examples in which it functions in a maladaptive manner.

A rifleman pulls the trigger of his gun and then hears a loud report which elicits blinking of the eyes and a startle response by the whole body. The end of the loud stimulus is closely associated with these responses and has a rewarding effect.[9] On subsequent occasions, the cues involved in pressing the trigger tend to elicit the blinking and the startle. These anticipatory responses are likely to occur before the gun is actually fired and to cause the bullet to swerve from its mark. This tendency is maladaptive, but, as all marksmen know, is so strong that it can be inhibited only with difficulty. In this example, it should be noticed that the cues which touch off the anticipatory response are proprioceptive ones which the subject receives as a part of the act of tensing his muscles to pull the trigger. Thus, the maladaptive startle can be eliminated readily if the subject squeezes the trigger so gradually that no specific cues precede the explosion in a regularly predictable manner. That such a practice has been found desirable is a tribute to the strength and the involuntariness of the tendency for responses to become anticipatory.

A small boy comes home at night hungry from play. He cleans his shoes on the doormat, comes in, passes the door of the dining room, where he can see food on the table, hangs his hat carefully on the hook, goes upstairs, straightens his tie, brushes his hair, washes his face and hands, comes downstairs to the dining room, sits down, waits for grace to be said, and then asks, "May I have some meat and potatoes, please?" Eating the food is the rewarding goal response to this long series of activities. On subsequent occasions, there will be a strong tendency for responses in this sequence to become anticipatory. He will tend to open the door without stopping to clean off his shoes, and to turn directly into the dining room without stopping to hang up his hat or to go through the remainder of the sequence. These acts will be likely to crowd out other preceding responses in the series because the connections to these acts have been strengthened relatively more by being nearer to the point of reward. If he secures food, the anticipatory responses will be still more strongly rewarded and will be more likely to occur on subsequent occasions. The response sequence will be short-circuited. In this way, the principle of anticipation often leads to the adaptive elimination of useless acts from a response sequence.

If the response of turning directly into the dining room without stopping to remove the hat and clean up is not followed by food, however, it will tend to be extinguished as a response to cues at this inappropriate point in the series. A discrimination may eventually be established. Similarly, the acts of washing, brushing the hair, waiting quietly during grace, and saying "please" will tend to be abbreviated and crowded out by competition with anticipatory responses unless the latter are either punished or continuously extinguished. Those short cuts which are physically and socially possible will be strengthened by more immediate rewards; others will be punished or extinguished. Thus behavior tends gradually to approximate the shortest, most efficient possible sequence.

Like all other discriminations, the type which results in the elimination of a non-rewarded anticipatory response from a sequence becomes easier as the cues to be discriminated become more distinctive. According to the principle of generalization, anticipatory responses are more likely to occur the more similar the cues in the different parts of the sequence. Thus, the boy is most likely to make an anticipatory entry when passing the dining room door if his hands happen to be relatively clean and his hair well brushed. If the cues are too similar, anticipatory errors will regularly be expected to intrude.

Anticipatory responses may play an important role in communication between people by providing significant stimuli to other persons. An infant not yet old enough to talk was accustomed to being lifted up into its mother's arms. Because often followed by innate rewards, being in the mother's arms had achieved an acquired reward value. As a part of the response of being picked up, the infant learned to stand up on his toes, spread his arms, arch his back in a characteristic way. Subsequently, when the child wanted to be picked up, this response moved forward in a series; the infant performed in an anticipatory manner as much as possible of his part of the sub-goal response. He stood on his toes, spread his arms, and threw his head and shoulders back. He could not, however, bend his knees, which would have been a part of the next response, because this would have conflicted with the activity of standing. Since his parents rewarded this gesture by picking him up, he used it more and more often.

All of the stages in the evolution of a gesture have been observed in pairs of albino rats. The hungry animals are placed in a cage in which there is a single, small dish of powdered food. The first rat discovers the food and commences to eat. The second rat comes over, notices the food, braces himself, and violently bats the first rat out of the way. To the strong stimulus of receiving the blow, the first rat withdraws and is rewarded for this withdrawal by escaping from the blow. After a number of such episodes, the response of withdrawing becomes anticipatory so that it occurs at the sight of the second animal's starting his blow. As this procedure is repeated, the second rat's response of returning to his food becomes more and more anticipatory, so that the sweep of his paws in batting at the first animal is progressively shortened. Eventually the whole process is reduced to a mere gesture. The second rat raises his paw, the first retreats from the food, and the second goes directly to the food without attempting to strike a full blow. The tendency for the responses of both rats to become anticipatory has caused a gesture to be substituted for a fight.

A similar type of communication by means of involuntary anticipatory responses occurs when an athlete unwittingly "telegraphs" his punches or points his play. The clever opponent learns to observe such gestures and respond appropriately. The role of anticipatory responses as a means of communication is enormously elaborated by the conditions of social life.

NOTES

[1] See Hull (1934a; 1941*), Hilgard and Marquis (1940), and their references. For more rigorous theoretical formulations, see Hull (1929; 1930a; 1932; 1939a).

[2] This assertion is based on data to be published by N. E. Miller from a series of experiments on acquired motivation and acquired reward.

[3] Guthrie (1940) and Wendt (1936) have maintained that extinction may be a process of learning responses incompatible with the original response. But they have not suggested any way in which such incompatible responses could be rewarded.

[4] In the case of glandular responses, such as salivation, the source of stimulation which is present when the response is made and reduced when the response is stopped is more difficult to discover. This, of course, does not mean that it is necessarily absent.

It may be that "escape from the stimulation of fatigue" is only one of the factors which may reward extinction. Another, similar factor could be "escape from the stimulation produced by conflict." In the case of extinguishing a rat's habit of running down an alley for food by removing the food as a reward, the conflict would be between the responses of eating and those elicited by the sight of the empty food dish. See Miller and Stevenson (1936).

[5] The behavior of infants definitely indicates that the response of stopping eating when the stomach is full must be learned. These

observations are confirmed by unpublished experimental results secured by students working with Miller.

[6] This fact argues strongly against the position held by the old associationists which would seem to demand that every repetition of an association between a stimulus and response, whether rewarded or not rewarded, should strengthen that association. Guthrie (1935) attempts to escape this dilemma in a very ingenious application of the principles of association to the problems of motivation and reward. To date, his statements of assumptions and deductions of consequences have not been systematic enough for us to convince ourselves of either the soundness or unsoundness of his position. If Guthrie's principles should be adequate, they would not contradict the importance we have ascribed to rewards, but rather explain it in terms of more fundamental principles.

[7] The gradient of reward is what Hull originally called the goal gradient (1932; 1934c).

[8] The functional significance of anticipatory responses has been pointed out by Hull (1929; 1930b; 1931).

[9] This rewarding effect of the termination of the sound is clearer in cases where sounds of this loudness persist longer. Then the individual may try a number of different responses and be more likely to repeat on subsequent occasions those which were more closely associated with the escape from the sound than those which were less closely associated with the escape.

BIBLIOGRAPHY

Adler, Alfred, *The Practice and Theory of Individual Psychology*, New York, Humanities Press, 1955; also in paperback: New Jersey: Littlefield, Adams & Co., 1963.

Adler, G., *Studies in Analytical Psychology*, New York, Norton, 1948.

Allport, Gordon W., *Personality: A Psychological Interpretation*, New York, Holt, 1937.

————, *The Nature of Personality: Selected Papers*, Cambridge, Mass., Addison-Wesley, 1950.

————, *Becoming: Basic Considerations for a Psychology of Personality*, New Haven, Yale University Press, 1955; 1960 (Yale Paperback).

————, *Personality and Social Encounter*, Boston, Beacon Press, 1960; 1964 (Beacon Paperback).

Dollard, John, and Neil E. Miller, *Personality and Psychotherapy: An Analysis in Terms of Learning, Thinking and Culture*, New York, McGraw-Hill, 1950; 1964 (McGraw-Hill Paperback).

————, *Social Learning and Imitation*, New Haven, Yale University Press, 1941; 1962 (Yale Paperback).

Freud, Sigmund, *The Standard Edition of the Complete Psychological Works*, James Strachey (ed.), London, Hogarth Press 1953–.

————, *The Interpretation of Dreams*, New York, Science Editions, 1961.

————, *The Basic Writings of Sigmund Freud*, New York, Random House, 1938.

————, *New Introductory Lectures on Psychoanalysis*, New York, Norton, 1933.

————, *Three Contributions to the Theory of Sex*, New York, Dutton Paperback, 1962.

Fromm, Erich, *Escape from Freedom*, New York, Holt, Rinehart, Winston, 1941.

————, *Man for Himself*, New York, Holt, Rinehart, Winston, 1947.

————, *The Sane Society*, New York, Holt, Rinehart, Winston, 1955.

Goldstein, Kurt, *The Organism*, New York: American Book Co., 1939, 1963 (Beacon Paperback).

————, *Human Nature in the Light of Psychopathology*, Cambridge, Harvard University Press, 1940; 1963 (Schocken Paperback).

Horney, Karen, *The Neurotic Personality of Our Time*, New York, Norton, 1937.

357

————, *New Ways in Psychoanalysis*, New York, Norton, 1939.

————, *Self-Analysis*, New York, Norton, 1942.

————, *Our Inner Conflicts*, New York, Norton, 1945.

————, *Neurosis and Human Growth*, New York, Norton, 1950.

Jung, Carl Gustav, *Collected Papers on Analytical Psychology*, New York, Moffat Yard, 1917.

————, *Contributions to Analytical Psychology*, New York, Harcourt, Brace, 1928.

————, *Psychological Types*, New York, Harcourt, Brace, 1933.

————, *Modern Man in Search of a Soul*, New York, Harcourt, Brace, 1933; Harvest Books (no date).

————, *Psychology and Religion*, New Haven, Yale University Press, 1938.

————, *The Integration of Personality*, New York, Farrar and Rinehart, 1939.

Lewin, Kurt, *A Dynamic Theory of Personality*, New York, McGraw-Hill, 1935; McGraw-Hill Paperback (no date).

————, *Principles of Topological Psychology*, New York, McGraw-Hill, 1936.

————, *Resolving Social Conflicts: Selected Papers on Group Dynamics*, Gertrude W. Lewin (ed.), New York, Harper, 1948.

————, *Field Theory in Social Science: Selected Theoretical Papers*, D. Cartwright (ed.), New York, Harper, 1951.

Maslow, Abraham H., *Motivation and Personality*, New York, Harper, 1954.

————, *Toward a Psychology of Being*, Princeton, N.J., Van Nostrand, 1962.

Mowrer, O. H., *Learning Theory and Personality Dynamics*, New York, Ronald Press, 1950.

Murphy, Gardner, *Personality: A Biosocial Approach to Origins and Structure*, New York, Harper, 1947.

————, and F. Jensen, *Approaches to Personality*, New York, Coward, 1932.

————, and Lois B. Murphy, *Experimental Social Psychology*, New York, Harper, 1931; 1937, rev. edition.

Murray, Henry A., *Explorations in Personality*, New York, Oxford University Press, 1938; 1962 (Science Editions, paperback).

————, and Clyde Kluckhohn (ed.), *Personality in Nature, Society, and Culture*, New York, Knopf, 1953.

Rogers, Carl R., *Counseling and Psychotherapy: Newer Concepts in Practice*, Boston, Houghton Mifflin, 1942.

————, *Client-Centered Therapy: Its Current Practice, Implications, and Theory*, Boston, Houghton Mifflin, 1951.

————, and Rosalind F. Dymond (eds.), *Psychotherapy and Personality Change: Co-ordinated Studies in the Client-Centered Approach*, Chicago, University of Chicago Press, 1954.

Sheldon, William H., *The Varieties of Human Physique: An Introduction to Constitutional Psychology*, New York, Harper, 1940.

————, *The Varieties of Temperament: A Psychology of Constitutional Differences*, New York, Harper, 1942.

————, *Varieties of Delinquent Youth: An Introduction to Constitutional Psychiatry*, New York, Harper, 1949.

————, *Atlas of Men: A Guide for Somatotyping the Adult Male at All Ages*, New York, Harper, 1954.

Sullivan, Harry Stack, *The Interpersonal Theory of Psychiatry*, New York, Norton, 1953.